For Oliver Reynolds, true relater

However, to palliate the shortness of our Lives, and somewhat to compensate our brief term in this World, it's good to know as much as we can of it, and also so far as possibly in us lieth to hold a Theory of times past, as though we had seen the same. He who hath thus considered the World, as also how therein things long past have been answered by things present, how matters in one age have been acted over in another, and how there is nothing new under the sun, may conceive himself in some manner to have lived from the beginning, and to be as old as the World; and if he should still live on, 'twould be but the same thing.

Sir Thomas Browne

Sixfoil One

Humpety hump. Thems were my very words, No point in spittin, I said. Yass, yaas, Oliver, Olleeverr. Kin? No, Conn. Con? No, Conn, ye dolty. Jes a story, no more en that. Ye bleedin steam-wiper, I says, what a story. Do you want it? Or is it all the same to you? Here's a fire, I admits. I did. Grey granite. What other bluedy cooler, I axes. Conny. Oliver Conn. Man of his tribes and tributes, eh? I was sore in love with im. No I were not. Wree did I learn me English? Sure it was di army, you know dat place. Listen, Moll, drag up. Here's a one. Long time ago, maybe. Mebbe not. Scittish? Not at all. Notatall, he was of the West, a man in his black boots. How do I know? I seen em, I smelled em, I polished em. When was all this, Mr Apostle? It was long since, I'm tellin yer. An don call me dat. Moran it iss. Hold your tongue, your tongué dont come out right. Yas, yas, he was a rum one, last of his lineage, went into the gutter of histyre shortly after, and no place for a soldier-boy, I think. Did he rise out of it? He did naat, he fixed there for good, nothing else heard of him. And how did all that come about, who caused that? A great conqueror he was from that time, those places beyond over the morning bit. The dawn? Aye, the dawn. Sit closer, Moll, if you want moi hand on yer knee. You hopeless skieser, skittle, skittle. Will yez begin? I'm greased by yoor expectoratin. Do stop, the doc says, stop expectoratin on them linoleum flor. Good for me bowels, I said. I, I said. I, I said, Doc, me hearty farty give over them verbs from the doctioneery, becorse I am agin all that. Avv no intention now of any of the sort. It was in the West, I well remember, before the last and final conflict, that did put the kibosh on the nation, that did hurt it sore and ever. If I may call it the Catholik revolving, the King of Rame's work, an excellent man, but none of ours, and wanted none of us. Moll, your hand is too cold for me shins. Your hand is too cold for all and aught. Moll, in the West, pay yer heed, and incline your showy head all the same. What year? Who can say? Lassy year perhaps, lassie. What odds? And odds goings on he had. An ancestor? Not at all, twas me meself, it was I there in the foretime. It is a history of myself I yam peddlin ye, what else? Me younger years, sure you know how I was. A man of sustinance. Never a cabbage to be wanted in our household. Not in ower, to emphasise that. Hooly gawd, he was a handsorme fellaugh, he was a howel, no. Piddled in his puddles like the besht of em, oora lady, I am about to be explaining to you. To you. Hold while I get me steam up. And me whereabouts.

Yer see, he wus one man of parts in them parts, aye. That oul clan ad been about fer too manny yeers no doubt. An fate did clobber im an all. But before fate did there wer this to say: he had a daecent life, what wid fine cloths and the like for the time. And I only mean for the time that was, for our cloes here, Moll, be perhap finer. But for the payriod, don mistak me, he wus a gennelman, but gennelmen got characters too also, and he had one of them, of a sort. A fiery boody.

Now Oleever was a set up with one dame, his woif, but she were half daft an carzy and no one liked her. What could you expect, Moll, from the Queen o Connaughts daughter? You feel me, you guess me oot. Well, yer great mistook, for that were moi station in the pasht, and olny Galluc we spok them years. When was it? It was long since, lass.

Olleever he was a mon of sum height, he were six of feet if not mur, and his frame was guid and his healt. He was prime of his timber right enoug, par dally, Moll, leave orf, and his home was a leetlt tower built o granite, from the granite quarry, where els? But a handy one, by the by, and some oul mason made grand job of that dwellin. A wee shite cauld in de wunter, o course. It was sited schmack i the muddle of a greet wood, an oaky wood of those times, since demoved, Moll. Guid-bhe to de trees, we used ta saye whan we wus younger. Member it wal. Not ta say it was not damp and queerish, with the surroundin cantry offside o the forest meerish and boggish. Now it was, yas. Sowa yee can pictoor the extent of it, leddy. We half Oleever Conn in the cinter of woods and disolation, desert widdout sun, and lick of water. Becorse, gord above in his hiven, there waws sun niver seen year start to year puff. This dominoon of shadoo Oleever loved slightly, but the idee o power he adored, lik and it were a seecond gord. A christian man, a catoolic by law, bit by natoor he wasint but a pagan, with his poetic priest and his odder catoolic bishop from the modern times. And now the modern teems were coming to somewhat else. It was the pattern that the owl bishopps were achieving that was woorying the herts of is like. For, be it that he were a pagan at heart, at law he were a catoolic, and pledged in his coort to stay near and besode it for ever. This ever did na lay heavy on im, he were a brave podunk but not any ero. He present to the wurid a calmish face, and inside he was full of the fright we hoomans call necessaire. Why fear be invented will not be known hardly. Grave but nat brave yon man. In prime of decisoon, and al the rist granted. His favoor fud was deer meet and rabbut, a narky mixtoor. His prefer suit of cloes was the skin of them both, combined, for effect. Most people under im treated him much, becorse he had the seed of fear for to grow softyness.

It was a green garden. Then green was green, and shadows of colour were as mysterious as the difference between Mrs and Mr. When the milkman passed I made my choice, but mostly called him Mrs.

'Hello, Mrs.'

He didn't laugh. A chalky scowl came over the perfectly green hedge, and stabbed me on the perfectly green lawn.

The landlady of the house was mad, of course.

A piece of square park continued idly across the tarred road. Its emotional life was considerably more assured than mine. The granite steps represented the bridge between sudden fear and possible soothing. So here was the sky and the hedges and the lawn, and the standoffish birds. It was ordinary, and my clothes were so too. The house was the usual middle-class place, in which my dear family had a flat only, and whose landlady was cracked. I based this on the fact that the roof of her kitchen was made of corrugated iron, wavy and inexpensive. She shouldn't have had waves over her head. She might have been engulfed. I dug her flowers up, in the bed under the kitchen window, and she planted fresh ones. I probably never set actual eyes on her. Or I forget.

This heat here in Florida would make you forget what you forget. It is so unlike this time, all of that, that it seems ludicrous to think of it, pointless and distant. But it is not so distant really. All that backs all this, and informs most of this too. How I see a gull now is how I saw it then: a dark broken noise coming slantwise down the sky, from the brown gloom of the church roof. The church roof which was truly the whole world outside, the edge of the planet. And the balconies on the houses carried trains in the night-time, big silent travellers in them. I heard the noise of them also, in the early evening, under the kitchen table, while the so-called servant washed the knives, and her legs grew for a while in the floorboards, and then plucked up, like the landlady's flowers. Her own noise was a miserable clutter of country songs, and songs off the nasty radio. She had this thing going all day. Between her and the radio it was a hard time under the table, till mummy came in and said goodbye.

'Goodbye, mummy, goodbye.'

If I was able to speak at all. There was a lot of brown too in the hall, but I wasn't there much. And a lot of brown in the nightsky where everything stopped. Everything. Goodbye, mummy, in your brown coat. That's a mighty long night you're going out into.

A city I missed, being so small. A whole end half of a decade never seen, because only quarter born at the time. Late Fifties city. With god knows what because I never entered it, the square my boundary. All else had to keep. And having seen it all, what shall I say? Be glad of it? Hardly. Weep for it? Even less appropriate. All these children out of their Edens. If they were Edens.

But very muddy mud there was under the sheltered houses of the hedges, where it was sticky and pleasant to play. The sister did not involve herself in these sections. She was contentedly elsewhere, after the job she did on my thumb, or was it my nose? She pushed me down the steps, my holy lovely sister. And after the hospital. But never mind the hospital for the moment. But after that she pushed me down the steps. Curious repetition.

But here I am. Milkman herds his horse and dray up the

Fifties road. Being only that and ever that, and never to be again, not just so. Stuck out there in history with no chronicler, and no need of one. Each cobweb, each ant, each old cigarette-pack, each piece of dust, each gob of spit on the country-minded pavement. And the milkman goes by with his bluest hat under the moony sky. It is morning because the moon is in the quaint evergone blue sky, the fucking moon. Flying over and over and stopping still, at the same instance. The milkman with the fucking moon on a string, and his horse a horse, a h-o-r-s-e, a drawing in my eyes of a horse. Not a breathy engine with oats in his belly, and mares on his gelded mind, distantly, but four legs and a head and a virtuoso tail in a book. The milkman is going by with his bookish artistic horse, with the moon on a string, and the bits of rubbish on the road are being forgotten, nor ever remembered. Hands that cast the cardboard. Eyes that noticed the ants. Tut, tut. They'll be in all over the bread in no time. High summer, Mr.

'Hello, Mrs.'

A high summer morning in the town of Dublin, thousands of children and half a million moons to float by without gender. Hello, Mrs Moon, how's the milk?

For all I knew the milk came out of the horse, or my mother. One or the other. Never having sighted a perfect drawing of a cow. Hello, Mrs milkman, my sister has materialized in the garden among this stuff, and she is saying in my ear rather loudly and sorely: *Mr*.

'Mr, Mr!'

'Hello, Mrs.'

The scowl drops on the grass like a moonstone. Bounces ever so. And enters my side with a nimble skip.

'Ouch.'

This merry milkman has good taste, but I wish he would greet me with a required bonhomie. Even now I wish he would. Reel this back and replace with intelligent child that knows the difference between Mr and Mrs, milkman with white countenance, no moon, sister present and proud. Get my steam up. Include the wavy roof, and the scuff on the road ignored. Never stepped in the mud in my life. Hold your breath. Here he comes. Clamm, clamm of the hooves. That's the leather shoes he's on.

'Hello, young fella.'
'Hello, hello, hello, Mrs.'

There is a long road ahead of me and this is the place to be setting this down, and I can do it in my own time, because I want to get this old piece mapped, and not go back there again, no sir. I had it with all that and now I'm ready to wander, but in the right direction, that is to say well away from, you know. Now Sue is a nice girl and I found her not so far away from here and Sue is coming with me. Sue is nice. She's pretty. She's got a look in her eyes now that I've begun to notice and I kind of like it. We're a long way even from where I found her. I was kidding. That's what we like about it.

She didn't have anything there. She was starving of every-thing except food. She could of stayed there, but she didn't, she came with me. Now, I respect that, and I'm keeping her, and I hope she stays. If she wants to go, okay, we'll manage that then, but for the moment I'm glad she's here. Maybe we're stuck at the moment at some stupid junction I never heard of before, but Sue's out there, and her thumb's stuck out, and she looks pretty, and she'll get us up the road, wherever we're going. I think Cincinnati is a good place and Sue thinks it might be too. But she's never been there. And I haven't either. So we're heading south and soon we'll get there if we keep on going. That's the main thing.

But I haven't always been here, people.

Once upon a time I lived in Paris, France, and the going was bad. What was I doing there? I was there on account of Art. Now Art, with its old capital, is left behind, and I'm here on account of myself, and Sue.

You can't know what a little dog I was in those days that I'm running from, because you've never been told. Now I'm telling you. Well, one day in Paris the war was over and I went down to the corner shop to get me a paper and read about it. That was not the best war we ever had. No. It was the worst. Would I tell you a lie? I already did, once. That was the worst and I'm glad it's over. What the hell, it was no good that war, and now it's over.

I was passing the brown pipe at the bottom of the stairs where I was living, on my way back in with the paper, when what should I see but two letters. Could these be for me, I thought, and they were. One was from what I used to call home – my little joke. And the other was from a girl.

Now that girl was a very distant girl at that time. She came from Germany, and no, that's not true, she came from Switzerland. And I'd met her some years before that, at a train station. I was young in those times, or younger, and at the train station I fell in love with her. It was the least I could do. She wasn't pretty like Sue, she was beautiful. I'm through now with beautiful, but in those days I wasn't. I hadn't ever even had it.

And then she got on the train after we held each other a while, and I noticed how long her breasts were by feeling them against my chest. And on the grass, which was dry and damp with autumn, I noticed other things about her. For instance she moved once away from me to look at the mountains, and her ass brushed my hand, and it seemed round and warm. That was fine with me. I liked her more because of it. Here was a warm-assed long-breasted woman and I fell in love with her. Her face was dark and her hair was dark and she couldn't speak any English at all. She knew *yes* and *no*, and a few other things in a godawful accent. But I fell in love with her anyway. I wasn't after her language abilities. I loved her for her warm ass and her long breasts. That's the truth.

Now Sue has fine breasts and a slim body but I don't love her. So I say. That's why I'm with Sue.

This other woman she got on the train among all that steam, and the southern-minded porter he shouted something in Greek and what happened but the train took her away. She was going to come back to that town which was a white town under its sky and I was sure she would. I went out into the countryside and stayed in the house of a barmaid I knew. And in the night the dead people of the farm came to the little door and wanted to come in. I had only the blue wood and a bit of fur and linen between me and them. I said no. There was a well beside the house that went right into the earth, to the centre you'd think. But it hadn't been lucky and never held water, which is why the barmaid, who was a foreigner, had the house, because the farm was dry. Next day I packed my water-bottle and my cheese. It

13

was meant to be a cold water-bottle but even the morning was getting to it. And I strolled into town a bit annoyed by the heat and the stillness along the rocky mule-path. I was stumbling along but the Swiss woman was coming back, and I didn't care when I thought of her. There was a letter in the little post-office, where the man made a mess of my name. And he looked up at me and brushed his young face back into place, because he had been asleep. And he, he was happy for me because I had a letter. I was always looking for letters. I opened my letter there and then under his nose and it was from her, and she had found someone else, she said in her version of English, and wasn't coming after all. So I walked out under the sun again, on the track beside the biggest church of the town, a town of churches, and I thought, well, well. I got to the graveyard, where there were pictures of the dead in metal frames, looking as dead in the picture as they were in fact. And I conversed strictly with the dead portraits, and asked them a few questions about how things were, sometimes. They said little, but the squirrels and the birds were in the cypress tree, and they said a lot. So when I turned up the stairs in Paris and saw the letter from Switzerland, I was a mite more than interested to see what she had in mind. It was all stamped and franked, and the town it came from was Berne.

Today I was lying in my room, thinking I was imagining something. The bamboo chair stretched out, already like a man lounging or sunning. I was thrown back sort of on the bed, and the rough Indian blanket. All the furniture blacker than its own black, its mysterious veneers.

It was siesta time for the town, only a few of the black people moving in their familiar time. I was imagining this condition and then half woke up, and knew I was fooling myself. That was myself there in the dream or the daydream. My red shorts in the strange cool and heat were the only live colour. I was imagining the road but really I was thinking of the road, where I had been with Sue. And she was so unreal in the imagining of her that for a while I had considered myself to be making her up. And then with a slow feeling I missed her.

Missed her right there where you do miss people. Where it's hard to find them, but so easy to imagine them, too easy. I wanted to go down the street, out among the blanched houses with all their shops of flowers, dripping with tropical nonsense, painters gone mad, or sane maybe, past the white church in its mocking wood, by the musical façade of *Fast Buck Freddie*'s, and discover everything again in the Jamaican Village, where the Blacks were pretending to live. They were too. A damn good job of pretending.

But I didn't. I fixed myself like I was staring down on my own body, and I said: Go on then, my sleepy friend, dream her back.

Not that I missed her badly, I didn't, or not exactly. It's too easy to say that. Well, I missed our time together on the road to Cincinnati when in fact we were heading south. This is south but somehow Sue seems a long long time ago. Now this is what they mean when they say time passes. Time passes itself out. So many cars on the highway. Each man eager to prove himself against the next. A homely philosophy.

So I must have been younger then, and I was standing on some road in Virginia, not long out of New York where I started, the most foreign of all local habitual cities. Like trying to move forward with your coat caught in the subway door, and the train beginning to inch away into the black tunnel, a well on its side. No, I was standing beside, you might say, a long blown-out hill. Just a road nowhere, and everywhere – everywhere to whoever lived there. Whoever lived there was this girl with a pretty face and a slim naked look to her.

She was quiet but not shy, and she said, straight off:

'Where you from?'

I said I was from down the road, and she laughed and said:

'You go to the Movies much?'

And I said, no, not too much.

'Ever see a picture with Gregory Peck in it?' she said.

Oh yes, I'd seen one, I said.

'Good-looking fella,' she said.

I looked at her. Didn't say anything.

'I mean Peck is,' she said, 'you ain't.'

'Why are you talking to me, then?'

'Because you're just a kid. It doesn't mean anything.'

15

Then up the road a bit I heard a voice shouting, and I glanced down, and a car had stopped, a little sporty car unusual for the country. I was pretty sure the arm waving was black.

'I got to go,' I said to the girl.

'Hey, not without me,' she said, and leapt the fence, and we both hared along to the car, and flew sort of into the back seat. She was glistening with happiness, and the man in the driver's seat let out a great laugh.

'Got some smoke in the dash,' he said. 'Want some?'

And I said yes, and he reached it back and made the car leave the green hill behind him. Far away behind him. His car was all plastic but it smelled like long distance.

'Roll it for all of us,' he said, the man.

'You're from New York', the girl said, 'aren't you?'

'Yes, I am,' the man agreed, but he didn't look round even, when I handed him his smoke. That man drove us way way into the world to some place, and we had to get out at dark. I hauled us into a field, or what I hoped was a field, and we crept in under my blanket, and I kept my suit on, and she certainly kept her dress on. Of course it was a cotton dress, all the country girls wore them.

'Aren't you worried about leaving just with nothing?' I whispered.

'I didn't leave with nothing,' she said, 'unless you're nothing.'

I thought for a bit and thought to myself: Well, you are nothing. But I didn't say so to her. She might never find out if I didn't tell her. So I let her fall asleep against me and she was sure of me and slept warmly. I listened to the owls or the owl, and asked everyone I knew in my head how things were with me. Everyone I knew said in my head that things were going fine. She was a pretty girl and had left with less than nothing because she had left with me. I didn't know what father or mother or even husband she had abandoned or freed, or ruined or celebrated, and I never did know, not for certain. She was Sue, and Sue appeared like that at the side of the road. And I thought Cincinnati was a good place. So we went south though Cincinnati is not south. Maybe going south to Cincinnati lost her for me. She was a gentle little animal asleep against me and I wanted to sleep myself, but even so it was sufficient and restful to have her there like a soft oven, a real rabbit. I wondered of course what I was going to do with no papers and no passport, and not even American, though trying to be, and only the one suit of clothes, and now Sue to take care of. And it didn't worry me a bit. She was Sue to me and I had been waiting for Sue. Nothing had gone right up to Sue for a long time. So she was like money in the bank from the start, and for a good long time.

In the morning, my field was a chilly intersection. Just a wedge of green between the tar.

Imagine, Moll, being pushed to the top of a huge blue picture and being told: You stop there. And down at the bottom the man paints a distant dark sea, a bay of islands mile after mile. And you, Moll, are still the black bone at the top, a little aeroplane. A forgotten bit. When you look out the tinny window you see only bright bright dark, and you remember the cities with their exact grids, thousands of yards of activity littered with colour. The carlamps going up shine yellow, and the carlights going down shine red, so you get a swapping of red and yellow on the straight promising design. But here above the sea there is only bigness and the littleness of the plane. As a consequence my ears are gone vicious on me and I can't enjoy anything. The miniature plane thunders tinily through the minutes on its way to the end of America, a raisin sinking through flour. I was on my way there, Moll, because the army had almost done for me. I had my few pounds or dollars, I had my few bits of clothes.

I'd wanted the wife and kids, all the notions of them. But it wasn't for me, not in the upturn. But the thought of a baby, that was the long thought. Never mind. The old brain was not the best, not the sort for that sort of business. I couldn't have looked after a lassie, and a kid might have been ashamed of me, and, great christ, it might have taken after me. And that wouldn't do, Moll. I'm just an old parrot, and that's that, so I thought: The end of some place will suit me fine. So let it be the end of this place. The bottom of England, the bottom of Ireland, the bottom of Europe, all would have attracted me equally.

So I came in with my battered ears. I couldn't hear a thing

17

except the remote buzzing of nothing at all – and the hum of the other passengers, a big hulk of a fella and a fancy lady. But as soon as I had my old boots on the ground I smelt that fine forgettable thing, the rich half-rotten thin military smell of the sea. Land that is the part and parcel of the sea, land that was covered once or nearly, the butt of the Atlantic, where the storms have to stop for lack of resistance. Because there was nothing there, Moll, only the drunken smell and the shed for an airport.

I had me a big taxi, driven by a lass, into the town. Imagine any American city studded through with palm-trees, and everything on the flat, and imagine the ordinary streetlamps lighting quare-looking colonial houses, white-porched and white-walled and white-hearted. And the taxi on its big black wheels pouring through this welcome like a smooth liquid, and me perched up in the back, fingering my dollarbill in my palm for to pay the girl. And worrying about what size of a tip would suit her in this faraway place. But money was the same there as anywhere, and her turned cheek, watercoloured with a fight of shadows, seemed happy with the few extra cents.

It was late at night and the moon had taken over, and she left me at a broad wooden boarding-house near the middle of the town. Everything there made of wood, except the trees were made of cloth, hairy fellas on the pavement.

Well, Moll, it was a young girl let me in. That town was made up mainly of young girls, or so I was beginning to think. In fact it was a place of whores, fishermen, killers, addicts and smugglers, with some of them all these rolled into one, and then young girls, and the Blacks, and the few respectable types in their flighty mansions, and their servants, and the moon at night.

She put me up in a fine big quarters, with a fireplace that you'd never use, and that was a never night for the never moon. And confident black furniture, and a bed with a blanket like the ones you'd shoot Indians for, if you ever shot Indians, Moll. I put my few things on the bed, and considered myself well-landed, with a few dollars and a nice cheap kip. I clapped my limbs and hoped the town was waiting for me. And I found myself the nearest bar, The Bull Bar, where they had a famous killing once, The Bull Bar Killing at Key West, if you ever heard

18

of it, and looked over the inhabitants.

A whole whack of Texans and southern types, and all of these drinking beer, and nothing in the way of a local. I decided they didn't have locals there at all in that locality, besides the Blacks. I established myself on small currency up at the bar, and had my beer pulled for me, and I drank in the barwoman's arse, as she bent like the best. I examined her public features too, in the bad light from a faky silver lamp, that hung like a ship's lantern in the surprising breeze. She was breezy herself, from somewhere like New York, but she wasn't friendly. In fact, no one was friendly, and I got speaking to no one. The way the old head moves a bit put them off, I suppose. So I hunched there, absorbing the guitar player.

He had rolls of good obvious potato-fat over his dirty shorts, and he was standing snarling happily or unhappily, you couldn't tell, into the microphone. He was singing into the red light, and all his songs were about Texas. There was nowhere else for that fella. The others, who weren't speaking to me, liked this singer and clapped him well, and lurched up and pin-pointed bits of change into his glass, and bulled to the barmaid to bring him his drinks. God, he was a big fat man with a broken dog's voice, and he knew what he was about on the instrument. And I sat tight with the beer, feeling pretty lonely for a lot of things, even Texas, where I'd never been, and wondering about the Boers, and whether they'd be holding on to South Africa after all my trouble. But no one was paying my trouble any heed, neither the red lamp nor the arsy girl, nor the wild men chanting after the screamer.

And I got up when it was low time and the night was gone, and my instinct seemed to have failed me again, and I made it home bushy in the head from the travel and the beer. And wanted my woman, or any of the women I was supposed to have had but hadn't. That's the worst of me, drunk. I mean the one or ones I might have had, Moll, if I hadn't had myself instead.

Wherever the vehicle went from that time, till this time, if you could call it a time, I, in the natural way of things, went. Not

19

out of passion exactly, perhaps duty and circumstance denote it better. If it was a hard passage, it was what I was paid, though not in kind of course, and designed for. Nothing brought me up or trained me in its cause, to speak precisely, no particular light backed no particular course. But nevertheless the vehicle reached the certain impasse of getting himself born, and therefore I came into the picture. Came into the picture is right, except you would have been hard put to pin me, or point me out. Indeed, keep your greasy fingers out of my direction.

What lies before the vehicle, or lay, I forget. It is not an archival head, mine, obviously. No one would confuse it with a computer, in its day-to-day memory. But periods I do recall, blocks of whatever, pieces of fate as it were. And if my duty was to follow the vehicle, *in* the vehicle you might say, then my duty I calmly obeyed. Not for me brilliant reaction, or world wars, or successes. I am those in antithesis, and what would some have done without me, the mirror, the familiar – a mirror broken in the celebration of seven years' ill? Eh?

I address the night, the small jumble of greys and blacks, and the night is very critical of my use of such words as *address*, when *talk with* or *speak to* might have done. The night is at heart normal, and hates circumlocution and euphuism, but the night has no character, and I don't criticize it for that, so let it keep its comments to itself. Actually I give it life where it probably only has semblance, you know? Or so I would wish, if the dictionary would let me get away with it.

In the course of the years I often asked myself, why this vehicle in particular? Why not a statesman or a robber, or a whore? Someone of especial interest, even a prurient one, appeal to the parts or the heart. This, apparently, is my fortune. I'll let it go at that. But please note this for future reference, Mr night, and god bless *address*.

So here is my mixture of tremendous secrets and tiny motives, merely to pass the time. If I am moved by the absence of importance, all to the good. It is a long time since I properly catalogued what was not in need of cataloguing. Let it go, I always think and fare thee well. I may be celebrating a parrot and a carrot, for all I care. I'd rather do this than propagate the special, because the special is a spurious manmade commodity, mere metal. Here's the stupid soil, and I'll be engaging in a stretch of strip-mining. It will be bones for us all, sooner or later, but just for the moment I'll say: Long, long ago, in a small town of the west of Ireland, namely Sligo – it doesn't matter what town it was, it was a small sewer of a place, and the people were gruel-minded and often unusually mean. The silver wind, that had no real currency, caused this in the population, because it scoured out their decency, and what was left was a clean whistling bone of smallness. They despised the country people, with their soft turf, and their tough marriages and non-marriages, and their puerperal muddles, slipping into all sorts of wrong-doing, by way of courtesy.

When the countrymen came for their few groceries, they felt a rain of invisible spit, like pebbles and stones, falling on their reddened faces. And the pubs were slow to serve them even – even the money-careful publicans.

To be, then, a legitimate son of the small farms was no good. And so to be an illegitimate, a dropper, a baster, was the last end of humanity, when, of course, it is really the first end.

In the light of your mother's bad luck you were doled your days, an old mule before you were out of shorts, if you had shorts. If you were a child of normal intelligence, you were considered an idiot.

The first trial of Batty Moran's life was the poor house. Far be it from me, a mere chronicler – a small joke – to say what he suffered there. But he did suffer, and it left its mark. In some foul ditchy manner, he was addicted to the place after he survived it. Hundreds of babies from all over the countryside went in there, and from the bleak town too. And the gentle motherly nurses – still ferocious in their ancient photographs, that spoil their graves – dosed the brief mouths with mercury to cure the syphilitic little childer. Now, whether or not they had this disease was impossible to tell. But the nurses *knew*. So the babies got their dose of mercury, and it killed most of them, about ninety-nine-point-nine per cent, as people say. That's a lot of little corpses to be rotted in the lime-pit. But then it was a great guard against the syphilis, and Dermot the butcher and his wife could feel safe for another generation. Their pale broad children, with brains like paper hats, could feel certain of a disease-free wife or husband in the coming happiness.

Maybe Batty Moran had a liking for mercury as a mite, but

whatever it was, he got over it. Perhaps it didn't do his head much good though, because it trembled and shook even as a one-year-old. The nurses were shocked by this survivor, and were sure he really did have the syphilis, what with the unsteady crown, and they shoved a bit more of the ever-running stuff into him but he got over that too. And all that happened was his head rolled now and then, instead of trembled.

The poor house was divided into three parts, like Gaul in the school-books, Moran noticed many years later: the invisible Men, the invisible Women, and the visible male Children. Female babies never prospered, as a rule.

Sixfoil Two

Oleever he had no son, he had no ditter. He didint have no nuttin of alla dat, Moll, he were a lone ool feelo, except his quaen. But he did possis his awel poet and is bishopish man. These two werena bruder and nor wier dey cousin, and fighted alla the time, Moll, ara yes. Lord Conn he loved dem not the same. He loved his awel poet, the mangey chap, furst beforn all. Twenty generations he hadded had this lad his famuly in the way of poet, to be sining the oeld song of the tribe that Conn were top to.

Good enoug, youill say, Moll, but I was sore fit in the days of them to be putting it up between meester Owl and the bishop himsel, Larentius. And when one ud be whustlin on the tour of the place, the other ud be singing in the chapli. No, no bother on this, septin when thase two ud maet in the stablin, or mate under the arch that led into the castle propero, when there might be a ferrce rowin of a very bad repoot, with exemplins from the biblio and examples from scriptoot on the one side, and on the other sad sade, alla the learnining of the ancunt peple. For then it was nasty and hot under the arches of this time, and the grooms did complain bad and black, and the nighttimes were all kept up from their snorings. The thunder and the yellow wedder would come a little pace, and set off for odder parts ares quick as bad noos.

My oel poet he were aon oel man, and he had travulled all over till he came back to Olleever, the chieftain man. Becorse, lass, in the oel times, first out, the blackness of dethe had lain over dem perts, as taulk has, and it had dishpersed the popule with the oel poet man include. But dethe he had decided to pull over to Galloway somways, and sometin had recovered its head about the shalders of Sligey. And poet and herdsman heard fine noos of it, and were after caming bok in the drooves of their delicht. And meester Owl he came spritest of most in the cause

23

of his dear man, the holy Conn. And he had many a fair lick of new song, that were old in his baggy, but new to Olleeve. And the songs were wandereres stuff, and it made some fair contrastin to the present pacefulness of the princish dominoon.

'Yer a boutiful returnin, Mastra Owl,' says Olleever Connn, with some show. He had three peegs kulled from the group in the peig spot. And messter Owl lad his nakked boody on the grun, and let the clothes of the late day cover hos oel limbs, that had no attractin left in em. The womin he had luved, and had melted him, were oel in their time, and alla dat, Moll, was spruce finish. But dem new clothes put new manner in his lep, and his mout seemed all the ruddier for it, and the lines were again brookish, and like the pleasant oel ocean. And the babbs and the childs and the lassy women remembered the dance, the blue dance they knew afor the dethe, and they bluely did cross the gras, and all were felled with juice like a little forest.

Bishop Laren he wus faar from joyed. He cam to the door of Olive, and asked permisoon of the hairycoat for audience with the maister bravoon.

'Come in, oul bishop,' calles Conn from itherwards, where the black flies were in the sad heat and roast of noon.

'You have it fine now,' says the learned moan, alluding to the newest carvung and such, that had occupied the workmen from the muill.

'Are you good?' says Ollever, and:

'Not the worst,' says his bishop. 'But the ole man has cum hame, as you well collect. It will be many things: viz, the end of chastute peramong the ladies, and the end of sobernis among the lads. He will be in amid their defence before the holy pigs can scream et. The black dethe will rejourney. And I'll be called to count for it all among the servoonts and the salves. He hiss no fearing min uf gawd, and that heartily, and he doant know one ting aboot religoon, apart from ooman sacrifeece, and spillin insides of good animools. All of which is nat churchwise or reasonable.'

Ollever glanced most greyly to the foine little winder he had newly put, Moll. And asked himsel wehere patioonce were to be had, efen dearly. And he turned to the highsmellin bishoop, and he stoop to him, and he said:

'A little beet of bletherskiting on yern part, Bishop. The oel poet and his fathers have bine on this pert for a thousand year. The place, such as you see it now, is of his creatoon. He made the trees and the castel and he madde my fathers. He kepte them all from hurnt, and kepte them Coons in rightful breadth. His oel faders took the seeds for de trees froma their puckets, and sowed dem. Dey are de seeds of distant oak circles.'

The quaen, his hold bride, cam in, as alays withoot the holy brood Conn woulda liked for his age, and taked the part of the bishop. And Conn said:

'Ye see, man, yer the womanes favoorit, and so I will have not much to do wit ye. Ye are the power of the present time and so I leave ye to yer office. But poet he madict this prisoon for us, and poet is honour for our bottoms and our hersts.'

The bishop went off, with his body steamin sorry he had spekn at al, what with the ire he ad awaoke in the headest man, which he hadna seen before. And the poet was safe enough for the avenire. Conn said:

'Little queen, you are brave and half nasty to take with him. Here we have disputes closin in the far off, and even we are warrin.'

And the queen lifted her clothes, and the Conn remembered whoy he had linked her, notwithstanding the politic of it. Because she had a solid circular bottom that was his delicht. So they hove into the bed straight off, Moll, and the Conn, lord Olive, dogged her as she desired. And he loved the great smell from her, and hated it also. For it was the smell of the middle woods, where everything was growin and rottin at the middle time.

Last night, in the noisiest bar I could find, I was thinking about the green garden, about how old I would have been then. And I decided I would have been three or so. I couldn't for the life of me remember two things: my father or my mother. Well, my mother as she left in the evening for the theatre, but never my father. He just isn't there. and yet that not being there makes him there, somewhere, mysteriously. He didn't register on my circuits, that's all.

What was the house, then, was it male or female? Standing

25

on the steps wanting to get in out of the fright, what was that? I was looking for my father when I was talking about the milkman, but no matter how far I took it, my father didn't appear. A funny child, who remembers the milkman, and not his progenitor.

And there was the stick woman also, whom I don't think I ever saw clearly, but whom I certainly retain an image of. It might be evening in the summer, which, if it was a good summer, showed as watery yellow on the tops and tips of the houses in the square. The bird in the distance is not a bird, but the tap of a stick, regularly against the caging railings. As the sky is a little brown I am confusing it with my hair, which I know is also brown. I am being painted into the moist sky. The mousy clang is coming up the square, and as I realize what it is I climb up the hilly steps to the summergreen door, and tremble the wood ever so slightly, with a bright hush instead of a knock. My eyes like snails are twisted, and my neck is mangled, trying to catch a sighting of the stick woman, the mad evil crying stick woman, who will do something or other to me when she arrives. Better my grandfather on his old bicycle and a bag of purple rocky sweets than the sweetless stick woman. Far better: my grandfather will go down on his knees in his worst suit, which he puts on to visit me, and I can be his rider across the faraway carpet. I want the servant to appear, to come like air, to be in front of me. Even to lift me out of the stick woman's path. And the tonk-tonk on the railings is a tiny bit fuller each time, and the roofs are a tiny bit yellower, and the space above most things browner. She's almost here now, and she'll have me. So I hurry down the steps, and run around the greenest grass in long circles, to make myself vanish. If I run, I might take off like a dirty gull. I get my arms flapping well, and hold my breath, and I am surely almost afloat. I can't hear the stick tapping anymore. And when I fall, I pluck up again. And hum like mad. If she's here now she won't see me, because my hum is very white and covers me. And then I stop like rain and open my leaping eyes, and one leg poises like a crane. Because the grey head on a fat cardiganned body and a tonguy bag is reinterpreting everything about the hedge. The old hedge keeps her out, and the railing keeps her stick going. I see the grey trouble of hair very clearly, like it was painted on the brown late town.

And I'm still, and all I want is the house, the insides of the house, I don't want to play in the garden, or anywhere else, just the house, and if I wake the landlady with my thumping let them not mind. The grey hair is passing, but it won't pass. It goes slower and slower and slower, and the hedge seems to stumble to keep up with it. After a long time the hedge can't keep up, nor the garden, and it stops all together, and the grey hair rushes on further up the square, where the other boys are, one to each garden. And certainly we all want the same thing: to be inside the walls with the crabby servants who call you *a bitcha*.

But it's the house I wanted, I see that, not my mother or father in particular. I stood in the middle of that fear and shouted:

'House, house, house!' instead of *mummy, mummy*. And the house never answered.

Once upon a time I was away down the country with Auntie Anne, and when we were coloured back in the Volkswagen after the six months, I do remember my mother. She was passing time at the top of the steps and the door was pleasantly open behind her, and I know what I thought, I thought: She looks older. Why I decided she looked older is difficult. Obviously *I* had become older, and saw her better, or even for the first time. There was a grey fall to her skirt, and her face was exhausted. It comes to a halt there, because whether or not she embraced me I can't remember. It is her on the steps, a trifle greyly and tired, that has stayed.

I didn't miss her in the country because I didn't retain her, not among those narrow lanes and greedy grasses, where the calves were full of milk and the horse full of calves, too fat to escape from the stable up the lazy falling field, and into the forever trees.

But when I found my mother anchored loosely at the door, me peering at her through someone's car-window, and discovered her older than she could ever have been, then I missed her. And now even I miss her, never having reached her at the top of the steps. According to my memory, she is still there, and I am not even still in the back of the car. She is still older and older still. What can I do to help her when she doesn't shake off her quietness and her greyer self, and run down the steps

27

and out the iron gate and wrap me round? She doesn't and she remains so. So it's not her I miss truly, but her opportunity to be alive properly, to gather her children and make them alive too, to make a central place with an ordinary light so memory can have a chance to work, so you can miss then only your own opportunities and your own felicity, and not just the possibility of theirs. But never mind the plural of parents. Because even here, which is nowhere, my father isn't.

I hadn't shaved. The era of the stranger was already afoot but I didn't know and I hadn't washed very recently either. The room had no shower, only the most complicated compromise between a sink and a bath. A fat white container could be brought to the sink for balancing in, and a shower-curtain hooked up to a pattern of string and coat-hanger above. I trained a shower-nozzle into this, and the main job was not to get clean, but keep the water from reaching the floor, and appearing unexpectedly on the ceiling of the rich apartment-holder underneath. This was a major complaint of his to the landlady, though I had never seen him. I only lived between dirt and the expectation of him having me kicked out.

The shower-nozzle always dripped, and I had to be terribly careful not to leave it on its notch, from where it could drown the underflat if I left the room for half a day, as I often might, but in the sink, safely and gutteringly.

Washing took place then in the kitchen, so-called, because that was where I lexically kept my food and the little electric rings kept court. My room proper stared blankly out over everlasting grandeur: the Hôtel de Ville and the churches, and if I stuck my head out and craned, Bastille, and away in the other direction, the remote aristocracy of the good end of the rue de Rivoli.

This room was fine, except for the traffic all day and all night, which was worst when it was motorbikes. Four traffic-lights grew far below my seventh-floor window, and the air brought up their decisions and hesitations crudely and generously. In the sunk night the bikes bulled with melancholy at the lights, and the thoughtless glowing lay like an idle tramp against the panes.

Once, passing the Tuileries, I saw a tramp like that being rolled up in plastic by the police, and brought away to his warmest dissolution. The tramp of the night festered and growled, but didn't give up so hardily. And each midnight leaned against my window-glass, while I lay in the blue-covered bed, and tried to sleep emptily. I never could sleep till the white bureaucratic morning brought the civil servants with their *lettres de cachet* to their lives across the gap.

And when I slept figures visited me – my sister swept in once, and pushed my shoulder to wake me. But I thought if I woke up, it might not be her, but another, so I kept on dreaming.

But that was the beginning of the stranger too. Before her my most familiar companion in the city was my fright of dying. It was bound up nicely with the brown water of the old river, that moved as gracefully but also as fast as it could through the beautiful careless houses. It flowed through because when it reached the sea it could journey incognito and spread itself into safety. One afternoon I stopped in the middle of a bridge, and wondered if in the rain the water was warm, like seawater is in the rain. I remembered my sister entering the warm rained-on sea below the houses years ago, and the heat of the water allowing her to enter the present also. I felt on the bridge I had no present, or one I was allowed go into. And I wondered, for a moment, about the temperature of the river and the temperature of my life. Then the letter came, and its papery information was a new leaf for everything. It was only a leaf, but I thought I could see the tree behind it and then the wood, and even maybe a forest. The forest would have to be on a hill away from the city, so the letter was both distrusted and celebrated.

I wrote, and said any time she wanted to come to Paris, or was passing through that way, I would be very glad to look after her, as long as she remained and needed protection. I knew how frightened she could be among strangers, though she was the ideal stranger herself. I also recalled how much an idiot I had considered her at the vanished station, but hoped it was on account of her English, and not her personal intelligence. I was flooded too with cinematic recreations of how it had been with another girl before, and how it might well be just the same again. So I pulled back from the idea of her coming and needed to welcome it at the same time, because I was almost in that

29

river on my way to the sea.

I was expecting her to bring her lights and leggy gifts the next day. I told myself she was the most beautiful woman, or one of them, I had sighted in my white life, and certainly the most beautiful that had ever shown any interest in me. This was a constant talisman: the most beautiful woman, the most beautiful woman, a reason for everything. Her name was Xenia, which in Greek means the stranger, so I was probably suffering from a mixture of xenophobia and whatever its opposite is.

Between these two bulwarks, she had arrived early. At the top landing it was clear that, at the end of the unmoved glimmering corridor, my narrow door was half open. I suddenly was very aware that I hadn't known the girl for more than an hour or two, and over a year ago into the bargain.

My room and a half was in darkness, a sort of moody darkness I didn't recognize from the place, usually so much itself and unwelcoming. Vaguely I distinguished her shape on the mattress, twisted unnaturally, and hopefully asleep. She seemed more murdered than asleep.

I sat on my blue chair and leaned on the thick desk, and wished not that she would go away, or wake up, or that all would be well, or that this time would be the beginning of the golden time. But only that I had shaved.

She was curled in a sleep that I suspected was faked but didn't mind. It gave me a chance to look at her silence first, and gauge her possible noisiness. She had cut her brown hair to the skull. It gave her body a suggestion of extraordinary heat. Her skull was breathing heat and immediately I was confused. I was calm enough and was trying, faithful to her possible memory of me in the other country, to be chill and silent. In the other country I had been happy and didn't need anyone, and on the chair I was working myself back to this point. She only had to stay asleep for a year and I would reach it.

I stood in my grey dry coat, and wished I had shaved, and crept over near her. The white walls, hung with blue cloth and their six assorted mirrors, stood up with me. The traffic's concert was gone. For the first time in that room I was really in it, and not in space surrounded by discord. She was pretending probably to be asleep, and even with that gesture she had centred me. I was sure I was dying, and I wished I had shaved,

30

fervently. If I was dying, still she was here now, and the god of Notre Dame might let me live a few weeks with her. When the rotting began I knew I would have to leave her, because she'd notice. But I prayed that the only god there was, the god of stony top-sainted Notre Dame, might allow me a small stretch of colour.

Her *Hello*, when it issued from her mouth, was made of stretching plastic, which flew in a pulled cone to my own mouth – which made it easier to answer. I didn't recognize anything about her and I dreaded my death, but I recognized the childish whisper and flicker of her voice. She had no extra English in her bag, anyway.

I didn't touch her, though I considered it, as a gesture, as a danger. Part of my worry about her coming was the undiscussed nature of her visit. Was she to sleep with me in the blue coffin, or was I to make up a bed for her in the far corner, beside the eternal radiator? This had been a terrible concern, which I now regained forcefully.

She was gripped by a remote close smile, and the strange long *Hello* appeared in the room again.

'Are you early?' I said, as if Early was her name and I was overcome by a peculiar distant curiosity. The coolness of my attitude shocked me, because it was the first unnecessary barrier and I was building it singlehanded. I wanted in some way to ignore that she was here on the bed I had mumbled and felt myself for death in, at which the electric clock had spat its lit numbers, against whose wakefulness the tramp had filthily leaned and not cared. I was so unused but accustomed to being alone, not only in the room but the city too, apart from the river, that I almost couldn't accommodate her presence. In fact she was, in an untrue manner, not there at all, as insubstantial as my dreamed sister.

We got the hell out of there, and ferreted for a restaurant, and on the way she linked my arm, and was very excited and beautiful. She was excited and she did link me, though much later she denied that. I was unafraid and wondered if I really was finished. And I could barely make her out under the enthusiastic lamps of the street.

'When I was young,' Sue said, and I stopped her with:

'Sue, you are young.'

'You mean now?' she said.

'Yes. Aren't you? I mean, don't you feel yourself so?'

'Oh I'm young enough,' she said.

She had her legs stuck up on a piece of tree-trunk that had drifted surprisingly onto the edge of the road. There wasn't a scrap of a tree in sight besides it.

'Don't be staring at nothing,' she said. 'Listen to me. When I was young I had four uncles. Three of my uncles were very boring, but one of those uncles, whose name was not Sam, smarty, but Goran.'

'What sort of name is that?' I said, with a stupid loud part to the *that*.

'Yugoslavian,' she said, 'Yugoslavian, will you hush, I'm trying to tell you?'

'Oh I'm listening okay,' I said. I was also watching her legs where they were appearing from under her light dress. She knew well I was doing that, and she didn't touch the hem. She spread herself ever so slightly more open and casual, and the story she was telling idly was part and parcel of the dead piece of wood, that must have fallen off somebody's pick-up. But why in high summer someone was hauling wood was a mystery to me.

'But we called him Joe for short,' Sue said. 'And anyway he didn't like his name, much. He was a big, big man who always wore black and worked hard as anything for his family, and one day he came to see my father, are you listening? My father who was his brother, naturally. And I was just born. And he looked around the little house my father was pretending to live in, you know, and my father looked at him, and said he didn't know where he was to put me, since there were already four other kids spotted around the house. This was in Kentucky because we didn't always live where you found me.'

Sue's legs were smooth like the belly of the wood she was resting on. They were wooden but there was also something alive in them, a sort of slow liquid wood. They were extremely brown, and were brown even deep under her dress, I could see. She had a little pair of dirty white socks on, that didn't cover her ankles. She was so neat and ordinary and brown that I didn't

32

even want to touch her. I felt like waiting, like you tease your-self with chocolate when you're hungry but respect the taste of the brand. Not that I wasn't getting very hungry. I was.

'Well,' Sue said, and her ordinary fine hair fell back because her chin thrust up. 'Buddy, you know what happened? Why don't you fuckin listen, you crumb?'

'I am listening, go on, will you?'

'Okay, my father,' – she said *father* in a queer way. It was queer even that she said *father*, instead of *pa* or *da* or something – 'my father left the room to itself and the uncle and me then, because he had an errand to run. Now my old ma was dead at this time, you know: stone cold and sober dead. So my father was thankful to have the old uncle to look after the babby, that is to say, me, little Sue. Should we get something to eat, hon, or what?'

'Go on with the story. In a minute.'

'Oh it isn't any great story,' she said. 'I've bored myself with it. Where was I? Well, when the father returned in his hasty way that did for the old ma, I suppose, all he could see in the bright little room was my big uncle Joe, in his black clothes, and no sign of me, where I had been resting on the red chair. I was very fond of the red chair, sugar. Don't underestimate me, I have feelings. My father stoked up and said, where in hell is my daughter, what have you done with my girl? And the biggest uncle in the world laughed with a steamy noise, and reached over to the chest of drawers and pulled a drawer that was a bit open already, and my father crept over like a cat and peeked in, and there I was. That, said my uncle is what we poor people do, when there's one too many in the house. And when I went to Uncle's house, years later, it was true. Most of his children had slept in drawers at one time or another, and the youngest there by his second wife was just growing out of his drawer at the time.'

'Sue, can you step out a while, and see what you can do about a lift?'

'Oh, sure,' she said. 'Now, how'd you like my story?'

'I like it a lot but it's late now.'

'Okay, I'm stepping out.'

And she made her brown brown legs lay a sudden colour against the ditch. We were still in sunlight.

'Wait, Sue, where you going? The road's this way,' meaning the road was just beside her.

'Naw,' she said. 'Wait up a little. I've got to, you know.'

And she rustled away into the secret cornfield, and I was left alone on the dirt. A huge car started up on the brow of the slowly inclining earth, and my eyes flickered, wondering whether I should try it or not. There weren't too many cars and we were getting hungry. I couldn't exactly smell the hamburger I pictured in my brain, but I could smell the sauce. But I hated standing out like that, because they never stopped for a man. I had a pain in my backside from pressing it against some pretty unfriendly ground. I pulled up and got my thumb out.

I could see my thumb like a wretched little animal against the immense fields of corn, going away like travellers into the next county. The car was so big, nothing could have passed it going the other way. But it was a city car and from some city far away because it was layered in dirt and dust. I didn't believe it was happening when this great beast began to slow down, roaring itself and me into a fright. The driver got it to halt.

'Sue! Sue, come on!' I shouted, and the middle of the field started to tremble. I shouted in to the driver to please wait, half expecting the shaking engine to pull off again. But the driver stayed.

I was on the ditch scouting out over the field. And for a second I pretended that the car was mine, and Sue was mine, and I was calling her impatiently to hurry on with her peeing, so we could travel on. But the car wasn't mine nor the ditch, nor Sue, so I bellowed out to her hidden shape, deering away through the corn. And I cursed the girl for going so far in just to relieve herself, when the fine car might juice up and leave us two wretches to whatever would've happened next in that husk of a place.

Even though there was a strange cut to the room the next morning, and a strange cut to what I had left for vision, I was content enough with the return of my ears. Apart from a narrow dullness at the bottom of my earlobes, I felt they had pulled themselves up again from the well. I thought I'd better stay on in

Key West a good while, rather than go through all that again. I must have been good and drunk the previous night, and achieved that condition quickly, because it was only now in the mess of lights that the room attracted from outside, through palm-leaves, and across a little covered balcony, that I even remembered the miserable veil and thrum. I must have presented a wonderful sight to the bar people with my old head and deaf to boot.

I crammed myself into the boxlike toilet at my disposal, and disposed of beer and what might have been the remains of bar food. I knew I had got home fine, because obviously I was in the room, but I didn't remember how or when. Something about women trickled back, and I tried to regain any memory of a café or stall where I might have eaten. Well, Moll, I didn't feel exactly hungry, but you try and pinpoint the origin of your shit anyway. I don't like to think of myself staggering around gorging at strange counters. Maybe I had munched on some victual in the bar. Funny how confident I am when I'm drunk that I know what's what, and then in the morning I can't recall a thing because truly I'll have been in a ruinous condition under dark.

Behind the lattice of thin white wood the green plants held stock still in the warming air. I thought: but had I been drunk? Or do I just forget what happens, drunk or sober? I flung an old shirt on me, and the old blue trousers that were easy and loose, which I used to have for the tropics.

The mirror on a desk drew me, and I dropped on the stool in front of it, a queer stool like an African's, painted a feminine blue. Of course, I was still there more or less. The ugliest face in christendom. It's not that I was a monster, but my eyes were far too small, and my head far too large. It was a nodder too at the best of times, and sometimes I plain hated it. I poked at it that good morning with my fingers and held it and half-caressed it. You can grow very fond of a big unloved thing like that. My ugly duckling on top of my own body. But very little likelihood of it turning into anything of the swan variety. I began to sweat, like I occasionally do, with a sort of boggy fear, a bad feeling that the head is getting even bigger, even more astonishingly otherwise to the normal. I slapped my ears on one side, and struck my lips and teeth in front. The same old flush blood trickled out to surprise me, and I leaped up off the chair. I was at that trick again. I stuck my hands in my scanty pockets, and after a moment threw a dollar in with one of them, and fled the shadowy room.

The girl was at her table, writing on slips of paper.

'Hi,' she said, 'Sleep okay?' There was something wrong with such friendliness.

'Oh, yeh,' I said, very jaunty, forgetting immediately about my head.

'Breakfast?' she said, and opened her hand towards a sideboard of brown cakes and coffee.

'Ah, yeh,' I said. But I didn't like the idea of her being there to watch me. She wasn't eating herself.

'Help yourself,' she said, and followed some notion of her own out the back of the house. She could hardly have known what I had thought.

I tried the brown cakes, but there was far too much dry wheatmeal in them. No juice, Moll, you wouldn't approve of that. The coffee did a lot of good, as is its duty in the world. Then I got to wondering how most mornings of my middle life, that's to say after childhood, I had worried about my head. And yet it never did get any bigger, but, all the same, was always the same, and never smaller. I supposed I was waiting then for it to shrink. But how could it? A head once grown couldn't shrink if you had your vigour. Now, Moll, of course, my head is quite the usual size from age, and even if it weren't it wouldn't bother me, because of you, and how friendly you are. This isn't much of a place, but it's our place in a way that somewhere else wouldn't be, eh, Moll?

I gazed at my legs, which weren't as straight as a ruler either, and attempted a few minutes of plan-making. But with nothing very much in mind or decided, I strolled out onto the main porch, and had a gawk at the street. A couple of Blacks on bicycles, very young girls, were on their way somewhere, but not in any hurry. Their bottoms looked like cushions. It was already wood hot, you know: when you lean on anything and it has started to burn. That was very pleasant.

So I leaned on the wooden railing that was in the new sun, with my body in the inquisitive shadows, and watched the nothing that was going on in the street. I relaxed splendidly, felt

I might stay there for ever. I knew though, that forever has to be financed, and set off from the grainy steps to the stone pavement, to find my fortune you might say.

I was sober and clean now, and the houses impressed me in the daylight with all their silent clamorous blooms, and the shell-white paint on a few of them. Even the run-down places were happy in the sunlight. Why wouldn't they have been? The Blacks didn't live about that quarter at all, it seemed: the two girled bicycles vanished away into the muddled sunny distance.

I wanted to find the sea but didn't know where it was. So I got myself back into the suddenly cool house and called the girl. She was just behind a door in the long shippish hall.

'Hi,' she said again, as if she hadn't seen me for at least a day. I puzzled this a second and then asked her where the sea was.

'Do you want a beach?' she said.

'A beach?'

'For swimming.'

'No, I don't know how,' I said. 'No, I just want to see it.'

'Well, all roads here end up at some part of the coast or other and it's never far.'

'So if I just wander along someways?' I said.

'Well, if you follow the street just outside the house,' she said, 'you'll reach the ocean.'

'Yeh,' I said, 'the ocean, that what I want.'

'It's right there,' she said, 'at the end of the street.'

And then I liked her, a bit, because she sounded like she had arranged for it to be there for my sake.

There were some older children in the poor house, right enough, those that had arrived already grown in this brown world, with a grey sky outside the crumbly windows. Again, they were all boys, because the girls got their breakfast of mercury no matter what age they had managed to reach.

Moran continued on – it was not quite living in the proper sense. He had a moulding sack on the floor for bed, even as a baby, in a puffy room whose most vigorous tenant was the forest of brown moss that lived on the walls. Even high up against the old beams the moss existed, a strange mole-coloured plantation at the edge of Moran's universe. A fire like a dream of falling was stuck up against a corner of the room, where the bigger children spent their days before the marbles of coal.

Batty Moran, and I, lay on the sack and examined the distant ceiling. When very young he forgot the ceiling as often as he looked at it, but after a few years he began to foster a memory, and the ceiling was his memory. Everything of any note that happened in his life happened on the ceiling. He really didn't notice the bread and the soup, and the milk on Sundays, and the nurses and the attendants like drunken spiders, or the other half-mad and half-dozing children. His small black eyes fixed on the gloom of the ceiling during the day, and even at night, when the unwanted dull smudge disappeared like so many faces ducking from the windows, Batty Moran kept right on staring. It was clear he was miserably backward and empty-headed.

Possibly he was backward. But his head, which was thought to be empty, was silently full of narrative, and the stories happened quietly on the ceiling. And Moran as a boy knew this was perfectly natural. He had his stories and his man and woman and his boys, like any other child, but they were things that breathed properly at the top of the walls.

Moran presumed that this was family life, and growing up, and he was happy enough. His surroundings after all were thoroughly unreal, and he only looked on all that as dreams, bad or bearable.

The woman's name was Sug and the two boys were Do and Da. He couldn't often see the man, and sometimes he didn't see him for so long he forgot he had one. After a while, though, La would show up again on the ceiling, but he never did much, only scratched himself. Moran scratched himself, so he knew what that was. The doings of the woman and the boys were often inexplicable, and sometimes he had only a white idea of what was going on. He had no language for any of it, anyway, except a queer daft squeeze of words he liked to say out loud: *Sug, Do,* and *Da,* and then the man *La.*

Sug spent most of her time holding the boys in her lap, and talking to them. Moran tried to hear what his woman was saying – he spent years straining to catch her words. She sounded like a bird, like one of the owls that were only doors opening quickly to Moran outside his world.

When Moran was fourteen the man La was always away. He might turn up a rare time, but it was only to eat with his family. His family kept crouched in one corner of the ceiling where things were darkest. La talked without stop, a goosy gabble which was quiet and even, but seemed to terrify Do and Da. Sug put her skirts over her blue head and tried to disappear, but she couldn't. La finished with his food, and approached the coiled woman, and the snakelike boys. The woman pulled her limbs in tighter, till she was almost round and complete. The boys entwined themselves around each other, to make themselves impossible to lift or separate.

But La of course just stroked the skirted head of Sug, and whispered forgotten matters to her through the material. The boys raised their faces, and they were snarling without a sound. The faces surprised Moran because they were extremely fierce. When La turned to them the faces cleared like dawns, and smiled at the big man. They nodded their foreheads and then twisted their hair from side to side, and sang. La patted them also and looked very pleased with himself, and left the ceiling.

Do and Da had a knife from the plates. They circled the ceiling with the knife clutched between them and they looked again like reptiles, elongated, like shadows in the morning. Moran made up this idea of reptile and had some other name for it: *wyrmlic* – but he meant a snake, the notion of a snake.

In fact, the boys Do and Da were turning into Moran's idea. Already their feet were joined, or one each of them, and as they covered the room they stumbled now and again on a beam. Sug still remained covered by her skirt, and didn't seem like ever budging again. Soon the boys were on the ground, writhing effectively, and they were joined into one, seamlessly from nose to toe.

The snake couldn't carry the knife, so it swallowed it carefully. Moran was fascinated by this swallowing: it seemed suddenly to him like a wonderful action. *Swallow the knife, always swallow the knife*. It was a lesson to him.

But the glittering reptile was also shrinking, and after a bit Moran could see the knife inside the belly, with its point thrust out one side, and the handle the other, but not breaking the skin. And the snake twisted even more, but not with its natural movement. It was in pain now. Its body was dwindling perhaps

39

because it had eaten the knife, or because it was normal for the boys to dwindle now they were a snake. Whatever the reason, they were only half their first size now. And abruptly the point of the knife pierced their grey side and pressed out. As the snake thrashed the wound was sawn a little more widely, and at last the knife slapped out wetly, and fell from the ceiling onto Moran's bed. Still Sug didn't shift an inch. Moran thought she would never move again, unlike her panting sons with their luminous gills, who were dying as one on their invisible floor.

Soon after this Moran was forced to get up and try to walk each day. In a month or so he was as proficient as the rest, which wasn't saying much. As soon as he could reach the lake, that spread beyond the door of the workhouse, he flung the knife away into the weedless centre. It was the end of his childhood, because he never glimpsed his family after that.

Sixfoil Three

Bishop, Moll, he were not mich luved be the paple of the toor. They loved the hoary pote, who was much licker their oon natoors. They knew his songs and is songs of family before. And from cradel along they were of is cercel.

Not, ya ixplore, Moll, thaten thiy adored the min himsool. No. Et was de werk of the fellaugh itsel they treasoored.

But bishop they ced nat unnerstind, but were feary to him, in he were put on eart be gods or the one got. The gots of the poet wer their oulde goddes, tha the peasunt paple stull hankered after, and kept the wells and rivoors to. They, the grat min of the toor, had admire for de vanishe goddes, for in that, Moll, tha wur fighteres figoors. Whereus the newe wan wus anly a secreting quiet man wi ghostes attached to his persoon.

Ovveller Coon knew this, an more. It was a ting upside in his knowin. Perhap he hadda it alla square, he whispurred to himself, but better there shoulda be a settlin for it.

So he rode oot to the wilderpart, where the sun was in his vanished dance. And when a gud mile was covered, cam to a villoog in his protectoo. The rain was tryin to make a buckit of the skee, and also overspill her, so on first glances the village was inside out. I mean, if you had pulled it throo like a gansey, the paple woulds have ben found stickin to the hid pert.

His hors was a flighter, so he tied her easy to a tre, which was drawin life from a litool holluck. In the village were nat mur than five huses, the doors of whach he tapped at and made sure noises. It was the thurd hoos that came open for him by the hand uv a leetel boy. These boy, Moll, was a peculiar wan, becairse he was naked, and his instroment of pissung were a foot lang. He had it hangin from his underbelly lik a snaak. Tha instroment were limp, and tha boy nat mur dan seven. So Conn chukcle to himself, and drave all thotes on the boies futur oot of maind.

He pushed his wae inta the hut, which was madde all of grisses and dirt, and stank of the paesoont or slaves kind. It wass one enormoos stench that brak upon his nostrool. But his awn rame were not much better, but that it were mare big and brightened. Thes plas waus unly a tinee refuge for the humoon.

In de muddle were a albeen of muddle-age, nat wuman an nat man bit bothe, Moll. Ites pricker were smal and is cunt part were narrow also. This were displayed be the open thighes of the bastie. It wus a lying spred for the door, on many stinkin owl skins and meterials. Ollevver stood quiet and examined all silent the ting he had fund. Perhap he has herd of this monsteer afor, bat he had no memoire uv it now. The perts of the creatoor were much slimed and doorty. He or it was not much too handsoom, but stil Ollever felt his mannes blud storr, and wanted to lie wid the albeener. But the albe spakk furst and said:

'I see what's in your eye, master. But it can't be. You would break me.'

Coon decide to hold hissel from the rood hermaphroditty. He was astonished by the quare natoor of ittes speech, that seemed most barbaroos to Olleeve.

'What do you want in my village?' sedde the ting.

Conn drewe his height to de toppe, an fellt much aboov the aboorte.

'I iv cum,' he sedde, 'to aksen yer aboot the trubel in me castel.'

'The trouble,' wispeered the cratur, 'you have trouble?' It was so allurrin in its speek at de promis evva trubel dat Coon feel agin his blut rannin likke hates unner has skoon.

'I luv my oel poet,' saz Olliver, 'but I messe haves elso meine Bishoop. Bishop camme frum the god uv Rame, with pooer to destract me kinder. Withouten bishop alles is herd and cold. Bat he iss a leetel fellaugh, that sleepes my wifes night through, and his smalnes is becam mar to her than moi gratnes.'

'You couldn't look at me like that, if it wasn't true, master.'

'Til me then, creatoor moi frende, whar is the goodes uf Masiter Owl, and what mus I doon?'

The cratures facce was growin a scrub of greye harr. The licht increased and Conn came clear to see how furzy the skin was with harr, and nat grey bat blanched. The pinkish skin wass runin with many a soor and scab, and the sex wass manny messed with mannes seed. The hermaphro stirred its bellie with a blacken hand, an de slime slipped and polished unner the softe fingoors.

'I will tell you, as I know,' the halfman sed. 'Sit by me for a while, and listen.'

The lard pushed his oel buttocks by the shalder uv the ting, and stared out to the fluttery door, and the cald dey of watter beyant. He wus aeger to knaw wut might be to what he aseked to kno, bat the ting hadde him bad excite in his perts, and thise shammed him. He knoo iffen he slep on the cratoores bello he woode dee.

'Tal me so, moonster,' he murmoor.

'Your poet's gods are gone. Your house is almost gone. Your poet's gods ruled here for eight thousand years. The bishop's god has only ruled for a handful of hundreds. But still, the older gods are gone. I don't know where. They won't be back. The people here in the village, and all over the province, worship the rivers and the hills and the stones, but they don't know what has happened. It doesn't matter, because the old gods were not much use. They were only colours. But you can see that the colours are gone from your lands. Your poet still has much power, even the same power. That is why you love him. But he is like an underlord whose lord has died without his knowing, and everything outside his strong estate is tightening and closing. The poet will be gone soon as well. Your wife, the queen's daughter, is right. She's playing the stones that will win out. She'll not have you only for a husband, Oliver, but she will be your only queen.'

Coon he gat uep, and nad his hed.

'I dremmed all thiz,' he sighed. 'But it iz nat matoor.' An he coverede nat the fouly bast wit hes deseer, bat leve it quik.

So when did my father first try to murder me? It must have been building up in his head like a small castle, the ramparts from which he could throw me, in some room greenly sitting and hatching a plan to dispose of his hatched egg. Or it may have begun welled in his head and memory, where the worst things swim with the best. He knew I was the enemy in

43

embryo, and so he made sure I would have no recollection of him. Then when he killed me I wouldn't be able to give him away.

Do you know this man who has knifed you?

No, sir, I don't.

Would you recognize him if you saw him?

No, sir, I wouldn't.

He was your father, wasn't he?

Yes, sir, but no father of mine, sir. Mine memory, that is, sir.

You are a queer child, boy. Perhaps the sympathy should lie with your soon-to-be-electrocuted da.

Later, after the first effort to be rid of me, he often said in jest:

'That boy will hang!'

Something or other to do with Oliver Twist, I expect. It was also clever of him to send my sister as his agent. My sister loved me, of course, but because I had arrived after her, in the normal way of these matters she was always on the look-out for an opportunity to bump me off.

On the steps one morning, smack in the wet sun, we were playing or waiting to go out with the servant. Yes, the servant was swimming through the deep brown of the house's interior, down the impersonal hall. She swam by the shoals of the wallpaper and waded through the seaweedy linoleum, a little woman from some barbarous part of the West. She used to wash her feet in the lavatory bowl. But then I used to wipe my shit on the wall behind my cot, so we were equal enough.

My sister saw the servant struggling through head down, and turned to me and gently pushed me off the top of the granite steps. I dropped like a bean-bag, and struck my face on the second or third step, and there remained, not rolling or falling any further. At the same time as I could see only redness in my eyes, I could also see my sister's face framed by the redness, a suddenly bullish wicked face. The image remained while I screamed, and the servant screamed with me, and something was done to wipe the blood which made me howl louder, since my nose was broken.

'What have you done to the critter?' bellowed the servant, and knocked her country head against the wall, probably for fear of what my father would do to her. She was terrified of him. She didn't know my father had wound up my sister at the

44

back where the clockwork handle was. In fact she couldn't even see the handle.

I could still only encompass the red explosion, and my sister's face there in the middle for ever.

I was fixed up by parent and doctor, and my small gristle reset. But my father didn't give up so easily. He waited till I was lulled into my normal fears again, and then set my sister after me a second time. I might have learned by then, but I hadn't, and still trusted the girl, and played with her as often as she'd let me.

Some time later we were idling near a low little window that let out on the garden, with a drop of about a foot. I was very involved with something at my feet, when I looked up at her, because she had started to hum. I knew well what that was. It was the mechanism taking her over again. We had a mechanical bird that gave the carpet a race, that is the design of the carpet, and she was now much the same. She came whirring over to me, and though she was the same size as usual, she was bigger than me. Her face had changed, and she had bristles on her chin like a man that hasn't shaved. Her mouth champed open and closed, as if it too were on a clockwork hinge, as of course it was.

I shouted long and blackly in her face. Despair had got into my legs like woodrot. Her arms stuck out stiffly in front and took my shoulders like a big hawk or vulture. My father's face on her shoulders was smiling benignly. I gawked at it and tried to strike it, but when I reached it with my pebble fist, it was made of wool.

'Dor,' I moaned, 'Dor, Dor, Dor.'

And Dor inched me over to the window, and Dor with my father's face started to drive her head back and forward like an engine. Her hum was loud, and was going to fill the damp room before she was finished.

It was really the hum that pushed me out the window, a weird distortion of my father whistling on a walk. I arced out the little gap in the world, and for a while fell for ever. I never landed till I woke up. It was the similar old thing all over. The servant was in fits, and Dor was scowling, and the red sun had got into my eyes, but this time of course the framed face was not hers, and this attempt had been more successful. Certainly I wasn't quite dead, though nearly, but when the nose healed I couldn't-speak except through it, and was a nasty addition to a quiet evening. I got on everyone's nerves now with my whiny nasal diction.

And I was going to be an outcast, except some doctor or other advised an operation. This must have been part of my father's plan all along, because now something began that didn't stop for years, even though it only went on a few weeks. What happened in hospital I do not remember at all, apart from there being many eagles there, but they didn't bite. In the end, at the end of my tether, I hoisted myself to my jellied legs and gripped the bars. I don't know what I wanted to do, but I wanted in some way to go back, back before the nose breakings, and even before the stick woman. I couldn't manage this business. I saw I couldn't manage, in a diagrammatic manner, and therefore gripped the bars. My head was lifting off, by a lid at the top, and my brain floated out and the eagles flocked for it. Just as they did, someone very like my mother started to appear at the back shadow of the room, and step towards me in small strides. The eagles clamoured, and winged into the corners again, to the plaster, and my brain guiltily hurried in again, and the lead lid shut.

My mother, or something like it, wrapped me up, and tried to bring me back. But she couldn't do it. We went all the way up the steps, and into the raining house, and she put me in my cot, but I wasn't there.

A long café, with a new bar too intrusive for the place, and an inexcellent barman, bent on earning the town a further reputation for rudeness, was our final stop. She was conspiratorial in her friendliness by now. And she had been very kind about the loathsome vegetable stew they had served her, in my supposedly favourite restaurant – favourite meaning cheapest pit in the district. She hadn't concluded anything from the circumstance that I didn't eat anything there myself, at least not in English. Yes, she is beautiful, I was still saying to myself, in a mixture of unease and admiration. But she was also somehow other.

I got as much wine down me as my francs would allow. Poor

as I felt myself to be, it was somehow very important that she didn't pay for anything – not gentlemanliness so much as some brand of keen insurance.

Her black leather jacket was a ditch against all the waiter's lack of enthusiasm.

'Hey,' she said. 'I'm here. I think maybe I even love you still.'

She had given me quite a few details about the Spanish boy she had gone off with instead of me. So with the wine in my head I was having trouble distinguishing between her old love for me, that she had somehow forgotten in the face of him, and her love for him that had been so horribly returned, and now her new love of me that was, in some important way, her old love back again, unspoiled by the middle love.

When someone is fashionably beautiful, you tend to take their word with editorial seriousness, and throw your life down, for this word to step on, rain or no rain, puddle or lake or land. This benevolent face was talking benevolently about benevolent matters, such as her possible love for my benevolent face. And I followed it, and, as Americans say, I bought it. Why wouldn't I have? The night was metallic outside the moistured window-screen, and the severe square, that I had crossed in so many troubled afternoons, was kept from attacking me by her confidence inside so large a leather coat.

My mind grogged back to the café in the station where I first found her, among cardplaying roadworkers and an autumn. And I even recalled precisely my notion of her idiocy and the dismissing letter. But now, under the new rules of the rain, I believed her again. But I didn't believe myself. Myself I took for an idiot, not worthy of her beauty.

This always remained true. I was not. But then neither, in some respects, was she. But never mind. You can lie on a corny ditch in Kentucky somewhere, with a strange but probably sweet lady like Sue, and think what you like. That's what I'm at. I can't be got at here. Like my old pal Netta, the barmaid in the white bar, I have no expectations. Even when it rains here it's different rain than that heart's blood stuff in Paris – like all the dejected Arabs were opening their veins in their verminous rooms, and their grey life was jetting and spurting over the roofs and squares that hurt them worst. I'm glad I'm on this road because there's nothing at all at the end of it, except another

47

road, joined by a brief similar town. Paris has history and history is unliveable. You have to get away from it. That is what I've done. I just wasn't so enlightened in those times. Maybe Sue isn't the Mata Hari, but she's very much present, even if hers is a quaint nebulous kind of presence. Better cloudy than opaque, at least there's something there to muddle over.

Look at me now on that cold green bench, just near to where I had my coffin rooms. I watched my reflection for a second in the glass, and tossed up my hair so it leaned over like grass, black grass, and imagined I was so fine-looking. I reminded myself of that picture by Degas of the absinthe drinker, but the drinker was me, and more pretty and romantic and doomed. Doomed, doomed, doomed. The word doomed brought me up glassily, because I wasn't really capable of entertaining such pictures without scaring myself badly.

'Oh, Oliver,' she said, 'I feel I have done you so bad, you must not be afraid of me. I am not such evil person as you must think. I dun know why I did not come back.' She leaned in earnestly, and quite movingly: 'I am sure I loved you anyway.'

We were quiet while the waiter came over, not to serve us but to whistle beside our table with a wretched air. He was almost sitting on my shoulder. Eventually he padded away to discuss something with the clowns behind the bar, severe black-haired clowns, all slicked and white-aproned.

'If you tired of me I can go walk out.'

'You mean now?' I said. 'It's raining.' I was drunk.

'No,' she urged, 'we say we stay together if we can for a while. When you are in trouble in me, when.' She put her thin hands on her leather-covered chest, and touched the tips of her fingers against it firmly. 'You are tired of me, I go for a walk.'

'Okay,' I said, 'thank you. But it's okay, I won't get tired of you ever. I mean I wouldn't have the right to send someone out into the night, just because.'

'Well that is what I say.'

So I smile at her gradually, very conscious of what it might look like. In the window it looks ghoulish. She reaches over the battered table and grips my hand softly.

'You remember the station,' she says, 'eh, you remember?'

And I glow, very happy to remember the station.

'Oh,' she said, 'the station. What I love was the way you

holded my hand so soft.'

When she said *soft*, her mouth, which was extremely and naturally red anyway, reddened. If she had removed her mouth and put it on the table, the waiter would have charged us for it as some sort of victual.

'Let us go,' she said, like a curious playscript, or the poem by Eliot.

Outside the evening *was* spread out dutifully upon the sky, and I was feeling etherized by her mouth and the wine. The square sloped yellowly.

It was a long mile down the track before the driver spoke to us. There was dust in that part of the world over most things. Handles of pumps stuck up, like huge green sprouts, out of it. The houses sometimes were enlarged to mushrooms or some devilish plant of the brown clean dirt. The black car swept on with a sunny gleam over the young dust. An empty farmhouse winked at us across the still empty surface.

The inside of the car was casual with good leather to sit on, and a few old old cushions, like ones you might have found in those very houses we were ignoring. Some frail lady had put a lot of trouble into stitching and embroidering them. There were strangely savage scenes needled on the covers. Looked like massacres of holy men. At least the white men had white collars under too-bright pink faces. The blacker men had the hatchets stuck in the white. Underneath each cushion-picture was stitched: *Samoa*.

'Samoa.' Sue fingered the lines of the thread, and chucked her chin a bit. She was getting talkative. 'You come from Samoa?' she said.

The driver swung his head to the right.

'Nope.'

'Where you come from?' she said.

'Not important. Up the road.'

'That's what *he* said,' she said, and threw her cushion at me. She was still. She took the cushion back, politely. 'Seem to be having a few race riots in Samoa,' she said. She took in a bit more dust scenery.

'I come from up the road too,' she said, without stirring her-self. She sounded pissed with us. The driver turned his head, because the road was dead straight. The car seemed to know its route anyway.

'Chicken,' he said.

'Eh?' I said.

'That's all. Chicken,' he said. And he lifted his hands off the wheel, and turned them flat at the wrist.

'I'm going to ask you a question,' Sue said.

He clenched the big marble-looking wheel again.

'Sure, go ahead,' he said, very like how Sue had said she was from down the road.

'My question is,' said Sue, 'what do you mean by chicken? Chicken what?'

She nodded to me, as if she was sure she would get something out of him now. His dashboard was sparkling with polished instruments – even a clock, that must have run off the battery. When I looked out at the world again I was a bit blinded. His instruments were very bright and important, and I liked this car.

'Just meanin,' he said. He rolled the window down with a slight screech and spat into the dusty air. A handful of affection-ate white powder arrived on Sue and myself, like a wonderful Eastern cloth.

'Must oil that,' he said.

Sue threw up her eyes to her imaginary heaven, and said:

'Well? Chicken, what do you mean, chicken?'

'That's my name,' said the man, 'that's my name.'

'*Chicken?*' said Sue. 'Ha.'

She toppled over to me on a pretend corner, and whispered: 'I love you.' She made me wake up.

'What's yours?'

'Sue,' she said. 'Uh huh.'

'Oh yeh, Sue's a good name. So's Chicken though, you'd be surprised.'

'I would,' said Sue.

'What's your friend's name?'

'My friend,' said Sue. 'Oh *him*. His name's Owl. Or so he says.'

'That's a good one,' the man said, glancing at me in the mirror. 'Chicken and Owl. I like that.'

'So we're all happy,' said Sue.

The road ran straight as a carpet right into America, or nowhere. Sue, though, had another corner special to her to negociate. This time she licked my ear briefly, and said: 'I want to sleep with you, Owl. How about it?'

I stuck my shoes tighter against the passenger seat, and tried to accommodate the landscape with my interest.

'Well,' she said out loud, 'how about it, Owl?'

'My name's not really Owl,' I said, 'she calls me Owl. It's Oliver.'

'Oh, yeh, mine's not Chicken, but I like it. Pa used to call me Chicken.'

'Because you were so brave, right?' said Sue, with a sort of friendly sarcasm.

'That's it,' said the name, 'you got it.'

'I thought so.'

It struck me that Sue was just a little strange in the head, but not foreign strange. My own sort of strange at times. She had asked me to sleep with her, and as we licked up some more miles, that's all I truthfully wanted to do. I was watching her thighs when I could, where her legs stretched the cotton tighter. I just needed to get out of the car with her and into some field, where we could begin. On the other hand there was something very agreeable knowing she wished to, and us not being able to act on it.

We were losing the daylight and there were upholstered shadows beginning to drop over her deep head.

'Are you going anywhere?' said Sue to the man, out of the new shadow, a shadow that wanted to sleep or wake with her too. The driver who liked the name Chicken leaned a bit and flicked on his headlamps.

'I'm going with you two,' he said. His lights were the slightest jerky yellow on the gathering track.

'No,' she said, 'we're going with you. You one,' she added, as an inspiration.

I immediately didn't trust him. I tried to see his browned face better over the leather seat. He had a denim suit on, a very weathered denim suit. It didn't go with the car, and then again it did.

'I'm broke,' he said, 'completely broke.' When he admitted

that I trusted him.

'Completely?' said Sue.

'Apart from a hundred dollars. After that goes I will be.'

'Well it's not gone yet, Chicken, call yourself rich.'

'Ah I don't want to be rich ever,' he said.

'I have a little,' I said.

Outside the car the sky had gone wild and silent at the same time. A great colour had soaked into it, like a light red ink. It stood on the horizon, a wall of red. On the very tops were whiter fields of magnified cotton plants. It exhilarated the three of us to drive quite quickly towards it in the black car, as if we were bringing the confident neutral colour to the hopeful red.

'That's where we're going,' said Chicken.

'Where?' said Sue.

'Straight on.'

'Things are really looking up,' said Sue. 'Jesus Christ.'

She almost flung herself on the back of Chicken's seat. Her elbows spread out, and her knees, and she trembled herself. I hadn't seen anyone as happy as that since childhood.

'Jesus, I love your car, Chicken, I love it. Thank jemimy you came along and picked us up. Yea!'

And she dragged the window down, and shouted at the fields:

'Chicken, Chicken, Chicken! Sue, Sue, Sue! Owl, Owl, Owl!'

She dashed herself against her seat, and her bony back bounced away again, and she made her lips severe, and she laughed. Then much quieter, she said:

'It *is* a nice car. Where'd you get it?'

'I stole it,' said Chicken.

When night wakes in the tropics you're still in your shirt, you know, Moll. If you're wise you wear old monks' sandals, or pad around on your good soles. For the bar perhaps, the sandals suit better.

The inhabitants often put on heavy suits in the evening, but that's their privilege and look-out. For northeners, the best was the least.

The houses on my way to the bar, through the grey-blue, were solemn and girlish. Faces on the porches stared briefly but interestedly at me as I ambled by. I waved to a tousled little girl who waved back, and a woman snatched her like a rag and slapped her gently. A Chinese machine chimed in her hair as she straightened into it. I smiled in the seaworthy air. Maybe I looked like a bum. I was a bum. I wanted to be nothing else in that town. Those settled people didn't work up any curiosity in me, apart from the settled Blacks.

I'm always a little afraid when I enter a bar I don't know well, and I felt that as my soles slapped in. The singer was whispering gently into the microphone as no one had arrived yet, no one except a black man with curious hair, up at the pool-table. I said to myself: I wonder who *he* is. I paid the barmaid hardly a second's attention at first, and then I remembered that you never knew, and smiled at her, and she returned it. But she really had a bad face. It's funny that I with my head can say so, but it doesn't change how you see. I wouldn't have been against her for the scarred face, but I noted it. It caught my interest. She had an identical streak on each cheek, and I knew a knife had done that. She must have been a bad or unlucky girl somewhere, at some time, or gòt mixed up with a right hoodlum. I didn't care either way for law and order, but it can scar you just he same.

'A Ströh's,' I said, and she raised herself on her palms a bit across the counter, because she mustn't have caught the name.

'Oh, yeh, Ströh's,' she said. 'Coming right up.'

She didn't care a damn. It made the world seem empty and unhappy. She had me unhappy in two seconds.

'Here you are, baby,' she said to a dowdy beer-belly on a stool at my elbow. I hadn't quite noticed baby. He was an ordinary-looking fellow, but you could tell he was her man the way she placed the beer softly on a mat for him, and didn't plonk it, as she did mine. I didn't care. She made me unhappy.

The black man attracted me like a moth to darkness. But the light over the old pool table was the sort of gleam that moths like.

'How are ya?' he said, resting his cue on the edge, and then poking it at a ball that went nowhere in particular. 'You play?'

I can't really remember how he spoke, Moll. It was nice

53

though. I'll pretend I remember. His hair had been drawn into messy plaits, and hung long around his face and on to his shirted back. His trousers had the sea in them, and flowed in a worn-out pleasant way around his long legs.

'You play?' he said again.

Now I was staring at his face, Moll, which was stone-black, with a rather Jewish nose, or what we think of as Jewish. I remember a Jewish acquaintance somewhere or other getting very angry about that. His features were sharpened by something, or seemed so, as if he had put a polishing instrument to them. Where they didn't make edges the bits and pieces curved elegantly like good chairs. He was casual but very friendly.

'Now look,' he said amiably. 'You either play or not? You want a game here?'

'Yep, okay,' I said. 'Billiards is my game but I can manage maybe.'

'Oh yah. Billiards. I played that, mon. But dis table is too smal.'

He forced two coins into the side of the table, and something gurgled inside it like a rocky stream. It was just the balls. He picked them up expansively one by one. I had seen them before, with their many colours like jockeys' silks.

'You wan to break, mon? I don mind.'

'You do it,' I said.

While we set to he taught me the rules. I could see he had two styles of playing: very good, and very bad. When he wasn't concentrating himself he couldn't do anything.

'Dis game needs your own magic,' he said. 'You play how you feel. Tonight, I feel both okay and not so okay. You know? The game tells you how ya feel.'

I had to pay for the second game, and by then I had an inkling what was required. I forgot about my head and gathered what I had for that night. Like he said, you played how you felt. It was a good drawing of our two moods, the games we got through together.

'You from north of here?' he said. 'I'm from Jamaica.'

'Ireland,' I said.

'Ah, yas. Good country. Not like Jamaica. But de same in many ways. The same history, mon. My name is Ali,' he said. 'I'm a musician, but not in Key West.'

'Moran,' I said. 'Just a traveller looking for work. Any work down here?'

Ali leaned on his stick, and though it was his turn to shoot, which was a little frustrating, he thought about it.

'Maybe, maybe,' he said. 'We'll have to see. You want a beer, mon? Have a beer.'

Now the other customers were starting to fill the unlit bar, and the singer increased the volume of his songs as they did.

'He can sing,' I said to Ali.

'He isn't bad,' he said. 'But don lend him money.'

'Why?' I said.

'Because, mon, he's got plenty of it.'

And Ali laughed on his heels and shot the black rabbit – straight into the far-right corner pocket.

'Do you live here?' I said, defeated again.

'Oh mon, I got a band in Miami that I'm trying ta find money for. Good money.'

He was watching me while I struggled with the coin slots. His hand slapped my shoulder gently, like the woman had the child's, and he edged me slightly away from the sliding bar. A large foot in a torn canvas shoe tapped hard, and the coins ran for it into the machine. His trouser leg smelled of some open-air laundry, such as the sea.

'Everytin has its way,' he said. 'Everytin.'

I warmed towards him for saying it, not for any clear reason. It was just pally. He reminded me of one of my army friends, a fellow who knew we were only here once, Moll. That's what makes the difference. Mean oul bastards don't realize it, which is their great loss.

'Mon,' said Ali, 'we'll play one more game. Then you go home where you're livin, and tomorrow we'll find your work.'

His face was high over me. And I believed him, because he looked exactly like a tall black heron.

As the knife was gone, and his family too – because at the churned edge of the lake he was sure they wouldn't be for him any more – Moran had only one complete idea. The lake was bordered by a tumble-down wall that kept in nothing and kept

55

out nothing. Even if the sky appeared green beyond the wall, he couldn't bear the thought of traipsing back into the poor house, and seeing that he was alone by the emptiness of the ceiling.

The sky sprinkled a green rain on his large face, washing the part of him that he knew least. He couldn't see his image in the mirroring lake, because the drops were shattering it. Still, he wondered how brave he was, in his interior gobbledegook. He flapped his arms but they didn't lift him away. He laughed to himself with the sound of the rain. He couldn't spot any of the keepers about – only the familiar moonlike faces peered here and there from the ivied black-stone windows. They were not moons to stop him, or moons to light his path. They were the moons of what he would be if he stayed.

He stood on tiptoe as long as he could to try and gauge what lay over the wall, and plonked down again, and felt the wet-tened grass under his soles. Now where he had been standing was sodden too, and he realised he had to go. He took off in a heronish run around the brown sandy beach. He wasn't used to it, and he imagined himself in the form of a daddy-long-legs, trying to escape his own hand – the leafy way they had of running and half-flying up the walls.

Leafily half-flying he came to the abrupt wall, which was much higher than it had seemed from the other side of the scum-med lake. He glared back at the dark buildings. The moons lit and darkened as a cloud's shadow swept over the great wall of the poor house. The green rain had become white and bright in the sudden sunshine. They can't see me, he thought, they are blind moons enough. I had better translate his gobbledegook, or even I won't understand it after a while.

Moran applied himself in spider fashion to the ancient wall, and a fear of falling back into his only world urged him upwards. If he could only have continued upwards, for ever grasping from ledge to ledge, he would have been content. The upwards movement thrilled him.

At the top was a long train of ants travelling somewhere, with ears of grass-seed and such. He crossed the army carefully, and rolled to the drop of the other side. He fell simply and tidily onto a very squelchy surface of bog-grass.

For a while he lay in his first position in the new world. Only his fingers stirred a little in the chilly grassy muck. He was on his back and he watched the scrubbed sky, which watched him with two curious small clouds. The rain had passed over to other poor houses and other Morans, he thought. The rain has gone and it's left me here to be Moran. If Moran was a fish he could stay right here, and live against the damp boundary.

His language and the chaste imperfect sky moved him. He cried without murmuring, and added his own moisture to the empty bog, an empty bog full of water and harsh grass and small birds.

Moran balanced his head and set off.

It would have been more convenient to carry his head under his arms, as the bog was difficult at first to make his way through. Where am I going? he asked himself. Where is Moran going? He couldn't tell, which surprised him, because always before when he questioned himself an answer surfaced. He was pleased. The world of answers was lifting away from him, and his head was becoming lighter every moment. He was Moran without answers, whereas in the poor house he had been his poor opposite. He loved his family but they had vanished for good, and now he had his lack of answers, his patrimony of unanswerable questions, to keep him company. Soon he would stop even thinking of questions, he thought, and then his head would carry him into the different skies of the new world like a balloon, a belly filled with dark air.

'Moran, Moran, Moran,' he chanted, as the bog slanted up to the horizon and the ground got firmer.

By midday he had reached a broad empty common, with thick white bushes dotted about it, with legs. He didn't linger in this wonderful region, but plodded on through the stretching afternoon. At length he was on a muddy road that oozed over his feet and between his toes. The lined mud was cold and refreshing, so he followed the hedgy track to the unanswerable question of a village.

At the end of this he wasn't so fond of his new ignorance. He did really want to know what this group of buildings signified. It must be a poor house, he thought. But he was certain at the same time that he was wrong. There were no flashing moons, and the buildings were small and separate. There was no wall and no lake. The road entered the houses and split itself up among them. He felt the whole pattern of the place was sleeping, and the workhouse was perpetually awake.

His head dropped without his noticing to one side, as he considered the village. He didn't care for it as much as the bog, but all the same it made his small eyes narrow even further.

The village had the sun on a string, and was pulling the impossible balloon slowly down into some field beyond the roofs. Moran said:

'Hum, hum,' out loud, and immediately on the other side of a low wall a dog woke up, and tried to recognize him over the brick rim. Moran saw the dog's eyes unglaze gradually. The animal was very old, and its bark could be heard starting up distantly inside its slim stomach. Tinily, tinily, and then hugely it burst out of its narrow head to honour Moran. Moran began to bark as well, which sent the animal into a deeper register of distress. The boy caught the tone and shut up. The distressed note frightened him. He felt he had made a mistake. He approached the wall and reached out his arm to the hysterical creature. His arm above the elbow was abruptly clenched by a sodden sharp jaw, which twisted and yanked on Moran's flesh. He toppled into the garden and tried to bite the dog back, but the dog was bony and couldn't be gripped.

Sixfoil Four

Under the blak rain misser Owel was walk, Moll. Eh, he knowes dat insoid hes hert he iss smal, but outwards he bin grat wid the solac and de histoire of his faders. Fer himself he be emptien always. Bat wat succors ti emptinesse iss de tres.

   Ass he walked he trod out a rytm. An de dey were over black, an cowled his hed wid cloakish memor. Moll, in me owen hert dis man lives grete and lithe. I honoor dis fellaugh for dat he loved al equal. Dat he is past is hard stone for al to ate. Lisun, Moll, and take his owel talken song inta yer brest:

> Iffen musse lard Olleever vanished
> alle know the dooer consequed.
> We al be numboored amang the been
> an seng we wull for no breathy man.
> Leet et be soo and let uz go among
> feen tree dat groo in grun amaze.
> And iffen des tres are nat uf lif
> we wull be nat of gut lif nor.
> Olieve is nat man abuv al man
> but makes ee ech man abuv himself,
> for be hus cheftan way he turnes most
> inta hes ful potential uf streng.
> We hav no countroo inta empir,
> we hav no godde leden al.
> Coon iz no springer frum godes hed,
> no bluty emprer oot a Rame.
> We bring na harvoost abov enoug,
> we healt no thoro deyin corp.
> But smal batel but we fete,
> but litul hap to gossup of,
> but smal bab from de muteres loin
> to shaw de wureld we ar heer.

59

If so it is yet so we lif
and az de treen spring so we.
Ye tak de treen and ye tak al
inta forgut domaine over lant.
Norrmal ower lant and ordinaire,
normel ower prinz and uzual.
But lave uz be wit hem wid honoor
so wureld it mai kep it ane honoor.
Dreve us orf and poverish de gren
an mak yern droory parish ina sted.

Meester Ool had no gret judgement uf his effoort, bat it wass
the passer uf hes journoo. For he waz gan ta see dat sam owel
whited cratur in ites den, its fowel villooge. It waz al the heelp
dey hadde ta seeke in der trooble. Uf curs, Moll, he did nat
unnerstan dat Olleve hat ben wit de monstoor afoor hem.

The glade of dis stankin pleece shimmereyed in a broken
downpoor. Ol Owel hesitate on te bordoor becorse dat smill
hurted his tender. nostrel. It were a shape to em, a kinder grat
dragoon. He met dat stunk wid grapplen armes, and conquereed
hes stomuch. He sowed a largess compasioon for de livers of
sich nastinesse.

And wan he put seet on de hermaphrodit he fund it slapin.

'Ho, noo, gret lamb,' he sayed. 'How are yer, wid yer
important magooc?' An he stirred the sleepan boody wid his
skanny feet.

Wan de daurk fledded the liddel chamboor, der wass a fat
rood inseect on de nack of de cratoor, liken it were a leech or
sich, Moll, an meester Ool lookit at et wid curiositee unfeigned.

'Wat, moi monsteer, are ye nat aleeve no loanger?' he asked
wid stupiditee. For ites throt wus parte wid some vanished
kneefe. De white heed dropped bak to shoaw de workins uf de
throat, dat wase alla dree and bar, for so it wass dat some
animell hadda drink de blut offa et.

Der lay in de cornoor a smal blak pup uf a hound, al milky
softe and yang. Bet tho Owl lookit der, fond he na lavins uf
gore. Samtin elsey hadde lapped the free juice of dat ded
monsteer.

De wund stratched and began to spek, as it were lippes of a
true mout, an de face in muddle-age stayed still and white

above, like so mach hair an scalp.

'Why do ya cum in my deathes time, lord Owl?' it said.

And meester Owl shrank half back to the sunles door.

'Why do ye nat speke?' asked the wound.

'Who hass don thes ting to our beloved hermaph?' said Owl. 'He muste be killed in yer honoor, or dis lant is over.'

'Dis lant iss over,' echoed the wound widout hesitatioon. 'This bluty dethe of my liveliness is nat concerned wid sich consequence.'

'But who has sneaked in an hastened everytin?'

'My hert,' said the dede ting, 'it was necessar for I to do dis, in stead of Oliveer. For it wass cler he wished me dedd, for I herd him in his rowal hed, as he leved me for final.'

An Owel he fun an olde eeron dagge from long ago in de stull hend of his oracle. De wund sad nuttin after for a wil. Den it bulgen and panted, and befor Owel knaw wat was de case, sontin was floodin furt, an swamped de wanton baste. Owl he vomitet fram freet, and de bowel mater mixed in a spraye wid de visioos liqid.

'Mey oulde gots,' said Owel in wekness, 'wat is dis occasioon?'

An as he spake, furder stuf broke oot, and lad inches of jooce onta de flor. An slawly appeared de hed of a cratir dat was been borne frum dis dethe. It brak as fram a womanes cunt. It wasse de heed of a yang dag, likken the specie in de corneer, shiverin. Soon al de boty was der, an it shak itself fre of ites strange mooterly fater.

De wund gadered awau an awau an disappear, an de boty crumbl. Anly de facc wus remained, whach said, widdoot movin leppes:

'Owl, my friend, take these two hounds, because they are your own death.'

An den it were ever quiett.

The light seeped out of the tall cinemas. The street of houses clung to their warm official whites and greys. Our taxi, from which we had just clambered, reinserted its square of excellent black into the dull bright herd of traffic. Winter travelled in the

round red lights at the back. The street kept exploding without
any hint of an explosion. Only the colours fled up and spread.
When they reached the tin roof of the sky, everything stopped.
The street became a picture arrested like a breath. My mother
had to drag me slightly, not because I was reluctant to walk
with her, but because I was overcome by the sights of the town.

The thousands of high heels spiked against the pavement. I
listened to that sound alone, and it was more alone than anything else.

'Child of grace,' said my mother. 'Don't drag.'

Her handbag under her suede arm held the drawings of such
as we were. She had a pencil that she could place down my
throat and into my incurious heart, any time she liked. But she
never liked. Her hair was not old, and she was younger now
than the older she had been in Dublin, after the country. Her
hair dipped in the yellow night, and painted the air above my
head. But the brown mixed with the yellow already there, and
it swished in streaks over her thin back. As it swished, the street
shot up again, full of yellow.

Black coats and grey coats and red coats stood in long lines
for the cinemas. The lines were drawings too. Something had
reached down and smudged the mark of coats on the pavements
and the walls, dimpled steamy pavements.

In a way the light of that street reminds me of the light here
in Key West, but Ali and his Aliness is so far from the
geographical dominion of my mother.

When she flicked me from the yellow pavement into a department store I couldn't question the change, because it was natural
and of her. And in the cramped room with the high racks of
skirts and dresses, it was her forest, and unobjectionable. I had
the enamelled white chair for my own existence. And she had
the epic assistant, to hand her what she desired to try on.

Between skirts, my mother stood in her stockings, but the
assistant didn't appear put out. Perhaps the key was swivelled in
the lock, and the three of us, and the big iron cash-register with
its halfpenny sign stuck, were to be for ever the citizens of this
domain.

My mother dragged her horse-tail of solid hair back from her
breast, over her shoulder. As she was bent over to step into a
skirt, it had dropped like stiff water and clouded her eyes. I

would have liked to have such hair and look through it, out at all passing things. I would never cast it like that away out of sight.

The cream skirt tubed up her frightening legs, and wrapped tight against her. The light-bulb shivered and glimmered as she smiled vigorously at the appalled assistant. The horror abandoned the shop-woman's face, and she translated a measly one-candle version of my mother's happiness onto her fresh falling cheeks.

'Ideal, Mrs Conn,' said the curious woman.

'It's the right one, I think,' my mother allowed.

We all agreed it was. They looked at me on the suddenly rocky chair, and I nodded for a while, and ceased nodding. My knees were glowing whitely. Could the bulb not break now? I thought. Just for fun. Then we'd see what the right one was.

I knew I was beginnig to melt in the cottony confined room. Let them unlock the door now, and let the yellow street be king again. The yellow street was king just shortly after.

I remember, years later, and not so many ago, in a porno cinema in Soho, a short little film about an assistant giving her beautiful customer cunnilingus, and then servicing her even better with a wide snubbed dildo. I wonder is that a popular scenario among the desperate patrons, because of similar and similarly-stuck memories? The customer was teased by the assistant, because the dildo wasn't being thrust in all the way at first. But at the end of the clip, the solid plastic was pigging in and out, and the customer's head was thrown back and forth, and the assistant had her own hand on her thespian clitoris. Most strange, and attractive, in a completely male manner, probably, a male version of a nonexistent female desire. So in our unhappy heads we create the machineries that are the minus of an impossible minus.

The customer is sweaty with delight, because the black dildo has explained itself to the lining of her cunt, and is seeking entrance on the euphoric back wall.

My mother conducts me into a more silent adventure than formerly. Only two taxis are making lion noises at the faraway curb.

Minutes later, that is to say thousands and thousands of minutes, that are leaves on the ground now, under the tree, and feed the roots, but have softened too much together to be distinguished as leaf one, leaf two, leaf three, or three hundred, all these particular fashioned minutes later, another rivery taxi ferried me either to or away from the house in Highgate. It may have been to, as the journey ends at the house. Though on the other hand.

London has become a question of hoardings in my absence, or my nonexistence. On the hoardings are the new songs, the pithy blue and red posters selling shows at the theatres. My mother *is* the theatre. She represents it for me, so all the posters are either for her or put up by her, a lavish self-advertisement. London is nothing else except these posters, or so that taxi journey wants me to believe. Just for a change it displays a block of severe grey flats, and then says nothing whatever about them. This is the journey either to, or away from, and both ways it has an importance I don't retain. The customer comes waterishly, and dribbles something synthetic on the dull slow dildo. It had been prepared for a long time, the journey, many leafy minutes, under the dear tree. The dead tree, I mean. My mother is not in the taxi. She has claimed elsewhere as her estate, without me. Whether for ever or for some over-lit minutes is not clear. Nor is my father about, but then he is never about. He is about, but I don't see him. On the seat beside me is the cat-basket, without the half-Siamese cat. The half-Siamese cat has vanished, in anticipation, or in memory, of the plane. So is rather like my father.

The credits don't mention her name, as there are no names.

Drunkenness is a spring of sorts, and will kill the deadliness of seven flights of a Parisian mansion. But drunkenness refuses, quite, to blot out any over-riding tough toxic worry. So you may rise and float but not tread easy at the top.

Like actors with some plot-advancing asides to deliver, we made for the two-hearted window. Now the cruelty of the ordinary traffic was banished again, and only our own clamour persisted in the theatrical hovel.

Without her leather jacket she should have been soft, as in later months, but she contrived not to be so, in this whirling night-time. The station and her remembered roundness and heat stood at our sides, and watched us with some superiority. There was no necessary order here, and we were for each other's enjoyment if we wished it. But some signal section of me had been sacked for the moment. My unease wouldn't shut up in my tired ears, and was a more visible presence than she was. Her cloak of visibility was off, and she became a pillar of some divided substance.

What my wasteful hands found they found with no white interest. They reached her with an amount of whispering that she could not know about. You are dying in your crotch, the whisper said, your balls are swelling and belumped, and soon you won't exist for such things as this. This pure business will be out of your squalid diseased domain, and the likes of her will abandon you necessarily.

Her health was not in question, and she was inside this time as surely as a hare is in its proper field. But I didn't stand outside it with any sort of detachment. She stood outside of me, and I stood outside of me, and when my stupefied body headed for her, it was alone and ignorant. My brain had decided to keep narrating in face of everything. Any green clear morning, any pleasant cake. It wouldn't even stop for her, whom I considered the most arresting.

With a number of superfluous strokes I sketched her over again, as ugly and disturbing. When her clothes, shaped by an unknown geometry, looked for the reversed image in my own distressed corpse, all my movements were clear and menacing to me. I was involving myself in my own killing, and I was to be police and judge and victim all in one. For as surely as she advanced normally, and it seemed joyfully, on my insufficient state, I shrank away, and tried to fold myself in and in, where I could cower half-contentedly, and suppress her kind damage. My phallus was paying no attention to me, which proved somehow its desperation and separateness. It knew the future as well as I did, and in its two crumbling brains it was, without hysteria, thinking out some passage of escape. It wanted to run inside her, this place, this last cave, to bolt, and desert me. I needed to restrain it, to teach it proper fear.

Her mouth was brimmed with language now. She had words for each electric sad second that the clock was programmed to offer.

'My big love,' she insisted. And without any hint of holding me or mothering me, she tried to cradle me. And then she was back to the detailed expected progress. She disappeared clumsily into a creature of long breasts, that in the gloom seemed to end at her waist, and in the light did end at her waist. And oceanic legs lost their red tights in three tumbling ticks.

Some memory of normality stripped me too. The mocking window, very amused and cool, measured its meagre colours into my eyes, as it had done so often when I was alone and sleepless. Now it laughed at me, because even with her, who had arrived too late, too late, I was more alone because more frightened.

I cheered on any sign of real enthusiasm in me. I cajoled my bullying neurosis. For the first time with Xenia I felt my continental distance from her centred vitality. Lord, I was an Eskimo to her Greek. Her knickers shocked me. Even in the so-called dark, that was only a newer better glare, I saw the nestled bulge of her sanitary towel. Knickers and towel were swept away in one dancer's gesture, and her hair sprang to my crotch, like a puppy, and took root in the rusted skin. I begged my copper gods of Notre Dame for an hour's gift of the present, the on-going still space of being alive. I was dead on my live feet, and only my disinterested phallus considered her at all, and she was kind and kin to it, and washed it with her crying mouth.

The blue-covered mattress received her form, as if she had thrown herself accidentally and naked on a deck-chairing spinster. My instinct told me to put my face in my hands, and make use of the window for an exit. Such horror was no longer horror of my own making. Her usual human normality was like a rape to me. The window roared with laughter. There was no stealthiness, no pornography, no hatred, that would have made it recognizable for me. God, was there no bulletin that might have informed her, and metamorphosed her brownness and nudity into half-clothed rounded lust? She required me to make love, as she presumed we must. So youthfully and freely that it seemed a vice and a cell to me.

I entered her sore prison without either cowardice or bravery. I pushed my soles across the violent warm floorboards, and knelt beside this monster of normality. Her skin to my fingers was as leathery as her coat, and appeared to wrap her loosely and thickly, like a person who has been lying for some centuries under a bog. Her breasts stretched long, long, with great unfolding nipples, and her ancient grandmotherly thighs were half-opened already.

I realized then what this disaster was. *She* was making love to *me*, something that had never assaulted me before. I was clear in her head as a progression and a logic, and the filling of the list was what made her so oblivious. I had a man here with crazy breasts, a parody of breasts, and the moon had got into him, and was bleeding him like a nineteenth-century doctor.

I couldn't fall on this man without phallus or voice, or this woman without discretion or need of direction. I couldn't make use of her in her unbound uncluttered use of me. I only wished to be perpetrator, not unreluctant victim and instrument. What vast machinery was I lacking to manage her perfection? My phallus as before ignored me, and computed her desire in its own secretive knowledge. The board it was attached to, it ignored, and left me to fend for myself, above the vanishing diagram of her name, and memory, and arrival.

The whole moon dribbled and drabbed through the scrapy branches, and the lake had only miniature Atlantic breakers to push to the soft shore. Sue waded through the bright dark of the water.

'I hope ta gawd there ain't no fuckin watersnakes in this damn place,' she said, but only to herself. The words swam back to me, as I watched, in two minds, on the suddenly splashing sand.

'You going in too?' Chicken said, walking down from the car.

'I might just do that,' I said. 'I'm in two minds about it.'

Chicken watched Sue's buttocks disappearing into the echoing unknown.

'Might be a few moccasins here, at that,' he said. 'Knew a fella came up to the surface, months after they got him. They'd made a thousand holes in his skin, I can tell ya. Don't think I'd swim in these southern lakes, no sir.'

'Well, I would,' I said, a little annoyed by his caution, and I

67

dragged my shirt across my ears, and dropped my trousers. I thrust my braces into a warmed deep pocket.

'Skinny bastard, ain't ye?' he offered, sticking his hands in his own pockets, as if in answer.

'You think so?' I said. 'Better than a pile of old fat.'

'Oh yeh,' he said, 'better'n that. Well, I'm watchin the both of ye.'

Sue had travelled out to the centre of sombre water, and was waving clearly at me. When she waved her body dipped, with a second's gap between the wave and the dip. Her form was a strange white in the distance, and her hair had flattened, so she looked like a real creature of the lake.

The chill enveloped my balls like hands, and I plunged forward, and began to stroke out to her.

'Lord,' she said, as I puffed near her, 'lordy, lord. Hey, Chicken!' she screamed, exhausting me a little more.

'Hey,' I said.

'Hey, Chicken, get in here!'

A long far-off *Naa* bounced over the surface to us.

'What's the matter with him?' she said, her mouth sinking under in the middle of her question.

'Sue,' I said, 'you're so beautiful. You're so beautiful.'

'You think so?' she said. 'You really think so?'

She began to laugh, and struggle because of the laughter, and when she came up she was in a bit of trouble for breath. We treaded water, and she said:

'Hell, Owl, don't make me laugh. Don't make me!' and she giggled viciously again, and it drove her under, as if a hand had pressed her shining head. My sleepy otter was half drowning now.

'Woah up,' I said, swimming to her, and trying to raise her by the floppy underarms. But she was making me sink, perfectly, also, and for a moment I saw her in the moonlit underwater, her eyes pebble-dark and terrified. She terrified me too, and I wanted Chicken to rush and rescue us in a damn boat or something. Just as suddenly though, she calmed, and was floating about as before. She spluttered for a bit and got her breathing going again, and was churning her legs energetically.

'God, you just can't laugh in the fuckin water,' she said. 'Tell me you think I'm beautiful on the bloody shore.'

So we stayed out there a while under the undecided sky, with its eloquent moon, and Chicken was a small distant bush, taking his own notes from land.

'A bit strange, isn't it,' I said, 'out here?'

'Yeh,' she said, 'but I love it,' she said. 'God, I love it.' And she struck out her arms at me so the brown water washed my lips.

'It tastes like something,' I said. 'Like wood, or something.'

'Of course, darlin,' she said. 'We're in the middle of a damn forest, you know. Oh Jesus, don't make me laugh.'

And to stop herself she started to breaststroke back to shore. I thought as I followed that I didn't really like Chicken waiting like that for us, with a complete view of Sue as she waded out.

'Ouch,' she said, 'I've stood on a bloody rock.'

'I bet that was a snake,' said Chicken, and chuckled.

'A snake it wasn't,' said Sue. 'A rock it probably was.'

She tottered on one leg to look at her wound, and then put her hand against Chicken's denim jacket, and got steady and decided.

'Well it's nothing, not even bleeding.'

I noticed Chicken gazing openly at her breasts, and when she unbalanced him a little to move up the bank, he took the opportunity to follow the twisting movement of her bottom as she clambered. The black hair from her cunt peeked out at both of us, and Chicken chuckled again:

'Fur-burger,' he said to me, as I passed him.

'Right,' I said, and gave a laugh, which was directly the opposite of what I felt. I didn't want any camaraderie of that sort. But Chicken didn't seem too bad, and it wouldn't have created much to get annoyed at him.

In the night, under the pines, when we were almost dry, but still slightly damping my blanket, Sue lay calm and breathy with my arms about her. She had the slim bones of her back to me, and my lower arms naturally crossed her breast. Against my thighs and belly, her smooth moonish bottom rested.

Slowly, in the wordless rustle of animals, and barking of old enfarmed dogs, she circled against my skin. A quiet perfect moan sang in her mouth. Without thought my body gave a tiny thump against her, like a heart, and then again, and in a while we were pressing carefully together, and the blanket warmed and gently lifted and waved above us.

Away the other side of the car I heard Chicken cough in the darkness.

All through the intelligent moon, we moved only like that, with the smallest sighs and murmurs. My cock lay in the damp cleft of her bottom, and she had herself tilted a little so her cunt touched it now and then. Each movement was thoughtfully and thoughtlessly stored, and remembered as the next circle took its place. Like travellers in no possible hurry we enjoyed our tiny dance under the glowing blanket. All night we danced for ourselves, and the water and the moon and the peace that was to be discovered in the dance. No characteristic of our separate selves intruded. Everything nasty and quarrelsome locked itself in voluntarily, and that particular asylum slipped full and forgotten into yesterday. The moon climbed into us, and rowed his new boat across the integral lake. Everything silvered from its nets of trouble and age, and the whole small world of the forest stepped forward out of all that scarred skin, and stood under the moon and whispered: This is tree, this is clay, this is good water.

You can't always rely on what strangers contract in bars, to say the least. Among the cards of the identical morning, I didn't really expect Ali's face to turn up.

I remained on in the big bed for half an hour, just to think. You arrive in a new town, and there's a special excitement that makes the first day or two special and out of your life. But then your own self arrives that bit later than your machinery and body, and very little has changed except the streets and the weather. If you're lucky your tardy self is happy to see you again, and happy with the shift in the climate. On the whole my rags and tatters of a character were smiling, Moll. After the queer war, down the end of a queer continent, this no-place-at-all suited the sort of burnt-out condition I had reached – a trading-post between yesterday's sweat and tomorrow's.

It's not often I can lie in my bed and doze, and consider this and that, because sooner or later I start thinking about my head, and wondering if it's swelling today, of all days, just when I've got a bit happy, etcetera. Which is a merry-go-round that, once on, is lethal to get off of. So I do my level best to avoid it. The fairground beauty spins most of the hours without me. Anyway it's too attractive a refuge from the way matters stand sometimes. Like a kid wants to keep turning and turning among the late-park bushes, because his parents hate each other, and scream in bed.

I have a stupid-headed enemy inside me, like a war traitor they were always hunting for. That traitor isn't in the Boer or the British or the Bushman or the Anything. He's right there in your own camp, and you can recognize him any section of the diagram because, Moll, he has your own drawn face.

Something had happened to me in the so-called dark continent, and it confused me, and was the why I got out of the army. I was musing over it under the light sheet, which was connected with the light morning in my head. And Ali breezed up the porch, and clonked along the wooden corridor, and brought his wakefulness and swing into my dark room.

'Mon, you ant up. Hey, it's seven of the clock, mon.'

In the deep room my cheeks deepened.

'Hey, wat you want wid al dis clothes? Mon, I ain't got mor an jes dis trousers, and ma shert. An wan der derty I wash em by de boats.'

Moll, I'm still not certain if I can truly tell you how my old friend Ali spoke. It was very complicated and sometimes I didn't even follow him, because though he was using something like English, and probably better, he had a lot of new words for his own private and national use. But I'm translating him here, because it's the best I can do and anyway I don't really remember exactly what I said either, and in that respect I'm translating myself also.

He seemed taller and much skinnier today, but I could see he was strong. The untangled tangle of hair made him look heavier than he was. He was so certain of himself, sitting on my bed in a room strange to him. Everything straight away became somehow his, and worthy of his attention.

'Mon, look at dis werk,' he said, raising like a wooden statue sprung to breathing and pointing out. He lost his curious long-distance expression that fell into his eyes when he was thinking. It was like an iron mechanism which shoved his thought from the back of his skull to right behind his black eyes.

'You know how much dis werk cost nowaday?' he said. His hands were running the length of a section of wood, which was carved and grooved.

'You like wood?' I said.

'It's ma trade, mon, dat's what I am. A carpenter.'

'You work at that?'

'Sure, I work at it. I don werk here in de town. Bat wat a know best is expensive, mon, becas it takes a long time to do.'

I don't know, Moll. Somehow Ali impressed me only because he had turned up when he had said he would. And now was stationed in my room, discussing the woodwork, that I hadn't even valued correctly. He was a carpenter, whereas I was only a failed soldier. Now that wasn't true, Moll. Don't listen to me. Listen to me, though, don't sleep. I'm not, Batty, I like your new friend Ali, he puts me in the world there with you, when you were not so young and not so old. That's it, Moll, that's what he did for me, too. His confidence and sense of things, the wood in the wooden room, pulled me those few inches forwards, the inches that keep you from being alive even in your own life.

'Hey, Moran,' said Ali. 'Wat you do? What's your own trade, mon?'

'I was working a little while in Africa. Not a lot.'

I was getting choked on my own vagueness. And I wanted to dress myself, but not for Ali to see my ungainly whiteness. Not, I mean, Moll, in relation to his blackness, but there was very little in my distracted corpse to admire. Of course I didn't need him to admire it, a man admire a man, but I was conscious of being, you know, a bit ungainly, and naked is never my favourite condition. And then I thought: Well, he won't even consider it, he won't even think one moment about it. So I hauled out of the sheet and muddled my clothes on. We headed out into the sun then, the two of us making a nice clatter on the front steps, between the tall bushes.

'Right, mon,' he said. 'Here we go.'

'Where to?' I said.

'Mon, nowhere special. We'll cruise around a bit and see wat we can see.'

His walk was a species of pad, because his feet were a trifle

72

flat. The long body allowed the flat feet to progress without criticism or reference of any kind. Ali was always just Ali. He was doing my head a lot of good, or at least my cracked notions about my cracked head. Sun sat on our shoulders, and we carried it like a child up a long avenue of the white silent houses. I put my morning into Ali's keeping, and he banked it quietly with a private promise of interest. He knew well what my mood was, and that also he ignored. He just progressed, conscious of his own unconsciousness. He didn't need to overthink, because his world was slotting just fine. He had it tame, like the killing tiger it was, not with a whip, but with his special trick of ignoring something till it came with him. The tiger couldn't bite Ali, it seemed to me, because Ali had pulled the tiger's tooth, as a gesture of extreme friendship on his part.

A yellow river is the only thing that runs in my head any more. Here other colours have absconded with the usual meagre patrimony, and the little ferry tweezers the bruised handful of passengers from one bank to the other windy bank. In my head the river is as real as it is imaginary in itself – a game of long standing that it chooses to play with me. It is not a perfect river, because it neither looks for the sea or any sea, nor drags its first drops up some flute of a fissure.

Moran, in after years known as the Blessed Apostle in the accidental town of his unchoosing, is also of course much on my mind. Between his odd self and the urinaqueous river I eke a certain living, or at least a certain peacefulness. While not expecting this to last any useful amount of time, I allow it in the meantime to have its day.

In bringing Moran's life to light by means of a poor and uncooperative language, I am staining that river further, and more than I should. Whether there is some punishment set out for this case will be of some interest to me in the future. For the moment I am content with the interest I seem to retain in Moran.

He doesn't fascinate me, he is me until I peel him off piecemeal, chronicle by chronicle. I could worry about him without his investiture in me, but then it would be futile to worry so. And why stop with Moran, when there have been so many others, more worthwhile and less worthwhile, but occasionally more engaging? Moran's existence was utterly without point, and everything he said, and everything he thought he did, was stillborn in importance as it left his mouth, or fell behind him to represent his past. And such a terrifically unromantic brain as his hardly ever dwelt on the past. He hardly knew it was called such a thing, as perhaps it is not. Most of Moran's life lived in his head as an impossible and tattered scrapbook to which he never referred, and to which he added only because he had to, as long as he remained breathing. The consideration of death did not occupy him, which was lax, nor why he had been chosen to be among the living, temporarily as is the way. The question of his mean beginnings and his mean ending and meaner middle-life he never bothered or thought to ask. His friendship with the Jamaican Ali, and his partial revelation in Africa, were the single and remotely singular highlights on his sombre apple. Who could have loved such a creature? The final years he spent with the woman Moll in a squalid house of his own construction, a gloss on the idea of poor house – and perhaps Moll was mostly of his own making also – were inexorably implied by his birth and his appearance. He was incapable of getting on in the normal world, where a human being must get on, or imagining the condition of having a wife and off spring, of restocking the cages of the circus. He had some notions on these matters, but they were ludicrous guesses from other people's stories. A child of his own would have loathed him, his smell and his difference. But he would have worshipped the child with a stupid, detailed and highly burdensome simplicity of mind. Any child of his would have ended up an enemy of family and society, and probably have murdered a number of innocent and guilty individuals, and composed himself or herself for the gallows, without humour. Only on the seedy perimeter of all agreeable things could Moran make his way, neither despised nor honoured, because invisible.

For instance, when he fell into the garden on the invitation of the dog, it was the vegetable patch of Jane Smith he arrived on. On the day of Moran's coming she was about fifty-five years of age, and was just ending her career as the town whore of Sligo. She was not, I might say, a pretty sight by comparison with anything except warthogs, but the men who made up her customers were normally the beery older crew, who made sure to be so expensively intoxicated when they tottered to her bed, that they could make anything of her that their magnificent imaginations could manage.

So Jane Smith's, or Jane McGowan's, contact with the town proper was with the town improper when in its cups, and family life was as foreign to her as Rome. She had no education, no sense, and no bath. She was the ideal mother for Moran.

She dragged his slightly-chewed body into her cottage, and wrapped his hand in a piece of scarf, and rushed the dog out of her garden. She had been keeping the dog as a substitute for something or other, but the boy looked a better bet. She examined his limbs in the moist dark of her room, and judged him ill-made and of poor mind, because Moran only babbled at her with the miserable pain in his hand, and he wanted to vomit up the tuft of hairs he had removed with his teeth from the dog.

Her shoulders perpetually shrugged with fat, as if of their own accord, and two curious bosoms kept pushing in Moran's face. They were heated like sunny bogwater, and they calmed the small flames inside Moran's fingers, which looked as if someone had been shooting at them. Jane McGowan didn't intend this, but it was so none the less.

In the boxy room the plaster attempted a leaflike effect, as if the room were walled with mouldy hedges. Many of the minuscule leaves had dropped in quite deep dusty drifts to the edge of an old carpet, which was entirely worn in much of the centre, letting the bare earth become a famous feature of her pleasure dome. Newspapers were heaped for mattress on a sturdy wooden frame against one wall, and from this the autumns of plaster were evidently swept regularly enough. It was, after all, the source of her few shillings, and even with boozed customers she couldn't have the site of their grunts and thrusts so abhorrent as to impede their imaginations.

Already Moran's wound was festering a little, as if Jane Smith's room were a tropics all to itself. And she took the trouble to place some lengths of cardboard on the floor under the bed, which was more than she had done for the dog. She pushed him in under there, as if to get him out of her mind, and sat at a strange little table thrown together with stumps of trees.

There was a small gathering of pots, and an insectivore brush, on the indistinct surface. She settled on the little bottom she had – because, like some large-breasted people, she had a slim enough rear – and divided her legs around the castle of trunks. With a stomachy whisper she bent her face to a geometric oddity of polished metal, and began to improvise a ruby mouth around her severe lipless grimace, with some ruby moisture she had bullied out of wild poppies. It was getting on to early night, and sometimes a depressed afternoon husband forced his steps to her shilling edge of town.

Sixfoil Five

Eetseed a lutel sturm hadde riss, an in de cinter offa dat viloog stoodet de teeny boi, of years in handefil. He was creased be de sturdee rain in hiss har, and he weepid also for de ende uf hes hermaphrodit. His specal cock it hange ner the grun, and Mester Owl was mich affrad be the gloomy grey cloud that hang on de hed uf the boy. It fillud the volloog, like a miste do. Soon nuttin cad be deiscern except at de levul uf de boyes stoney eyen. De bratte creed lunge and herete, soo al de birdes and deer an oddere bastes might have news uf der pitfall. Owl he squatted dun nar det boyes fase an asked him:

'Wat was here, dat hat caused de cratures finis?'

'A bigge mon,' said de boy, in the ditche uv his sobbes. 'A bigger mon rad uppe and mad dis villogg trimble. Whan he lefte, moi craftie mooter madde one howel in her throte.'

'Wall,' said Owel, 'and wat did yoo doo ta halp?'

'I dranked de fowel blut uf her nack, bat it wasse soon drree, an a liteul dogge cam barkin oot, and I sped off inta de treen, an noo I stande here al emptee, and ould. For I bin siventee, nat sevin, of summoores time, not regarden to moi ragard. I hald de scared seed uf yer treeb in me middel, and dat is ale I have lefte naw. Betwan de hermaphrodit and me, ye surveev.'

An meester Oool wasse angred at de boy, becass his tribes soorce wass so strange. De phalloo betwan Ooles awaen ligges ris, and as it ris so did de fallus uf de tribes boy, and Ool wass confused badlee, an gripped the boyes cinter wid horroor.

De childe who seemed childe were entranced quate, an his bellee throbed and beate lik a drum, and in Ooles fingoors de lange phaloo bate wid blut.

'Take dis hooly ting inta yer mout,' saidde de boy, in mannes voice, dat shockit Ool. He did nat unnerstan wat was require.

'Be de ancun goodes,' sadde de childe-nat-childe, 'takke de sede uf yer tribbes life an continoo.'

Bat meester Ool shiveret bak, an did na whoosh ta dreenk. De clood lowered over de hed of de boy, and the figoor starte ta vanoosh in de swirls.

'Takke, takke,' sadde de boi, 'or be amang de consequeenz.'

Meester Ool he serche his side fer his stik, an befoor de mist hadde encompoasse al de boy, he battred de phallus wid his muscools al gathered. An de garson clossed his lampish eyes, and de grun sede shattered fram his branchleek pert. Et fal to de pebbly flur. Ool he strak now de heede, till it were nat more dan a mushy crown. De boy neder moved nar creed, bat seemed nat touched be the progress at al. On the sandee grun de gren sede lay, wid a litel steam procedin oot lak de smok uf a town. An sur it wasse, Moll, a towne indade, de freshe toon of de futir for Olleve Conn. An Ool hadde niver knawn such an articool as townes. An naw de town of Olleve wasse spillet for all teem.

Ool he drave the boddee inta de safte surfoose, tal alle de boy was easilee burit. Anly de blut uf his skull circled as a marke in frant uf de drien sede. De gren an de ruddy cud nat mingle.

At his herte meester Owle knew de grep of sodden disquite. Al his angoor an swete dreed fram his armes, an he asket himself wasse he woke fram a slepe. For he thoght it wasse nat his armes dat slayde this boye. An he knew that then de villoog hadde filled wid daemons.

He raced wid a wile clamour out and aloong the homin path. Behint him a litel blak flowr grew on de grene marke, an a smal white floor on de redd. Bat be nighte dey had withered.

Ass Ool ran fer his dethe, de two yang daggs skippet at his ankools, and fallad his miseree home. On de ootskirtes of the castool place, Ool halted and watched de animals waddle up. Dey raced forward, and under de high arch uf the castel, they transferred their outwardness ta a peer uf hares. Dey halted as if in worree. An in place uf enterin de hame of Conn, dey skeltered awaye back across de litel bog an disappeared.

The grat frame dat his distante muter gaff him at birt, thunder ta de mucke, an teares uf humanitae washed his feece. His whate harr brak fram a litel goulde bande, an hid his waterish eyes fram de aire. Has fingerez grappit at de dirte, an he creed for has reliece:

'Gute mooter,' he sad. 'Why haf ye lefte yer sune fer dis trooble? Alle my hert will bi assonder be eveninges sang, wan bleke neete brangs hes coat ta coover has bedd. I haff na candoll ta litte puer Ollever, moi lard, ta resste. Mooter of di goddes dat rein in de skee an de ert, turn in circle all yer opinoons, and lat uz bee as previoos!'

Da rain it clossed quack, an Oel he begint ta hoope, an tuooka hes legges ta himsel and haulled hes sorro up. His armes stratched to de cloods an di emptee bla skee.

'Figor most poorfal,' he bellooed, 'mooter in pooer uf all, do ee har ma shoot!'

De castel shan in de verry ston, an convince de warroors on di battlement dat de gute teem hadde stert. A shooer uf teeny briddes appar on de edge uf all, an plucked a plac on de shoolders uf Owl. Al choored an shooted on de castel, til soodan de tinee basts shatten foule on heem. De mannes noo wat it mant, an itta seelenced dem, bifor dey forgat et.

'Goddes in der gratnesse,' Meester Owel whuspeered ta himsel, 'it iss closs ta ovver. Thes will nat breng mich yeers ta passe.'

He had a spinne in hes braines fram portant affta porteent, an had noo differonce ta consodoor. Was et a smal dreme he had to soofer, like in hes darke chilhood? Wad he wook in tre secoonds, or wat?

'Mye lardes goddes,' he sadd wid teerfalnesse, 'my lardes goodess, ye arre writched soones uf notting.'

De cloods mooved apparint to all eyes, swaepin in a theek clar movment, till dey gatherer in da viry topp, where alle de goodes were livven. And it was shutte, dat peece of clar dee, an did nat oopen mare dat timme.

In de blakke mudde Owel remaened like an orphann boi. He was sik, wid water invaddin hes ees so soor.

'Wy?' he stert agin, an den al dat he cad manoog wass Wy? again. De min abuv hem on de walles tarnedd off, an want to dar offeec an buznes, as ef evertin wass normool, tho wance dey knoo. Anly oul Ool waz leftt ta tak reccaning, an he wuzz too drere tyrede. A clothy neet, like nuttin ivver beforr, lade de lant ta slepe dat nigt.

That big confident bristly creature, singing falsetto between the hilly church and the speckled town is my father: I have him now. There is a road that loops and rises, and rises and turns, which we knew as the way to school. It involves gravel and tar and old paving, and weariness, and the chocolate relief of the downhills. Up over our tight heads, he schooners my sister and me.

'This way, my children, this way.'

'Alfred Deller, daddy, sing like Alfred Deller!' my sister insists.

So at the footed steps of the quaint houses, which all hold their green plants and their green mornings and their green faces, he clicks his voice into the top storeys and pipes like a girl, an expansive secretive man warbling wickedly and thrillingly between sparkling grey windowpanes.

'Wake up, wake up, ye citizens, our father is afoot and abroad against the earliness!'

He shakes all sleepiness out of his great sky, and the pavement reddens for him. He won't greet anyone who greets him. He thrusts out his nesty beard and ignores the ordinary.

'You may grow, my children, but you will never be as big as me.'

Sure of this, he inserts our noses and cheeks into the kind sunlit eight o'clock, and encourages us to our bewildering education, whose wilderness is overgrown with alphabets and pens, and exercises for our skinny bodies.

'Grow, my body, grow,' I whisper, as I come amiss on the unscalable peak of the vaulting-horse. 'Be like him as soon as you can.'

Our great man, our falsetto singer, he whom nothing and no one confuses, who will scream in your nostrils before he will allow it – scream in those two miserable traitorous holes, and put the scream in your hard narrow belly. Ouch, daddy, your scream has reached my innards, and now I may not grow. Perhaps that will please him. He is easy to please but he is easier to enrage. But at least he has appeared, which is something beyond expectation.

Now everything materializes, the Highgate streets and the chipped houses, and the vanishing faces of the other schoolchildren, and the long silenced voices. All of it races and turns still in a proper place of its own, still continuing after a fashion, not to be erased under so light a hand, nor ever possibly, by so pitiful a weapon as the passing of years. More real now than it was then, when all things were only suggested by a number of conflicting and faint-hearted phenomena.

If I crouched with a book in my lap in the drawing class, was it really because I had pissed in my trousers, and didn't want anyone to know? Or was it, in reality, because I had a pain in my belly, as I thinly claimed? And if I scuttled to the cloakroom with the chair grasped to my bottom, and the book to my coloured lap, why did they not understand my subterfuge? And if my mother was sent for, and led me home to the impossibly lost house, where the boards were made of the present, why did she get me to change my clothes under my white plastic raincoat? And if I walked the rest of the way with her sans pants and underpants, but red-naked beneath my coat, why so, when it was only a pain in my belly? And if I was there, why was I not elsewhere? For instance, the son of the new Indians, or was it Chinese, who first showed me chopsticks and gentled my mouth for me? And why was that scenario and any scenario written so for me? And who was viewing it, in what remote country cinema? A closed off film, where the child who was me and never me, believed in the life of his mother, and himself and his sister, but only imagined his father, in the absence of good continuous proof, who never had a conversation of any length or meaning with him besides rage or silence or condescension, who willed his body to copy his father's, created or uncreated, but who most of all could not imagine anything beyond his father, and had no sense of other lives, millions and millions, repeating his or borrowing freely from his uncopyrighted script.

And why that continuous drama of things refusing to happen once, but always? Of things, streets and corners of shops, beginning to become familiar, like a family that is, and to be always on the verge of speaking, recognizing for certain the child in the white coat, with his bottom naked and not naked?

'They'll think you're wearing shorts,' my mother said astutely.

Mummy, I was wearing shorts, the clothes of the emperor's boy. The emperor's new clothes do in fact exist, mummy, it is the emperor himself who is invisible. Could you not encourage

81

the emperor to appear more often, as I have an engagement and contract with him to be his son, and himself, believe it or not, I know it seems inappropriate, to be my daddy?

Hey, hey, and a bottle of rum. This is a queer line of thought for the noonday of Key West. God bless its distance from itself and itself.

At the brown late party his friend the grey man sits on me, covers my bird bones with his cat bones in the dark-blue dusty armchair, that is famous in the sharp living-room. But my, here comes my old dad, it is evening, and the grey has changed places from the man to the volcanic garden below the windows, and the yellow curtains slide like dancers and priests to the middle of themselves, and sleep. And the flat is changed completely, as he is home, and the black cat is eating very fast and delicately, and talking to mummy in the narrow toffee kitchen, and he, the old hero, has brought pies from the shop on his way, for us, for us, for us. He has paid money in trickling silver for individual pies.

'In-div-id-uals,' we moan, in our London-County-Council accents, no posh for us. We moan and our hearts beat for our great invisible cat, and he hangs from his branch for us, and trapezes, and brings pies. Sweet hours, sweet fellow. You are thrusting the responsibility of delight on your kinder's crowns. Your children love you as their pieman, against the grey window-light, all smiling and present. Of course, no, they can't actually see you. But they quite clearly can see their notion of you, such an excellent notion, which freely grants you the reputation of a lion.

Rinsed blessed fucked-out five o'clock, in the bluest room this side of Boulogne. An enormous life has arrived in my second of first mornings, and it's not gratefulness and relief that bricks me in, but disquiet and regret. Not because of her beginning, but because of her endlessness. She has turned up, out of scale, to my diminished half-settled fiasco.

What the road doesn't know wouldn't broil a hare. What the room knew baked my early-morning bones till the flesh was soft, and inclined to slip off to her insidious practised knife.

Watch her with a fish knife some day, friend, in the long attitudes of tomorrow, and you'll catch what I mean.

I never claimed singularity for this. It has happened and recooked and rehappened to you and the distant them, in this time and that time and lost times, and in periods outside the weak definition of time, with its expanding and contracting divisions. A minute can last an hour, says the idiom, and it does not deceive. A minute can be relied on only never to last a minute, but something more or less. These minutes as perfect as a selfless intention – never met the creature myself, never lay among its hairs.

Unwashed in red tights she lies sleeping, and much service it does her. As for myself, a shallow unrested condition greets me. Thought you'd got rid of me, it says with a profound belling wink. And the clock on the church-tower trembles its stones for Sunday, and sways the old building-brick campanile. St-Sulpice, sweet darling, I was so glad to see you the first day. And so sorry to live near you.

The edge of the mattress is my portion, as my new animal demands unthinkingly her rights to graze in sleep. If I was to get to dream again, it would be her sheep I'd need to locate and count. Or slaughter. Xenia, I must take these sheep to a market of my own making, mea culpa, for death is rottingly on my conscience. My lady, you have bruised my worrying parts, and between my no-man's-land is a soft raw idea. This idea is chock-full with sentences and clauses, which I sift through carefully in the rainy dawn. Should I slip down my hand to investigate? Or is control in order? What damage could three hours of three comings do down there, in its current unenthusiastic exile, and her crouching over it with her largest of cunts, and her dancing on it? Her pressed-out bottom choreography, with her accidental slips which would snap my old cock if it were woodenly constructed. This unthinking eyes-shut satisfaction of her linings and endings.

What reckoning is there now for her assuming ease? Why does her being inside life drive me out further? What is this lack of gentleness in my beloved bull? A female bull is an hermaphrodite of some threat. It is not that, in the night sanctified by bells, she abused or raped me. It is that she could not recognize my faceless progress. I was not there except to pay for her

83

expensive poverty. My god, call out some army, some American cavalry, and let this Indian be shot or honoured with citizenship. Throw a few garlands to this bull and leave me in my treasured segments.

But still, when all is unsaid and undone, I flower my good sense of hope, and climb up the few mountainous feet from mattress to standing, scoop a clatter of coins, and dress, and spiral down, down, the brown sunk gloom of the stairwell, my bucket, my bucket. With happiness my companion, I step among the shops purchasing a baguette here, and good butter there, and mille feuille cakes over yonder, and Coca-Cola back across. This granite celebrates my earliness, to which it is not used. I loved my being up so bright as much as I hated it. A curious happiness then. I couldn't stop that literary yellow rivering down from the sun, and filling the gap between the houses, even if I had a sponge. My, but legs can be happy too, if you get them up and out early enough, and youth can be a palpable idea, even a certainty, against the insurance of a long day. I do not love this bull but I do wish to content her. This is an evil desire, oh doubtless, but now Perrier, and now instant coffee, and now milk, and now oddly-packaged sugar, hard to recognize. And I am glad to recall the two new big cups, with their smart blue saucers, which had the fortune to be chosen yesterday. That was a fine move, in their tinsel and thin paper. That was a fine bloody stupid extravagance.

No, that was a gift to someone who didn't arrive. Wasn't I expecting that woman from the station in old Greece? With the warm bottom and the idiotic language and the travelling breast? I was. So who is this I have behind me, above in the frightened room? Asleep on my stolen acre, unwoken and unasked? A demon has come in her place perhaps. The same face, but this body of hers is a weapon, not a counterpart. Her sexuality is a woman singing falsetto with her hand gripping a castrato's balls. A rather confused thing, you might say.

My grocer, you have such fine cabbages, but you are not friendly, and I have no flower-pot for them.

Kentucky, Kentucky, you are a useful distance between these two so-called times, a handy eight-thousand summers, a post-Celtic rescue. To think my murderer was on my own sweeted bed, whose calm sheets I had laundered carefully in the Arab shop, opposite the alien dignity of St-Paul. And if I had danced, I had danced for nothing and for myself. And the wine shop could not be found. But it was too soon for the wine shop. I was tired of wine shops. Let the wine-shop rot. Let the whole rue de Rivoli rot. But let my poor childhood and allhood balls not rot, please. Hey, Notre Dame, good morning! I'm going to feed my love! A likely story. You don't believe me? I don't believe me, but we have faith. You'll have heard of that. That's what built you, pal, and it's what'll build me now. Never mind the middle-ages, what about youth? Take her out, you say, and I will. But first I'll show her the dignity of an asexual breakfast. Tweedledum.

'Bon jour, Maria,' my pretty concierge, how dark you are at the bottom of this well. Have you been much bothered by the busy insects that are born from the muddy bottom? No? Well I have, I am terribly bothered, my sweet. If we spoke a common language I would certainly tell you.

Everything in early morning was describing rough-and-ready. The clouds now had an obvious painted look. Certainly they were not true clouds. And the lake was mere daubs of light-blue and grey, and the trees were shot-green smudges. A lot of ink also had apparently been soaked into the paper. A nice strange feeling to wake up in a paper place, Sue and myself joined together by a slight sweat, and the colour she flung against the rooms of my old head at the thought of her. And as I woke I reconsidered. Wasn't she just an accidental girl, who had uprooted herself from her front yard for no good reason, and barely for my sake? Yes, yes, but. The thing was redefined by what had happened now after that. You can start out in idleness and proceed with meaning, eh?

I heard Chicken starting out in idleness, the other side of the sunk sleeping motorcar. He muttered and hawked, and crept half-crouched and asleep down to the small music of the shore, a tiny distant muddling of the scales. And then I became aware of the full political noise the birds were concocting. They were driving each other to revolution, by the sound of it, just a hint of threat in their happiness.

Chicken seemed now to have fallen into a dream again on his feet. It was warm and chill at the same time. Something was working to wake us and something to drug us – the wild civilized singing of the hidden birds, and the card-shuffling of the lake, were in conflict of a sort.

She woke like a child, and turned and opened her mouth as if to cry, but she smiled and giggled and pulled herself round to hold me and laugh.

'Owl,' she said, 'Owl.'

'What?' I said. 'What about me?'

'You're a beast,' she said.

'I am not.'

The trees heard my pretty lie, and stared at me from a number of boled arrogances.

'Owl,' she said.

'Yes?'

'When I was asleep, I dreamed you.'

Too true, I thought. Tales of dreams usually bore the death in me, but tales about myself, even in Sue's dreams, didn't really.

'What did you dream?' The question was like an endearment: What did you dream, what did you dream? Like asking a child if it knew what the coming time would be.

'What did you dream, Sue?'

My arms started to heat. Something turned up the birds' performance.

'You,' she said, 'I dreamed about you.'

'But what?'

Our whispers were diagrammed by a kind of amusement, the amusement I suppose that new lovers feel who don't regret each other. Each thing we said moved off like troops against the other's doubting, and hollowness. Hollow is right.

'You were waving,' she said, 'waving, waving.'

'And where were you?'

She squeezed up her face.

'Well?' I said.

'Well, well, well,' she answered.

'No, come on, tell me, where were you?'

'Not there,' she giggled.

'Not there? I was waving at nothing then,' I said, 'I was

waving at the stars?'

'It was daytime,' she said, 'in a little wood.'

'Like here?'

'No, not here, later.'

'How do you mean, later?'

'Later,' she said. 'Darling?'

'Yes?' I said.

'Darling, darling.'

'Yes?' I said.

'I love you, Owl.'

'If you do, you're crazy,' I said. The seemingly automatic sensation flicked into talk inside me: Don't let this woman stitch you up, Oliver. But it melted, and I educated myself with a little hope.

'You want to get up now,' she said, 'darling?'

'Okay.'

'Where's Chicken?' she said.

'Why?'

'Because I don't want him to see me, that's why.'

'Oh yeh, well, he's trying to root himself into the lake.'

'Oh yeh? Well, cover for me, bud, I'm getting out.'

And she took her slim secret life which had held me as its life all night, and she put it out in the open before the suddenly miserable trees. To be still morning trees before such movement. But they relaxed as she plucked her knickers on, and dragged her cotton dress roughly over her night breasts. She wriggled it in place, and tossed me her own look which involved a thrusting-up of her eyebrows and a crooked mouth.

'Will you excuse me, please sir, while I go and pick flowers?'

'Take a shit, you mean,' I said.

'That's what I said,' she said, She left her laughter for a moment struggling behind her, till it dropped to the grass and rolled down to Chicken, who swung slowly and rather dourly in our direction.

When he came up the slope though, he was creased and easy.

'Mornin,' he said. 'How's my buddy?'

'How's yourself?' I said, and tottered to put some cloth between me and the fresh day.

'How's the girl?' he said. 'She sleep all right?'

'She slept fine,' I said.

'How long you know her?' he said, smiling.

'Oh,' I said, 'you know, a while.'

'You live in the same town?'

'Do I look like I live in a town, Chicken?'

'Well, shit,' he said, putting his hands in front of him, theatrically. 'You must have grown up someplace.'

'Nah,' I said, 'I never grew up.'

'That figures,' he said, 'No, you see, but I like her, but maybe you're steady, you know, maybe.'

'Well we are a bit, Chicken. Yeh, it's true. What're you driving at, Chicken?'

'No, I'm not driving at anything,' he said, 'Shit,' he said, 'I'm driving *in* you, know what I mean? Listen, forget I said anything. I was just, you know. Let's hit the road,' he said. 'Jesus, I get sick of this forest after a while. Saw a whole flock of moccasins cross the lake, too.'

'You sure?'

'Something or other made a few snaky circles. Maybe it was fish.'

'Well I hope so,' I said, 'because I'm thinking of a swim.'

'Shit, fella, you have your clothes on.'

'Sure,' I said, 'I can't wander about naked.'

'Sure you can,' he said, 'sure you can. The animals do it.'

'Chicken, what's your second name? It wouldn't be shit, would it? Fuck you, Chicken,' I said, and laughed with a small choke.

Sue reappeared and smoothed her dress, with the embarrassed politeness I might feel if I'd just been vacating my bowels on the open ground nearby. She probably feared we could smell it, because she said:

'Come on, boys, I'm hungry.'

'You're always hungry, sweetheart, ain't ye?' said Chicken.

Sue gave him a salty stare, but her friendliness bobbed up like an otter.

'I could eat a watersnake,' she said. 'Come on.'

So we gathered the stuff, and left the anonymous lake, which might well have had a name and a history, but, almost like ourselves, we knew little about its picnics and its drownings. The ground tried to remember us, though, and light grass where we had dreamed each other held on to our shapes for an hour or two. And as we manoeuvered the big wheels away, and sped up on the cloudy brisk track, already the blades were starting to lift again. And by afternoon all trace of us would be gone, except for Chicken's cigarette packet, travelling out to the centre of the concussed water.

'I have a fren, mon, I'd like you to meet,' said Ali at the boats. I had discovered an open mirror of water, and Ali had reached it. It deepened good and dirty.

'Here?' I said. 'We're to meet him here?'

'No, no, mon, not here. And he's a she, you know, not what you're tinkin.'

The fishy sun, strained through the linen of the clouds, twisted greyly on the water. The port was stacked on all shores with smacks and smaller boats, but for the most part motor launches, with their high platforms and important-seeming aerials. We hove down on the concrete curb in this sunlight, and watched the slow business of the boats. Ali's frayed ageless trousers caught the simple shadows thrown off the surface, and the simpler lights. His richly black beard ringed his long-distance gaze more than ever. All of him had grown in the unnarrated night – my friend was a bigger friend even than yesterday. Thinking of growth made me consider my head. But I slapped the thought away in the interest of the moment, and then I surged with a minuscule contentment that was the reward for my control. The water flashed better. And the imprecise actions of the one or two fishermen in their vessels became involved with a more optimistic story. Now they were men in the middle of their breath. Their breath cloaked them. And they pushed their lives on into the undesired and undirected future. What they were doing now would not exactly inform what they would do the next week, but it was the necessary preparation. In other words, they had a real life, as I did for those minutes on the concrete in my wooden firmness of mind. I felt a roped con-nection with them – like them I was pursuing a sufficient-unto-the-day existence.

The morning was certainly beautiful, and the sun on my face took the opportunity to tell me stories.

'Yas,' said Ali, 'I'd like you ta meet her, an we might get some work there.'

'Oh,' I said. I didn't care so much about toil just then, but I was willing to listen, no matter if he wanted to talk about lobsters.

'Yas, she is a good woman,' he said, and marbled his features out over the lip of the dock a little further.

'Oh,' I said, 'okay. Where do we meet her?'

'You know dat topless place, mon?'

'Yes I think I do. Back of the mall there.'

'Ya, dat's it, I tink so. Hey, Johnnie!' he called out over the water. 'Wat's de news?'

There was a medium-sized fishing boat being swayed softly by the new movements of a blue figure. Perhaps he had just woken up.

'Dat's de boat I sleep on, time to time,' said Ali to me. 'He's a good mon too.'

'How do you get out there?' I said. He didn't seem to hear me. He was keeping an eye on Johnnie. I was going to repeat the question. But I supposed they used one of the cramped rowing-boats stashed up against the wharf like coracles. Cranes appeared blackly in the distant reaches of the harbour, or rather I suddenly and without point noticed them. And then I noticed a smaller clicking sound, that was the tapping of all the wood and wharf together. It was a fast sleeping beating noise out of its own Africa. I thought of Africa, and then I swung back and thought of where I was. It was nicer to think of that. It occurred to me that Ali in a way was an African, or someone behind him must have been.

What did they have in Jamaica? Was it slaves had been brought over, or what?

'How'd the Blacks get to Jamaica, Ali?' I said.

But he still couldn't hear me, and had his cat's gaze fixed. It was a stupid question anyway. I was glad he hadn't registered it.

'We were slaves, mon,' he said, even after the pause.

'I didn't think you were listening, Ali.'

'I was listening, but I was tinkin too. Yer better off tinkin for a while, when someone asks how sometin cam about.'

'You're dead right, Ali,' I said.

'Hey, Johnnie!' he shouted. 'How about bringin us two out

90

dere for the fishin?'

Johnnie stopped his preparations, and placed a hand over his eyes against the sunlight, and said:

'That you, Ali?'

'Yeh, it's me, mon,' said Ali, swinging his tattered legs. 'How ar ye?'

'I'm fine this mornin, Ali. Yeh.'

'You fishin today, mon?'

Ali's voice already had all the satisfaction of a day's hunting in it. Somehow he included the chapter and verse of the probable catch in his tone. Even from his distance, the man couldn't fail to be infected by him.

'I wish I wus, Ali. But I ain't got the gas.'

'I'll get you gas,' said Ali.

'Where would you?' said Johnnie, not disbelieving, but rather trusting.

'You want it, how much you got to pay?'

'How bout nothing? Will that do?'

'Sure,' said Ali, 'an you can have my grandmammy too.'

Then I began to suspect they were talking a language I didn't have the sense of, because it had veered away from that commodity for me. They chatted on in their code, and I examined the purposes of the brief black fish that seemed to make a living between the planks of a sunken boat at our feet.

'Hey! We'll see ya, Johnnie!' said Ali, drawing up. 'Catch yerself, Moran.'

As we wandered away, he said:

'He didn't want us coming out, but that's fine, I like him.'

'Is that what he meant?'

'Yeh, I know wat he means. He wants the day for himself. Dat's fine.'

'Does he use those big rods, the thick ones, I mean?'

'Oh ya, he uses everytin he can.'

And when night began to arrive that day, Ali and I had walked, and drunk a bit of beer, and eaten a pizza, cheap shiny pizza, and swum in the affectionate sea, and greeted all the people he always knew on the street, and snoozed a while in a shadowy corner of the town. And for the most part we were slumbering on our feet, and even the seawater was heavy-lidded and afternoonish. But there was no complaint to make of any of

91

it. And if some other things were worth a great deal more than our meanderings, they couldn't have given us more pleasure. Ali had filled out his application form for being alive, and some unofficial someone had granted that to him.

Our strolling ended up near the Topless bar, but we ducked into another to prepare ourselves, a den of folding shadows. A fellow about my bad age, or older, with a heavy grey stare, was feeding his guitar with whines and sliding. And his old woman was beside him, like a crushed cushion, playing rhythm, and looked like she had been stuck there at his more busy elbow for ever. They gave us *The Yellow Rose of Texas* like a record player that had something amiss with its workings. But behind the too-slow music was the original music, fresh and sad, and it was the youth of this pair it was singing of. And I could see them setting out together, with their words and their notes, and now their journey had become a spinning.

The breast is so alien to a man, more alien than his own phallus, that it can not be a mountain or an idea or a cushion. It can only and ever be itself. And because it lacks imagery, and seems to persist somewhere out of everyday language, and is not often allowed any daily place in talk, it is full of the unmapped power of a secret. If Moran had graphed the movements of Jane's breasts, he would have been dealing with the world's most intricate and wilful drawing. During his years with her, he watched them swing and cross and dip up in their room. He saw her washing them once or twice with despondent splashings of old water. He often saw her picking the hairs off the saucer-big aureoles, with an ancient tweezers. But these hairs might grow quite long before she did. And she trimmed herself when the customers complained of them in their mouths.

Moran saw the hoary men try to eat these unsymbolic breasts. He saw the quiet speechless masses being pummelled and bruised by the rougher shilling-boys. Sometimes the men just liked to sit on them with their skinny hard arses. From his accepted place in the corner, Moran notated it all without willing it, or he received vicariously the tremors of old desire, under the faithful bed. He didn't care for watching the older fellows. He hated the way their balls hung sadly, further than they should for prettiness's sake. He hated their sorrow, and meanness, when it came to paying for something that was mostly memory, even when it was taking place. Most of all he hated their distance from him, and their distance from Jane Smith. Who in turn was distant from him.

She didn't know why she kept the lad, she said, as her legs were opened yet again, and another sheepish but advancingly rough attempt was made on her passiveness.

'No,' she said, 'I don't know why I keep him. There now, Jack, don't strain yourself.'

It was the stillest life Moran could imagine, even stiller in a way than the poor house, because there he had had his roof family, and here he had only a vaguely precise circle of trade and tea. When Jane had no men she drank tea in black cups, with many spoons of sugar, and much slightly-blooded milk. The milk was blooded because she got it cheap from one of the flaccids, who carried it to her from one of his iller cows. That cow seemed to live a long steady life for a creature so sick. After the years she got well-used to it, and probably would have missed the small taste of blood if the cow had passed on. *Moran, my Blessed Apostle*, she often called him. He didn't know what an apostle was, nor what it meant to be blessed. After a while they called him that in the town, when he went on his own, so he knew that the men talked about him and Jane Smith to everyone. The children even, not much younger than him, jeered him from the corners with it.

'The Blessed Apostle, the Blessed Apostle. Well if it isn't the Blessed Apostle.'

They never got tired of this, Moran noticed. It suited them as a witticism from one end of the year to the other. But he preferred rolling into town, than not, as an antidote to the unbelievable stagnation of the room.

Jane never went out, unless it was to urinate or defecate in the back yard. And as the years increased, so did her bulk. Her arse remained as slim as always, and her legs. But her stomach and breasts swelled. The customers loved this, but they didn't like her getting old. Her face was a strange army camp of creases and oily marks.

In the end, the customers stopped coming at all. Only the

very old ones turned up still, like strays, either to sit on her endless breast, which was always a favourite with them, or to suck on them like puppies. But she couldn't charge them more than a few pennies for this tiny service, and anyway she felt a great disconnection between her face and her upper torso in general and hardly considered it a part of herself at all.

Her only fault in Moran's view was that she beat him. He didn't like her beating him. He liked the dirt and the smell of tigers and the sugary food and the younger men performing, till they stopped turning up. But he didn't like her hitting him. She hit him, she said, because he enraged her. But she never looked enraged when she was striking him. She looked preoccupied. She bound him to the bed with old coloured scarves, remnants of famous presents in her younger days, and slapped him lazily, but quite viciously, with a pan. The metal pan made dull sea-weedy sounds on his belly and legs, but when it met his head, it sang out. *Rashers and eggs, rashers and eggs*, said the pan, rather tunefully. As she proceeded, her breasts of course billowed like sails. But they weren't like sails naturally they were only like breasts. She never knocked Moran very forcefully on the head, but she liked to have him good and bruised on the thighs and stomach.

When this was over, and it took place on average once a month, as if it was his wages for doing nothing, she brewed more tea. As the customers dried up, so the beatings increased, and the tea wetted. Moran didn't know exactly why he endured it and allowed her freely to bind him and punish him. But he realized he had no choice. The breasts were in control of that room, and the breasts could not be denied. If he had attempted rebellion, they might have devoured him. He didn't know about them. He had no images or ideas of or for them. For all he knew, they might have mouths hidden somewhere under the creases. He respected the breasts, and he even respected, just a trifle, the yeastily enlarged belly.

He watched Jane Smith swell, and accepted the pan, and time took care of itself. Time passed, insisting on the verb, and soon, it seemed, Jane Smith was old. Then she was old for many years, and not even the ancient men came for her services. Not even the dead in the graves troubled themselves, as they might have done, as she would have accommodated them, *the poor same people.* A younger woman flowered in some other edge of the town, and that was that. Now she depended on what could be stolen. And as she never left the premises, she despatched Moran to perform this necessary dance. As a substitute for the dog, on her own instinct, he made sense at last.

Sixfoil Six

Wel, her leddy she wus setteld guit aginst herr hides an velvut. She had a litul wud barnin in her fier — oakes branchen and harrde oul walnutte tre. Her walls were very stoney and bar, and roun abut whar har huntin peeces of receunt timme. An they war nat curred proper, and the heds of deere an bor hang on de wal wid beets of fleslh an blut, dree but stunkin. She did nat minde dis, but wasse radder fonde of ittes perfum. It lay in her braene likke somer.

Di leddy she semed smal bat it wass anly in har statur: in pooer she was grat amang the servoonts. For har owen smel wasse thicke as an animool, and de min wanted her for der spoort. But have her thae coold nat.

De door was rapped wid mousy knacks, an de hooly bishoop scattled in. Hes cloth were greezy wid ateings, an hes bellie pressede oot, as dat of a wimin wid chillde. He putte himsel on de eddge uf de seatin, an lookit shylee at hes quene.

'A littul seek todye I fele,' he spoked.

'My pur litul feelow,' honeyyed de ledy.

Der was sileence den, as dey gazed likke deere inta eche odders eyen. Dey were bothe so smal, and barrelly the bishoop, 'an firm yer lasse, dat dey madde de walls wid animools blushe. For he was no strang gud man, de man uf Romme.

De yeng quene leanned forwar, an rubbed has bellee quietlee, an a brun belche riss oot, and falled de chamboor wid stinke.

'Yar feels batter noo?' askit de womanne, wid a birdushe laughing.

'Tank ya, ' he groanned, an he sprad hes legges a bit, to reste de bownes which war hertin hem. In wintery Rame he hat suffirt fram de rheumatee, becasse hes hoos der hadde ben damppe. Noo he wass in de mast dampest cointroo in de wurel, an hes painn marterred hem. Al nicht an dee de throbbes occupeed hes secunds, an it companioon hem fram bedde ta tabool. He atet as

96

muche as de tabul offert. An soo hes stomik burstet alway. To eese hes sore procissoon in liffe, he madde his peece wid god, an slept wid womun. Fer he funde dat dallioonce wid cuntes and botums cawsed hes trooble to slep. Tharfoor he expectit helles flammes fer his desoort at dethe, an wasse a hooman sorelee advancin. Bat aboov al he desiere de quaene uf Conn, whach wasse nat kinde.

An shee noo anly wunted hes boody an barrul, an shart flab-bed erms aboot her in de blak interim betwan sunne an sonne. It seemt a luv dey possesset, bat it, in trut, represence a devilishe appeteet, far de dowel himsel habited de rounde bishap, Moll, in mine opinoon.

'Lovve,' he sade, 'I amm mar worrit aboot yer keengly man, den all de warres of foren cuntrees.'

'Shishe, mye fren, he isse a gotte felloo ta mee.'

'Bat, laedee, he wull keel thee at de ent, becarse yee at nat in faethe ta heem.'

'Soorly I amm,' she tinklet. 'He cann havv moi corpse whan he willit.'

'Yas, bat in neeht yee arr nat far hem, bat in mee chamboor, as ye knoo.'

De quane laff wid memorees iv blisse beneet de bishapes bel-lee.

'Donat laffe,' complan de rued mout, dat defiledde ittes got. 'He wull keel us bote in teem. Ass I amm a runed man uf Rame, an denizoon if dat citoo, lat me advisse my quene.'

'Noo, noo,' she spatte. 'Be queet. Lat me fondle yer perts in secrette herre.'

De bishap strak her hande offe hes lap, an raised uppe hes meaty selfe.

'Ye arre madde,' he said, 'lik a demonne. Lave me bee whil we talke aboot oure saviance.'

De quene jes giggulet, becorse she did nat care for talking dat wasse fulle of a badde futir.

'Bat it isse my softe botoom ye wante, is nat it, moi liffe?' An she dragged her skert uppe har lags, an madde of her lower lant a moone. She tarned it al to de bishop, and he fixet his smal eyes on de strange fullness of her cheekes.

'Fer gooddes goodness, cover thie gloree,' he sadde, hes hert stonelee sunkin in hes hed. An inne her hedde wasse a lake uf glasse, Moll, wid no wedderes interferren. She sanke doon an creed, an pullet her skeerts to thar polite posisoons.

'I amme gan dafte,' she moaned to hersel. 'I am for ruine too, moi bishoop. Bat moi bordoom hasse dun it al.'

An de bishoop take her tinee heate in hes armes, and she wepped lang lik dat. De crows outseed filt everytin wid feelthee ceremonee, for it wasse cam ta evenin his teem.

'By liffe,' croaked de movede litul fowelman, 'we arre a rotin pare uf craturs.'

'Noo!' scremt de quene, an knocket hem bak. 'Noo,' she saide, an plucket at her faece. 'I amme nat. I amme a goodly lasse, an ye haff tampered wid moi perfectoon.'

Her screm wanderet oot de windoo, like a bolte uf an horse, an fell on de hed off Conn, dat was strollen in de coortyard. He paused himself, and gazzed up de roughe walles of his castel, and akset nat what he herd, bat stayed walkin after a minoot. An in de stabel de licht of yellowish humoor wasse cuttin throo de beets of strawe an sich, dat floated in de lightness uf de evenung. He lingeret lik an animool der, til de finall blaze uf de owel sunne dampened on de hills.

In tru de gaet cam meesster Ool stridin, an hes legges ate up the seely mudde.

'It iss a true evenin,' said lorde Conn. 'My fren, how are ye at all this dee?'

'My lard, I am ruddy an feen,' sadde de beardy poet wid a gromoce of chucklin. 'An can ye saye de saem yerself?'

'I can nat,' spoke the Conn himsel. 'I can nat. But nae mater, lat it bee.'

'Why do ye stande here amang the dustee stabelin? Can ye nat go in an reste yer bowens?'

'My owel house is full uf praistliness, an it is nat kinde,' said Conn. 'I haff no patieoonce lefte to me wid dat portlee gentilman de bishopp. Soorly if he canterres on in hes manoor I wull steek a litul kneef in hes corpulanz.'

De poete roared in delicht.

'Dat woud nat despeleece de min, my honoor, no. Lat ye be aboot dat.'

'Yesse,' said Conn, 'I mighte. Bat he iss de man of Rame, and shee is pooerfool alway an ever.'

'How iss de croppes dis saison, my hert?' said Owl, his man

of menne.

'Dey will doo de jobbe dey must. We wall nat go hungery. Dat is nat moi worree. It isse mare de questoon of yoo, moi fren, and dat worst preest.'

'Nivver minde it al,' sedde Owl. 'I haff ben ta see de hermaphrodeet, an all is welle, she promissed.'

'Is it soo?' said Conn, very surpreezed. An for a mimint he beleeved. An den him memoiry did nat faille hem. Bat he saidde nottin.

Out of sight in another place, that claims to have passed itself by. Only then the word *sky* becoming a tag for what was above my head out of doors. Whereas before I knew that mess or smooth tangle was never the same thing, or capable of the same word. And placing these names on everything, like a foreign child's English lesson, only made it easier to say hello to everything: Hello, sky. But as soon as addressed, each thing disappeared for the sake of convenience. Now the sky was blue in my head, and anything but true blue in fact. The sky could assume all the livery of my grandfather's water-colour box, but I stopped half-noticing that. The large pictures became of little importance outside the idea of them. A wood was a wood, but the unhappy root of one tree, exposed in the rain, gained in size. Pity though that the rain had to become its word also, because each rainfall had previously been very much proper and special to each arrangement it fell on, and could be relied on to code and key the present when needed. Because even a child requires his memories, albeit slim fantastic and exact ones.

And there is nothing longer than the feeling of having been alive for ever, that seems to get shaken off after puberty, the conviction of being alive in a world, or some world anyway, supplied I suppose by the solidity of parents, or, if not available, of a parent. Which is why, in the disconnected new backyard of Key West I even consider the matter: because to win a sense of your parents is to regain a sense of yourself.

More calm, perhaps, to look for those diagrams in your grandparents, but possibly, after all, that is only a fragmentation of an available whole.

Except for the slight problem of the father. Vacuum abhors a nature. But the shadow is there, or here and there. Wily woodsman, I suppose, who when he crept, crept always through the undergrowth – seeing as he carried a sample of such twisting vigour on his cheeks and chin.

We could play as noisily as the progress suggested, until the usual catastrophe, and there might even be a traditional look in my sister's face, as she aimed her roars and battle at the cracks in the adult doors. *Let him come if he dares*, she seemed to offer. Come he did. Not before the perfectly late day had a fine time of it in the garden below, with its longness and tagged greenness, and the real jungle at the bottom, where the toothbrushes were.

There were words strewn, teacherly, all over the dominion. In my head the sign came up.

What is this word?

It is Father.

What is the father doing?

He is getting his belt out of the cupboard.

And what is this word?

It is Fear.

And what is fear doing?

It is having a holiday in my heart.

Come now, child, heart is a word for that silly pump of gristle and muscle you carry for safety's sake under your ribs.

Excuse me.

Well, what is this word?

It is Blow.

What is the blow doing?

It is proceeding from a great paternal height, and approaching the bottom of my sister.

What is she doing?

She is shouting at him, at first, but suddenly she goes quiet and allows it.

Allows it?

Well sort of. Actually she is harbouring a Grudge. She's great at that.

And what is this word, child?

It is Exit, which my old da is now doing.

Where is he going to?

100

Back into the completely undefined place where the brown is, and the possible glasses, and the rumble of talk, like a lost radio.

And this word?

That word is Tingle. And if you would hold your next word up, it is, I expect, Regret.

Good boy. What are you doing?

I'm making a hole here in the wall beside my bed, because it may be a good idea to reach in to the next house.

But, little fellow, that wall has only the air of the earth on the other side, and will lead you, with something of a fall, to the garden.

Oh.

What is your sister at now?

She is counting, sir, right up to a hundred. And I will have to continue on where she stops, or there will be trouble.

Your father might come back.

Yes, but she is counting quietly, and the cat is asleep on her legs.

You mean this word here?

Yes, Cat. The black cat that my mother knows how to talk to. The black cat gets into the sister's bed at night, and burrows down where it can't breathe. I don't know why.

What is that great patch above your sister's bed?

That's where the ceiling fell down one evening, when, luck-ily, we were in the sitting-room. But it's fixed now. It's fixed, but you never know. It fell, it fell, it fell, and it might have killed her.

What is this word?

Relief.

Ah, you like this female child, she who is but one among millions?

Extremely, if it's all the same to you.

But why?

Well, she is rather large, and has my nose twice broken, and yet she has a certain I-don't-know-what about her that suggests the salons of the.

Stupid child.

But now this worded sky has quite taken off, and has shaken away any semblance of vocabulary and is a storylike great cloth high over the Heath. The path enters in, and as it does, it becomes groups of children with their makers. And even between them in the dry chalky parts, it has talk and character, because the spirals shrug up of their own accord, and my parents' feet consume the yards. And the stone wall is mostly asleep, and is able to be in the future before I am, because I can see it away up the track where things have still to happen yet. The things that haven't yet occurred are smaller than the present clutch of puzzles. Mummy wears her suede coat, in memory also of the future. The man of men is only a black mark, a door, in my head. This may be the beer last night, and I am willing to see it as my own shortcoming. The painted door and the suede coat with the stockings walking it, carry the knowledge I don't have, which includes the clew of our way home. Since others are looking after those keys and details, I can concentrate, and learn to be friendly with the numerous stones and dusts of the journey. And when the lawns sweep to vanished houses, I just ignore them. Too many imprecise words. The trees too attempt to shake off their miserable tags, and start up conversations that they can't finish. Tree becomes oak, becomes the fellow with the score of rough servantlike arms, that might hold me idly.

All the blessed afternoons. Eight thousand what? Eight thousand afternoons. One of those hardly a motto for all. But so. Still the green affair, a leather jacket and a magazine face, on a park bench in the new past, and the troublesome images all hidden.

I heard her say *château*, when in fact she said *chalet*, and saw a modest stone castle beside a Swiss lake.

'We go there,' she said, 'in the summer, the next one. We have trouble my father with me.'

The park-keepers mix in with the noise of French dogs and French enthusiasm, which are almost the same thing, and strictly reserved for the French. And this colour of the afternoon hangs modestly as a back-cloth to her and me, on the wooden seat.

The hoops at the edge of the path are not as ordered as the lost order of my progress. Or should I admit, an inherited progress? Never mind all that, I say. What she had outstretched on her pocketed hand was a history of notions, just a museum, very nice at that. Xenia on the park bench, telling me how much trouble her father was to her. Now could that really be called representative of the truth, in hindsight? Well, if she had only been the product of her own P.R..

And why shouldn't she be allowed a continuous life, at least in my consideration of her now? Let her be. She was not the most wicked. No, but she was there. Funny, she was there on that Sunday, inside that afternoon, in that particular park, in that city, where many were, truly, but no one like her exactly so much as herself. At least I hope not. Not very pleasant to think we might have been duplicated all about that spot, like nodding butting pigeons. But possibly only too likely, eh?

'I have old ladies,' she said. 'They come and we teach them to move and sometimes they are younger ladies.'

This is only too fascinating when issuing from such an historic mouth – the sort of lips that history gets only too uncritical about. So what chance to hold back had I? A mere chronicler, and private at that. And amn't I a tiny bit invisible beside her, in the manner of le père? Ah no. I want to get her back there, but not cast aspersions on my poor self. Still, I wonder what my motives could have been? Survival, pride, and a useless brand of desire. Rubbish, it was merely survival. She was the cavalry to scare off them injuns. She knew how to blow her bugle with the right Hollywood timbre, with the Indian–scattering guarantee.

Mind you, I do think she looked on me as a regular discovery. She maintained some notion of my character, that was never there, obviously, but certainly survived more than a few revelations. She was a connoisseur of belief in that respect. Perhaps I even forced her hand at judging the old pelt as it was.

You'd almost love her, the way she forgave the rash of ruddy spots on my back that had sprung up in the intervening months of petty terror. Actually, I wonder what I have against her, really. It was what I became under her admiring gaze that I don't care for. I knew well I couldn't be that fine an animal, no sir. The necessity to show my hand undid me there, I suppose.

And now, one of those intervals between clear-sighted erroneous memory and the next scene. Such a cinematic experimenter, the selfsame memory. Not a stickler for continuity, but quite a perceptive director, if in its dotage. But here we are at the lake, among the barren plots of the park, and the attendant is calling unhappily to the lost or late rowing-boats, a shepherd to young dogs, tiny catastrophes of extra francs and embarrassed bravado. Six francs for the rowing and thirty for the insurance, just in case we haul out on some distant shore, and scarper with an oar. Sweet god, but to pull on the wooden poles, and have her in the centre of the boat, balancing it, and the world was not the pointless lack of exercise it may seem now. From her head to the sky, a pillar of invisible heat built itself, and so I had to draw it too with my unpractised arms. Come on, little breeze, conspire with me now to carry my new love and her incommodious pillar. Under the well-footed arch of an iron bridge we think to pause. Now what symbolism could possibly lurk in that? Since symbols seem to lantern us out of our frights.

And the single signless difference is, that we spoke in friendly ignorance, and continually granted each other the benefit of belief. Whereas later that was not humanly logical. And if we were as wrong-headed as all that, it might have served such paradoxes better to have gone on bestowing the benefit, in face of the slowly-becoming-clearer flaws. Where she was a fool I was a worse fool. And vice versa, if possible. So pity these two boaters under the bridge, moving away from each other even as they forced their lives closer.

Emptiness is a terrible man for filling an existence to bursting point. Can't our words, her confident nonEnglish and my Hibernoenglish, be allowed their imagined meaning still, even though what happened after proved them pretty overbrave and curiously futile? I mean, those two might have loved each other, satisfying all the paragraphs of the textbook, and there might have been as much chance of success under the bridge, as there certainly was of its accident, as her bottom influenced the movement of the boat, and as mine did. Which unnoticed dance may mean more that our foully-overheard gabbling – because if my words fled out of pretension and cowardice, hers rabbited out of self-confidence.

On the other hand, I would like to call up the true arbiter of this matter, he, she, or it who knows the inner machinery of us two, as we worked then. Why leave it to me, an amateur in the matter of human history, and holder of one side of the story merely, when there were not simply two sides even, but probably a number of hundreds, or a fraction of one? And to describe the water and the green people might be more fruitfully done from the point of view of our bottoms, rather than of our so-called minds and memories. What went on still exists, whether I noticed it or not, and, more likely than not, inside that ignorance. The ignorance being a perfect map for a genuine country of knowledge.

In a little while I began to think Sue's face was a bit horselike, but when I translated that into my idea of foals and stallions it was all right. Anyway I knew everyone seemed awful from time to time, and I wasn't such a bloody fool as to think it didn't apply to me too. Who said I was handsome in the first place?

I suspected Sue never even took note of my appearance, as such. She responded more to how I said things, and how much I listened to her. And I couldn't get tired of listening to her, because it was always bound up with the desire she could evoke by casually spieling off stories. I got a good grip of her father and her uncle in the end, though I probably confuse the two of them a little now. But they were true baggage to her, and part of her, and she was passionate in a quiet manner about remembering them. She needed me to be there, so she wouldn't let any of the details slip. And of course I could soon ask specifically for a story to be retold, for instance the one about the drawer.

So the old woman dying off so silently like that in the farmhouse, was a double shock. Because I had been resting there, wondering if Sue would be like this when she was old, when it happened. That was the farmhouse we got to, towards the evening of the third or fourth day in the big black car. It was one of the most uneasy things that have ever passed quaintly in front of my curious eyes.

The façade stuck up in the middle of all those dead miserable fields, a simple clapboard building with no pretension and no future. But Chicken turned in along the troubled track, and we were too sleepy and thirsty to stop him. I should have tumbled Sue out of my arms and lap, and got a bit of going-on-further enthusiasm into Chicken. He had a tendency to swing in sideways in that way, like a car with its wheels out of alignment. You had to keep your eye on him if you wanted safety to feature in affairs.

He roared the car up to the farmhouse, and let it die suddenly in its own dust. He swung around with his dry lined eyes, and just shook his head at me.

'You don't give a shit about anyone, Chicken,' Sue murmured. 'You just drive in, where you please. I was going to sleep for a few miles.'

'Jesus,' said Chicken, and sort of bolted out the door.

And then we got into the house together, and the old woman was there with her tins, and she thought she knew us. She thought we were her family just come in from a day's work. But there can't have been anyone about besides her for a while, because the house was under a linen of dust.

'Sweet Jesus,' Chicken whispered to me. 'The old lassie's gone daft.'

As we padded about her rooms the dust danced for us badnaturedly. It wasn't a good feeling. We couldn't understand the woman being there like that on her own – unless we had walked in on a recent brief piece of her history, that was odd in the ways bits of my own history have been odd. I mean, sometimes if you walked in on me, you might think things were a bit peculiar.

Her peculiarity was all confined in a big colonial armchair, and she was a large-boned lady herself, and had got through a good few tins.

After a bit we grouped around her on the other filthy chairs, and listened to the unstoppable nonsense that she served up:

'Got the grey, and I said to Jill, it wouldn't be as smart now as a good gelding, but she would insist.' And so on. She was a big clockwork toy, and even we could see that she was winding down. But she didn't stop mumbling for a second, and all her mumbles were obviously stories. We soon felt absolutely as if we didn't exist, not even as much as the little she did. Yes, she drove all the importance out of us since she confused us with some other people. We wondered where the real ones had gone. With all that dust it wasn't hard to guess, but still it was a funny thing to do, leaving the ancient dame behind like a half-broken radio, or a gramophone, that kept on repeating itself. And such big bones for a woman, and a face truly like a horse, not in Sue's way, but a serious working horse, the kind that would plough you a field, if there was ever any rain in the world again. And just at the point where we were all three of us beginning to disappear, by sheer dint of her gabbling, she disappeared. Her voice withered away and stopped. And her breath stopped. And her fingers stopped tapping. It was only when they stopped that I noticed they had been perpetually stirring.

'What the fuck is this?' said Chicken, and Sue laughed. 'The weirdest fucking thing, Owl, isn't it?'

'Who is she?' said Sue, with a queer texture in her voice, like she didn't want to know.

'Just some old corpse washed up here,' said Chicken.

'Nah,' said Sue, 'she's been in the house a long time, this is her place.'

'Off-beat her just dying like this, though,' said Chicken. 'Never saw the like.'

And then Sue sighted a little metal box, and there was money in it.

'Not much,' she said. 'About twelve dollars.'

'It's a lot for these days,' I said. 'Worth killing for.'

And Chicken and Sue looked at me.

'What do you mean?' said Sue. 'We didn't kill her.'

'Yeh, but we're here and she's not breathing,' I said.

'We only got here an hour or two ago,' said Chicken, very neatly.

'Sure, I know,' I said. 'But I wish we hadn't driven in.'

'She was a weird old dame,' said Sue. 'Let's not stick around. I don't like dead radios.'

And we crawled back into the car and trundled off. But we couldn't get it out of our heads all the way up the road to the next town.

'I mean that's one hell of a fucking strange story,' Chicken kept saying, with variations.

'We dreamed it,' Sue said, 'we dreamed it.'

'Wouldn't mind if we'd murdered the old piece. But just dropping off like that, without a by-your-leave. I don't know,' said Chicken. 'What the hell did we eat this morning?'

'Not a hell of an awful lot,' said Sue, with meaning.

'Ah, it doesn't matter,' said Chicken.

'Not much of a way to finish,' said Sue, and she let a syllable of breath out of her mouth.

We flooded on through the little town and into the minutes beyond it, and when we left the town behind, we left the woman. Maybe Chicken and Sue forgot about it immediately, and in a way I did too. We never heard another word about that death, till later. Probably the old woman boiled and bubbled and dried, and stopped stinking, and became a sort of leather cover to the homely armchair.

A wooden wordless man kept the door of the bar, with its elegant sign, leaning *Topless* into the mauve evening. His skull was shaved, except for a rabbity run of hair in the middle, and his eyes had a raw bladed look too. But he wasn't connected with the warmth of the place – not quite the heat of the ordinary night outside, but something by the way and solitary added to it.

The moving nakedness of a dancer was the first thing to avoid staring at, at least to start with. Entering with Ali gave me the sensation of being a regular friend to the bar, not a gawking patron. But Ali paused open-handedly and watched the dancer for a few moments.

We perched up at the counter and as always Ali was saluted as a fixture, and I got the little side honey of that. A popular dance record was being given a new surrounding and meaning, and a careful exact lighting steadily made sure to reveal all angles of the performer, without shadows.

The drinks were on the house, as the bar woman presumed I had no money, since I was with Ali. This made no difference to her.

A tallish server stopped beside us, and complimented Ali on his dreadlocks. Ali replied smoothly and pleasantly to her, drawing her into his geometric benign friendship. I tried to concentrate on admiring her face, but the lack of clothes made my old eyes topple to her body. And the way she was decked out had me thinking not of making love to her, but of fucking her. The verb fitted the clothes, or what there was of clothes.

And yet her palliness was distant, Moll, and quietly fenced, and looking was the order of the night. We were there to gaze, and even if in other conditions we had been allowed to touch and possess, here everyone was reduced to an insular voyeurism. Actually it gave me quite a sensation of freedom. I knew I didn't have to attract any of the women in here, or plot to make them not see my strangeness. Because they tried, as much as possible, to treat all the customers in the same prejudiced manner. For the sake of sanity, the basic reason of the establishment was considered within the boundaries, but further lowering of things was invisibly prevented. Any notion of a hand reaching out to finger was quickly made shameful and rather awful, as if touching might cause a severe disappearance or suchlike in the toucher, or as if touching might suddenly call the procedures of crotching and bottoming on the sanded floor into question.

Ali and I preserved our professional position at the bar, which was a little outside the main area of heat. The pattern of dancing was straightforward. A girl appeared from the dressing-room when her predecessor had done, and began to thump her body to whatever rhythm the music could imagine. She danced in her cramped square and the young men occupied the seats at the table-height railings, drinking beer and almost filming the dancer with pleasant blotting-paper smiles. Most of them had a little sheaf of dollar bills beside their drinks, and when they wanted to draw the dancer, they waved one of these greenly. The woman moved through the clear shadowless glare, that bared her even to the pimples on her bottom. She paused with her crotch thrust out, so the happy man could slip the folded bill under the drawn line of her G-string. Then the dancer turned her back on him, and dropped straight over, so her arse was stuck neatly in his flooded face. Off then to dance, till the next carrot was raised. I was fairly certain that these tips were the wages of the dancers.

It was a bit curious for me to watch these transactions, all done with smiles on the part of the women, and bigger smiles on the part of the young men. And they were very young men, not bad looking, and probably sailors in port for a few days. There were none of the grubbier types that you see in such places in the big cities. In fact there was a sinister sense of innocence about it, a quaint obscene ceremony that wasn't obscene because it didn't belong to humanity – and yet there it was. Its accepted boundaries made it real, but only inside the alien bar.

Mostly it was hugely exciting and attractive and I was completely shuffled into it after a while, and waited impatiently at the bar for my 'favourite' dancer to come round and round in her turn. For there were only three women in all, and the one I liked was the server who had spoken to Ali. Her figure was ordinary and her breasts took a brief stretched dip just before the nipples, but she seemed overloaded with energy; and her particular lure was a mad scatty smile that she reserved for her tippers. It really was the most hair-raising and cock-raising flourish.

That was the business of the place – a sort of ordered protracted arousal of the men, which became after an hour or two a clear alternative to actual fucking, and gained a satisfaction and addiction of its own. It didn't lose its potency because there was never any form of climax. Given the stamina and the right measure of beer and food, I might have sat there at the welcoming bar for weeks. The lack of furtiveness was reviving, and because I hadn't spent much time in such joints before, I was surprised by the everyday way the show progressed, and the ordinary and even special camaraderie of the people enclosed for the night among the green performances. It was a love affair of a kind, and when I was eventually locked at the pit with my single dollars, and had tried the action of tipping the dancer, my head was quite lost to its whole logic. It wasn't money in my hands but a sort of language, a formula to beckon over the symbol of simple desire. And under the crippled music, and after a fair number of bills had been bestowed into the strings, the premium among rewards was a plain pat on the head and a muss of the hair from my beloved. No gesture could have a more supreme value. Because as touching was barred, the act of touching on her part became a profound expression of her acceptance and her admiration. I began to feel both privileged and rather handsome inside that cocoon, and confused myself and my life with the abrading lonely troubles of the briefly-contented young sailors.

So my unprecious vehicle became the vehicle of Miss Jane Smith's nourishment. If he didn't succeed in stealing something decent she went hungry. Her obese old age was a festering necessity back in the cottage that was gradually abandoning itself, even before its inhabitants could get around to it. The outside walls grew a variety of unnamed mosses and plants, and the thatched roof turned colourful and luxuriant with seeded grass. It turned into a bearded cube that Moran left and returned to, in a plain pattern of hunger and satisfaction of hunger.

This went on quietly and undetected until the afternoon a baby was found in the quarry with a needle in its stomach. It was not claimed by any woman of the town, and the mayor decided in conclave with his men that either the child was a casualty from outside the parish, or an unnatural being altogether.

Immediately the older men who had often made use of Jane Smith thought of her, and the possibility that she might be involved with the death, or whatever it was. Why she in particular sprang to their minds must be left to others to explain, considering they had individually and frequently expressed their beery love for her, hedgehog face or no hedgehog face.

Some of these men were quite senile, and blamed their condition on their excursions to the edge of town. They were old now, and they were sure Jane Smith had hurried the dilemma on, not paying much heed to the fact that seventy is often quite a debilitated age, whores or no whores.

It doesn't matter that the true mother of the baby went unfound or unsought for. After a few hours of consultation everyone was sure Jane was responsible, and indeed couldn't understand why it hadn't seemed obvious from the start. The younger members of the town-council didn't know much about her, but they tried to guess a possible character for her from the new whore their generation had discovered.

Moran was out after a chicken in a fairly distant farm, when a group of black-coated gentlemen arrived outside the incredibly overgrown dwelling. Few of the former customers could recognize the place as the object of their merry pilgrimages, but one old butcher was certain of it.

The mutilated child had been buried clumsily in the pauper's grave outside the church walls, and there didn't seem any reason why the vicious unnatural mother shouldn't join it as soon as was convenient. However, this was only a preliminary visit, and they fully intended to bring the 'auld witch' to trial in the usual way.

If the elders were surprised by the antiquity of the cottage, which was a fine image of the antiquity of their thorny loins if they had only thought about it, they were overcome by the ancient appearance of the mound of flesh inside. She was decked out in coverings of sacks and flour-bags, because it had been a long time since she had been privileged to move. Her stench was that of a beast that has been shitting into itself for some time. The hair of the creature was very long and white, where it existed at all, and her eyes were almost shut in the acred blub-bered cheeks. This was the life that had been the care of Moran for the preceding years, and probably he didn't notice her extraordinary metamorphosis, nor she either. That sort of change is so gradual it is almost no change at all, and there were no mirrors in the gloom to describe her anyway, because her own version of a looking-glass had tarnished long ago.

Her bizarre shape and advanced age made it seem all the more likely that the murdered child had been hers. She was the very picture of pregnant evil, or evil recently pregnant, at least to the townsmen peering in at her from the door.

The butcher whispered to his fellows:

'Why, min, de ouwl baste is did. Sher her eyes aren even open.'

No one said a blessed word.

'Dat's de stink uf dethe,' said the butcher, 'an I shud know. Eh?'

He herded the men away from the cottage, and under the late-evening bluster of the sky he struck expertly at a matchbox, as if about to light his pipe in the wind. The old men stared at each other with some kindred of doubt, and linened closer together like a muddle of puppies on the road.

'Where's the Blessed Apostle?' said one of them. 'Is he in the house, do ye think?'

'Arrah no, he'll be away at his mischief somewhere.'

'Do you think he might have been the father of that poor wee baby?'

'No, no, the child was devil's fodder, I'd say.'

'This is the Christian Era,' said the bank manager, who liked to say phrases like that. 'The Christian Era. And it's very doubtful whether a devil might make a child on a human woman these days.'

'Ah yes, Mr Flynn, on a human woman there might be some difficulty. But how about a creature that is half devil in herself, to say the least?'

By this time the butcher, a Mr Clancy of Main Street, had managed to interest a pile of straw and papers in his flame, and he nudged this little conflagration till it blossomed, and then he added to it with boards and dry brief bushes. The smoke began to travel in among the men, and they smelled an unusual herbal aroma that confirmed them in their progress – no natural house could possibly smell like that. But it was only the wild thyme beginning to smoulder, which was among the bunches of kindling the butcher had chosen.

Somewhere away over the fields Moran lifted his head like a dog and smelled the air. He didn't know why, but he started back home without the chicken, which he hadn't been able to entice as yet to the edge of its netting. Feeling very much like a fox in the red night, he ran with his crooked speed towards the papery light that was growing in the neighbourhood of his home. By the time he arrived, he saw it had become parcel of the old walls and the extravagant roof, and had a voice of its own too, a large round-bellied screaming from inside the flames.

One of the dark men chuckled, and said to his companions:

'Well if it isn't the Blessed Apostle, looking for his Magdalen,' and everyone broke out into a slight laughter. Moran smiled at them agreeably, and then looked at the fire again. He flicked his head at it and started for the door. Two of the townsmen promptly sat on him and suddenly Moran understood what was afoot. The scream was not the fire's scream.

'No,' he said out-loud, 'it is not.'

Then he bellowed too, and all the time Jane Smith was ceasing he accompanied her with his smoky lungs.

Sixfoil Seven

Wat a baer feelty owel place hes aetin room wass nowe, Moll.
Leet me tal ye. It iss de etin rum of Conn, I meen – my sweete
Ollever. Manny owel stoens were most hardily embasted in de
walle. Bat dey weres fidgety wid speeders an roaches. Snakkes
der war none in dem perts, natoorly, bat rattes and battes and
cattes and seely litul meece played al ovver de rames uf de cas-
teloo. Whan dey sattes doon ta dinoor dey were carfal ta kep der
feetes saffe from de knaws an appetoot uf de unkinde rattes, for
dey hadde beeg lang oily yallaw teet.

At de mane tabul satte Ollever and his ledy an de bishoop an
de pleasante poete man. Hes lange durty beerd was most visoo-
ble to da mar minoor eters. It semt ta flood his chinne and
cheste, and sprad ta fille de roof. De rattes nivver toucht sich a
riche-in-pooer man.

De quenes peculoor snakkey face mad upp far de lacke of sich
craturs, far it wasse de anly liutl disfavoor in her aspeckt, dis
wide sneaky levl to da eyen.

Dat neet der wasse a fierce quieet on de gaddered companee,
becorse nowan wud speke ferste, except de lowere paple talkt
ruddily enoug. Anly de soond uf de bishoopes balching lik a
tyde allooed of a smal respeet fram notin. An wan he cud he
winkt at de quaene or narly. Bat Olleve hidde his hed in hes
thoght an fud, and wasse unknoon in hes idees.

Meester Owl did natte suppe nor stomich de victool as wasse
hes waye. Only sich a vuery tinee peece of mate he did slepp
inta his mutte fram teem ta teem. Dis wasse a fashoon dat de
jung min foolawed, bat dey war nat as thinne as he becorse dey
et in secrit after ivery meel. It wasse known as *de yang manne hes
manoor* in honoor of Owl.

Wan Owl lokkt at hes present frends he didde so wid no glinte
or rainboo uf recognitoon. He was vury royalle in hes eatin. He
maght singe and prance aboot wid the beste at close of

114

swallooin, bat whil hes larde wus satisfyeen hes hungoor Owel wasse distoont. So an aire of solemnitee an dignitee an rowaltee reinned in de halle, an whan de cloons an de singoors of dat hoor war performen, der was no happee lafter nor clappeen, whach wasse harde fer de workes dey presentee, bat so it wante in dose teems.

Bat sodden outa de sileence de quene saidde to da bishoop quitte lood:

'My bishap, will ya tal mee aboot dis habeets dey haffe in Rome for de ettin ower?'

An de bishoop glancced softlle at Oliverr an at Mester Owel hes better-be-farre, and begant.

'Bug forkees dey usse for de luftin of alle,' he sedde. 'Likke de forkkes for de hay ites harveest, and al isse cuttet oop wid kneeves of silvoor, and de grat pappe hasse in especool hes owen properre wans.'

De quene oppened her bodeece a lituel, an frede her stringges jes sleightlee, an gavv a pebblee belche. Bat she sed:

'Wat good is itt ta spere de fud wid forkkes, my gutte freend? Soorly dis waye of oors is baste?'

An she dragt uppe a lang peece of coowe and lad it unner the noos of mester Owel de poete. She wipped de jointe slawlee and greezily on de berde uf de owel mastere.

'Unlesse,' she sed, 'ye havve a beeg owel feelty berde likke dis fowel manne.'

An she lafft wid a gratin cheesy roor at de sileent nobel.

'Ya knoo,' she addt, 'ye havv a neem for de laeddies, mester Owl. Bat I wander iff de origeen of all dat is nat oonly yer seely storees?'

An at dat de eyen of Owel glitert, becarse he hatted dat sort of tawk. Certanlee he hat gan too farre in hes dealins wid yang womin, an de wureld wasse ovver-riche wid his childer. Batte to havv hes streng pat in doot be a madde reptiloo quene wasse harte on hes hert an preed.

'Woamin,' sed Conn wid a fervoor dat all cud here, 'soorly ye canne be quiet, evven iff I do nat cuut thee throte.'

An de quene roared oot wid happinesse, it semt, to here her larde speke.

'Oo noo,' she sadde, 'ya cud nat cutte ma throt becaorse ye wud nat havv de beenafitte uv ma arsse den.'

De howel rume begant to larffe an argoo acordin to dere taste, til Conn bete upan de woode an husht dem all. Bat der facces were de facces of dem who will nat obee for lange, for dey warre a foolishe grup too free in der wishoos.

De quene smilt in her strang fase, an mumbelt sumtin to da bushoop, and de bishoop grint an sturtoored wid glle. Olleve roze fram his char a litul, an tooke de beefe fram hes wifes hant, and as de bishoop gurgled wid joye he slapt de hooly manne wid de meate on de moit.

'Whisht, me owel bishoo,' sed Conn, 'or I wall nat love yer morre.'

De bishap blusht to be soo trated, bat alsoo he wasse nat prood ta be ill-considoored be Conn, for in a thinne ways he wantted the afectoon of de grat lorde.

De quene did nat understande dis, and she grabet de mete, and startet ta et it feercely wid her tethe an tong.

'My,' she sed throo all her wrenchin, 'but, groo groo, ye are a high uncivvil manne, my lard, ta streek a manne uf Rame, de grat quene uf de christoon worel.'

'Nivver minde,' groant de bishoop. 'I amme not herte.'

'Ye disapoont me den,' sed Conn wid mich lacke of affectoon. Perhaps, Moll, he wasse a bit childeesh here. And all the peple taut he wasse childishe. Bat stul he was speciool in de eyes of Owl, an de bony makar lafte de halle in gloome.

Soone de dreenk an fud madde al vury merri an loose, an de argoomant wasse forgatten. Evven Conne shooted wid de resste, becasse he cud not cer aney moor.

De feerce comand uf hes place an leef were weekent dat dee. Somtin uf Olleev vanisht, an want upp de chimnoo wid de wispes an flavoors of de mete. He putte mich ween an beer inta his bladder dat neet, an wasse loonly and dafte on hes bedde widout hes ledy. She did nat cum ta hem at all. De roome swepte roun an roun in birdish cercles, an he wasse seeke to hes boones. He falte dat all hes life wasse a grat black berd, an it wasse fleein away ovver som hil he hadt no neem forre.

'Smal grene goddes,' he sed, 'why moost moi felds be made so bar?'

Noo answoor arreved, an he dropt lik a tre inta a grimee dreme, wahr anly his mooter wasse sangin to hem, wid a daggere in her breste.

116

One imaginably large bare plain, myself with all the clothes I have ever owned and worn, strapped and wrapped to and around my frame. The wretched optimistic booms of Bach's cello concerto, number whatever, probably one, loudly and thinly, like a seaside flock of exigent seabirds over a mechanical-looking pram. The gouty breaths of the aged cellist like fat on the music. An aspect of hopeless fright on my small round face, the inexact oblong of a passport description – I mean of course oval. The clothes neither heating nor chilling, because the element of weather is absent – and consequently most of verbal life – as is smell and touch. Only a pictorial visual and aural environs.

At the far edge of the plain is a remote familiar figure, tiny but clear. It is the old daddy.

There is a very difficult schoolroom geometry to this place, which overcomes a certain desire it has in itself for being known – so a lonely science at best.

As we start to trundle towards each other the music pulls about, like it was constructed out of melted plastic. Its distortions put in my mouth an idea of being filled with rubber, a sensation that has haunted me all my life, but only from time to time. If I clamp my teeth on the idea they pierce it exactly, and form a cast, as at a dentist's. The idea streels from my mouth like connected spit, and I am reminded distantly of being in a hotel in Barcelona as a boy, and encouraging my mouth to form moisture, which I can use to drop blots on to the parched pavement below. If there are heads passing when the spit is available, all the better.

Memory is stopped there, because as usual it would prefer to keep pushing further and further, into the catalogues and slides and tapes, not necessarily deeper into the past, but deeper into detail and similarity, the enemy being not chronology but comparison.

There is a decided lack of human reference on the plain, I notice. I mean, it is neither habitation nor geography. Only a pair of tracks appears above the surface of the water, which I have just observed. So it is some flooded plain, without name,

117

and without proper European meaning. Because the greatest shock is that in the Far East our home is the Far West, and the Far East is home for there, the heart of the compass. This is unfair. However, better keep an eye on the approaching da, because my wheels are bringing me quaintly, and on no schedule that I have agreed to, in his improper direction. I see that out of his head flow ticker-tapes, with women's names written on them, or printed – and so he resembles those eighteenth-century cartoons by some slaving hack painter, whose name was lost even as he signed it, and took the king's shilling.

Here then is the dialogue of his poor-hearted head. He wishes to be remembered merely for the Herricklike roll-call of his necessary mistresses and monstresses.

'And why not?' says my pictureless frame, as the gap between our bundles echoes less and less. But alas he is not lagged with clothes, but his nakedness is a kind of accepted experiment, amid so much useless unexplained water. It is slightly cumbersome that, as I approach him, I diminish in reverse perspective, while he unfolds and enlarges at a greater rate than is normal, in normal procedures. The printed names fly back from him, and his head is tilted so the back of it touches the muscles of his neck. He appears to be holding the pose of a picture by one of those highly unromantic romantics, but no one has driven any heroic spear in his beery stomach, that can be noticed. Not that my unsweating eye can bear to linger on his over-symbolic form.

He has increased hugely by the time he is only a few streets distant – a veritable statue of liberty, or the lack if it, to the unpromised land. Some flooded plain may host this encounter, but it does not provide any reception or party after. This gripped swollen shape is alive, but not a thing given to movement. It may have danced once but it will not dance for me on the plain. How bloody sad. And I know what bloody is the abbreviation for, *by the blood of our lady*. A most inconvenient etymology to enter the head, for it produces a flood of the same stuff, which increases the height of the water by an inch or two, but at first only away on the undefined deeps or shallows. And the redness moves towards us like the calm additions of an estuary or a mud-flat, a very wide thin straight strict line from one side of the canvas to the other, which when it tips the rails obscures them. And soon we will not know where to place our feet, my pa and me. Unmovable pa with his head thrown back for ever.

I am so small I can not straddle the rails any more, and have lost my wheels, and must trust to the undecided sleepers underwater. When the slight wave has passed, the red wet plain is uncontrasted by rails. So we stand, the two opposing engines, on the limitless red mirror, myself much too little, and himself, the lord of nothing, much too large. My movements are negligible, because of my burden of good clothes, clothes for the winter and flags for the summer, and bootees and socks and boots and school shoes, splattered with cereal and pear-juice and ketchup. And we are held there not by our choice, certainly.

And as usual we have nothing to say to each other, whether or not my father can in fact talk in his present condition. Someone appears to have enlisted him in the great catalogue of unloved statues – some embarrassed statesman discredited by revolution. But clearly he is resisting this immortality. He is a great one for being alive yet not for being great, obviously, as would be any man, eh? Held, held, held, till I am far beyond the point of not being able to put up with such closeness. For my ears may be covered by a flapped hat and other headgear, but not my impressionable face. Perhaps I have a red ten-shilling note stuck on my chin, like an Egyptian drawing of a beard. But still and all, the tip of my nose tips the tip of his calves, or whatever that part of the leg is. And there we are for the moment, though all things pass. Of course the Bachian celloing has changed long ago to the grindings and swallowings of a family dinner, which is only a music of a sort, you'll understand – not among the bearable items. Yet even at this shunted extremity we are distant from each other, and I find the officious information, telegraphed in my head, that he is asleep, the poor man, and does not realize we are here together.

Xenia removed her spirals and patterns from Paris. Five unusually noncontracting weeks were agreed on, as an unknown country of endurance. Alas for my silly head on the gangplank of my always-alien brown corridor, where on one side the Arab

119

sang quietly and on the other the inhabitants were religiously wordless and never seen. And in the unholy toilet with its rich mop of trees in a far-off nonexistent park, a difficult view from the small window, whose mad metal sounds I still hear among the clutter of this American road.

In the little paperless jacks my fingers grew too fond of mauling my worried balls, softly plucking at these doubtful items of vegetable. Rotting or not rotting? Swelling or not swelling? Natural or unnatural, these minute lumps below them?

Xenia's loving rapes had bruised me further and worried me into a razored condition. There was no sleep for that particular young man in his blue room. The clock as always stuck its numbers unconcernedly on the brightened dark, and the emptiness of the room without its newer stranger, was imaged by that curious drumming music that silence scores.

In a moment of savage complacency I stood in the centre of my possessions, while Paris spinned and hurried like air to my ship. I had seen a doctor's plaque while walking the day before, just next door and so convenient. Wouldn't it be a weight off my mind if I toddled up to see him, and know for certain I was imagining things? For after all I was not unused to my neurotic hypochondria in the least. And so I descended from my nest to the washed normal street, where the distant people moved like views of parks.

The double-doors of my chosen expert were so daily and expected that I stuttered away back down his stairs to the living street, and was half-way up my own ladder again when I spun about, and without calm retrieved the dustiness of his door.

One foreign face above a shroud of fading linen allowed me enter in my own forbidden foreignness. She threw me against the silence of a bare waiting-room, where true to its title I had to wait a half hour. During this generous period I considered alternatively fleeing or complaining, but I was too unsure of my French and my position for either action.

When the doctor looked in the door at me I had become so used to being still and unwanted in his rooms, that I could not react to his stare. He had to come back once more, and once more beckon me with his curiosity.

It crossed my mind that it was odd there being no other patients, and no prompt service, and nothing really but a colourless slightly-fake quiet in the apartment. It must have cost him much money in rent, unless he owned it, and it was a piece of annoyance that he should circle in so spacious and useless an area, when I was confined to mere inches.

I followed his skinny back into another equally fateless chamber. Only his desk tried to define itself below one window, and an old rather rusty-looking examination couch had parked itself by a pictureless wall. The doctor was quite young but curiously shrunken, like one of those Indian heads in the National museum in Dublin. His nose was in an advanced stage of pinocchioism, and his eyes were tiny Etruscan coins of self-containment. But the emperors' heads were worn away, and only a rough brown surface examined me where I sat. The rue de Rivoli outside made several attempts at sounding quotidian, as I did myself while I described my fears.

This was not as straightforward as it might have been, since he had rather poor English.

'J'ai des, well, lumps, vous comprenez, underneath les testicles. Ils sont très petits – mais, je voudrais savoir quoi ils sont. Eh, excusez moi, mais ma française est très mauvaise.'

'O-kay,' he said, with the idiomatic correctness of a Tuileries Gardens duck speaking goose, without being aware of its inabilities. 'Mebee we shall look at you?'

He herded me over with a disturbing too-friendly smile to his ancient couch. I wanted to ask him about the deserted nature of his practice, and who he was, and why did he seem so sunken in manner.

It was sunlit outside, but that sort of light couldn't penetrate the simple whiteness of his surgery – a ruined technical pallor. While he poked briefly and birdily at my parts I noted the extreme regularity of his desk-top. It was crammed with marshalled oddments: a desk calendar, a black notebook, a telephone from the Forties, a few tombed books, scores of pencils in an ivory holder, but all of these things elderly, and not so much worn-out as neglected. The bare just-moved-in-look of the place was clearly the result of many years tenancy.

'Yes, yes,' he said. 'It is – swollen, here.'

'No,' I said, 'c'est pas ça. Il était comme ça pour beacoup anneés. I mean ans. Mon docteur en Irlande a dit que c'était bien.'

'Arr yoo shoor?' he said, certain I was mistaken.

'Yes oui,' I said. 'C'est pas ça que concerne me but those très petites choses ici. Regarde – are they normal? C'est normal, ou non?'

'Non,' he said. 'Not normal. Come.'

In clattering silence he got behind his desk again, and wrote for some time on crackles of old notepaper.

'You see a specialiste,' he said. 'Okay?'

'Okay,' I said. 'Is it alright? Not too serious?'

'No, not too serious,' he said, 'but I do not know what, truly.'

His wooden nose had come alive somehow. He was animated now by his certainties and the delights of his idle profession. It was almost as bad as I had been fearing, and certainly my mind only wanted to believe him and understand what the trouble was.

'There,' he said, leaning his bodyless body over the table.

'Do I owe you money?'

'Yes,' he said, 'fifty francs now. You go to the hospital of the good god, le bon dieu, and my colleague will see you. You must telephone first.'

'Could you not telephone pour moi?' I said. 'Il serait très difficile.'

'Ah, monsieur,' he said. 'I can not. Forgive me. But you have my letter. It will be okay. And now.'

The distance between his desk and the entrance door had augmented, and the surrounding walls were even more undefined and blurred than before. I moved towards my escape and he trailed out after me, like a dead man walking in a winter wood in a dream. He became excited in his small barely-noticeable manner again, and seemed to be trying to make some joke or gentle remark, so I asked him to repeat himself.

'Répétez, s'il vous plaît.'

'You must not be worry,' he said.

'Oh no,' I said, 'of course not.'

'Don't, you know. Because even if we must remove, there will still be one left. And this is enough for les enfants and so on.' He smiled historically. The effect of such a remark has to be experienced intimately for full appreciation.

But you forget, you forget. The big bulled car pulls on through the podunk towns, and you forget. Direction doesn't have much to do with it, only the possible distance you can arrange between your heated body and the dead ladies behind you. And even the accidental deaths are our fault, and the accidental lives. The car passes the night trees, investigating the dirt and the tar of a new state. And Sue lies cuddled in your bad arms, and Chicken is absorbed and steady in the front, where the radio gives out a babble of half-talk and half-music – a Viking to my peace, but the ladder I'd pull up is a snake when I touch it.

Chicken's head is silent and hard, like a new planet, and the gas he is made of drives us away from what we didn't do, but didn't want to be caught not doing. My perfect silly Sue as idle as myself, walking through some dream she won't remember well enough to tell me, but which she will tell me anyway. And that was my life, of that hour, and those hours, my simple roaded allotment, with the usual discontent as a jam to that best bread, wondering what would happen next up the way, and hoping it might hold some profit for me, and the whole idea of trains and travel and dark towns almost mathematical on my lap, in the shape of Sue. Desiring her, but at the same time agreeable towards her sleep, and able to hold her with a gasfire sunken affection, as if that whole period of looking forward, which you get with a blaze in the grate and a bottle of wine and the soft girl soon to come, had been extended and catalogued and epicked into a long moment of hours in a stretching black car. As if we had agreed to forego the trouble and the sweat for a damped-down passion suitable for the back seat of an automobile.

Chicken may whistle *Oh my man, I love him so*, but he doesn't mean it that way, and the radio is his accomplice and enemy anyway. He likes to leave the dial between wherever and where-ver, though even if he homes in on a single station, the pro-gramme soon drifts as we extend further beyond the reach of its small-town signal. Chicken is in love with the jangle and stress of voices talking on top of music, and underneath that blanket the bleeps and codes of government dispatches, possibly, or else it is sea creatures calling one to the other through the unimagined land mass of America: the Pacific seal to the Atlantic. My best Sue losing this part of her life to what Shakespeare guessed the nature of, but all the same granting my drifting-through-it a neater chapter and line. Her hotter brother breast coming sideways at my chest, and her brave arms raised up to moor themselves around my neck, and cling there even in sleep, and her shoeless feet on the leather seat under her tucked legs, reminding me constantly of the gesture she makes when she kicks her red shoes off – how the shoes might hang and hang under her catapulting, but not annoy her, and then they drop, and she tucks, and reaches for me, and heats and dreams – among bushes and roadside trees and a riding moon that are part of her finally only through me. I transfer what I see in little boxes and books to her gentle silky head, and tie them there with invisible threads like small presents on a Christmas tree, so she might have them when she wakes.

If this land is dreaming then the dark blue it owns is the dream. And Chicken may have his head at an angle, but some-where his eyes are fixed and blue on the blue road, and he looks like he's travelling to some place he's leaving behind at the same instance – he doesn't appear to be headed anywhere except a forgotten nowhere that he used to call home. Chicken doesn't know where he's going at all in the black car in the simple dark-blue night, but he's taking us with him, and that allows his head its angle and authority. But he doesn't mind really, not the night, not the absence of destination, because he knows he has a whole continent of destination if he requires it, and the road is as good a place to arrive at as anywhere more structured and named. The road is his destination, so he holds his head at a bony angle and aims for it – which grants him the privilege of steering Sue's being-far-off. And the glass and the metal and the leather of the car doesn't so much frame us as fold us out into the nonexistent outside, where the world probably stops at the shadowed trees and the suggested grass, and if there are cornfields, or tobacco fields there, then they are not there truly, not for Sue's dream, and not for my waking. They spread only for some farmer's feet and his tiny sons', not for Sue's breast that is trying to explain the meaning of my shirt to me, and in that way dispose of it.

And then in the private beat of the engine I want Sue's

important skin to be medicine to mine. But we are not in a century of secret but of public difficulties – even in the car Chicken is our audience, as all non-lovers are to lovers. And if I am gentle now to Sue, Chicken is also gentle by proxy. And his noiseless clapping reaches me as a form of transmitted approval.

Chicken is calm and doesn't disturb me now. He has lost his long eye and his uneasy double axe, and if I can't trust him, even so still I can let him bring us as distant as he chooses into the coloured minutes, not ideal but idle. I hear in the confident engine a confident complex music that only seems a full growl to begin with, but soon starts to contain the information it has always contained, the diminuendo of childhood, and the maps and muddled tracks of what is coming up quickly in the barrier of darkness and hardship. And the hard farmers are explained by the music too, and their dogs are walking and sniffing around in it, and we carry them as efficiently as bees carry pollen, to drop the barking and the snuffling on a new farm rapidly up the way and rapidly down the way. This dog's bark gets distributed casually among barns and strangers, and after a few mornings the farmers believe they have never been without it, behind the clicking of the old clock their grandpa purchased but which their sons more truly carried in at Christmas time, and the faithful moaning and considering of the sad hens in the great barns.

And, Moll, out of that dance of breasts and bottoms came a careful conversation. I wasn't nervous of my rattling girl, because I had the little bit of beer drunk. Maybe the shadows in the room had a lot to say about the lit faces at the pit, but the induced bonhomie made much of the small true happiness that was there. And the other women were like portraits hung against the gloomy edges, with their nipples like nails, and their neat stomachs quite painted in their rich night way against the brown canvas. And I had to let it be so and accommodate it, and had not great trouble in the doing.

There was a little jiggly girl I watched closely also, whose breasts were tight and young. She shook out her bottom like a mongrel skiting off seawater, but only the slow colour of her light-brown skin travelled off her in imagined drops, and when she was down to her G-string her body grew even more alive, and she created a sort of perpetual miniature dance for her skin: her breasts bobbed and her bottom quivered, and she ate the music with nice long gulps of her reddened mouth. That was her style and, although I preferred Ali's friend, there was much in her notion of performance to consider and remember. With my broken head, my lover is my hand, and my atmosphere is my memory, or for the most part anyway. A prostitute is the only accomplice to my huge love, and even so I am for ever afraid of going to one. It embarrasses and thrills me at once, and that is a very powerful condition to be dragging like suitcases through the red streets. I am afraid of their real opinions under the monetary smiles, and want too much for them to love me, to pledge themselves against my pledge. Perhaps I fear to fall in love, and be miserable and destroyed by them. To see for a moment the possible woman behind the theatrical necessities and need her.

So it was more probable in those times to satisfy that particular all-colouring logic under the sheets of whatever hired bed I found myself in. And there was only then the fright that the landlady or cleaning-lady might comment on my maps of semen, under some unhappy light of tomorrow. And so I always tried to spurt on to my belly, like Horace, where my life might dry and be a thin sail to my entrails, and we might row into the proper harbour of sleep and rest, and not be found out in pleasure. To be found out in pleasure!

And in the Topless Bar with Ali we could not be found out, because we were a tribe of conspirators, with one exact and bathroom conspiracy in our favour. Let us slip out among the policemen and the travellers, by all means. But at the same time it should be known that in the room we were not inflamed but merely drinking, and all was normal and familial, and that we fell in love with our paid dancer was not so true after all. And that we were young was not true. And that we were important was not true.

The young sailors flew their desire as pennants over their brushed heads, and the dancers were mesmerized by the fluttering cloths that were not there. And the little dollar flags were stringed to their bodies, and danced with the dancers.

When it was over and then over again, Ali gathered me with his habitual indifference. I suspected him as a connoisseur only of the best individual performance, since he could probably go as far with any of the women as we could only dream about doing.

In the late night that was having none of its own lateness, the sailors were gone to their ships, or the ships of the high-street whores, and the bar had the air of a betting-shop or a cockpit when the men have trailed home to Sunday dinner. The bottles at the counter and the tinsel decoration, the cheap wooden tops and the plain borderless mirror, reappeared as if from somewhere, and the shaved doorman became calmer at the pin-ball machine and played succinctly. Ali's blackness stuck against the bar, like tar on a piece of whitened tree, along a beach, and he possessed a bright bottled moon in each eye, through which he watched nothing gently, as irregular as clockwork.

The swirl was over, and we waited for his friend to dress and return. She arrived in our midst as if for the first time, that day in that place, with clothes not too whorish and not too streetish. She must have bought her mad smile in a foreign shop, because really she seemed quite plain and brief and restricted. A Jamaican girl, a dancer who hadn't danced, whom Ali had no relations with, diplomatic or otherwise, came bitterly out of the dressing-room, cut by us, vanished. Ali's friend stalled. Knowing her body under her skirt and shirt didn't mean I knew it at all. Out of sight was out of knowledge. Her legs were now a real woman's legs, not to be stared at, and the idea of reaching under her skirt to slip a dollar bill in her knickers was terrifying. She wasn't pirouetting and pretending now. And there was a slight paste of bad temper over her glance at me. Possibly she was tired out by anything remotely resembling a customer, and she only wanted to speak to Ali. But since I was here she offered me a blue stare, and left it at that for the moment.

'Hiya, Mr Ali,' she said. 'Jesus, I'm whacked out, buddy, I'll tell ya. Hey, Maggie,' she said, almost waking up the older server behind the bar, 'would ya give us a beer?'

'Where you from?' I said, and heard the blotting-paper that had got into my gills.

'Where me from?' she said. 'Fort Lauderdale, yeh. How are ye? You the friend of Ali? Yeh? Okay. How ya doin?'

'I'm doing fine,' I said. 'That was, well, some dance you were doing tonight.'

'Oh yeh, some dance, sure. Listen, Ali,' she said, 'let me go to the bathroom, and then we'll have a talk about things. Okay?'

'Okay, Susan girl,' he said.

She carried her curious loaded cosmology to the other pittance of the room.

'You want her for the night, Moran?' he said very softly to me. 'Maybe I can fix it for you, mon.'

'Would it cost a lot?' I said.

'She likes you,' he said. 'I can see it.'

'Really? Me?'

'Yeh,' he said. 'It shows she likes you. Wait now till I discuss this with her, mon.'

'Don't we have some, you know, other business to discuss too?'

'Yeh, yeh,' he said. 'We'll do that. Don't worry.'

The barlady smiled at us sleepily, not sure of what we said, but agreeable anyway.

'Want another beer, boys?'

'Yeh, sure,' said Ali.

'Thanks a lot,' I said.

'Sure,' she said, thumping the glass bottoms on the damp wood. 'You bet.'

There was a small greedy planet beginning inside me. I could feel its gases bursting out from the centre, and the edges hardening, and under my telescope the floor moved, and the planet that was also myself was proving hard to focus.

The town decided it was neither fond nor otherwise of the creature they called the Blessed Apostle after his devotion to his female saviour. But still it wasn't the poor house that reclaimed him or a new poor house that claimed him. He was let drop in the water and find his leafy path to the bottom.

Naturally enough, Jane Smith's chief dispatchers, Messrs Flynn and Clancy, both of Main Street, kept their eyes principally on the boy.

At sixteen years of age he was a patch of mouldy colour that

128

passed up and through the town, shedding a bit of mould here or a scrap of straw there. The real children of the place feared him singly, and mocked him simply when in groups. They cast bits of tin and dusty stone at him, in the half-knowledge that the offerings might well pass right through so unimagined and unnecessary a body. These were not complex enemies to him, and the vehicle accepted their missiles as an instance of notice and even affection. Batty Moran might enter the church square and shout his name at the dull stone façade, but still they persisted, and screeched *Blessed Apostle, Blessed Apostle* after him. This he minded. He lay on the grubby flagstones, and he minded. They didn't know about the lice that were a soup over his skin, or the festers and patterns of skin fungi along his arms and flat belly, and his blind thighs. He was sixteen and he wanted his name.

He couldn't remember where his true name came from, but he desired it, the small tune it allowed the air to hear. And as he lay and waved his arms, like the dark seaweed he watched on the floor of the harbour, and as the pigeons quietened in their holes, and the swifts became mathematically sophisticated in the space between the shop-fronts and the church, he begged the grace of his name from the memory of Jane Smith. He knew that if he asked this favour in the correct manner it would be granted to him.

Whenever he passed a bollard on the perimeter of the little town park he had to touch it three times with the middle finger of his left hand, in order to be sure of building up sufficient luck for the great change back to take place.

As he swallowed the rather ancient lights that the butcher Mr Clancy cooked for his benefit, and stared at the grey and green wall of the alley, where the wooden bins of skulls and bones were, he prayed to the future definite ghost of Mr Clancy to leave his name in some cow's belly, where it might be found and returned to him.

He also was keen to get the seagulls out of his own hidden skull, where some had taken root, and seemed to need him as a nest. The gulls bothered his night-time, which the stars fled through in the clear summer, and the moon rolled through in the needled winter. He had nothing to do only juggle his lost name, so he wouldn't forget it, with the handful of never-seen birds. He might have eaten his way through the bird's bellies, if he could only have got his mitts on them. The bellies would hold the first permissions for his name.

At the harbour, where he could sleep best, the moon lived in a wooden building on an old island, a man-made one, at the centre of the channel. When he wasn't looking the white biscuit vanished out of it, and struck into the sky, to ride the clouds like a lost football on the late-afternoon tide, when children have wandered home without it. It was important to Moran that people understood this sly mannerism of the moon. But they didn't, if only because he couldn't tell them.

In those years he stopped speaking altogether, in lieu of having a name. He was fastidious in that way, and dreaded the insult of being called by a made-up label. He didn't know what a Blessed Apostle was, and he didn't care. Even if it was a saint in heaven he didn't care. He was sixteen and he wanted his name back.

And the parish priest, now that he thought of it, was the first man in the world to call him wrongly, and the parish priest accompanied his insult with green graveyard laughter, which Moran had heard the rooks at in the cypress trees above the beds.

Jane Smith's name lived in the graveyard, but she did not. They had eaten her body for Sunday lunch. Moran had watched them at it through the frosted windows, and every Sunday for ever without end they ate her, section by section, and carved his old mother up with big clumsy knives, and the seagulls wolfed the buttered scraps, the greasy leavings, at the back-doors, and then screamed back into Moran's head and digested. So what they shat in his skull was Jane Smith, which was the reason he wanted so much for them to quit him. He pressed against the bad windows after dark, and the fires in the poor grates excited him, till he had to walk about with his phallus like a ship's rope holding an old spent trawler. Tied to the world in that way, his eyes widened, and he stared forward for the release of the church building, or the caress of the blind rats that shared his night in the wharfhouse.

The hours flew from Main Street to wharfside, complaining always of their lack of welcome and the stupid weather.

All day Moran talked liplessly to himself, but he was unable to recall the conversation of two sentences back. He rushed forward in his mind to reach the parts he would eventually remember, and this forced speed gave his nights a collection of small boulders on a long unknown beach, as a headache. The boulders clustered around him, and when he didn't guard against it they shifted nearer to him, and tried to make him look at the sea. The sea attracted him, because there was an orange light at the far side, and after that a purple, which grew richly and affectionately on the other part of night, the sea part. Yet if he enjoyed the lights the boulders took full advantage and edged up stealthily. He hated that, and so brought himself back to the wharfhouse, where he really was anyway, and locked out the beach dream, and talked about something else.

When he shat, he was careful to kill the worms with his soles, and not touch them, because he guessed the white wiry creatures might know how to penetrate his fingers. He didn't want white worms for fingers, though he often expected he might end up that way if he didn't retrieve his name eventually. He was sixteen and he needed the name back badly.

Sixfoil Eight

Coon by accidoont ded invente de miroor, Moll, bat natt by de complicatoon uf de mathematuc. He warre no man fur dape larnin. No, he anly had in the brite marning to fallaugh mester Ool upon the brad rode, amang the quieet treen and bushes whar briddes of gutt coloor hadde der parliment: for trulee dis Ollver wasse miroor to ower Poette, despeet Owl havven one berd mare den Conn.

And dis you maye finde amang menne and feamales, Moll. Characterre iss a litul bagge uf points and movements, whic wull falle dis waye and dat to telle de proper storee uf a manne or gearl. In de pouches of derselmes Ollever and Owle braght similoor componentes, and de sunne admirred dese, an shan likke a soupe inta dere vitalles and madde dem whowel.

So whan dey walket, dey walket as one in too halven, which de berds acknowledget wid coloored creen. Oleeve pacced sileentlee by de shulder uf hes frend, and felte de moistoor uf de firste hoor uf de newe dee fully entered inta hes bonnes. Dey did nat car den for all der dificultoo. Na, dey warre agreeabel an softlee shodde amang de grasses. Owel his minde wasse lik a quieet buckit on hes necke, and in hes hed he sawe de poor saveg pictoor uf de initiale peeces uf hes paste. De busynesse uf poete in de lante wasse lik the flockes uf swallows to de hotte southe counttree whan home dey come. Batte no wan knew excepte de poettes wat it includet to larn de secrets, whic whar as bigge as a whalles gutte. De darke moldy roome hes fader hadde locket hem in surveeved in hes memor, evven now in hes famoos majoritae.

'Ah, it wasse a strangishe teem fer mee,' he sadde alood ta Ollever, and Ollever, wid a tinee curving if hes chin, shawed dat as welle as watchin de swannes theire carful steerin, he wasse attendin also ta de taulke.

'Yasse, moi frende, moi keng, we hadde naw windees for

ower plesur, an culd nat converse in lattin, nor in speech, to ower fellaugh pottes. All lae in der narra beedes, an de oldeste woomen uf de accadamee fedde us dey through dee. Curtainnes uf de dede sadde deere kepte us to ower intente, an throo our heddes we ledde the dogges of metters, and de footsteps uf beate an rithem. Catul wasse moi favoorit, evven de nonsense belles aboot de sparroo. Turdus wasse de namme in dat lingage fer blackeberd, an it becam moi tinee mornin joke: fer I hadde anly a narroo buckit for ta plac moi turdes as nately as I mighte, an dey did nat stunke liken to a blackbird, no, moi Oleever. "I havve two blackberds for yer pie, moi loif," I might saye to da ouel gerl, as she geeked aboot de plac. An shee did nat kno wat I ment, bat laffed wid her toothee spede. Dat wasse in de seely silenc uf de hooly christoon marning, as I sedde. Bat I noo dat it wasse de romanne goddes, an ower full-poowered frends uf de above skee, whach werre allies to moi laboors.

Propertu hes pome aboot hes unkindlee ladee hurte me hert in de yang dee, for I was missin in me perts de silber paine in moi darkenet eyen, dat wan liteul fingoor canne bring quicklee. Soos an Goono an Posighdoon flitteret aver moi halve slep. It was hardde ta drenke moi soop wid der lothsem chetters. Bat I amme nat compleenin uf dat. It helde de tinkels an perfectoon uf toons and creatoon, an turnet us alle fram drery boyes to greyishe menne.

In sumoor de antes foght fer lant on moi skinned bedde. De blacke sterted oot ta congoor de poor vicoos redde. In lines an fishin-nettes uf bodees, they marcht fram ole oaken ende to old oaken ende. Acrass de smoothe skinne uf a whitte deere dey passet, lik de smal perts of dirte atte de edg uf a calme tide. An de unseein watter surget de litel beests, til dey mette all togeder, an slashet at der idees of wronge coloor wid sords inbilt to dr arms. Walle, Ollever, perhappes ye knoo wat these creturs do fer sporte in de lange blak dey.'

'An arr we redde or blak, my hert? sayes Olivver.

'We arr bot,' splutters Owel, 'bote, my lerd.'

'So why den do wee ete our owen bowens and fles?'

'Becarse we arre nat wize.'

'Yoo ar wize, my frend. Yoo arr wize enoug fer dese lants.'

'O wal,' he sedde, de poetman, 'yoo arr kinde, bat I am nat wize enoug for to savv moi blut fram decaye.'

133

'Dese tings happent befar.'

'Dey will happen anly ta uzz on dat accoont.'

'It iss nat falt uf oure eyen or ower affectoons,' sed Con.

'A tre dat graws uppe ta inhabit de slippy cheek uf an hille is nat foolish den?'

'He iss foolishe whan he iss too bigge ta stande.'

'An yat how canne he stoppe to growe, an wasse nat his downfallin well-hidden in hes start, dat gren curled sede?'

Coon stapt, an lokt awaye uppe de hill at ther lefte side. He swang hes brode arms oot, and flapt dem to hes thiys.

'Owel, we must leeve moi place ta rotte and travul to anudder contree. It dances, dis wan, wid fowel partners, and waull nat lette us walke aloon. We havve no coloor nor no sunne this more, an widdoot dese two de croppes will nat be for very lang helty, an ower liveliness will wither lik to de ol man hes skinne.'

'Enjoi soo de wavy fields we see belo uss,' sedde mester Owel calmlee. 'Do nat frette those sileent browes you ware abuv yer worrysome eyen. Luk in de distanc: der walks a gerl. Jumpe herre inta dis dree ditche, and we wull playe a treek on de lass.'

'I do nat wante to do it,' sedde Olleve.

'Yass, yass, do it,' sedde Owel. 'Hied yer bones.'

So dey crunched inta de waterless place, an wated fer de figoor to approch. Throo de frendly wanderin brambels an grasses an delicat wedes dey hadde her clerly, but nat she they.

It semt lika purty jolee lass dat movd slaw an slimly to der coverin. After a minoot Ollevve gript de hairy sleeve uf Owel, an sadde nuttin. Bat Owle felt hem shivoor, an de wave in de lardes bodee recht hem too.

'Wat ist?' he glimmered.

'She duss nat tuch de grun,' groant Ollever.

'Ehh. What?' sedde Owl. 'By Lug ye ar true.'

Dey hugt ech odder becass dey knue wat de gerl muste bee, a verry dangeroos demonne oot of somewan his bibel.

'Who hasse been openin hes biblos in dis distreect?' fethered Owel.

'Now see wat trooble cams uf bishoops an mutterins.'

'She iss a verry fowel demon. Luk, her hed is on fire.'

An a citee of smoke riss songleslee inta de greye placcid mornin, out uff de pale ears uf de nameless gerl. She passt lik a fedder on her owne wint. An in de bodees of Conn an Owel, a feelthy tide uf miserere washet.

Befor her, in her bluty hant, she carried a rottin onione.

Studio, circa 1962, Highgate. Indian nationality or Britishized. A limp possibly. Certainly a wife. Studio mixed up with those who read the Sunday papers in certain Sunday attitudes. Very much so.

And a long tarry walk through bright clean grass. Where that is god knows. Might be a cinema or a porch or a tiled corner, and then sirens for good or bad measure. Bad measure this.

In the far-off undreamed dreamless studio the paint is still mountainous and moony, as in surface, on the surface of the painter's table. If painter he truly was. What he is doing now remains unrecorded – no news from the slums where untrue painters dwindle unto newspaper items, which duly dwindle into scraps in empty lots, as the song goes. 'Look, mummy, a leaf.' 'It is not a leaf, boy, why 'tis a newspaper item: Singh Shukla is dead.' 'Who?' 'Sing Shook-la, you dolt.' 'What did he do, mum?' 'Says here he painted shop-signs and a very good job he did. Loved in the district for his mannerisms and his Eastern politesse.' 'Oh.'

Père-moi-dans-le-temps-qui-est-foutu did not know I was among the curdles of the Indian's paint. Mr Shukla had a squint, or rather a bend in the river in his right eye, through which his world attempted to enter but could not. His wife was wearing a tent or a parachute possibly. His son was not there, he had no son.

That was elsewhere. The curiosity of the old dried colours on the table and the edge of the easel being that they were all of them grey, or dark and pastelly. What he painted there was anyone's guess except his own.

But that is the little tragedy of failed painters. Where his canvases are, that his wife at least I hope enthused over – well, it is not said among the vials.

Into this space my lack of space was inserted, as a rabbit into a burrow. Whether convenient or not, the ceiling rained dryly onto his begun-and-spreading enthusiasm. He spent a number of lives converting my truth from face to façade, during which

135

time I watched *The Beauty and the Beast*, and other features less memorable. The granite persisted mildly in the street below, reminding me of things that had not happened yet and could not happen. However it is a symbol of one's safety that most of the real outlines have blurred, and bestirred themselves in some other capacity than memory.

My unpaintable youth. But in the bedroom there was a cupboard, where many items mingled, and it is much on my mind. Imagine the audacity of the morning we left England, when some hand thrust in there and simply vanished everything. But I don't remember. A very quick exchange between pink and yellow and a great imperial shopping arcade. Possibly. My mother like a linesman to the colours, a herder of palettes and choices, a kiter over the positively proven buttercups: that did after all show yellow under your chin, the yellow of a neglected daffodil. Just as, if you put blotting-paper into your shoes, preferably someone else's shoes, you could make yourself faint. Really? Yes.

'Oleever,' says Mr Shukla in my benighted memory. 'Can you please still stiller than you are so far?'

However, you must go on tip-toe to help the effect along.

'Oleever! Stiller.'

But Mr Shukla, you are merely painting me out with grey and blubber.

'It is the least I can do, Oleever.'

Very nice, I'm sure. As in *noice*.

Take your tent, madam, and impress some other bedouin, but also:

'Please turn up the television.'

How red roses are in black and white. Such a sad rich beast, and such a white girl for his trouble.

Mr Shukla, you are not hurting my image?

'But of course not, my little friend, my little English friend.'

Watch it, brother, I'm Oirish.

'But you have a little English accent.'

Yes, but I'm not aware of it, see. I got it off the pies.

Mr Shukla stands so much behind his canvas, as if he is ashamed of it, or me, or himself, that most of the time appears to be spent alone in the room, with only the yellow conversation of the traffic, between the daffodil beds of the houses outside. Mr Shukla lives at the top of the white wooden stairs, you understand.

'Are you still with us, Oleever?'

'I am.' Sir, I am. God bless America. I mean the queen. I mean the Tuatha dé Danann. I mean King Bess.

'Are you well at school, Oleever?'

I am, sur, I am. The girls are not massive, as this word is unknown to me.

Sir,

'They are building a swimming-pool in the classroom.'

'Yes?'

'Yes, but I won't be there to see it, because we are going away.'

'Yes, I know you are going away,' says Mr Shukla, with his eye on his wife's posterity. 'Which is why I am.' A bird larks a moment. 'Painting your portrait. A goodbye for you to your father who I understand is not going for the moment.'

My father is very forward, sir, he never goes anywhere. That makes two of him, eh?

But you see, Shukla old man, this swimming-pool is much on my mind also. In fact, it has made an exraordinary impression on my tenderloin years. How tender are your years? Not to mention my ears. Eh? At school, eh? No. Well, I am possibly seven, probably six, and I feel like fifty. However my memory is engrossed in error. In fact, it is primitive. This studio is not an example of attraction.

And years later, in the moon of the best that followed, the other studio of my young acquaintance, of him whose hair embered whitely, could not connect with this one. Due partly to a defective or rusted memory. And partly to a sense of style.

'Your papa will be very pleased. No?'

'He might.'

'Ah, I think he will be very pleased.'

Why, Mr Shukla, does that slimness in your cheek suggest to me that you have been courting an aeroplane? After all, you might as well tell me now, since I wouldn't have understood you then. Key West is really a better vantage point for any words between us. And how much nicer for you to proceed, and not have even to paint the more futuristic version of myself, that has compassion for you, albeit misplaced, and apologizes for my seized memory of the period.

'There. I am almost finished.'

Yes, that is a genuine feature of portrait painters – they are for ever 'almost finished'. Even when one is quite finished oneself.

The picture seemed fine to me. But I didn't see why he had bothered. My old pa did though.

'Mr Shukla,' says my mother, idling with a pan of world-hard toffee by the drawing-board, 'wants forty pounds for it.'

They don't seem to want to pay it, beautiful as the work appears to me, and the canvas is placed in the cupboard, mentioned above, and lives there until some disagreement can be reached without the artist's feelings being reached simultaneously. Exact current whereabouts of picture unkown, but an intimation of embarrassment lingers after twenty-five years.

In the face of simple fright, building up tick by tick to fear, flowering in stony terror, the politics of recollection, if such a phrase can be deployed among the swept reaches of a journey, give way to the pleasant anarchy of how-things-were. How-things-were rules in its new clothes that memory stitches for it – memory usurping the sites of strict progress, and supplying a more gummy progress in place of the largesse-afflicted expansiveness of how-it-is. How-it-is now, between Sue and the wrong roads we are learning to love, will never be so again, not in the generosity of my own particular memory. It allows a mere shadow, a slight frame of what happens, to persist without glory and without true muddle into the sections of the future that are set aside for the hunting of the past. Etcetera.

What I mean is, I was out of my life with terror when I crept back to my room – of that I am fairly certain. I can see myself, very clearly, standing at the curtained door, half in my bedroom and half in my kitchen-hole, and not knowing whether to believe the present or get out of it or to pretend or to run. Instead, I dropped on my bed and rested my forehead very gently on the back of my hands, and discovered a syntactical groan at the back of my throat. The blueness of the bed seemed purer: it came up to my blown eyes with a soft rivery innocence and seemed verbal and far away. It was my childhood, where the possession of virility was never an object or a considered necessity. I feared disease with an architectural loathing, but I feared sexlessness in far more detail. If I had been threatened with the state of an hermaphrodite, or androgyne, or femininity, I might have gulped and turned and even laughed. After all, the boxes that contain the most unexpected, most potent horror are really quite funny in the endgame. You imagine yourself in a skirt, and you know you haven't got the legs for it. Or have you? And that is funnier still. But I was a church threatened with despoliation, even a sort of minor demolition, that would render my edifice repugnant and dangerous to visit. A black cross would be painted on my doors, and pilgrims and penitents would henceforth pass me with appropriate disgust.

To say now among the wheatfields or the cornfields or beneath this oldest tree that I was over-reacting is pointless. A threat is more powerful than an action, especially when the threat is to all of what you are. Because I dreaded that if a surgeon's blade changed my body, my mind might alter to accommodate the adjustment. And even if I was a wretch and a nobody, still I suddenly loved myself and my character, such as it was, and didn't want to be dead to it by being made alive to some other. Death was bad enough, but metamorphosis! I hadn't worked hard to create myself, but I had worked hard to bewilder it. You can't bewilder nothing and nowhere, you need a bit of fairly decent scrubland at least. I had that. I didn't want not to have it. Simple perhaps, but my fear was simple. To think I had wandered down to the doctor just to reassure myself, and get on with things in that way. And now I would never perhaps be able to do anything again so lightly, and so trustfully. A measured mulish trust in life!

I rinsed my soaked cheeks, noticing among my many arms that my scalp was heated and itchy. I swivelled my neck to make my eyes stare through the window, out to the clerkly sky beyond. Let this be true or untrue but let it not live on my breast like this, eating me.

I sat down on the mattress with a babyish bump, and tightened my fists. Take it easy, kid, I said, take it easy: you're still here. God, I said, give me a few weeks so I can have my time with Xenia. Please, my dear God, give me that.

'Anyway, that doctor is mad. I don't believe him, he's out of

139

his mind.'

But then so am I: that bastard has driven me crazy. God, let me not be crazy.

But who this god was that I appealed to I don't know now. The idea of him became more succinct, rounded and bright like an apple. I decided quickly that he was making himself ready in the cathedral of Notre Dame, which was not so far away across the river. I would see the polite bushes and the cold trees and the considerate water as I hurried there. But I suspected they would already have lost such adjectives.

Xenia, Xenia! Might she save me from this? And the telephone. I must telephone the specialist and make an appontment. To the telephone and then Notre Dame and then. And then. All right.

And this is so unnecessary, and why I am being subjected to this is beyond me. I might have been sitting up here, normally mooning over her absence. And now I'm plonked here, terrified of my own absence. There is everything to be done in this situation and no reason for doing any of it. I mean, if it's true, why go to any trouble at all, beyond the good brown river, and the deep breath it will give you to stop breath?

But there is still Xenia. And there is still. What? There is still daddy. Daddy will save you. God and daddy. Holy shit. God and daddy and a stranger. Or God and daddy *or* a stranger. Reasons for this, reasons for that. I pulled to my desk and put my buttocks carefully on the seat – balls, balls – and ruled a line down the centre of a calm gesture of paper. *Reasons to head for home. Reasons to head for the stranger.*

The stranger won. There were no reasons for either, but the stranger won because I belonged to her. If she hadn't made love to me all day, I mightn't have worried about the discomfort. Discomfort, laddie? You're dying! Young men get cancer down there, it's a fact. You read it in *Time* magazine, eh? You did. Fuck off! Telephone. Don't panic. Why not? It is the correct reaction this time round. You're right.

Telephone kiosk empty in the street, having reached there by some magic. Hospital. Specialiste.

'Je voudrais parler avec monsieur le spécialiste d'Urologie. Oui. Quand?' Or do I mean *con?* 'Trois semaines? You're joking! Est-ce que c'est sérieux? Non, c'est pas. Je ne sais pas.

Non, no pain.'

No pain, buddy, just terror. Three weeks. Okay. Three weeks in doubt. I come from the citadel, and there's cinnamon growing on the top of it. Some arrangement. And how will you pay for it? Avec ton coeur, sirrah. With ichor, if you were a god.

Notre Dame, the same mysterious speed. Didn't even get a chance to greet the old river. God in your heaven, protect your stupid son, though his courage is ignominious. The granite or stone roof was loquacious and silent. *My son, my son.*

Yes, it was a house. Not *the* house, or a house I remembered. Even the photograph album it was in, was a possible entrance. Not that it was truly in the album, it just ended up there. And it is only here that I can properly confuse the two, among the shards of old leaves and the wandering lumps of granite.

It is a helpful wind that blows me by the cottoned back up to the door, which can't welcome, but allows at any rate – a very blue wind, like the surface of an estuary in late light, stripped off by a clever knife in the thinnest layer, and hung up by its fists in the sky, where it struggles and where its feet toss, and reach me, and get me up the unmusical steps.

This drumming possesses the qualities of a drunkard reseeking his wife's bed. The door close-up is a picture of the house's façade in miniature, so the same door is tinier than it might be, with still another answer of steps up which I am to be carried by the breeze.

And then I understand I have imagined this, because the door is more exactly an old neglected surface, where there are no pictures, besides the remote gallery which time has made of the panels. If there are people walking there with umbrellas and prams in the London or otherwise afternoon, then they do so in black clothes because I can't find them. Is this a sign here that says *The Haunted House*, or am I anticipating that also? No, it is not, it is merely the old letter-box that used to live on a pole at the front gate, where the walls used to be, anciently, even though it is not a district for walls.

If this is America it is a very tiny America. But that depends on how you look at it, I suppose. The full orchestra of perfectly-bowed and blown music turns out to be the same fisted unhappy wind in the old curtain rods. The non-music hobos from the big broken brown windows. This is sepia then, or tinted. And a bird has fainted, and rotted on the rotten boards of the porch. So be it. The winter wind has ejected it as a superfluous character in its already repetitive novel. Very small fists, I might add, so small that lineage and family and such matters are either contained in them or ignored by them. If the silent intelligence of a baby realized for a moment the ignorance of its parents, it might well refuse to push on out: bankteller's bathos.

You could not use perspective to construct reality itself, at least not on the page of reality. It may be that painting before the discovery, or the dreaming-up, of perspective is the truer to reality, for among factual shapes lines do not proceed to one point, but are parallel, if parallel in perpetuum, and if not, not. But lines that live in parallel in truth, meet in paintings in seeming truth, or tend to meet, as this house does, which possesses the perspective of a painting, in that its hall, now that I look into it, is narrower at the back than here at the door, not only to the eye but to the head, which I prove by proving. The internal doors are both open and closed at the one time, or perhaps in two times that occur together, which is not nice of them. Because how can I now decide which they are, and accept they might be both, even though they are for a certainty both?

These brown doors neither bar my way nor let me in, or possibly do both, as I say, which comes to much the same thing, which only goes to show. So how will Sue find her way to me, and how in god's name will she get out again when she does? The second being more of a dreadful mystery than the first, in that the first is impossible, and the second therefore the philosophy of a philosophy, monstrous.

The idea of Sue finding her way to me is such a gentle one, in which I catch sight of her picking a path between dangers and daffodils, with her long cabaret legs. Such a white thing: the palest canvas, with herself the merest daub but brilliantly imprecise, to the border of precision. Love in a perfectly defined state without its confused accretions.

The state of being on Sue's side and longing to be at her side overcomes me in the brown hall, and I curse the doors their logic, and the great painters of the Renaissance have done me an ill turn by their discoveries, and are worth something less than the melting smallest brushstroke of her hair. She is a painter without considering it as she weaves among brambles and fullstops to reach me. The house beats with the engine of decay in the kitchen, where the milkbottle, which was once full and ready, has dried up to a mousy scum on the telescope of its bottom. This process hums still, and provides a recalcitrant electricity to the vanishing bulbs, that hover so fruitfully and unplucked from the tender wires, wires that have examined the insides of the ceilings and the patterned walls with a thin wormlike curiosity, and have abandoned their Nautilistic sports to hang themselves quaintly and fiercely – surrounded by impassioned stucco, manned by helpless cherubim, redundant cherubs down at the labour exchange. But they find they can not be exchanged for any true labour.

Decoration of that sort is neither admired nor necessary. Such houses are left to the infrequent bladders of the ghosts. Ghosts do not keep their bathrooms clean, I notice. How do they turn the handles without polishing them? Theirs is a very science of neglect.

But here is Sue asleep in the armchair, naked and strong. Her dreaming limbs are not to be watched lightly. She makes me glance away in gentlemanly embarrassment, or is it something more primitive and pure? Such an English notion. Her limbs as they dream are clothed by a more private cloth than our clumsy weavings. She dreams whole and without end. Such metal as flesh is can't wither or rot. It sleeps on in the woken memory to be taken again and again in your empty arms, till you might cry true original tears – collectors' items for the collected works of any one night. Her body lies into the chair with a different existence than the chair owns. She is stronger and whiter than any white or strength in the room.

I press my admiration, bordered by my trouser-legs, against her smooth picturing toes, and gather her with verbs and broken grammar. The dry case of a dead old woman is all of her that I can reach with my imprudent arms. It has a little stuck wrenching sound as I pull it, and I wake as perfectly as the bag of skin does not, and the train that has disturbed me owls in the narrow distance, and Chicken flares our moving cave with his

143

match, and Sue in my arms sleeps on.

There was a curious upended feeling about the town when we added ourselves into it, as if we were all a great fish that some greater fisherman had beaten, and we were hanging tail-up from the frame at his docking place. The weird southern Atlantic was not content to remain bound inside its boundaries, and seemed part also of what we were offered for breath. The houses looked long and white even under the purple and blue cloths. The palm-trees were so expensively green that they constituted a kind of cry or calling, and stood up from the light road in a sudden painted greeting.

Between this unexpected geography, the late cars swam smoothly, with large rocking music removing itself from the glowing windows, in the guise of wooden flowers. Ali's feet were the pads to this place. He progressed along it with title and appropriateness, whereas I was only the most perfect interloper. This was his domain where he could plan his living, and his future living, and here his brain worked best.

Susan hung rather distantly beside us, glooming along after her night of grinding and invitation. She had sucked all the wet noise of months afloat out of her brief sailors, and wherever they were, her image was bouncing inside them like an inflated raft. She seemed sleepy and ordinary on the tropical street.

The colours streamed past my ears like water, and I walked through the muddle of engines and the last songs of bands with a notion that my ears and heart were battened down. There was contentment in that. I didn't feel quite so full of my map of mistakes as usual. I must have dropped that casual faithful pencil-line somewhere behind us, where other lives were not moving, and where I hoped no one would be so foolish as to pick it up.

Groups of desperate people were stuck against doorways, like honey bees in their raw hives on skylight windows. They were trying to peer in and appraise the performers, whose fingers would be bleeding now on the guitars. Our Texan in the Bull Bar would have flourished all his songs all over again to the old ears and one or two pairs of new ones. That was how he would have managed his clutch of new hours. And when people die, they seem so desolate about it, and yet they have killed themselves off, of their own accord, a thousand times in a thousand uncertain nights.

In the shadowed bar with the glowing white pillars we arranged some quiet for ourselves by choosing the most distant table from the entrance, because at the wide opening the girls were sitting with their cheap drinks, and passing men and boys slowed up there like the strokes of cricket-bats, and turned and examined and tried their luck. Many of the men didn't realize the women were working, and imagined for a space that they had scored with their good looks on tourists like themselves. The sailors knew the game, but the tourists from Texas and further north still believed in themselves in that way. You could notice their eyes drift and police themselves as they understood measure by measure the nature of the girls' agreeableness: and then they either stuck for the hell of it, or plucked their jeaned bottoms off the stools, for fear they mightn't have enough money, and being afraid too to ask.

'You get the dullheads around here working on that door,' Susan said at my elbow, which looked like the pressed snout of a dog.

'Oh yeh?'

'Yeh. The trick goes sour on the nice guys. They think they've picked you up.'

'Yeh, I thought that was happening.'

'Well you were right, bud. Only the dullheads stick there because it makes no difference to them.'

'Do the girls mind, do you think?'

'Nah. They don't mind. They're workin. It's money you know.'

'But Susan don't do dat kind of work, does she, Susan?' says Ali.

'Nah. I don't do it. I don't like it. I dance. It suits me.'

'You're a good dancer – you're a great dancer.' My voice has a lot of unwise enthusiasm in it.

'You think so? Yeh, so you said in the bar. Thanks.'

Ali lit up a smoke for himself and Susan leaned in to me. Her daft smile blew across her mouth like a swift in a squall.

'Hey. You got fifty dollar?'

'For what?' Now my voice had a lot of stamped-on surprise.

'You got it?'

'Yes, I've got it,' I said.

'Give it to me.'

'For what?' I said.

'Well, do you have it or not?'

'I do.'

'Well then give it to me. Go on.'

And she brought out five fingers till they rested on my arm. My arm registered her there on its instruments as a warmth magnified and changed by a quick but slightly drunken desire in my forehead, of all places. But it seemed like it was behind my forehead that my desire for Susan began.

'But don't you do anything for the money?' I said. 'I can't just give it to you.'

'Sure you can. What do you think I am?'

'I don't know, Susan. You're a dancer.'

'Look, I like you,' she said. 'Give me the money. I won't cheat you.'

Her eyes leaped into my eyes and started a silent quarrel there with them. She filled my eyes with such contempt that at the same moment I hoped she would never try to be an actress, and that I would be strong enough to resist her crazy demand.

'What are you talking about?' I said. 'I don't get it. I'm not rich. I don't have anything. We're the same.'

'Oh yeh?' she said, and shrugged, and pulled her body back slowly till she was sitting again alone and important in front of Ali.

'You dreamin, kid?' she said to him, like a kid sister.

'I'm dreamin,' he said. 'You work out something for yourselves?'

'Nope, but it don't matter.'

Ali put his massed hands together and twined his fingers and pulled at the join. He let a cinematic personal glance splash from his pooled eyes onto the table and into my breast.

'It's a,' Susan began, 'it's not a big house, and it's not a small house.'

'What house dat?' said Ali.

'What we're thinkin about.'

'Oh, dat house. Okay.'

A small neat bashed woman gave him a four-second stare as she bananad past.

'Hmm, *hmm*,' he said.

'Yeh, well, this house ain't so far from where you are, Ali, and I reckon that's pretty convenient all round.'

'Don't make any difference. We can always walk.'

'Well it's near anyway.' And she smoothed her palms on the warm beery surface, and leaned. Her breasts under cotton crushed against the edge of the wood, so I thought it might be painful. Then she straightened again, and sort of punched her breasts gently with her bunched fists. All the time I knew she was unaware of every action she completed. She was dreaming.

'What's your fucking friend going to do?' she said suddenly.

'He's the man,' said Ali.

'The man for what? He's a fuckin sore-arse. Look at him!'

Ali kept his peace for a few indifferent minutes, and whatever the girl meant by it was let drift like a bothersome wasp out into the belling night.

Mr James Francis Flynn of the Sligo Bank and Mercantile Society had no importance in the real town, because he was strictly and even nonsensically honest. The real town was where cabinboys made fortunes, where fortunes were spoiling for the grab.

Mr Flynn had a truly destructive vice. All the town blamed him for it, and knew it in savage detail. His vice was dogs. He had nine of them, large, inconvenient, and of no breed in particular.

In return for the shelter of the empty warehouse beside the metallic harbour, Moran was duty-bound to exercise the beasts of Mr Flynn each evening in the area of the cathedral. The bishop often sliced his gaze out one of his stuffy study windows and sighted Moran at the end of nine overly-thick ropes, being yachted by the enthusiastic unmusical dogs. The animals had the appearance of wide snub-nosed fish, the sort that inhabits the unplumbed shelves of the more unavailable oceans.

Moran for the most part enjoyed their joined power, and allowed himself to be misguided wherever the dogs wished.

The wishes of the dogs were full wishes. They liked ducks, in that they wanted to eat them, and they liked water.

It was happy for Moran that the town pond was shallow and marshy and not altogether lethal. It was jammed with offal and carcases end to end, and contributed in a generous way to Moran's general personality and acceptability.

The bishop loathed two things most in his little world: the parish priest and dogs. He kept a cat himself, and couldn't understand why anyone would want to deviate from the tastes of a bishop, in particular a small-town bank manager. That he himself was a small-town bishop he didn't allow to occur to him. Bishops are bishops, and indeed his own parish was in reality, or in ecclesiastical reality, an enormous district of Northern Africa, subject mainly to drought and inter-tribal warfare, under the rule of two separate gods, neither of whom were Christian. The bishop had never been to Africa, but he had been once to Spain as a very young man, and in Cadiz he had drawn his own burnt conclusions about the dark-skinned people of that white region. He knew what he preferred, and he had no desire to see his black lambs, even if they were apparently lost in the Sahara, or at least wandering there, and so had a connection of a kind with being hungry in deserts, which was such a feature of his own religion.

The desert appealed to the biblical part of him, and he had a genuine addiction to Hebrew prose rhythms, but Moran passing, and then repassing some time later covered in excreta and mud, did not. He felt it as a disgrace to his battlements, and would walk out in the deeper wooden evening to have words with his oldest friend, the embittered gardener of the cathedral close. The gardener was metal deaf, and fairly dreaded the indistinct mumbles of his enraged entreating master, of whom he had no great opinion. The bishop also had a stony Mayo accent that the gardener, even if he could have heard it, would not have understood, since he came by ill-adventure from a good merchant family of Naas.

Mr James Francis Flynn persisted in his ownership of the animals, and in the employment of Moran, and Moran, in his uninspired manner, persisted in being dragged across shallow water.

Syntactically speaking, Moran did not see things as I, in my

148

hollow innocence, have described. Since it is my privilege to present the vehicle as I please, or as I must, I allowed the character of the bishop enter my tone, and presented a view of Moran that he was never aware of, and wouldn't have considered of any consequence if he had been.

By this time my poor vehicle was seventeen, and had a squat lumpy aspect, not much helped by a slight but disturbing largeness of the skull, which righted itself more in later years, but in his youth gave him a lopsided about-to-topple-over air, that was only irritating, and frightened what there was of genteel ladyship in the town. There was very little of the latter however.

But I'd like to drop this tone because it fatigues me, and is not true to Moran, and Moran is what carried me for so long, and therefore I must honour him at least with the maximum exactitude. You see, for him Mr Flynn was only a bright shadow in a doorway, and of less impression than the incoming tide that made the seagulls nervous, and the mackerel dare their way in at the end of summer – mackerel being in many respects underwater gulls. He knew when the mackerel had got brave again, because they were tumultuous obvious eaters among the monetary shoals of the sprat, which they chased to stuff their tubes and stomachs with.

One day a seagull, in a fright at seeing Moran, dropped a mackerel on the boy's tufty head. Moran expected the simple creature to swim away over the cobbles but it didn't, and anyway had one eye missing already from the commanding attack of the bird. But he saw that it was a tight tube of smaller fish, and was overcome with pleasure and friendship for so neat and contained a personality. He stood on the cobbles and tossed his arms about slightly from the elbows, as if he were typing on a big machine, and didn't know what to write next. He had seen typists at work in the commercial offices at the wharf.

He knelt beside the buckling mackerel, and peered without touching it into the stretching mouth. The remaining eye of the creature seemed wild with hope and happiness. Moran shouted at the fish and pressed his nose against the seaweedy naked smell. The fish doubled its throes, and at each flip a little sprat or two slid dead and energyless from the singing jaws. The fish sang without a sound, but Moran knew the song well, because he had seen his old family on the ceiling of the work house celebrate things with the same procedure. Moran had seen everything and he knew everything and the fish was singing. Moran sang silently but expansively with the mackerel, clustering his bones as close against it as he could. He blinked in a sort of hairy delight, and wanted to roll, and spin, and flick his spine like the fish was able to. The sprat were still and grey, and had no happiness, but not the mackerel. And then Moran straightened his back, and got it into his head that the fish was alone now. The shoal would be gone and the other sad mackerel with it. He was more joyous then than he had ever cared to be before.

Sixfoil Nine

Wall, Moll, der is an oweld poem dat taulkes uf troobel. An it
sayes mich aboot de grat stoon beldins day ust ta finde al aboot
de anceent contree uf farr offe Anglelant. It makes mentoon of
envasoon and barbaroos calamitoo. Bat at ent of dis pom de
writterman sayes: *sich wass sich an dat past*. *Dis maye too*. Meenin,
Moll, whativer dradfil busnooz wasse aflote, it wud go bee at
laste.

An so it turnt oot wid Owel an Oleeve in de dits. De
demonesse she want bye an smokt off inta de ferther regioon.
De too dragt der cald lags oot a de dree unwhalsoom rutte, an
stoode noddin at ech udder uponne de shakent pathe. Noo de
wilde facce uf de barr cuntree semt drunke wid threts, an dey
felte muche de grat distoonse uf halv a dee, dat laye lik a poisson
betwan dem an hoom.

'We muste sufer bigly, it semt,' sayed Olleeve. 'I almoost
fanted oot inta de free aire dat teem.'

'I shud ev stuntet de animool wid retoreek,' sed Owel
gleefulee.

'An dat iss yer particloor studee, I knoo,' sed Oliv.

'Ah, yis, it wuss the delicta uv me yout.'

'Whar comt dat studee fram, moi beste herte?'

'It wausz fram de owel citee uv Byzantioo it ded flowe like
a rivoor uf grat importe. De bootes an bootmen uf retorik
flowet fram dat serioose environz, an cam her many yearn agoo,
whan yer grat-grat-grat-granfadded wuzz lard in yer sete.
Hermogoniz, a manne uv Tarsez, wrat al der wasse ta gif uf
dit somber scienz. An en Byzantee, moi frend, dey ust dis wiz-
dome ta pruvv de meanin an de colors uf ower gut bishoopes
god.'

'An by shit of henz, did dey now, moi Owle? An wass dat de
heade of ower hurte?'

'Wal, in dat contree de newe news uv Rame was all ta do wid

151

de lionz an de hurted menne, dat did in Jesu de manne of Nas-
saret believf. Perhap it semt difrent an gut to dem, becarse all
wasse newe, an dey did nat carr fer nor knoe ower splendit
frendlee gottes, dat make ower lant ta bloome, or wud ef teems
werre elder.'

'An wat, moi pure manne, izz lionnez?'

'Grat bastes dey ar, dat et de smaller beastes wid a naturel an
clivver patioonce, by dinte uf staulkin.'

'Why izz it den dat we cin nat ovverdo de bishoop by one like
dint?'

'Becorse, moi leeve lorde, we arre nat simplee lionz.'

An Oliv laft den, and it soundet jes a small peece like a leon
afftre al.

'I wod be one lion at dat,' sed Olivv, 'an et moi enemee.'

'Yas, bat wat iff al were lionz and der warre none mar delicat
beste, which you arre? De wurl wud stert ta spinne, an we wud
be flunge away fram ittes nastee edg. Dis ye muste heede.'

'It wud be so? An soo I will be lionz their meete.'

'Na, na, it wull nat be so necessaire, gud Conn. Ye can be
aspeckt of carful berd, and gard yer neste wid excelent politee.'

'Bat a cuckoo hass jammt moi nesting wid fowel dert, an der
is nat room for mee an moi power mare.'

'Nowe, Oliv, as in retorik, wan manne wishoos ta advanz
wid graz an dignatee, you cin winne yer batel wid worddes
alon. An I canne be yer mout if so you pleze.'

'I do pleze so. I nede yer wily canter an yer hed fer teems so
greye as dees. An iff I faile at laste, it wull be for the gloree of
noice coloor, whach maks de wuds so cheery.'

Der mar hopefulle fete want on alonge de trac, an braght uppe
litul towerz uf graeny duste in ther progressoon. Berds, lik fait-
fulle courters, strak der songes throo de prisoon bushez. Evven
de berds war drent uf der parfact color. Stil, color dwelet in der
tinee musik, an de brun lang facc uf Olleever reaganet a childeesh smiel after so manny dees uf soro. Bat hes soroo semt
always a sart of machine ta hem, an he herd de partes moving
an goin on ta der conclusoon. He sawe de walkin suune as ef ut
warre a fellaugh walker. An de sunne hes fac was happee it
appered also.

'Whie, Owel,' he sed, 'de sunne hasse ventoored oot uf hes
cave an iss cam ta fallo uzz.'

Bat Owle cud catch no site uf anee such sfere.

'My hert, I see no sunne,' he sed.

'Yass, luk, yoo dolte an cloon, do yoo nat wonder at itz sieze? I havv nat helloet my kinge de sunne fer one twig uf years.'

'I see no sunne,' repetitionet Owl. 'It iss nat der. Ya mak me gloomee wid yer seely tricke.'

'I amme nat trikkin, Owel. I see a globe uf yella feer, an he seese me. Hes eyez are opt, an wan grat grinne has possest hes cheks.'

Owel staret like a cowe in some fluded marning, whan de rivoor hasse come highere in de nite, an et her grasse.

'If ye trullee see de sunne, moi larde, I bowe to yer eyez. Der arre anly too of uss menly kinde her on dis tracke. One sese a globe, de odder nat. So sinz ye arr moi lard I bowe to ye, an say I see a sunne, tho none I see.'

'Of certaine course ye do, moi Owel. Sher certin ther it wawks wid a hidden bodee, an but hes smilin face iss cler ta lowere eyes.'

'I see yer sunne out of love to yoo, moi lorde. It isse a foine sunne. An dose it make coloor for ower lant?'

'Perhap. I can nat saye. Do ye spotte a trifel or a messe of sich, Owel?'

'I doo natte.'

'Nor do ei.'

'Bat maybee we ar bothe at fawlt thisse tiem. De reddes and blews an grens are dere, bat awer poor dottet blak eyen have loste de litel engeen ta greet dem.'

Whiel dey were trien ta invente de sunne itsel opon the softe dree sandee rode, a low manne hat come uppe as farr as dem ta spek. De fields he hadde traversoo warre mene an stubblee. Owle jumt a spaze ta dodge anee blowe de smal manne mite caste, bat der cam non.

'Tum,' sed de dertee pezant boldlee, 'si fortunae causaque Hannibalis ac vestrorum comparentur quanto haec vestra dis hominibusque acceptiora sunt!'

'Ach,' sed Ollevve, 'he speks sam filtee simpel lingage. Wat duss he saye?'

'I amme nat shur. He talkes so thicke an mudee. It iss too cloggt an curdelt ta unravvel.'

'Quanto laude ac sempiterna memoria digniora,' addet de

153

stinkin agricultoorer man.

'Izz it de lingage dat de menne uf de northe ust ta offer? Or dat fool his tongue uf de wilde menne, whoo lurke in quiet litul tres?'

'Certa lege temporum frateri certa lege temporum.'

De barbarishe figoor hadde fedders an strawe flingin oot uf hes har. He carriet unner wan arme a greye strugglin cock. He helte de unhappee animool oot fram hes bodee, an stuck et towarddes Coon an Owel.

'Do nat take et, lorde Oliv,' sed Owel. 'It es nat fer yoo.'

'I wante no greye chickens fram moi henz,' sed Con.

'Quis enim nunc sit animo tam humili,' sterted de strangeer, 'tam abiecto?'

Bat Olivv an Owel wud nat allowe hem finish, an hurriet off at a horsish gallop bak toards de castel.

Very few Sundays blackened by without a greatly preferred dish of my father's being made for dinner. At a period when I was a very old child in Highgate – by contrast with how young I had been at the start – which oldness on return to Dublin changed to a youngness after all, the green papier mâché hippo lived in silent but possible contentment beside the gasfire and the television, where Doctor Who mainly lived. It had been left, the hippo, by an emigré Polish sculptor, who had devised the powerful legs and body from an actual but less real hippopotamus in the London Zoo. I had never visited the protohippo, but enjoyed very much sitting on the quiet green back of the sculpture, which was not allowed. So the word *sculpture* meant at that time a thing of stone and warmth and blood, though the warmth was borrowed from the fire, and the blood was locked inside the hard glued paper.

The sculptor survived in my mind as the friend or owner of the hippo, but he did not survive the iron fortune of Poland and never returned from his stay, or his holiday, or his attempt to be Polish again, nor any news heard of him. So the hippo lingered on solidly beside the grate, and waited for his maker who would never come, but might all the same at any minute. Something in Poland swallowed the sculptor. But the jaws could not include his single perfect animal, the horse of the river: not even a clockwork system could ingest the mighty beast that the hippo seemed.

It protected the ambitious silence of my father's drawing-board, that hung latterly between the drunken armchair and the broad end-window, where the empty taxi blackness of the nights was removed by a curtain of air and cloth.

Between the curtain and the windowpane the temperature was chilled and avocado, the garden that I couldn't see precise and large in its dangerous cover. The rabbits inched in their hutches at the red side of the house, and the dark stirred unnecessarily around everything, threatening it, threatening it. I had to pluck myself back into the true night of the living-room with an heroic minuscule effort, like a toy soldier finally moving under the concentrated desire of a child's face.

The room was tracks of long floorboards, and a Christmas tree was always there in a memory of itself, but not in fact. The couch was dark blue and grey, and smelled of badgers and storybooks, and the marble table was a companion to and as smudged and old as the couch. They didn't look anything but new and fashionable perhaps, but in my skull they were ancient and otherwise, as were the leaning shelves of red Penguin paper-backs, sitting on the varnished yellow wood my grandfather had made for their cages – the lips of ice floors.

In that room of cold ocean I wrote out my name for the first time, servant of letters at last, and swelled it in the face of a tartan visitor, and was happy, and felt cruel and wicked at the same moment.

The electric socket was the place you died, and my father had seen his friend shrivel and smoke at another such socket, in an old time before that time, where I hadn't been.

He raised the boiled onions from the sunned white plate, on the bright hinterland of the table, to his long beard which hung redly and blackly from his solid lips. The onions gleamed on his round spectacles, and I watched the sticky soft fruit slip from the steel spoon into his brown cave. It was secret and happy in there, but I had never been. Whenever I pulled his wiry beard he was crossed, and pushed my hands away. But his beard wanted to be tugged, and you tried, and the onion disappeared, and the spoon lifted down for the next one, and the steady

155

desperate eyes remembered me at the other balance of the table, remote and among my family, and told me to eat my onions or, or else a loud banging shout would blood in my arms, with a heavy bottom-of-the-well sensation that heralded all devouring of pestilent boiled onions. As the spoon in my paw floated up, the fat stomachy layers slithered evenly and slightly, but would not fall off.

And outside the flat it was certainly the nineteen-sixties, but inside it was always. The child is still there with his mother and his sister flanking him without a word, and the hazelwood eyes are still at the other end, and the onion is still warm and soft, and ascending like a ludicrous star to drop down the deep endless chute of my body. The shadowed door is behind me, and the square hall with the flat-tyred bicycle that is mine but won't go, and the bathroom is there that we must never lock when we pee in it, because we are only children, and the kitchen is thinking of toffee, and the cat is abroad on the tossing heath among the highwaymen and the maniacs.

But here is the onion still at the lip of myself and it must enter. It is Sunday and so the papers are ready on the couch and the panting floor, and all Highgate has been for a walk up the Stony Way, or through the churchyards or over the generous green to Kenwood House. Hampstead remains and the villages of the district are home to their papers and their televisions, and their gardens breathe with notions of rocks and next year's borders and weeded black clay. The sherry joins the talking tongues, and the cars are ticking in repose on the neatly-tarred land of roads, where I couldn't cycle my new wrapped bicycle, but I did. The milkman growled he would tell my father up on the steep road to god-knows-where, though he didn't know about the onions on Sundays.

But I couldn't eat them, even if I had to, and there was always the watery pink explosion, which made the drops of his moisture leap like tiny dancers from his mouth. And after a while he stopped fuming like a garden dump, and played the finger game with my sister to show he hated me. He drummed his fingers close, and closer to her, so they looked really like a crab, and she groaned and cried and dreaded them, and then accepted the blunt travellers with a crazy squeal, as they rushed forward to rustle her arm. The rustling grew just like the school wind in the bushes beside the animal road, and our hair in the living-room blew round and round, and put lines of colour against the pale wallpaper, and we had to hold on to the table, all of us, and we were perfect at that. Then the gasfire got control of us, and sucked back its flames that had decided to join in the ruckus, and my mother was bird-happy and we didn't burn.

Green crosses in Paris marked the dead doors of chemist shops, and if you are in a morbid state then you find there are far too many of them, a Verdun for vials.

I remembered strange things the next day in the local laundry, and I decided I would set out for Switzerland as soon as possible or as soon as Xenia would let me. I phoned her while my few clothes balleted to the top of drier and stopped, mooned and dropped.

Every action I ground through was sung by a vague but immediate lack of point. My one interest was centred on the phone booth, with its grey metal and the hidden cache of coins in the self-important box.

Xenia's tone was very soft and asleep, like it had been long ago in Greece. She surprised me by the warmth with which she refused any sudden setting out, but suggested a week from that ordinary day. Indeed, she said we had been foolish and timid to have waited at all. The difficulty was, she had a dance-school to attend during the week in another town, and she wanted to be at her parents' house in Berne when I got there. I didn't quite understand this arrangement, but I was too excited and upset to think properly while talking to a baby of metal with the voice of someone I was sure I loved, or could no longer not love. In a way though, I was never closer than that to her again. Needing her because I considered myself to be in green danger had already changed the adjustment on our machine: there was no question of allowing any critical thought play in my egged head. She was all I had now, and I must get to her as swiftly as her roads would accomodate me.

Out in the hard street by the Hôtel de Ville I passed back among the green crosses, and my old footprints from other slightly less distraught journeys, and made myself return to the laundry. It was decorated with people settled more or less in a first-thought full geometry of being alive. They clearly had beds to spruce, and children to dust off, and meals to copy out of new recipes, and scolding to improve on, and showdowns to show down, and I had a dreadful feeling I would not be part of such matters again.

That sort of induced melancholy is quickly gained but less easy to remove. The paint of it dries, and you need a blow-torch of a quaint make to strip it. I didn't have a blow-torch of any description, though I hoped Xenia would fulfil that service.

I remembered reading a poem by Robert Bridges to a school-friend of my sister's, in an old rectory in the west of Ireland, when we were both still of school age. It was summer and the heat was confidently inside everything, including my head and blood, and I stood in the centre of an old bedroom, with its dark blue trimmings and a four-poster bed like a cave for child-hood, and ranted the same dull grey poem at her seventeen times in a row. The memory of it slipped back to me in the laundry for no reason, and it should have made me laugh. When you have done such things, really being in danger of your life is not that important. But it didn't seem so funny after all in the Parisian laundry among the dirty children and the mothers who smelt of clothes – it seemed remote and lost and ludicrously poignant. It had not been in the least poignant. But it returned now soft and vicious and as a kind of mockery of most elements I considered myself to be.

A young man in a poor quarter washing his battered clothes, afraid of losing even that status, and unable to overcome his fear for more than two or three moments of intimate pity, is a mechanism that dwindles and disappears like a watch made of ice.

I sat on the red puffy seat while stout black figures packed their cleaned lives into black plastic bags, and bundled them out, and said goodbye to the polished hands in charge, a lady in her own cloudlight, and left me unseen and unclean, in the Indian sense, while my life dried in the spindrier, and bits of an older family life skipped and lurched in my colourless head, like a bubble-car out of control. I couldn't shake it off, because there was no division of any clock to reach where I could walk away from what I dreaded.

There was no open room any more in me for bad temper or impoliteness, or for being amused or depressed: anything like that seemed the privileged procedures of the healthy and navigable. I felt myself to have entered a new capacity – the dangerous little I suspected I was had metamorphosed into some type of mouldy waiting-room. In fact, I had left my life, such as it was, in the rat-faced doctor's apartment among his out-of-date magazines, and the creature tossing with a mournful sound in the dryer was a remnant without metaphor or memory. If someone had reached out a warm hand and rested it thoughtfully on my shoulder they would have passed through and into some comical 'bottomless pit'. I had become a sex to the world of drabness. My limbs hung like old people's do in the tarry parks.

With Xenia I may have been frightened of possibilities, but I had glanced in that café window and thought my face like Degas' dowdy drinker – a sop and a consolation of sorts. The treatise of being doomed that I had formed from slouching in a foreign restaurant with someone of obvious popular beauty or power had been drafted out of a sense of my own inappropriateness as companion to such a prize. But the word doomed is not the same as the word sentenced. And I was finding that to have your punishment quietly and uncaringly read out to you is rather different than a borrowed suspicion that somewhere, sometime, in the great mulish future an end might possibly make itself known.

And still the image of myself grinding out the cold poem in the warm season, and the girl opening her blouse to show her neat delftlike breasts, to shut my hysterical calm, kept playing and replaying as an imposed reel across my misery.

An unreal feeling of loneliness and unworthiness stole about my noisy brain, like a something whose house has burned down with all its family inside. I was patently Without with a capital W, and the only even half-decent answer seemed to run to Switzerland – and an avoidance as much as possible, in the white interim, of any department whatever of my so-called personality.

My freed desire for Sue was a strolling troupe of moles that expeditioned into all possible earthings. The sightless movements were a clean opposite to the category of desire I had for her when we were dozing on the leather of Chicken's car, or when, tightly, she had walked in front of me from the car to the motel room.

As I lay against her in close night, the eyes of the three neon signs across the yard were more open and descriptive than mine, and I could see them more clearly then I could see her, because their message and redness floated into my stray glance at their planetary glimmering speed.

The three pieces of information were *Motel, Rooms,* and *Available.* While Sue and I improvised the most suitable sections of our bodies to rub against each other, the news of availability and motelship and roomishness travelled to my slowly blinking eyes.

But Sue was dark and uncollected under me somewhere, her face pressed warmly into the cheap nylon pillowcase that had become robbed of its material and was now only a forgotten shortcoming of the little brittle room. She was sunken in a contented undemanding dream, whether the same dream she had buried me in or another was not important or known. Her body ran, a fixed image of a warm pacific wave alone out at sea, neither looking for nor needing a shore to break on, but approaching such a surface none the less. The way her bottom raised against my stomach long minute after new time, was a newer version of being born, a wakeful ticking observed version. She birthed me with the silence and heat that would make me believe in the attraction of being alive.

As an introduction to the world it was ideal. The neon imploded affectionately behind my slow-motion head, and the colours streeled in very minutely, and wrapped in a fresh cloth around my hair. Sue's bottom strained up with a gesture a horse will make alone in an incidental field, with its muscled neck, and the brain of my thighs responded down the wires with a thick bitten movement against her. I struggled my arms about her white shoulders and made her blades imprint against my burnt chest. Her damp head engined under my cheek. I felt oddly but exactly like a large troubled animal that has just eaten some smaller troubled creature, and is digesting this catalyst to

160

happiness in a warm safe sunshine.

The varied facts of the room could only reach a boundary some feet around our skins, and they fell without disturbing us to the gritty carpet. The first thing was to move again and again to the same slightly shifting mathematic, to indulge with best instinct the lemming character of ourselves, that wanted to abandon responsibility and toss into a sea of the fleshy present.

The narrative changed tone when Sue's invisible cunt fluttered and beat like pigeons in their cot. Her cunt had travelled into the rooms of my stomach, and yet they seemed very distant birds when they vigorously whisked their wings, and made her ticker-tape a miniature scream from the corner of her dribbling mouth. My phallus was intelligent enough to try and follow, but I was disconcerted to feel like a tap filling a hose to the point where the rushing water reaches the nozzle, just before it divides out into the air. I was prevented from being reminded of anything more companionable by the insertion of a shadow between the three neon lights and my two candled eyes. This startled me, and while Sue surfaced and trod water on the hard little bed I had a wrenched cut-off sensation, like a child whose reaching hand has been unexpectedly rapped by an adult. I disentangled our various leads and valves and dragged the cover off the twin bed and twisted it around my waist. The still human shadow remained as exact as cardboard outside on the barrel porch.

There was a tussle then, and a few broken words, and the standing outline was disturbed and confused by another less defined blackness.

I opened the rattling door with a system of sharp tightness in my chest. The newness of the old night was like a reminiscence of itself as it met me. On the boards of the porch there was an apparently intoxicated man, and Chicken was trying to get him to his feet, but seemed so irritated with the floppy man that his yanking just served to make brief ripping noises in the fellow's shirt.

'What's that, Owl?' said Sue in the drowned room behind me.

'What the fuck are you up to, Chicken?' I said, and I shivered in the warm night soup.

'This floating ratbag was peeping in at you,' Chicken said. 'The little scumbag!'

It seemed miraculous that the fallen man could have been standing so still and quiet outside the room, when now he was floundering and flapping at Chicken's bare toes.

'The drink must have hit him suddenly, then,' I said.

'Not the drink,' said Chicken. 'I hit the bastard.'

However, a beery whisky ballad was meandering up from the fish on the ground.

'Old bastard,' I said, and I could see my spit skite against the backing neon.

'Small-town habits,' said Chicken, the red check in his shirt chosen and picked up by the gloom, so his compact torso seemed only a grid of bright threads. 'Watches everyone who books in here. Don't you, you big cunt?'

The drunk man sort of fell to his feet, and crashed against our wall. He was a curved bulky person with thin black legs. A light bloomed in the motel office and the clerk spilled himself out into the yard. All around in the night the cicadas were suddenly noticeable with their purring, their volume knob continually swivelled.

'Hey,' said the clerk, 'hey.'

He crossed over to us in his slippers and I saw that he was timid and doubting.

'Hey buddy, what ye doin?'

'I'm not doin nothing,' said Chicken. 'I'm just standin here.'

'Hey, what's the story here? Anyone want the police called?'

'No,' I said, 'it's all right. Just some drunk fella here. It's nothing.'

'What drunk fella? This guy?'

'Yeh,' said Chicken. 'This guy.'

'That's Room 305,' said the clerk. 'Hey, Room 305, why don't ya get some sleep? Yeh,' said the clerk, 'that's his car there, the Oldsmobile. Nice new car.'

'He ain't from around here?' said Chicken, surprised.

'Nope. Not a local man. So what's the trouble?'

'Ah, it's okay,' said Chicken. 'Forget it.'

'Sure I'll forget it. You just woke me up. I'll forget it.'

The narrow wiry clerk drifted back to his desk, where his tiny television thumbed the dark.

Chicken shrugged his shoulders precisely at me, and translated himself into his cabin without another word.

162

'Owl,' said Sue. 'Owl, come here and hold me.'

So I did. And the neon moons regained the empty yard, with all the personality and judgement of people. Or slightly more.

The morning was brilliantly coloured and dull. Every article under the worn white sky gleamed and richened. The boarding-house girl still reminded me of broken corn-fields so I drank my dreggy coffee on the porch. No one had decided to turn down the street or work in the gardens so early on a low-season day.

I tempered the fresh weariness of my legs and arms with a long direct walk between the lamped houses and the green fire hydrants and the generous trees. The flowering bushes were already unfolded and they signalled to me calmly as I calmly trod along. I moved as gradually as an old man and let the small pleasure of small loose strides claim me.

The sea was away off in the distance at the close of my walk, and it stuck up like a polished plate as if it were placed a little higher than the whitish tar. I was aware of the extraordinary efforts of the huge sun to dress my skin wherever it was bare in a light comfortable cloth. My head was almost nodding at the neck, and my body made a kept-in dance down the road, the steps of which were private and special to me, and whose effect on a piece of paper would look like the choreographic squiggles of a printer's border. I felt my feet were printing some pattern into the morning town of Key West, and I was unusually well-disposed towards the least of its possessions. Even the straggled cats, belonging only to themselves, that kept house in the tough roots of garden trees, seemed well-situated and opportune in themselves.

The sea kept glimmering like a simple metal fire, a damped furnace to decorate the distance, and I kept proceeding towards it, unhurried, unasked, and idle. Anyone still asleep in their lovely rooms was excluded from this my newest world. Only what was unnecessary and extra and inside nothing was part of the parcel of that morning.

The breathy stormed road and the swaying still beach were vastly empty. The sand gripped loosely between the sweating overgreen palms, and above and around these a watered moving brightness progressed like mobile brushstrokes. Who would have given anything but a copper halfpenny for all this would have been out of line. It was worth nothing in that way, a honkytonk liability. A money transaction would have forced the elements to vanish and reorder.

The overstuffed waste-paper baskets tacked on the trees were not beyond price but before price. They were something to do with me all right, and I could have talked to them softly out of a sense of comradeship. There was the ruined beach talking to the broken sea. And the objects that had wrapped yesterday's hamburgers and icecreams and pop wanted to drag themselves out of their places, and distribute their colours and associations over the scuffed down-at-heel sand.

Incredibly, at that hour, one of the food vans was already open for the business that wasn't there. A pucker of air hung over the tin chimney at one playing-card edge of the roof. Some oven was being heated, and fat was evaporating into the smudged sky. I had a great clean sympathy for the owner of the vehicle, and was persuaded by the minute clatters of activity inside the van to wander over and pause at the small slightly oily window. A starched woman between all states had her flowered back to me as she poked delicately at the blackening meat on her hot-plate. She was inside her van but somehow she was inside what held good outside too. I couldn't bother her for anything, and anyway I didn't require anything from her. We were more connected now than ever we could be under the uneasiness of a fresh conversation. We might as well have known each other for thirty years, so long as we didn't prove the opposite by talking. I already had a clear elaborate view of her character, although the only thing I could guess it from was her solid shoulders. Her van possessed a small animal of radio music, that didn't seem to want to travel much further than the open glass of the serving hatch. *So be it,* I whispered to myself, and stumbled as gently as I could up the sane border of the beach where it spilled thickly to the rasped concrete pavement.

I imagined unimaginable men making the flattened sand-castle of the pavement years before, and the winter storms making the ocean lie on it and wear off the spread evenness of the surface, so that the long plank of pavement had become grainy and uncomfortable for naked feet.

The colours of the sea had only the quietest things to say for themselves, like the hidden radio among the hamburgers. When I settled against the rhinoceros hide of a palm-tree the sea barely cluttered in response, but continued to waver and pucker as if some hand were constantly trembling whatever base it was laid over. The sun managed to lie for brief spaces on the offered sides of these crenellations, but was flicked off quickly, and the whole plain of the agitated sleepy sea flicked the plates of sun off like that for fifty miles right and left and to the familiar foreign horizon.

My rather more unfamiliar legs seemed to poke distantly out of their loose fawn trousers, and my shoes were abrupt and important at the end of these strange legs. If I could have flapped my arms and lifted off, to get a decent overview of the living sea, I would have. I tried to work out if this were the Atlantic ocean or the Bay of Mexico. I wasn't able to get the island or the key's shape fixed correctly in my unmapped head, or if I did, the right guess was as wrong as the wrong one, since I didn't know the difference. I made a map in my head none the less, and put Miami on it and Fort Lauderdale, and the town of Key West, and whatever of Texas I was aware of, and judged the possible distance of New York, and the impossible distance of Cuba and the Caribbean. In the centre of this crisp map I placed myself, a black x on a yellow beach beside a blue and white sea, under an aluminium sky. I distinctly heard the parchment make a beaky scratch as I appeared on it. And I perversely dotted the x to mark an ideal head.

The bishop was often seedy in his blood and had a repetitive pain in his shoulder. He prayed now and then for this pain to disappear, which it always did, but as surely returned. His housekeeper prayed for the pain in her legs to stop. Neither of them was aware of the other's pain or prayers.

He would have been busier with and distracted by the affairs of the diocese if there had been more of them, but each year the parish priest annexed more of the episcopal duties to his younger self, out of a publicly-declared desire to relieve the bishop of his burdens. But it only made the pain in the old bishop's shoulder worse, and this was the root of his severe dislike and despising of the priest.

When the baby had been discovered decorated with a knitting-needle, and the cottage of the old prostitute gutted by a vengeful fire, the bishop had wanted to discover all the facts of the case for himself, and be sure nothing was left unturned and unbaked by a judicious heating. The body of the baby had been long rotten by the time he was even suffered to read the slightest document on the matter. He wasn't sure how the parish priest worked this insubordination, but he suspected it had much to do with his own fuddled memory and galloping years. Every year was certainly shorter in effect, but each one pressed heavier on him when it had passed, and seemed to be constructed of a metal of an extremely dense mass. He was wary of this process and had to spend good parts of his rusted days mumbling to himself about the evil competence of the lowly priest. Because of this history he was determined for once to have his way with Moran.

The figure of the young idiot was a ludicrous element of the city and he intended to be rid of the spectacle. Without mentioning anything to his housekeeper or anyone else, he wrapped his black scarf about his chicken neck one morning, and swept as confidently as his frame would let him into the centre of the town.

On the flaking wall of the town barracks was a large well-printed poster, advertising the immediate need for men to go and fight in some war. The place was very distant, and hard and long to reach, and this seemed the ideal war for Moran as far as the bishop was concerned. The last thing he wanted to achieve was Moran's being wounded in some country near at hand, and being invalided home, or what passed for home, where the invalid might languish for ever, at the expense of the council and the church. Also the war in question was in Africa, and the bishop saw the aptness of sending Moran to the same continent that held his own neglected bishopric. He wished in a way that the area might have been the very same place in his enthusiasm, but even so he felt pleased and useful as he jangled the barracks' bell, and was respectfully admitted.

While Moran perched idly in the sun on the harbour wall some miles distant, the bishop leaned close to the Recruiting

Officer, and whispered in his delicate thin syntax the inspired purpose of his appointment. The Recruiting Officer was catholic and rather characterless in his answers. It didn't seem unusual to him that the bishop should suggest some young fellow's signing up. People often came to him on similar crusades, husbands and sons and dafties and wives, either recommending themselves at short notice, or recommending others. He didn't care really how he got his men and listened to the bishop's preamble with a firm *yes* ready for whenever the old rogue might be finished. He respected the bishop because the bishop had been successful in his career as priest, but he didn't respect the bishop as a man. To him he was an old white fogey in a black dress, and that was that.

'Listen, my lord, I'll go down to the harbour today and get a hold of this Moran chap and have him fixed up by nightfall. Will that suit you?'

'Eh?' said the bishop. 'Truly?'

'Truly. No difficulty about it. You just get yourself back to your fire and I'll take care of it.'

The office was glittery under its recent dust and the bishop was ruffled by the avuncular tone of the soldier. Did the man think he was senile? But he twisted out of the chair and nodded at the officer, and nodded again, and disappeared effectively out of Moran's life, having taken so great a part in it. For Moran might never have come even to the little he did come, without the fussing animosity and planning of the cleric.

And he did not of course know remotely what brought the smart bright gentleman down to the wharf to fetch him. He was still sitting there, dangling his pipey legs, and thinking about nothing much more than the colour red, which lived in tiny specks here and there about the water of the surging harbour. The hard high man stood for a while looking down at the unkempt object in a variety of inadequate rags and wondered for a moment exactly what the old bishop was up to. This chap didn't appear to have the full shilling, and didn't look like much of a candidate for the king's shilling.

'What's your name?' the officer said to the ragged head, and Moran peered up at the petalled shaven face and spoke for the first time in a few years:

'Moran I amme,' he said. 'I cum fram ovvir ther.'

167

As he didn't point anywhere in particular the officer wasn't much the wiser. But at least the boy could talk, even if his accent was odd, and even rather English for a beggarly Irish person.

'You have family here in Sligo, Moran?' he asked.

'Famlee? Yars,' said Moran. 'Oh yars, I have em.'

'Where?'

'Der ganne,' he said. 'Dispeered.'

'Ah yes,' said the officer. 'You're an orphan. Perfect.'

'Noo,' said Moran. 'I amme nat. Bat I wasse an orfan whan I hadde a famlee.'

'Right,' said the soldier. 'Right. Well, how would you like to join the army then? Do you fancy that?

He stared at Moran and Moran stared at him.

'Wat isse dat?' said Moran, with his face creased to find the word inside him. He was better equipped to discuss orphanhood.

'To fight,' said the Recruiting Officer. 'You know, war, and so on.'

'You wante me for dat?'

'If you want to. Free choice. Free world. Well?'

'Where?' said Moran.

'Not here,' said the officer.

'Den I will cum.'

And Moran abandoned the part of himself that celebrated the harbour.

Sixfoil Ten

The bishap his eyen, Moll, oftene reflected anudder pare of eyez, whan der was none udder ta bee mirroored. Dat iz ta saye, hes eyez hatte a strang dooble qualitee. Perhaps den, ye wull agree dat he were a ver dangruss fellaugh: smal folke ar many teems mare periloos dan grayter.

In de dingoon uf Olleve his hoos, de bishop helt a servante of his owen person, who hat spilt sam biling soop on de hooly manne hes fingoors, an paintet der a rounde redde scarre. For dis badde accidente de servante, who wasse in midel yers, gotte hes opportunitee to knowe de dree darke rooms whach floated in blaknesse undder de liffe uf de castelle.

In de litul music of an afternoone, de bishop Larentious tippled down de narro grene steppes, wid a dancin candel. He felte de wide warme medows spraddin oot fram de foldy castool, but also he felt de angoor still colouret on hes hant. He braght wid him a smal silber boxe, whach was deepe an lockt in hes foldy poket.

De servante was jest a pillow of clothe in de darkness, whar he was stratched and tiede on a lang wooden tabel. All perts of de manne war strictlee pinioned, an he cud nat move neider head nor legge. Twa blocks of wud at edder side of hes cheeks made sure he hadde ta staer uppe to da vanisht roof.

'Why, why, moi faitful manne,' sed Larentius wid a laff. 'I tink ye maye be sorree nowe, dat I wasse so sorelee burnt be yer stupiditee.'

De manne wasse betwan dreme an wakin, and did nat trulee here de bishap. Hes minde hat broght hem to some odder plac, and hes hert was given hem a storee dere, to companion sich a devize.

'Wak up, wak upp, moi ladde!' shouted Larentius, 'I wull nat haff you slep whiel I muste taulk to you.'

De mann returnt inta de boggee room, an stranglee smilt at

de rounde blak figoor.

'Ha, lorde bishap,' he sedde, ' I am sorre for yer hant. An it will hardlee be so agin dat I wud scorche ye.'

'Maybe, may be,' sed the bishap. 'I do half beleev ye. But here in dis foin boxe I haff a litel grup of tings, dat will finde oot de trut for uzz, moi palle. Let me laye de box at yer cheke almoste, so ye canne feel its gud chasin. Dis boxe is oweld an forin, an will nat let oot wat it holdes widoot me tellin it.'

De eyez of de servant tride ta swivvel an viewe de tooled boxe, bat he cud nat clerely doo it.

'Wal, pitee it isse dat you can nat examin et, Micel, bacarse perhap it isse sometin for me ta putte in yer mout.'

'Why, moi lorde? Iss it fuud?'

'It isse nat,' said Larent.

'And iss it swete den, moi larde?'

'No, no,' he sed.

'Or drinke? Iss it drinke?'

'No, nat drinke,' sed de bishap. 'nor fuud nor swete. But stil it maye go in yer mouthe, if we wishe.'

'I do nat wishe, moi bishap,' the manne whisperet. 'Do plese lete me fre an I wull serve ye beter.'

'Ah, beter,' sed the bishap, 'is nat always muche on yer accunt. Ye ar anly a litel uselez manne. But if ye will do my wholesomme biddine affter diz widdoot complainte, I wull nat put de contenz of dis silver boxe in yer silver stomik.'

The browen flur an de browen wallz an de browen ceeling sange in de mannes head, lik an oweled peece uf thunderre comin ovver hilles.

'Wat do ye mene fer mee, moi pooerfal preest?' he sedde, as a tinee tune inta de browen.

'Jest dat yoo be troo an gutt an, iff needz be, yoo will be quik and exacte to my deseer.'

'I wull, master bishap, I wull.'

'I see,' sedde Larentius. 'Wall, I am nat a harde badde manne, as ye knowe. I do nat wishe ta harmme yoo. Bat on de udder sied, I wud lovve ta see wat dis box mite do ta yer mout.'

'How so?'

'It mite kep it shutte batter den a promiz. An ye cud nat telle wat I haff dun to yoo.'

'I wud nevver telle a soule, moi bishap, by moine own sowel.'

'Ah yesse, yer sowel, moin manne. Yer soule is somtin elz. Who carres aboot de promiz uf yer sowel? Whan I havv me litul silber boxe an wat es inseid.'

De servante began ta fere like a smal childe, an hes cheste quivert lik a basin uf watter.

'Doant do some badd ting to mee, bishap, or yee might go ta helle.'

'Ta helle izz it, ye rascalle? Ta hell, did ya saye?'

An de bishap latte hes fiste falle softlee on de noez of de manne.

'I wull brak yer noze if yoo do nat shutte yer trappe.'

De manne kepte quiet, bat he felte all de dred an miseree of a nightesmere. As he cud nat waken, he wisht he cud slep, and nivver see de bishap again, whan after dremes he woke.

'I wante yer promiz dat yoo wille keel a manne fer mee, if I wishe yoo.'

'Wat manne?' sed de servante. 'Wat manne?'

'Leve dat questoon bee. Will yoo so acte for mee?'

'I can nat tak a lief, moi lorde – it wud ruinne moi soule, as yoo might saye, anodder tiem.'

'Ah, yasse, dat's soo. Bat stille I wishe it, an after I cin forgivv de sinne fer yoo, an yoo wille nat droppe ta hel.'

'Bat, bishap, if I do nat, den who will forgive this thinge fer yoo? Der iss no grater pooer of absolutoon in dis lant.'

'Wat arr ye, som grat philosofer, moi frende?'

'No, bat you friten my verree herte, grat Lawrenz.'

'Yazz, I ixpecte I do. Soo yoo will doo dis fer mee?'

'Bat I muste nat, bishap, I muste nat. An whach mann do ye wishe ta keel? Iss it moi eagelmanne, lorde Olevver?'

'Iss nat yer mout too bigge an fowel, yoo mousse?' sed Larentius. 'Bye heven, I tink ye arre a dertee litel traytor. Wud I stoppe de brett of moi kinge, ye smal fieldy bulle? Moi god in hes lant, bat ye are cruelle.'

'I did nat saye I wanted my gental lard ded.'

'Ye did, I herd ye. An nowe, ef yoo do natte be obediente as you muste an shud, I will telle hes axemanne ta role yer skulle. An I wull drye it, an tink uponne yer vanitee whan yar stinke hasse flowen. Ughe, I doant wishe fer yoo ta do a smalest ting fer mee nowe. Lat me unclicke moi boxe, an showe yee wat is dere.'

In de darke aire, a sound of smaleste metal flickt an diede.

'Dont hurte me, ye feelty bishap!' sed de servante. 'Boi godde an hes divilz, I wull curz ye til yer teet ete inta yer bellee!'

'Wall, here are teethe sinze so ye speke, an lette ye enjoi dem.'

'Wat teethe are dey?'

'Maggottes, moi frende, swete maggottes ta mine inta yer braine – an stomik too, if ye canne kindlee swallowe uppe a few.'

'Yoo foule shitte aginst de groun! Ye madde maggotte-manne, go waye fram mee!'

An de servante scremt wid a fulle echoin clamoor, an de bishap dropt wan gloomee maggot inta de wident lippes.

'Der, smal pette. Pleze ete yer hertes contente of moi badde servante.'

Batte de manne bitte on de sqermin ting to moorder itt, and begt:

'I wulle blade an batter whoo yoo wishe, moi larde!' he sedde.

Did you ever see him alone?

No, I did not. Or not that I remember.

That is rather a strange fact.

It is.

I wonder how companioned you are, as it were, by others who could report as much?

I do not know.

How do you like Key West in comparison to, say, Highgate?

Pretty well.

Perhaps you are an American at heart?

I do not think Key West is particularly American.

Perhaps not. But it hangs here, like a ravelled cloth, at the bottom of America.

Yes it does.

You are being facetious.

Perhaps just a little.

How is the morning with you?

It is counting, I suppose.

Perhaps you are a child at heart?

How so?

To judge by your light answers to my serious questions.
You dislike the light?
No, but it merely fills, if you follow me.
Ah yes, but I prefer that.
The heart of the matter doesn't interest you, then?
No, not as much as the light.
Oh which light did you mean?
The light light.
What was that about never seeing him alone?
What indeed?
Stand out in front of everyone here now and tell us.
I can not. It is breakfast time.
But the skinny girl is waiting for you, and she frightens you
a little with her unremarkable healthiness.
If only that were true.
She bores you then?
Alas, she terrifies me.
If you are so calm and simple as you make out, why then.
Why then what?
Why don't you get off your big dark bed, my friend, and
concentrate.
Like orange-juice, you mean?
If you like.
On what or into what though?
Take your pick.
I was finished with Highgate.
But you haven't mentioned the Heath.
That would only be a dream.
Perhaps you only remember it as a dream, and in fact it was
real.
I hope not.
It frightened you?
Alas. Yes.
What happened?
I can't remember.
Come on, Oliver, you remember.
I did remember but I've forgotten.
Shall I tell you?
Do you know it?
Was it on the Heath?

Yes.

Was it on the path where your mother taught you to fly?

Well. She pretended to.

It was a Sunday, wasn't it? A Sunday walk, and you found witches' brooms under the bushes.

No, that was another time.

Then you didn't take off like foxes and fly over Highgate?

Not that time anyway.

What did you do then?

You were telling me.

No, I was asking you.

Then ask me.

Was that the time when you were alone, and in the distance somewhere you heard the invisible schoolboys singing *The shepherds wash their socks by*.

No.

It was.

No.

Their socks by night it was, wasn't it?

Not really.

Yes it was. And you were very naturally alone on the dry brown track standing on top of dead leaves.

No.

Yes you were.

Maybe. Go on.

You want me to?

Not really.

Perhaps you prefer the story of the frog?

Hardly.

Well that is a simple story. You went to play with your friend, and the tool-shed was being demolished, and there was a frog there, and you were given it in a box. You wanted it. And his father drove you home, and the man was a doctor, and.

Why are you telling that story now, and so badly?

Because it has occurred to me.

You'd want to get yourself under control.

Well, anyway. You were pretending not to want to go home, and sitting on in the seat with the frog, and the doctor nearly blew your ears off with a bangy shout to jump the hell out of his car, because he was in a hurry to get to the hospital.

Why not stick to the Heath? At least the Heath had the merit of a dream.

What's wrong with the frog?

Because, I told my sister, and she told my father after all, because she couldn't help it, and he went down to the back garden to where I had hidden it, and he released it.

What's wrong with that?

You told it before.

Oh.

So shut up when I tell you.

We'll talk about the Heath then.

You will. I am not listening.

You'd do well to listen.

Why? It was only a dream.

Okay then a dream, and the black bushes were spiky, and waist-high, like in *Wuthering Heights*.

What do you mean? How does that come into it?

Like in *Wuthering Heights*. The thorn garden your man has.

You can't say that. You didn't read *Wuthering Heights* until you were fourteen.

All right, for god's sake, the thorns were waist-high and black, like nothing more than themselves, and you were leaning a little towards the brown sweep of the track, and you wanted to go home, but it was muddy.

You wanted to go home.

Not the same thing.

Not likely.

As you please. There was a large brown beard floating in the sky a few feet above your hair.

You're joking.

I'm not.

That's not frightening.

I didn't say it was.

So why mention it?

Because it was frightening in the dream.

Why?

Because the beard was very like the bushes, and it had eyes.

Children are too easily disturbed.

You're telling me.

So what happened?

Nothing.

Nothing?

Nothing. You were fixed there with everything in you dead as a stone, except your eyes, and your fear. You needed to speed down the hill and kick the leaves, and for your mother to be there, but none of those things was able to happen.

Paralysed.

What did you say?

You were paralysed.

Well in a manner of speaking.

What were the eyes doing?

Which ones?

His.

They were looking at you.

Did he speak?

No. He had no mouth.

Just staring then. Did he move?

No, like you he was stuck, or still at any rate.

It doesn't sound frightening.

No. But it was.

But it was certainly a dream.

I don't know. Maybe it was a sort of madness.

Maybe the picture has bits missing?

Yes. Possibly it was real, and the mouth was there also, along with his torso and legs and arms.

Precisely.

And we were paused for a moment there, and you liked him.

Oh possibly. I often liked him.

Did you?

Yes. I always liked him.

Really?

As a child.

And now?

And now I like him even more.

Why?

Because he's not simple.

But is he a good man?

I don't know.

Are you?

I don't know either. Probably not.

But you surprise me. I mean, saying that you like him.
He's just a bit cumbersome, that's all.
How do you mean?
I mean, to carry about inside yourself.
Oh?
Yes. His beard sticks in my throat.
Dear me.
Yes, it chokes me somehow. I wish he'd get out.
No?
Yes, I wish he'd get out. He won't though.
Is he very hairy?
He is impossible.

Any train that runs into Switzerland seems twice as smart as almost any train running almost anywhere else. Since Sue and I never take trains, it seems in a way as if I haven't been on a real journey for a long time. Trains, I suppose, to me, are true journeys.

But the Swiss train was so clean and new and well-lit that it reminded me more of fresh plastic-lined coffins in American death-parlours, than that old buried-underground-and-safe-from-everything feeling that most traditional European trains promise – even if it is only a tradition of fin-de-siècle morbidity. Victorians, of course, were quite fond of death, and their notions seeped on into the architecture of trains, more so than it did into the architecture of poetry. Most travellers probably would be natural threepenny novel readers, if such things were still on offer at station stalls.

The odour of perfect blue plastic made me vaguely nauseous on the journey, and when we tore through the advertisement hoardings stretched proudly on Berne rooftops, or rather tore among them, and began to reverse our speed for the station, I had a thin exhausted early-morning definition to my bones. The week alone with my catastrophe had rinsed and dried and shrunk me.

I had by now almost entirely taken over the character of Degas' café woman: she probably didn't miss it. I was walking around with a black scrap of canvas for hair, and my face was chalked and different when I met it in glasses. I felt spectral and lumpy and highly unsuitable somehow to be on that business-like train – so much inside what I called life, in my misty fashion, even as it streaked through it.

There were simple ceremonies to be gone through, between myself and the customs men, since I made the usual mistake of looking into their eyes, rather than gently passing by them in an assumed daydream. I was arrogant and curled with them because I knew I had nothing, and that they had only stopped me because my hair was cut peculiarly short. I had done this as a gesture towards the new existence with Xenia, whether it was to be short-lived or not. She could have me now as I had been in Greece, and god help her.

I knew she was looking forward to this strange lurching start of ours, and would have page-length plans. And I wanted plans too, except it was hard to believe in any that stretched beyond the next few weeks. I had made my pact with the god of Notre Dame and the copper angels on the roof, and didn't anticipate more than that.

In between intense sweating idiofying panic, it made me very calm to think like that. It was a perversion of the acceptance of death which gives peace to life.

Although I sensed my poverty and grubbiness by comparison with the other travellers, who were mostly shell-shocked businessmen, I also sensed them with what seemed a glowing comprehensive vision of their qualities: any gesture a mother made to a child, or a girl to her boyfriend, sent my memory out of control and careering across folding chapters of connected information. My fear might have led me all the way to Adam with the correct stimulus.

Xenia was waiting on the border between France and Switzerland, which appeared to be nothing more than a plate-glass window. She was also waiting on the border between herself and the green crosses and the long rain of Paris, and that huge second-packed-on-second species of time that I had endured on my own.

I had been caught between not sleeping till dawn and then dozing on into early afternoon, and then not being able to sleep till dawn again. The astonishing repetition of my brace of worst fears went rampant and individual after the dark arrived, and

coloured the noise of the continuous December downpour. I
had been even happy to abandon the senseless informative numbers of the lit clock, that persisted in telling me what time it
was, when what I wanted was lack of time and dreams. Asleep
everything was normal and liveable, and I never dreamed of
what troubled me – so naturally I longed to sleep. To wake was
a daft nightmare.

But even so I also feared the process of falling asleep, and was
finely conscious of my brain straining out into the normally-
slumbering little hours of other people's morning. And the
whole of Paris flew out of beds at seven o'clock and flooded the
undergrounds and put talk and chatter into the cafés and the
offices, while I finally let go and was let go of, and faded away
into the only possible life.

There was Xenia, calm on that border, and I crossed over it
with the passion of an illegal immigrant. I was shocked to discover the misery stepping over neatly with me. We embraced,
not for the last time in a station. Her long leathered breast
clutched me and I smelled the coffee washed hair against my
face. She was there right enough, but monstrously I was not, I
couldn't arrive. I hoped not too many young men upset themselves to such low degrees, and that someone knew how to
travel to their lady without such self-torture and sleeplessness. I
realized I was overdoing it in the normal sense, but not to have
overdone it seemed the mathematics of a genius. Having taken
fright I was running now, and only a high hard wall could stop
me. Xenia was solid and tall enough, but it appeared I had
leaped her with terrified ease.

We walked out into an odd city that I didn't recognize then
and never recognized afterwards, even passing through the same
spot. A raised highway served the same route as a lower
ground-level road – a remarkable bluely-watered arrangement.
At the restaurant I was more involved with the intense
geometry of the tables, and the split-level floor, than hearing
what Xenia was saying. I answered her well enough, but I still
had the very clear notion that I had not been able to reach her. I
was stuck in the doctor's waiting-room even now, and I should
have gone back to get myself. I should have gone back and killed him with his paperweights. But I felt slipped into a tight
envelope, with nothing to read except one unhappy brief mes-

sage in perpetuum. And she was beautiful without a doubt, and even if she frightened me she frightened me under a different quotidian category. I couldn't understand what she said to me but she was extremely important all the same, though she couldn't be the bureaucracy to my escape.

To rest the engine we stopped at an old café far from anywhere in particular. A hand of houses spread about the corrugated-iron shop, and in the porchless doors hard-looking old men sat with baskets of very large tomatoes. I supposed they were for sale, but who there was to choose and buy wasn't clear. The brown dried faces hung stiffly over the glowing painterly fruit. The globes gathered in their separate baskets like photographed fire. The men's eyes were mesmerized by the action of nothing happening on the baked street: even our dusty arrival didn't budge their enthusiasm. It lay as buried and as secret in them as the moist pips in the tomatoes.

The bar was lit mainly by the green baize of the pool-table. No one was going to such lengths as playing, and no one was serving behind the sunless bar. Chicken and Sue raised their eyebrows at each other in some kind of pantomime, but they pulled out chairs just the same into the shade of the shop awning. I waited there at the notched wooden counter, with my foot up on the rest, and listened to the small radio sound of their voices outside. I had been looking forward to a beer, and this was a hall of beer.

The area behind the bar was very neat and well-stocked. Someone had polished the beer-sticks and the bottles, and even the cans of Budweiser and Ströhs may have had a swipe of the rag.

Chicken laughed loudly under the awning and Sue cantered after him with a higher sillier laugh. It upset me for a second to hear her so friendly and happy with him. But then maybe she wasn't really feeling that. She was a good pretender.

The green metal lamp stretched down to where it would light the pool-table properly, if switched on, and it and the empty chairs made the place sort of cinematic and familiar. It was like a set for a cowboy film. But the old men with their silent faces

180

and the bounty of tomatoes didn't fit in with that. They were strange to think of. I hadn't seen any greenhouses or such, so I supposed the weather in this part of the country was clement enough for a natural approach to tomatoes.

Well, the barman didn't seem to be coming, so I said *Hello* into the blank barrier of the bottled wall. I struck the back of one hand against the palm of my other, and said aloud in the room:

'Fuck me.'

Then a little girl trickled out from an invisible dark door at the far recess of the shop, and clacked down to me, past the solid table. She had light wooden shoes on.

'You want somethin, mister?'

'Well, I wouldn't mind a drink. Is your pa around?'

Sue stopped listening to Chicken for a moment, and leaned her bright head into the room to get a look at the girl.

'Hey, come here, chicken,' she said.

Chicken's voice mumbled some words behind the plate window, and Sue turned back to him and said:

'No, I was talking to a little girl in there.'

The girl didn't respond much, but she relaxed on to her heels, and stroked the new baize on the table with a small white hand.

'Pa ain't here,' she said.

'Oh all right. Well maybe you can get me a drink, sweetheart?'

'Nope, I don't think so.'

Her clear dry eyes didn't leave my face, but they focused there as impersonally as a car-beam or a torch. She was extremely slim and a little crooked in her body. Her plain white dress looked a bit like coarse sackcloth. Her cheeks had the dull rounded glow of fruit.

'Then we have a problem,' I said.

Sue's head tossed in again.

'Is she getting us beer?' she said. 'The little one?'

'No, I don't think so,' I said, 'or that's what she says.'

And I turned my hands at the wrists, and let my palms lift the heavy air of the room.

'Hey, chickadee,' said Sue, with a funny Spanish accent, 'what's the trouble? Don't you like us?'

'But he ain't here, and he don't let me serve.'

181

'Who don't?' said Sue.

'Her old man,' I said.

'Oh.'

'I don't have an old man. I hate the old men,' said the little girl.

I looked at Sue, and said:

'It's an Irish expression.'

And perhaps I should have said it clearly to the girl too.

'You all right?' said Sue, and her eyes narrowed, and she slipped off her iron chair, and strode in from the different moving air of the outside. She walked up the the girl, who was half her size, and put her neat hand under the child's chin, and lifted the odd face.

'What you been crying about?' she said.

'I wasn't,' said the girl.

'Your eyes are all swollen, child, what's the matter with you?'

'It's the tomatoes,' said the girl. 'They make my eyes swell.'

'Is that all you eat around here? Tomatoes?'

'No, but I like em,' she said. 'I like em a lot.'

'So where's your pa then?' said Sue, in her unnatural motherly voice. 'Eh?'

And she held the small chin a little tighter, till the child tried to wince back.

'You hurtin me.'

And the girl plucked her face out of Sue's fingers, and vanished into the pitty murk of the interior.

'I wasn't hurtin her,' said Sue, and she leaned her breast against my arm, and her smooth stomach seemed to get hitched on my hip bone.

'Honey, that was nice last night,' she said, and her eyebrow flicked up and down once, like the humped back of a caterpillar. 'Like to show me how you did that sometime?'

I felt a laugh make an old pattern on my face, and held her strongly with one weak arm. She was slim but there was a layer of softness all over her.

'Podunk,' she said, 'I'd marry you now if you weren't just an old wanderer. My little wandering Jew.'

And she stuck a bitten-nailed finger into the underside of my nose.

'Shit, you do hurt people,' I said. 'No wonder that kid ran for it.'

182

I squeezed the tortured bit softly.

'I get a bit excited when I do that,' she said. 'It's like a rabbit in my muscles.'

'Do what?'

'Pinch you or make you hurt just a little.'

'That's very nice for you. How would you like it?'

'Oh. Probably a lot.'

And she put her face right into mine, so her skin was blurred. But her eyes were like stones in a river, and she laughed heartily, so it was like being at the centre of a tiny explosion.

Then the child was suddenly back again, and there was a man beside her in overalls and a cloth of dust.

'Which of you hit my little girl?' the man said, with a metallic Kentucky accent.

Sue stayed resting against me, but she turned her head and nodded it, as if it were on a spring, but said nothing. He pulled up his shotgun where it had been trailing on the floor, and he said:

'You better say, lady.'

'What you think you are? A cowboy, or somethin?'

The man let go the paw of the girl, and dragged back the hammers and I gripped Sue's soft arm to make her quiet.

Johnnie kept his shell-blue cap on at all times, because you could see, Moll, that there was no hair to slip down from under it, and the best guess was that he was bald. We were out on the deep emotional waters of the bay, and Ali held his short rod idly, but with a definite expertise. Yet another of his skills had become apparent. We fished in the thick-looking water, while Johnnie attended slowly to the wheel, and the light insect of the engine. A rich blue colour jumped off the water into the air, which was almost sore on the daytime eye. The blue gushed up like a huge geyser, but it was motionless too. Ali's hedgy beard grabbed his chin, but apart from that his body was dipped and switched-off in the chair.

'Hey, Ali,' said Johnnie. 'I wanted ta ask ye. You're what they call a rasta-man, right?'

'That's right. Rasta-man,' said Ali. 'Dat's what I am.'

'Right, but, now, what do you guys do when it comes to gettin marriage, or such?'

'It's like anywan, Johnnie: the woman is for the man, and that's the end of the story.'

'Right, right. I was just wondering.'

And then for a long while we didn't offer a word to the held blue energy of the bay.

'The children are important too,' said Ali.

Johnnie looked at him quickly, and said *uh-huh*, and let his eyes yawn out to sea again. The sun in the boat and the sun outside the boat felt like two different sorts of metal. Johnnie whistled in a little stream. The tune was *Alabama Bound*, and he had quite a few grace notes to throw against its famous monotony. He liked its monotony though. Then he sang a few lines of it all under his breath:

'I'm Alabama bound, I'm Alabama bound, I'm Alabama, silk pyjama, Alabama bound.'

He sang with a wooden private lack of tone, like a madman's whisper. His round brown face turned to us, and he laughed at something. The boat purred on over the careless businesslike surface. Johnnie made a noise in his teeth, and blew some tuneless air out of his mouth in a sort of sighless sigh. He was still talking to himself really, but suddenly he said:

'Well, Ali, what would it be now if a man in your place were a queer, you know, a gay guy?'

Ali lay calm like a big safe tiger for another bit. He didn't seem to be thinking it over, but rather waiting for Johnnie's words to reach him. The air was very solid, and the words had to be strong blue birds to cross the soupy boat.

'In rasta,' he said, 'in rasta it doesn't happen. No. It wouldn't be. The men go with the women.'

'Oh yeh, well, and if there is a guy, you know, if there just is one.'

'There isn't one,' said Ali, without any emphasis. 'It doesn't happen.'

'Hell, Ali boy, there's always queers, I'm tellin ye.'

Johnnie had got a little excited about this and only his hand on the wheel had remained as before. He spoke as if someone might be listening, and although he wasn't whispering, he adopted the attitude of a whisperer.

'It's nature's law, Ali,' he said.

'No,' said Ali again. 'It can not be, man, because rasta does not allow.'

'Okay, okay, and when it just so happens that a rasta-man falls in love, Jesus Christ, with another regular man, what then?'

'It doesn't happen, because if it did, we would have to kill him.'

Ali's words slipped over the side of the boat, and sank like a bait into the sea.

'You'd kill him? Aw, come on,' said Johnnie.

'Oh yes, mon, we'd just remove him. But you see, mon, it never happens.'

'It happens, of course it happens,' said Johnnie. 'Holy shit, you sit there like a statue with a tape-recorder stuffed up its ass, and you tell me one of the most, the most natural things in the world, in the whole world, never happens.'

Ali moved his shoulders in a cottony shrug. He was still wearing the exact same clothes he had on when I first met him. He washed them out every few days, and between their age and the bleaching sun they were looking pretty thin and light. His black skin rose out of the shirt almost aggressively, as if there wasn't any true connection between him and the poor clothes he had to wear. But this great self-possession of his was clearly a first-rate weapon in an argument, because while Johnnie got more and more sure of what he said, Ali remained as sure as he had been at the start, which isn't the same thing. I thought myself that Johnnie was probably right, but Ali, by dint of simple stillness, was making being right a very dubious value.

'So, did you ever have to kill a queer guy? I mean, you say it never happens. But did you ever do that?'

'No. Not me,' said Ali. 'But I've seen it. An it was all right to do that, because if we didn't, then maybe all of rasta would come to an end. You have to be clear, mon, you have to be clear.'

'God Jesus, I don't believe you,' said Johnnie, 'You're too fuckin much, Ali, you know that? Shit, you go around killin people because they're different, and you. Ah, shit.'

Johnnie glared out over the clean colour, and let his heart slow down for a while. He really hated Ali talking like that. Ali's rod did a quick strong flip, and Johnnie was over in a second, and talking to him like he was a lover. Ali didn't need the advice, and seemed to know already about the brake on the reel, and whatever else Johnnie had to say. But he listened with obvious attention. They had got themselves into a bit of a bad corner with the argument, and neither of them had wanted the argument, and now it could be forgotten in the arrival of the strike. They were close now, like lovers. But they weren't remotely that at all. Because since Ali had all borders and allotments exactly drawn, his brand of friendship could be as intimate as his silent belief wished. He and Johnnie could have slept naked in the same bunk, one on top of the other, and it would never enter Ali's mind that there was something sexual involved in it. It didn't happen so therefore it couldn't be, and if it did happen, you killed it. I wondered if Johnnie so was gay, as his talk half-suggested. But I knew from Ali that he had a young whore that he lived with noisily in the harbour.

Johnnie liked Ali, but he didn't like him to be so strange about such a straightforward natural thing. He liked him to be strange about most other things though. It was better to see them working the fish together.

After a full pulled minute the rod returned to its stiff passionless state, and Ali slumped back without surprise, in the canvas seat.

'Ah shit,' said Johnnie, 'we could have used that fish.'

'It doesn't matter. It didn't happen,' said Ali.

If you can imagine an endless train journey through endless difference, you will be at an advantage, as Moran would have been, if he could only have had some little seed of information to begin with. But the sides of the truck were high, and the soldiers were obliged to stand side by side, due to the lack of room and seatage. Also it wasn't possible to put your kit down, because then they would have had to perch on their belongings.

The great boat had taken a long time to reach the tiny continent. Somehow in Moran's eyes the boat was a larger thing, because aboard it there had been good room to feel ill and peculiar in, while ever since the dock and the dark billet, Africa had been only this cramped and ever-moving box. And as the uniforms of the men were a light brown, Moran said to himself over and over:

'Chocolate box, chocolate box.'

So some unseen strength pulled the chocolate box along, and only the scraping and winging of the canvas-awning above their heads suggested that there might be sky, and then possibly earth, to this new land. The trucks made such a rattle that when the men tried to speak to each other, the words got smashed up like chains of glass. And all Moran could hear was smashed cups of syllables and falling plates of words.

He had a great silent liking for the other men with him, and for some reason they considered him one of their own. They called him Moran as if it were a first name, and he was pleased in a white way to be rid now of the name that was not his, namely the Blessed Apostle. The recruiting sergeant had been the instrument of this change, and the sense of uneasiness that Moran had in him, like a cool room, was not encroached upon either by the oily queasy ship, or this travelling carton of men. He felt himself to be appropriate and new. He realized he was young, and much younger than most of the men. But he had never thought of himself as new, and now he felt it. He wore his uniform as an explanation of this well-being, and looked after it and the rest of his stuff with a freshly-discovered ability to preserve things. He wasn't smart so much as shining. His hairless face and intimately-cut hair both sat exactly and rightly under his helmet, and his helmet was a small manufactory of brightness. He couldn't have explained his plain happiness when he saw his legs appear out of his shorts, and quickly disappear into his leggings. It was perfect.

The men were mostly from country towns but none was from Sligo. As the Recruiting Officer had promised, the army was not *here*, but definitely elsewhere, confidently so. He was braced up by the acceptance and the seconding of the soldiers. They didn't think he was stupid, or if they did they didn't think he was different. Nobody knew he had lived with Jane Smith or in a workhouse, or that after that he had walked nine dogs and slept muddily on a wharf. They were as eager to find this out as they were for him to find out about them. No one asked and no one cared. Possibly Moran was affected more serenely than the others by this. Possibly some men considered themselves in a worse trap now than the one they had broken and bolted from and abandoned. And possibly the way Moran saw all this was simplistic and childish. But only he heard these tiny emotions turning in him, and what most of the men heard from him was ordinary efficiency and simple good will.

The train advanced towards its hidden end, and the dry graining of the wooden panels was maps that could not be relied on. Moran's bladder had been filled, innocently, just before being herded on to the train. Among the drab colours of the station, where only British people seemed to exist, the liquid had been bitter but refreshing. Now, under his shorts, he had a small circle of pressure, that could be more or less relieved by slight movements of his legs. The train shook at him, and the evenly-laid tracks made it run like a cart without springs. A flat tumultuous shivering possessed the truck, and eventually got into Moran's stomach and possessed that too. Pinheads of dull sweat pebbled on his forehead, and after a while they dribbled along the lines of his cheeks, and journeyed down under his ears. He could feel the drops enlarging and deciding to move, and he saw their trains in his heated head travel across the unseen country of his face. He could see neither Africa nor himself, and all travels were taking place in the dark of the bright canvassed carriage.

He watched the shaved black hairs of the nape of the man in front of him. It looked very clean and each hair lived separately and evenly. They were like metal pins inserted into the man's skin, a hairbrush. Moran wanted to reach out his hand and stroke the rough hair but he was afraid. And he was glad after a while that he hadn't. He had to preserve the acceptance and ignorance of his companions, just as he had to speak as little as possible, in order not to use what the bishop had called his gobbledegook. So also he had to move as limitedly as he could, because movement seemed to be some sort of language as well: and he observed himself thinking this or that about someone, depending on how they shifted themselves. The least of him moved, the least said. The least said, the soonest mended. He was a broken man, he thought, a broken dog – and now suddenly the parted bits of him were joining again. Except for the more unpleasant calling of his bladder this blind voyaging was bearable. But he wanted the grassy pleasure of pissing now. It was making him feel uneasy and stupid. His bladder was still very stupid, he thought. and now it was behaving like a fool. He had a fool in his belly, and there was no room to tame him or calm him down. He didn't mind his belly being a fool, but all the same he had nowhere to put his foolishness. Then a man said:

'Lads, what would you say if I had ta pee?'

And they started laughing after their silence, and Moran only noticed the silence then.

'Are ye in a bad way yourself, Jem?' someone said, and the rinsed laughter bubbled up again. Then they rotated gratefully, and any man who had to, sprayed his piss into the slipstream, through a small circular cutting in the door. Bladder after bladder with their different histories piped out into the continent they couldn't see. Only the padre declined the splashed hole when it came to him, and carried his shut blade to their destination.

Sixfoil Eleven

De horsse wasse derty whiet, bat stille handsomme. He hat streng and curious charakter, Moll: he hadd sum sarte of equous wissdim. He livt during winter wedder in a slopin feeld, dat hadde mich lite greye and midel greye an blak-greye and blak coloors in et, lik a tapestree.

In somoor whan de rodes war harde and beter fer travels, Con putte hes olde blak-golte saddel an hes foin rustee rug on hem, an wante ta see de bordeers uf hes lant. It tuk thre dayes ta mak a rider his cercle of al. It becam a sort ef rememberenz uf hes fadder, becarse wid hem his fader he had rid de distoonz in de flowenby teems.

De hors wasse nat gladde at ferst to bee callt uponne ta perfarm sich energetick milez, bat suen he setelt, an Con semt ta hem anly anudder pert of hes horsesh bodee. An nowe, Moll, I cum her ta descrieb a teem dat wasse Coone among hes peple. Ye muste reminde yerselff dat de min an wumen, whach livet in hes lant, whar natt wel knowen ta heem batt onn dis onczyerlee jurnee, an hes fader or hes granfader moight have dun as wel for dem as hee. An trulee dey sawe litul break betwan de sorte uf lardes dey hadde. De lard wasse al one, and sonne wasse de similar of fader. He lookt mare lik a godde ta dem, on hes feelty coloored hors, and dey greted hem wid liking, but also wid distresse.

These folke dey persistet inn grasse an muddy huttes, to which der were noe windoos. All day of winterre deye sate insied, an coffed amang de smok. In brite Hulee an de monthe uf Augustus de Romanne empereer, whach warr sesons by daffrent names to dem, the hooses becam mostlee placces fer sleepin. Ech nite Olleever miht lie wid whativver woomin he wisht, thre brests fer thre daies an no more. So hee lookt to dis periodde as a dogge dus to hes dinner.

An here, Moll, as hee trotz oot uf his gates, I feele thiz offten

190

confuzed ande seely manne ta bee mysel, but changt bee de grat rivver uv yers dat seperatez ower bankes.

De rode an wuds abowt de castel were bee natoor familier ta hes memoree. Dey remindet hem aboot hes childhud wekes, whan he ust ta slepe in one warme curle alonge de narro pathes. De smal barrels an tres of cloody sonlight fell throo de branches, an warmt hes hed, an he wasse veree noddin an droozy.

Aftir a bitte he came to a section of the wood he didn't recognize as easilee as beforr, and he knew that he had already drifted out of the well-known surroundings of his castle. The trees here were scrub-oaks and smaller growths, and when he had about five more miles behind him, he found to his great shock that many of the trees had been cut down and seemingly burned. This was directly against any wish of his, and he slowed his horse Jack to a walk in his astonishment. But certainly someone had gone through his forest with a ruthless axe. It wasn't a question of thinning out the dead or poor specimens, but each and every trunk had been hacked a foot or so from the ground. Soon he was riding through an enormous spread of topped and vanished oaks. It was as if a huge bird with a sharp-bladed wing had flown viciously through his best possession. As everyone knew, Moll, the trees were his life, and in some way him himself. His father had always told him to guard the trees as if they were his people, because, his father said, the trees were friendly to the people, and their roots were the roots of talk, and anything that was good in the Conn tribe. Once Master Owl had shown him a strange piece of parchment with black drawings on it. Each was the shape or borrowing of a tree, and this, Owl said, was the origin of men being able to laugh and tell stories. This tree alphabet was forgotten in its uses, but still it showed how important the oaks were to the well-being of the tribe. To see them hacked and removed in such quantities on his own dominion, made his arms weak and his stomach stiff with sickness. The ground around the hilled trunks was brown and dry, as if feet had been walking back and forth on every inch of it. The layer of last autumn's leaves had been mulched at first, and then rubbed to a powder. The powdery brown earth held the savaged stumps, and the grey low sky lidded the expanse of sameness.

On a different horizon he reached a clearing that he felt he had been in another time. The brittle houses had been crushed and razed, and the inhabitants had been turned into a bizarre form of roofing. Thrown up on the mounds of sticks and clay that marked a ruined house, was each member of each household. They had been quite neatly arranged to demonstrate the different heights of man and woman, and whatever children they had had. Oliver saw how often it was true that a woman is longer than her husband.

Even the village dogs had been tossed on with the rest of the refuse, and it was so odd and miserable to view that Conn didn't know if he was horrified or mad. All the bodies had dried out to nothing in the sun, and they were flat and loose-skinned, like leather bags. Still there was a cloudy stench in the place, and he remembered what he had seen before of corpses, and considered it probable that before they had dried to this state, the stench of corruption would have been enough to kill a living man.

About fifty people, from older shapes half-shrivelled when they were slaughtered, to very fresh babies, had been arranged on the debris. Oliver didn't know what he might do. He wished Owl were with him, who could advise him on the best ceremony, to make sure they didn't suffer in their darker deaths.

His horse stepped through the village with a muscular loathing. He shrank in his hide even as he was moved forward. Where the village ended the few fields began, and these too had been burned off, and still had their scorched blackings like old cloths. Then the chopped forest began again, and went on and on into the useless distance, over whatever the country there had of hills or folded ground. A blakberd scuteld oot uf a bushe wid sich tearin of de leves dat it woke Olleeve. He shivveret, an licket hes mout ta tak awaye de dry nighte cloth it hade. He wasse nere de ferst villeg in hes domaine, amang de riche darke oakes, an he wasse happee in dat berdy wakin.

Absence makes the heart grow ignorant, possibly. The night taxi peeled us off London like plasters, and stuck us down after the metamorphic plane journey into the inky bottle of a new country. The new country was the old one we had been taken from before. But now, miraculously, we were as much strangers here again as we had been on going to England. High-gate had given me a Highgate accent, and a long trailing memory of daily friends there and daily procedures.

This less interesting sort of taxi pulled in to a drive among shrubby rhododendrons, and a weak white lamp over a door. My mother was whitened and young and she grappled with her new landlord alone. The sea slept and woke to a cycle of time all its own, at the bottom of the hedged garden.

My father was at my school in spirit. He lay in the lines of the catechism I couldn't read, and smiled at me, godishly. He was the painting competitions I wasn't inaccurate and colourful enough to win.

I rang the bell of his skull in my hand each evening when everything was over. His breath was in the sandwiches the foreign boys had wrapped in sliced-pan paper, which was waxy and moist. The bigger boys had his clear eyes, and they raised me gently into the sky and dropped me just as gently from their laughing shoulders. Sometimes he was even the spiders that shrank away into the slim deep cracks of the bicycle-shed. The boys my size rolled his marbled eyes in the gutter outside the slaughter-house, and they had to wash sheeps' blood and cows' gore off the chipped gleams.

He had got into everything. And when I walked along the walled road home from school, he winked at me over the broken-bottle defenses of the expensive houses. Any distant figure, even if it were on its way to do something as incongruous as fish, would be a flag of his back.

In the night the sea-light talked at my window, and it had his whispers and his moans. When I knelt my knees on the hard sill, with its stripes of painted wood, the island reappeared in the same spot on moony water that it had been the night before. Something red had happened to the horizon again, and the metal underbell of the sky had been polished and buffed by our cleaning-lady. But we were too poor in that time to have a cleaning-lady, even though we lived in what was called a castle. It wasn't a proper one.

The island across the channel had a martello tower on it, like a hat resting on a snoring man's chest. My father slept with his back in the waves, and the late fishermen passed him gradually in their squashed boats. The window might have been a pane of

193

his glasses for all the difference there was between them. The windows perched on the castle wall like the spectacles on his bricky face, and the house watched me leaving in the bready morning, and slipping back in the bushy afternoon.

My mother was younger than I was, and took me home by a snaky route, that was assisted by fourpenny chocolate bars and talk. She talked about my father and how much he loved me, and I saw his love behind the low railings of the ducking cottages as we drifted past. She told me always how he praised me and liked me, and asked about me in his letters. I read some of those letters once, when I was older and less wise, and I was not mentioned. They worried about his career, and who they could get to help them in Dublin when he came back, but the long solicitous enquiries about his son have been removed or lost. There must have been pages at the end after his signature, that my mother might have put away elsewhere into drawers, which were not cleaned out when we moved away from the island. Where is that island and the white castle, and my mother among the bushes and her youth, and all his asking about me in letters? At this distance any of those elements has as much a chance of having been real and true. After all, the shop with the chocolate was only real if I was, and I was not as real as I might have been.

I was wrong in my eyes most of the time – as I still am. And yet the island was certainly him, as far as my elbows were concerned, growing a little discomfited on the ungiving sill. My mother wrote all the dialogue for his book, but the sea and the houses and the school supplied the simple bewitched narrative.

We were fond of the spring graveyard while we waited for him, and through the evenings she described the wonderful man who admired me, and followed my every action with unusual interest. To have a father was always big news. I was his best if only son, and he was bloody with reality and truth.

We loved the graveyard because the strange epitaphs were there always, as powerful as the day before in their ability to delight and unsettle. We wanted to scuttle like crazy people down the gravelled paths, and out the tall grave gates. But we lingered instead and intoned the serious memorials. When a child was marked, the writers could be quite gay and quaint: it was a different sort of seriousness. The trees there wore green suits like poets, and seemed to claim the composing of the information. The best one had on it: *Here he lies, Hid from eyes, In a sad Pickle, Killed by an icicle.* The victim or martyr to the frost had been done away with at the age of nine. This caused in me a mixture of gladness and horror: glad that an icicle could be so adept, and shocked that a boy of close to my age might be actually ended by such trivia. And then my mother explained the meaning of trivia to me: that it meant what is spoken at the tria via or the cross-roads. And she explained that it was Latin, though she didn't know much more of it. But she was able to make me see the people in white dressing-gowns, standing in the sun without their shoes on, or perhaps with Clarks' sandals, fitted in Nassau Street, talking trivia where the three roads met. The land was very bare around them as the graveyard was not.

The stones were like big spades stuck at various angles in the ground, and the handles broken off annoyingly – or they might have been lids of one sort or another dropped from a height out of an aeroplane, and none of them able to stick in exactly straight, which was equally irritating, in a bearable way. No matter what the stones had to say for themselves I could be fairly sure of one thing. In each pretty coffin in the leafy clay under our exacting and fastidious feet and the sort of connoisseur conversation we went in for, lay sums of my father with their eyes open.

Her parents' house was one of the cleanest and most folded houses in my world. It was smallish but expensively built to an extreme, among other similar houses, remarkable for the smoothing of their details, and the cost of the collective cars out on the pavement.

In the blemishless hallway were two almost human hats, topping a spare stand. One was grey and one was brown. A tall woman, so clean that she might have just been delivered from a factory of well-turned-out middle-age, welcomed her daughter rather religiously. I was inducted into the house with fingered politeness. I may have seemed peculiar and unpromising in my nervous state.

I never did get much further than the door in their house. Whatever their real life was had been perhaps long ago hidden to visitors as casual as her daughter's lovers. Indeed, she referred to Xenia as *your friend*. Xenia was hardly that.

At first sight the nature of the house and its people seemed familiar: after a while it appeared more alien than if I had allied myself to slum-dwellers. It wasn't the middle-classes as I had known them in Ireland. This was something richer and equal but never just the same. They had hundreds of years of trenchant practice and it showed. Even at the first meal I felt anarchistic, and as different as a gipsy might consider himself to a settled household.

They liked my name, which must have looked likely enough on the backs of letters. They mightn't have thought the insides so fruitful, if they had been given them to judge. My letters to someone I had decided I loved were always a mixture of morbidity and attitude, and alphabetical passion. I wanted to be with them, but I feared them too as a nucleus of family.

Her father made no impression at all when he slipped in home and was embarrassingly introduced to me. He dipped upstairs to do what could only have been wash the cleanness off his face and replace it with a new cleanness. He was manager of a small but consolidated bank in the town, and he was on some border between greyed and elderly. Both he and his wife were polite first and searching second. We sat in old wooden chairs at a blindingly-polished round table in front of a lacy window – but the lace had different associations in this elsewhere, and clearly had not been transferred from some old woman's lap in Sicily to the front room without a good many francs passing from pristine palm to rough grained one.

The father was so angled and exact, that he suggested by his merest remark that number eight spiegelstrasse was the middle palace of a small neat kingdom ruled apassionately by himself. He was dangerous in precisely the same way as Xenia was, in that he couldn't be crossed without a revolution. The meal consisted of an eating of smiles, while they excused themselves and talked in their most foreign of tongues about, I supposed, the details of another remunerative day. I fought a sort of sullen happiness in my head, and answered the questions when at length they came, across the geometric channels provided by the table.

The father began with a statement:

'You know, Oliver,' he said, with his nibbling smile, 'when Xenia was in Paris with you, we didn't know where she was there. We didn't know who you were, either. She just left like that, as easy as you would please, yes. Her mother wanted to get Interpol on to the matter: but even though I did also, we did not.'

The effect of this on my face was minutely to dumbfound me. Interpol on the tail of the unkown ruffian Irishman.

'She might have been murdered, you see, and we were worried.'

'Well,' I said, 'she wasn't. Luckily.'

'Ah,' he said, and placed a severe mouthful from his fork on to the perfectly prepared region of his tongue, 'many young girls now, or young women, excuse me, Xenia, disappear from their families: as if a family was of no consequence at all.'

'She would hardly have been in such a situation,' I said, as smilingly as I could manage. 'I mean, Xenia knew where she was. More or less.'

'What?' he said. 'A man she met once on a station in Athens? My god. I said to her: "Don't go," just like that.'

'Yes,' said the mother. 'We thought you might kill her.'

A pause occurred, which was, to my mind, the perfect place for them to say: *But we see now that our fears were unfounded*, or some such endearing adjustment. Nothing of the kind was offered, whether they were thinking it or not.

Xenia, in her red dress, and with a just-noticed flaking and redness, matching the dress, around her porcelain nostrils, stayed silent and even inscrutable in her chair. She ate secretly, it seemed, and paid little attention to what her parents granted to me by way of an introductory conversation. For all the opulence, or rather reserved richness, of the house, and the smart exact country surrounding me, I might just as well have been visiting a tribe of nomads in Mongolia. Because I didn't follow the line of their comments. If it was meant to cheer me up, or quietly insult me, I couldn't tell. This attitude was their form of the sheeps' eyes that traditionally throw off foreigners in other less foreign places.

I manipulated my shoulders slightly, to cast down the feeling of hearing an English that was yet another English, and tried smiling again. They drifted away from me, at least linguistically, for a bit, and ducked themselves in their personal investigations: a conversation that sounded, in terms of simple noise, as accusatory of each other as their approaches to me did. Except that it wasn't accusation, more a statement of things from this special royal point of view. I felt excessively divorced from my own family, and what culture they might represent at home. And as they suspected me as an example of vagabond Irishman, I began to feel like one, if there is such a thing.

After the table was ceremoniously cleared, and wiped by the father, and some television in German, Italian, and French was guessed at, Xenia and I got ourselves into her room.

'What's going on?' I said. 'They think I'm mad, or what?'

'You see,' said Xenia, 'my father imagine Ireland as a place with little houses, with ceilings in grass, and very very poor people, like maybe Yugoslavia. He thinks are no roads.'

'*There* are no roads.'

'What?'

'*There* are no roads: he thinks *there* are no roads.'

'Oh yes. You tell me when it is bad. He thinks there are no roads, and no, what do you says, electricity and water and so on. He is maybe horrified by what he see in his mind.'

'He's mad.'

'I know he is wrong, but he is not mad, no.'

'Xenia?'

'What?'

I was going to pursue the worrying matter, but I said:

'Where can I wash my teeth?'

I thought to myself that, in the face of this sort of trouble, the road was a much more judicious place altogether, and the less we stopped in future the better. If we needed to stop we should stop where there were no other beings remotely related to humans, though this charmer with the gun might not have been that close. The gun had been ragged and rubbed till the barrel burned, even in an interior shrouded and gloomily defined. It gave it a menace, as if it were the extended grinless gesture of the man himself. The child bloomed in grubby white beside him, and he waited for the answer to his miserable unanswerable question.

'I didn't mean to hit her,' I said. 'I'm very sorry.'

The child gawped at me, because I wasn't denying her lie, and even the man seemed a bit surprised. But he didn't have the sort of face that registers marginally complex emotions. He looked vaguely drugged, but it might have been stupidity. He must have been baking, since his knees were dusted with some powder or other.

'You're the one hit her, then?' he said to me.

'Yes,' I said. 'I'm sorry. I didn't think I'd hurt her. Maybe I swung too hard.'

'Oh shit,' said Sue.

The man wanted some action to proceed from this, but he couldn't find the right one. So he lowered the barrel of the shot-gun and stood there a second, very softheartedly.

'Okay,' he said. 'You want a beer or what?'

'That's the stuff,' said Chicken from the door. 'Listen, buddy, give us a coupla packs and we'll just move on.'

'No, no,' said the man. 'That's fine. Never mind that. Here, have a beer. I didn't mean nothin. Jest you hit my girl and I thought maybe you were dangerous sort of people.'

The small girl had the most disappointed scowl on her, and she kept plucking at her father's overalls, not so much to catch his attention, but to release whatever annoyance she was experiencing.

'What's this place here?' Sue said.

'Oh, it isn't nowhere,' said the man. 'I only been here a while. I'll be going back to New York soon enough.'

'This is your store?' said Chicken. 'Nice place.'

'It's my pa's place. But he's gone off to visit for a while. He's got family in the old country.'

'What old country?' said Sue, as she hitched her backside in her usual style on to the barstool. 'Is that Ireland?'

'Italy,' he said, 'Italy. What did you think? I never been there. But he goes back every spring, to spend some time in Assisi. Where he wus from, when he was little.'

'Never been there,' said Sue.

'Me neither,' said the man again.

'I was,' I said. 'A few old churches and houses, and a plain going over to the mountains.'

199

'Yeah, that's it,' said the man. ' I guess you've been there all right. Hey, Po,' he called to the silent girl, 'why don't ya just go and wash your hands, or play or something? You're making me nervous, honey.'

'I want my juice,' she said.

'No, no,' he said. 'Listen, in a while. Jest piss off a moment, will ya?'

I was relieved to see her clatter off, even though she did seem miserable about it. We drank on there at the bar for an hour or two, and thinking back on it, it was odd that no one else came in for a drink. The light was removing itself outside, and I wondered if the old men sat on in the descending shadows, or whether they picked up their baskets and dragged themselves inside. It was pleasantly warm after nightfall, and the blue papery light outside the plate window, and the decent beer out of the big confident fridge, made the barman more agreeable than possibly he was. I might have been wrong about him though, and Chicken and him and Sue got on very well, and the shotgun was forgotten in the calm drugging of the beer. The man matched us, can for can, and in an easy-going way we were competing. We had nothing much better to do than that, so we did it.

By the time the girl reappeared her father was mildly half-seas-over, like we were, and he turned on her tolerantly and possessively like drunk fathers sometimes do.

'What you want now, little rabbit?' he said.

'I want my juice,' she said.

It was hard to see her in the room, because only the beer signs were on as before, but the warm careless glow from out-of-doors spread on her cheeks, and I thought for an instant she was sweating.

'Hey, honey,' said Sue, 'what's the matter?'

'Ah, she's all right,' said the man. 'Don't mind her. I'll fix her in a minute. She'll keep.'

'Pa,' she said, just that, and stilled there, waiting for him to get her juice.

'Don't she have a fever or something?' said Sue. 'I don't mean to pry. She don't look as well as she did.'

'Here, have a beer. What ya drinking here, Ströh's, is it? Listen, don't worry, be easy. I'll see to her.'

The man stocked us up, and gave us a nod, and raised his hand, and did a few down-motions with it:

'Take your time with that.'

'You want we pay you now?' said Chicken, leaning in over the counter, because he was up-wind of Sue and me.

'Hey, no,' said the man. 'On the house.'

'What, all this stuff?' said Chicken. 'You're kidding.'

'Sure, sure,' said the man. 'Don't worry about it. You're welcome.'

'Well, thanks,' said Sue. 'That's really nice of you, mister.'

He pulled the girl gently to the back of the room, and they puffed away into nothing.

'Nice fella,' said Chicken.

'Yeh,' she said. 'Pretty decent. That's ten dollars worth.'

'Yeh,' said Chicken. 'Ten fuckin dollars.'

'He's nice, isn't he, Owl?' she said.

'Yes, he is, yeh,' I said.

He was gone a longish time, and Sue was feeling so friendly about him that she made her way to their door, swaying a bit like an old dog, and she peeped her head into somewhere: so all we could see was the gleam of the dark curve of her bottom.

'Yes, sir,' said Chicken. 'One nice ass.'

I looked into his cooked face, and his smile was clear and friendly.

'It is, isn't it?' I said.

'You got the luck there, boy,' he said, and pushed my arm with his elbow, and slopped his beer.

Sue came back quite straight, and she wasn't drunk anymore. She let her leafy hand fall on the old counter, and said:

'I want to get out of here.'

'Why?' said Chicken, fly-swatting the word.

'What is it?' I said.

'He's giving her a needle.'

'What you mean?' said Chicken. 'A hypo? The kid?'

'Yeh. A fucking great needle.'

'That's pretty fucking disgusting,' said Chicken, and he meant it.

We did nothing at all for a full minute, like soldiers on the edge of a trench, and we didn't even move.

'Right,' said Chicken. 'Let's go.'

201

And suddenly we were sure of it, and clattered out, and felt the open night as a different redeeming place after all. The car began to organ on the first turn, and I pushed in beside Sue alongside Chicken, in the front seat, and we drove.

'She was bent over,' said Sue softly, 'with her little fuckin skirt up, and her shitty ass stuck out. And he was poking her with this big thick needle. And she was so toughened up there, he was nearly breaking it.'

'She's been getting it a long time, so,' Chicken said.

'Hiya doin tonight?' said the Mohican doorman. 'Pretty slow business in here.'

He surprised me by coming up so matter-of-factly.

'It's a bit early maybe,' I said.

'Maybe. Where's Ali tonight?'

'He'll be in later. Playing pool or something.'

'Right,' he said, like a quiz-master.

Mona, behind the bar, iced a beer across to him. His thick brown neck surged at it as he gripped the can above him. The liquid vanished, and you could feel the new lightness of the can in his hand.

'Now, what they call you?' he said, pointing his finger at me as if he already knew, and only needed reminding.

'Me? Moran,' I said. 'Or Batty, if you like. First name's Batty.'

'Howya, Bat,' he said. 'How are ye? Hey, Mona honey, this is the Bat here. Make yourself known.'

'Oh, we know each other,' she said, with her pally miles-off smile, that must have been addressed to year-loads of strangers like myself. 'You were in here the other night, right? With Ali.'

'Eh heh.'

'Yeh. I remember. You had a good night.'

She had one of those popular country-singer haircuts that cowled her face artificially. She was hesitant but outward: a boat in a bad channel. And I wondered if she worked here because it was the right place to get immediate uncritical approval. When you put men through an evening like the inside of a porno-magazine, almost any woman becomes a receptor of burning speculation. Maybe she was in the correct sort of dream for her. And then maybe she just worked there.

'You been knocking around with Ali, then?' said the Mohican.

'Not for very long.'

'You didn't know him before you came down here?'

'No. Never met him.'

'He's a good sort,' said the man. 'Straight. No money, but straight.'

'Yeh,' I said. 'I've never met anyone quite like him.'

I noticed how my accent was beginning to match his. He had a seductive twangy talk, like a guitar string being pulled rather than pressed on the fret-board. He was observing, more than looking at me, when he spoke. But I got the impression there was nothing unusual in that: since he gazed at Mona in the same way. It was his method of being friendly. He was so friendly I was becoming him. This country was taking me over, as always. I would have made a very suitable immigrant at the start of it. In a few months I would have seemed the original item, more American than the Indians themselves. Did migrating geese and ducks and swallows pick up the habits and accents of their winter quarters? Did something in them and outside them alter in each habitation, so they were nothing except the image of the place they were – small littered mirrors on the riverbanks, or wherever they ended up? Except, in Africa I hadn't felt very African. That continent resisted any easy borrowing. Hard terms.

Susan high-heeled up to the bar, with a dull silver tray. She had been dancer a few minutes ago, which I had tried not to watch, for some reason, and now she was waitress again. There was a definite change in her somewhere between the two roles. I lusted after her trembled bottom as a dancer, but I quite liked her in her long-legged waitress disguise. They were probably both disguises for all I knew.

'Hey, Moran,' she said. 'I didn't see you there.'

A keyed-down version of her batty smile washed up on me, like a brief wave on a stony inlet. That's a pretty corny thing to say, isn't it, Moll?

'Good old fella,' she said, and leaned her satin waistjacket towards me, and hooked her arm about my head, and kissed

203

my nose.

'Hey, hey, hey,' said the Mohican, and Mona clapped her hands and laughed like a child behind the counter. Susan seemed to have earned herself some electricity by her gesture, because she beamed out for a second with a coloured energy.

'Hey, anytime you get tired of kissing Bat on the nose, you can start on me,' said the doorman. 'Start anywhere you like.'

It was his big joke, and Susan swayed back and forth with the tray under its new load of beercans, to show she appreciated it. The comradeship of the three still had its rustle of fright, though. If the bar had been a carriage in a train plummeting on towards a wrecked bridge, somewhere unspecified up the line, it might have been clearer why they behaved like that. Their friendship was the friendship of catastrophe. Like in those films when someone turns out to be the leader, and the other fella is the coward, and each member of the cast becomes the relevant stereotype under pressure. In the Topless they all seemed to develop into the same character – maybe the coward, maybe not – at least when they contacted each other with the distant plaintive morse of jokes and smiles.

Susan's valuable body carried the cheap beer down to three Indian gents at a table – Indians from India, that is, sailors too probably, though they wore very formal suits for their night out. She clicked her heels, and bent towards them from her warm waist, and said something, with a shake of her hair. The Indians fired up at her, as if she had turned on the switch of her vacuum gaze. She would have sucked them into her, like twigs and fluff. They wanted her to. You could see in their open changing eyes that they had no clear idea about what she might do for them, but they wanted her to do it anyway, whatever it was. When she unmoored herself from them, their faces painted all sorts of visions on her walking back, and they looked happily at each other, with a recognizable beery convention in their attitude. I recognized it because I had felt it myself the first night. It had been like masturbating, certainly: your silent owl-tight bedroom suddenly becoming the rendezvous for three ideal women. The Indians probably realized they were locked away by the rules of the joint into whatever tiny desires the dollars in their hands could purchase, and no others, but in their confidence they allowed, like all the others, the possibility that their personal sweetness and difference might spark the miracle. The miracle would be that Susan would treat them as anything but the necessary notions they had to embody to get into such a bar. But one moment of treating them as anything else, and her most likely reaction would have been to stab them, one by one.

The bar was not a rip-off operation. The beer was dear but not outrageous, though cheap in quality. And when a sailor was obviously throwing his bank-roll away, Mona always tried to stop him. I saw her at it later that night, with the Indians, without any success. Mind you, there was no question of returning the money to them afterwards. Whatever actually crossed from the 'customer' to the spider's cave of a dancer's crotch was a permanently transferred asset. You would have needed an excavator to get it back, from so fragile a place. Those women worked for their grubby dollars.

It is true, isn't it, that some people appear to have a fine expansive personality while you spend time with them? After a period of absence, this fine expansiveness dwindles. They are still admirable, and still contain all the details you valued them for: but you understand that you had them drawn on too big a diagram. You saw them as a map of the world on a class-room wall, whereas in perfect perspective they are only the reliable, if complicated, workings of a watch. It's a question not of intricacy, since most people are intricate, but of size and purpose – the difference, possibly, between a back-garden and a town. Both are highly organized but one contains more humanity inside its meshes.

Moran's vision of Africa was always an awed one while he was there. In his memory the substance remained the same, but he could sense the map of it reduce off its great chart on to a postage stamp. This postage stamp he carried with him, though, for the other parts of his life. Indeed, a rolled map might have been an awkward piece of luggage.

The camp had been established on a bare peeling plain. It looked like human skin after it has been upset by too much sun. It was reddened and sore, and there were crusts of dried salt all over it, that were exactly like killed skin. Each officer had quarters of astonishing amplitude, by comparison with the men's rough barracks: dust-caked, insect-ridden. This Moran discovered, since he was assigned to Captain Harry Collins as a bat man. What war it was, he did not know.

On the first day, he walked through the solid yellow light, surprised at each tread that the construction of the air allowed him to proceed. Away off in an impossible waving distance, what appeared to be mountains decided to rise up. It was clear the virulent energy of the sun would not let them gain much more than a few inches of the horizon. He could almost hear the noise of the low faraway mountains being hammered at the first sign of growth.

The captain was a thin figure in a small earthen room. The face, as it turned, was quite long, from round chin to the line of sulphurous red hair at the top of the forehead, a burning wood on two inlets. He looked a bit like the few African masks that were hung all anyway on the bumpy walls. The centre part of his cheeks was marked by the start of a garden of grog-blossom: and a whisky bottle was the most obvious object on the work-table. This was a shop of official papers, and paper with the letter-heads of obscure luxury hotels of foreign ports. There were volumes of poetry open and curling in the damp orangy heat. The captain was bent over these possessions when he swivelled to see his visitor, and the sole of his right boot crushed the sandy floor as it twisted. When the captain stepped away from the table to examine Moran better, Moran noticed the Celtic spiral that the boot had constructed on the ground.

'What you want, private?' the man said, in an ordinary here-nor-there accent, that Moran guessed might be Dublin, or a bit more south.

'Bat man, sirr. Repartin to yer selff.'

The captain nodded his masked features.

'Fair enough,' he said. 'This is all a bit of a mess here. I've been waiting for you for ages.'

Captain Collins dug in a breast pocket for a loose cigarette, but didn't seem to find one.

'I had them somewhere,' he said, but calmly. 'Do you see a packet of Sullivan's anywhere? Moran's your name, isn't it? I had you on a sheet of paper somewhere.'

206

'Yass, sir. Moran es rite, sirr.'

'Good. You're from Mayo somewhere, are you?'

'Em. Near thar, sir, verry ner.'

'Fair enough. Well, I'm a Cork-man myself, so we should get on all right. Ever been there?'

'No, sirr.'

'Ah yes, Cork's all right. Not like this dump anyway. This your first time out here?'

'Yes, sir.'

'I'm a painter, you know, really. Shouldn't be here at all. Nothing to draw here. Have you noticed?'

'I did notis dat, ser. Itz al yalla.'

'Oh God, it is and more. Yellow with a bloody vengeance. Well I hope you can clean this catastrophe up a bit. Just leave that easel alone in the corner is all I ask, and anything I have strewn around there.'

Moran looked at the corner, and saw a half-painted piece of paper on a makeshift stand. Gathered on the sand at its foot was a group of paints and brushes. But they were very neatly set out in brief rows, and wouldn't have needed any tidying.

'I haven't done a thing since I got here, a month ago,' said the captain, wandering over to the easel. Moran noticed there was a well-worn path to it. He began to put out kit on the bed that he'd have to polish, and pick up books here, and fallen objects there.

'It isn't a real easel, of course.'

The captain had a good line in ashtrays, which also bore the crests and names of hotels.

'That's Cove,' said the captain. 'I started this when I was just about to set out. Trouble is, I can't remember the rest of it.'

Moran wondered why the captain didn't paint some bit of Africa, but he didn't say anything.

'Maybe now you're here I'll have time. Mind you, I had plenty of time before you came, so I don't know. I'm going out for a minute, Moran. Bottle's marked, by the way.'

Moran didn't know what he meant by that. The captain strolled off into the vast low building. Moran heard his slow sleepy steps for a long time, as if the captain were walking down into the wooden belly of the earth. It was a trick of the heat, he supposed. The air was so heavy and yellow that it sat on the backs of sounds, and made them sink into the hard deep clay and sand. It gave him a funny breezy sensation on the skin at the nape of the neck.

He set about the room then properly, starting at one corner and spreading his attentions from there. He worked as if each square foot of the room were a room in itself. He made no reference to anything else while he concentrated on the little side-table, and didn't mind if the cleaned dirt fell on to the next pool of activity. Still after a long sweating hour, which rose up around him like water filling in a swimming-pool, and he was done, the room looked exactly the same. Everything was in its place, one way or another, but everything still looked haphazard and unpleasing. Moran didn't know why this was. He felt extremely hot and unhappy. The captain had spoken to him as if to a new friend, the captain had been waiting for him, and yet he couldn't straighten this crooked room for him. He tried to think what was amiss with it. He walked around the edges slowly, gazing very hard at it. He swung round now and again, as if to surprise the reason behind him, where it might be creeping along in his footsteps, a goblin. Eventually he saw it. He had positioned everything perfectly. But the four walls had been thrown up just anyhow.

Sixfoil Twelve

Diss viloog wasse de saim wan dat apalt hem in de dreme, Moll. Batt de peple war al reet, an nat kilt or dreed lik animools fer wintre etin. Oliver hes hert swam oot to dem, lik a swemmer sekin de shoor or sum hant ta grippe hem.

The men dat dragt hem gentlee off hes hors Jackk woar skeens lik hem, bat nat boare-skens an deere-skens bat de grislee oweld wans uf ancent dogges an sich beests. Der hants semt as slippee as woudan battes: a man cud haff med butter wid dem worne-dowen hants ta shape de yallowe briks.

He strode as kinglee as he cud to der fier, dat wasse the flowere uf der plac. Off in de felds he sawe de bent quiet backs uf de wimin lukin affter de croppes. De menne wer truly hes wilde pepple, and der were none wildere in hes cuntree. Evvn so dey made der deye wid tendin de ferms, an dey cud cook welle whativer they astonisht in de treen, or bewilderet into deylight fram de stremes. They foght Coon his warres fer hem, when warres der wasse, an dey foght der owen warres wid wad-dever pepple cam oot of der weye throo der districtoo. Certan dey war veri vicoos hiterz, bat deye hat mich gantle manerz alsoo, an der speche wass brite. Speres wer der wepen mostlee wan dae wente ta kille de prutty dere. But virree oweld ironn sordes dey kepte alsoo fer de skins an bodees of foez. It wasse a storee dat dis speciale bande ett somtiems de felsh uf der van-quisht enemee. Bat Coone did nat minde. Let it bee so, as it wasse so long agoo wid hes fader.

He felte himsel cum hoom amang dese viel menne, an satte at der fier wid thankes an laffter. De men wer verree cheeftanlike an bolde, bat calme in der eyes, an nat ruude to der prinz. Oliv-ver sharet de saem blut, becaus der blut wasse de blut of hes fader his ooncle. De moste manne uf de group wasse calt Amonn, a smal feelty ladde uf fortee yers or morr. Hes armes were all gut, and his bodee wasse veree perfecte an usefulle in fitin. Bat he wase nat tal. Hes feerce energee in batel gavv hem dis smalnes as a grat gifte: he cud cutt oot a mann hes eyes lik a jumpin dogge. Al hes folke wer smal too, bat he wasse de beste-made, as iss de casse wid cheften-pepple in dose distroocts.

Con askt dem wat truble an wat happeeness day had, and Amoom tolt hem in hes vicoos blak speche, as od as jette. He cud hardlee taulk widdoot groolin an spettin oot beets uf water: bat stil de wordz shan. He wass egsitable in hes maner, an cud nat contane hes tong. He spok uf grat harvets dat it was cler ta Conn dey did nat hav – but he let it bee. He spok of longe wiunds mad in de brests of enemees, dat nivver brethed at al. Dis alsoo Conn let passe. It wasse jeste spoort: an somtims Owle hes poete ded mich de saem fer himm.

Litul Amoon praezed himsel de moste, as wasse de customme amang blutty menne. He almoost sange hes worddes: aboot how manee wimin he hadde taken ta hes hutte an ravisht, an how manee husbants he hadde moordered, an how manee chil-der he hatt fram hes fien oweld woman. Hes wief, if sich she wasse, lookt lik de memoree uf a nothinne, a tre his shadoo. Her fac was as blanke an dreery, an her feturs war badde wid redde markes an coelds. Amon, Moll, wud haf killt me ta heer me saye dis. Bat stil de litul manne talkt of her frutful beutee, tho shee satte clerly at hes sied.

Whan nite stept ovvir de bumpps of der viloog, Olliver wasse brighte aftir hes slepe whiel he rode. An whan hes frens crept offe ta covver demsels wid de warme bodees of de wievs an de childrenne, he stracht unner de depe blak dark an watcht de skye fer starres dat seke der lowerr hoems. Der wer non at al, as alwayes in dis aftertiem. It pussled Conn stil, an he wondert wat hadde happent to da stars, an sich oweld thinges. He falt tho, veree warme an gut somhoe. He hatte hes gift-gerl prest agenst hem, unner hes hepe uf furres an skinnes. Al wasse fien in hes herte an wurld, an he did nat fere a ting dat nite. De blaknes abuv hem moved somho in de pooerfal spacces of skye, an he hadde dat movmint in hes armes. Ass de thik skye travelt he travelt wid it – an de gerl hunge to hem as if he war a rafte on som silente summere lake.

She wase a cretur as silvree as snowe in cloodlite, bat too yung ta kisse an fondel. He lat her bee. An shee warmt hem wid her yout an slepinesse. Her brethin whislet oot inta de colde foggee aire, lik tinee berds, an flutteret aroun Oliver hes facce. It wasse de depe welle uf de neet whan he slept hemsel. He slidde underr dat wunnerfool cloak, an al hes bones an mete war repared by dat solem magick. Under de coverins he laye, lik a thing in dethe, so stil an lange he wasse. De yang gerl clang to hem in her frostee smal dremes, an dey rowed togedder ovver de wied greye lake of der reste.

Sometimes she wasse in hes strang difficoolt pictoors, and somtims he slippet inta herz. Dey moved an swirlet an startlet ech idder wid der separat cuntrees. Hes greye fase moroored de deper greye emptenes abuv, an he lokt as ef he warre chippt inta stoen on a toom. In her dreme de gerl thoght he hadde in realitee becam rocke, an in her sunken armes he felt harde an lik metal. Bat wher her handes clutcht hem de fleshe stayt gut an softe. Onlee what shee cud nat reche thickent an got icee. This waye she protectet Olivver fram dethe dat neet.

Becass trulee he mite havv vanisht soo. Hes hert wasse badde in hem, and its chenels warre stertin to bee rottin an mouldee. Bat de freshe fingoors uf de childe, an her simpel affectoon fer her prinz, whoo wasse herz for dis wan neete, braght hes life fram memoree inta mornin.

De deye cud nat breke inta sprinklin sun. Butt de tres wok stil wid a brighte buznizlik instrumentin uf blakberds an ribbins an sparers. Evvne de peple flew uppe fram der wette cavishe snoorin. Ollivver sawe dem in hes clost eyen lik huge human berds, struglin an flyin to der clawet fete: bat it wasse onlee hes minde dat gav dese carvins, fer de fete uf de men warre ordinaire. In hes halfwakt conditoon de menne agen and agen rose. He wasse neder slepin or wakin. He wud tink he hadde gotte upp himsel, and yette be lyin der. He wud emagin bits of tawke an doins: an den suttenlee be backe on de litul latche uf usefule tiem.

De gerle pluckt her bodee awaye lik a watter-ratte oot uf a streme, an Oleever notict dat she wasse som yers oldder dan he hadde consideret. Her brests war neate bat formt, an all her slopes an turnin skinne wasse preparet fer nite as she shivoored inn a newe miste. In hes bones Conn sed: Wat perfecte fooles liv in me. Bat he wasse nat sorree eidder. Beter de gerl ta bee a shorte doghter thanne a shorte bried.

Every morning I made a letter to my father and sister that began, in its giraffes and hippos, with the formula that all good letters in the world jumped off with: *I hop you are wel becos I am well*. My mother took the pages and inserted them into old envelopes, and posted them while I was at school. I was looking for those two. I considered the memory of my sister a great deal, but in a different manner than my father's. I realized she wasn't here, and wouldn't be here unless she was put on a plane as myself and my mother had been. I saw her often, sitting very stiff and proud in a blue aeroplane, travelling back to us. But I still knew it was only something I was making up. The plane was real in my head, but could not land for lack of being real in the world. How still my sister kept in the air, and how like her to be so exact.

I had brought her spiral notebook with me in mistake for my own, and so the members of our secret club had unwittingly swapped codebooks. I often stared at her writing – not so much to decipher what she had written, but to watch how good and regular her hand was, and observe the words flowing bluely on, like the channel water between the castle and the island. Some of it she had composed in her once-new red biro. The idea of the newness of the old things pleased me but made me melancholy.

There was a good solid part of me missing while she was away, but in my letters I concentrated mostly on what I had eaten the night before, and what the garden was like outside the window where I wrote the letters. I didn't tell her that I felt like I was quite lost in the middle of a familiar forest.

She had never whirred and got dangerous in London, and I didn't fear her in the least. Games behind the couch were a little empty and difficult without her. She had always led the way and made the pure rules, and made sure I abided by them. I had some anarchic muddle in me, that turned any game on my own into a hundred conflicting puzzles. At my worst I wandered around the scruffy pages of the garden, and into the square of it that was hedged, by an entirely grown-up inspiration, from the sea breezes. There I climbed up on the green garden seat, and listened to the world breathing and seagulling outside the dense green walls. The gulls could strike high above my head too, and they went crying down from mad heights, like hawks without prey, unless the prey was me. They were large and loud and their beaks seemed too big for them, impertinent somehow, and dragged them down with their sharp weight. There must have been thin wires attached to the points of the beaks that I couldn't spot against the windy sea, and someone wound in the wire very swiftly, and the bawling gulls had to follow their hooked noses.

This was in my mind, because below at the little harbour one afternoon a bird gulped the bait of a fisherman, while he was casting his line into the waves. The sea was very deep and thick there, and the gull fled down and swallowed the worms, and the hook inside the worms. Then the astonished and angry man had an extraordinary flying-fish to deal with, and the equally astonished bird arced and patterned over an acre of sea, while the man's stiff hand reeled it in. I stood on the stone balcony where the mounded boulder was, off which I had once rolled in knee-scraping terror, and watched the gap between human and flyer close. The gull was making the man sweaty and upset, and a small collection of other humans bunched near him, to see this marvel. The fat old fisherman who mended other people's nets was there, and the boy with one arm from school, who could climb anything just the same. And the dark man in his raincoat found it in his sad self to note the horrors of the gull.

Finally the creature was spinning himself in the seaweedy air only three or four feet from the tip of the swishing rod. The man had to twist and curse and tug. He was like a person in a story, because he was below me where I idled, and was very much apart from me, in another kind of hour, in another kind of day. But the gull dived unheroically over the man's head, and landed shakenly on the old pier wall, and just hunched there on the cut stones, with the fishing line trailing out of his stomach. He reminded me of those toys that are worked by battery and move around on the end of an electric wire, except the gull had the appearance of an elderly man, and no one made toys like that.

The fisherman put his rod down, and the little crowd inched closer. He held the line lightly and moved towards the captive. Two brief tired hops brought the bird right to the lip of the

213

pier. He spread his wings, like someone shaking water off an umbrella, and folded them again, and gave a short irritated cry. He wanted nothing to do with the fisherman, at all, and wouldn't even look at him straight, but squinted sideways. Then he took off with a white swirl over the harbour and the rod slid after him, but yanked to a stop when it met the man's hand on the line. The man said something because the rod had hurt him. And it had hurt the seagull too, because it plummeted into the water and half-floated and half-sank. The fat net-mender laughed with a head-back theatrical gesture, and he seemed to me straight out of a comic book. He had a dark thick beard and it made his face seem overlarge, like the gull's beak. The gull's beak had got it into trouble, awful knee-scraping trouble, and the fat man gurgled so much I thought he might swallow the island, which at my angle began on the sea just after the fellow's mouth. The island would have a hook in it, the emotion of my father, and drag the man's stomach out, as the baited hook was doing to the exhausted seagull. I was in an extremity of affection for the bird. I was lost to this salted stored feeling at the low cold wall. If I hadn't feared the hopeless fearless laughter of the weighty net-mender, I would have run down and somehow saved everyone, or at least the seagull.

The man with the rod was staring now at the floating mound of feathers and misery. He didn't know what to do, and he shook his head at this mess. Perhaps he felt the pain of the bird in his own belly, since in a way the animal was connected to him by the umbilical cord of the fishing-gut. Perhaps he was impressed by the bird's ignorance. He held the green visible line gingerly between his fingers, like a violinist with his bow. He didn't tug it, but he seemed to will the bird to fly back up where some help could be given. It was enraging almost that the fright of the gull was preventing it from being aided, that it knew only one course of action. The man only wanted, as far as I knew, to clip the line as near as he could. It might even be only hooked into the fleshy inside of the beak, in which case the bird could swoop up immaculate and sound and free, with the merest tooth-ache. A narrow geyser of blood burst from the softly paddling body. The sea around it, in the clear sandy harbour, went door-coloured with the paint. The fat man went on incongruously laughing, as if he had forgotten what he was laughing at – or just couldn't be silent in front of a drowning.

Innocence is a great weapon in those who are not innocent. By
making no reference interiorly or otherwise to the right or
wrong of their rushing deeds, they create a robust artificial innocence, impregnable to question or archaeology. It is the innocence of amorality. Within the circles of a good action, if such a
naked notion has ever proceeded, this faked faculty can produce
all the reparative virtues of the real thing.

I was thinking this only as I thought it. It is probably vague
and untrue. I have been remembering our first entry into the
flat in Lucerne, and wondering if that, and one or two occasions
like it, were the true arguments for our being together. We both
had a hankering after special places to live, and in this case Xenia
had certainly provided an example of one.

We had spent Christmas in her parents' town, and it had been
a period of sudden mental changes. It is a difficult time for me
to think over, and my old head resists it. But perhaps after all it
was quite simple and ordinary, and I should map a little of it, if
only to know a place I will never return to.

A strange week passed, during which we wandered about the
decorated alliance of new banks and medieval buildings, with
small areas of painted colour on the civic architecture of the
squares: the crests of the old corporations. The cranking trams
went through these streets in such a ritualistic way that they left
streams of light and movement behind them. The sight of a
trout-coloured tram paused at a stop, and the people leaving
and finding these lights, was always at a distance, even a few
paces away. We ghosted into the cinemas sometimes twice a
day, sometimes three times, in what seemed the ideal method
of coping with our hours. We had come together to eye the
imagined lives of made-up people flicker and demonstrate
imagined truth. The only difference was that I imbibed the wis-
dom through the English dialogue, and Xenia followed in the
crippled subtitles. We didn't receive the same film. I was over-
sensitive to anything supposed to be sad, and might cry quietly
on her jacket at a cartoon or simplified love story. Then out
among the curiously toylike streets again, we crossed the cob-

215

bled surfaces arm in arm, at mysterious miles from each other, both of us for a change in signal need of subtitles, so we could follow what we knew of as our love.

Xenia was ambitious to leave off all her old friends, and anyway one visit to a former haunt, of pop-music and hugged greeting, was all my jealousy could manage, and badly at that. She tolerated an emotion that was a very old unloved habit with me: she understood it because she had it herself.

One afternoon we bumped into a couple she evidently knew in the style of the night-club. We were hunting for an eating-table which she could bring to her flat in Lucerne. The boy she embraced, like the most delicate and pleasant of bears, was fair-haired and attractive in what I thought of as the Berlin tendency: thin faced, and endangered, with a smidgin of the feminine and closely-bladed hair. He approved of Xenia's choice of table: and through the gravelly singsong language I surmised that he had picked it out for her himself, at some drifted time in the past, and had told her mother by phone it was there. There were courses of decision in Xenia I was not to be informed of, that was clear. I was stupidly touchy about this, out alone with her in the green town, and she faded away from me like a dream inside a dream. Then the town was even more underwater and childlike, because suddenly I was there for no good reason.

Later the same day I told her in a teashop about the doctor in Paris and my exact fears. She rapidly arranged for me to see her mother's friend, who was eminent it appeared in these affairs. He laughed at me, kindly, and dismissed the whole business as a piece of craziness on the part of young French doctors.

Catapulted out into the chill clean great world of the unconsciously alive, I was faint with euphoria, and kept making rather painful leaps into the air. Xenia was pleased too, and for the first time I had a precise difficult view of her as a stranger. I didn't know how I had got myself into that Berne street, with this unknown personality, who had taken me up as an act of rebellion against a father whom she celebrated with every other action, and who was partial exclusively to her own wishes. If she had just walked up to me on the pavement, I couldn't have known less about her. The euphoria watered away. And as joylessly as the release had been joyful, the hounding worries limped back into my partied brain in the form of: *Did he miss this*, or *Did he overlook that*, and *What if* one thing and another, like a pack that has been only temporarily wheeling and sniffing in a nearby field. These miseries I carried with me for the next year and a half. Not for one day did I let myself ignore their litanies and excruciating ceremonies, and a month did not go by without some new symptom being hair-raisingly discovered. I don't wish to go on alluding to it, because even now, on this journey with Sue, which seems set to become a continuing life of some sort, it makes me uneasy. It doesn't plague me any more, and I don't want to print any damned invitation for it to do so. It was an invasion more than a characteristic. In one way it was a legacy of a long deserved loneliness, and in another the effect of any unusual happiness coming up against the tightly-dressed wall of Xenia's self-possession. Very little reached her, least of all any quotidian mediocrity of my weathercock of a heart.

We went back to the teashop as a form of prayer, among the widows. Like the cinemas, we often went to tea-shops, for the sake of the hot chocolate, and the feeling that we got from being young amid the cleaned finished women. They were so polite that they glanced neither right nor left: you were able to be alone to perfection, a blade in a field of grass. They fingered their china cups so sadly it made you sweat, because their smiles were so well-mannered, terrified and indifferent at the same time. These women were survivors: their husbands were worms' meat in expensive caskets under the city graveyard. The banks were overstocked with their strong-boxes, and their pink hair sang.

By now, among the politenesses of that afternoon, my exultation must have rung more and more emptily, even to her sculptured ears. As if this occasion were an opportunity for confidences, she told me a wonderful Xenia-ish story about the couple in the furniture warehouse. After her return from her disastrous affair in Spain, with the seventeen-year-old Barcelona flautist, whose mother was mad and her lover a killer, she was in a highly depressed state, and used to drink so much in the music bar that she might be found spread over one of the town fountains by friends also tottering home: or she might be swept on the general haze of dope and wine into one of the topless bars, that discreetly lived behind rich stone façades. On one of

217

these nights she went home with the boy in the shop. They made love without feeling, she said, and then she told his girlfriend, who turned out in her story to be the best friend of that era. The best friend refused to acknowledge it had happened. Even when the same thing happened a week or so later she simply ignored it. And the boy too ignored the circumstance that Xenia had manufactured for him. These were the people she had embraced warmly and arrogantly in front of me, and the boy she had allowed choose our furniture. I was so surprised and hurt that my own impulse was to ignore it also. It was much too complicated and outside my former life to grasp. She looked at me when she had finished warmly and arrogantly. She had the same look for a number of rather varied situations.

I sat there, and the time between the Paris doctor and this began to bewilder my head. Streets we had walked through, alleys we had hurried through in the rain, street-singers chilly on pan pipes, long rises of stone lanes in the old town, the look of her cropped head above her babylon of a body, the very ease and slant of the downpour, suddenly became a sort of happiness, an ending perfect in its ambiguity, a flower only half-plucked. And I stared at her, and drank the chocolate in seeming calm. I wondered at myself, and at her, as if for weeks I had been a yard off the ground, shaken but alive in that colour, the idea of forever removed for ever, in fear of shadows, in love with misconception.

We were washing some of our clothes on a very bright big morning. Everything had disappeared only to come back again, renewed and content. The narrow bitter stream spun like a simple humble offering to the clumsy bank. *This will help you along*, the stream muttered, and the bank mumbled, inaudible, but possibly grateful. The three of us were stripped to our underwear, though Chicken's idea of such a thing was a generous swathing of cotton in the honoured shape of long johns. He peeled away the grey top of it by grappling with the stiff buttons, which hadn't often been disturbed, and let the gruelly sunlight in among the twisted black hairs of his upholstered chest. There was something cramped but strong about his hard body:

you expected him to unbutton that too, like an armchair. Obviously he had worked at something toughening for years, probably all his life. We knew so little about the man.

Sue's loose tight body crouched over the shallow water. Her breasts, like some other kind of stream, filled the soft lacy cups of her bra. When she shifted on her soles, her bottom feathered and shook like smooth water over stones. I watched these matters like other eyes might watch the movement of unusual clouds, or my own eyes might. I valued these still brief dances her body constructed for no one's intended pleasure except the lowering saplings, that begged like undernourished kids on the complicated grass.

Chicken was too aware of his own nakedness to bother about examining Sue's. He seemed uncomfortable but relaxed at the same time, as if he enjoyed this early informality but was having some trouble getting accustomed to it. Sue's back was unruffled and stony. It was a small shock when you noticed her flat muscles changing position slightly. The light made her quickly-brushed hair something apart from her, like an item of jewellery or costume she had high-lighted herself with. It was thin and metal under the passionate yellow paint.

I had a vanishing sleepiness still in me after the slow wide-awake night on the back-seat of the car. Chicken had murmured and groaned in the front. Through most of the dark I had been easy enough. Sue pressed against my skin without shifting, and I was falsely surprised when she woke that we weren't stuck together for good. My heart was confused with hers. I remembered her careless defiance in the bar the night before, in full disregard of an unknown trigger-finger, and it had me chuckling as gently as I could. The chuckling woke her, and she lifted on to an elbow with a sleepy smile on her best face. She let her head fall into mine, a shadow entering a shadow, and kissed me there in the little room of her hair.

'Perfect, perfect, perfect,' she said, 'perfect, baby.'

Now as we tried to rinse some more over-affectionate dirt out of our few clothes, she hummed a tune I didn't know, and threw a few words now and then in between the notes. A period of spinning sounds would have *Down in Memphis Tennessee* after it, and then another alleyway and city of a tune, and the half-remembered chorus. It was exquisite for all disillusioned gipsies

219

to be there and hear her. I wanted to rush out somewhere and tell some stranger about it. Chicken's self-distraction and our ordinary preoccupied nakedness was awarding the three of us a dipping few hours.

But happiness always sounds maudlin, or my notion of it is a brand of sentimentality. It's just that these casually-allotted happinesses are the poor filling-stations for this human engine. I may disapprove of the fuel and the attendant and the poor job he does of wiping down my windscreen, with its astonished flies, but even so without him and the place and the welled pumps you can't get up the bloody road. Anyway, for god's sake, if Sue was there and I was there and Chicken was, and if I want to think about it in some poor recovering room of words, well then I must. I wonder if Chicken has any reasonable memory of it, and if he has, whether it contains any similarity to mine? Or if he hasn't, what difference, if any, it makes to his existence and him that I do? But maybe Chicken doesn't want to remember it. Maybe he makes himself not. Wherever he is now, he probably tries not to go over it much, Chicken and his dirty long-johns – or companionable might be more generous. Chicken scrawny but powerful like a hungry mountain cat. My, my. Chicken stealing through the briars and the trees and Chicken pouncing on a sheep. That would be Chicken all right.

'Owl, boy,' he said slowly, like a thin fall under a well-used tap, 'shove me over that soap, will ya?'

The cake shone briskly in the early dazzle as it turned in the space between us. He allowed it to fall on his palm and settle there. It didn't move.

'That's the way,' he said.

I glanced at Sue's back and said:

'Pretty good catch.'

'Practice,' said Chicken.

I tried to think how any man might get practice at catching bars of soap, but nothing suggested itself. Pretty mysterious, my Mr Chicken.

'Jesus, Owl, what you been doin in these drawers?' said Sue. 'You been shittin in them or what?'

She said it so lightly, and with such a species of bubbled giggle at the end that I laughed too. Chicken roared.

'Shit, now, Owl's been shittin in his drawers,' he said, and the soap burst out of his fingers like a trapped fish seeing its chance, and dived into the stream with a smooth headfirst entry.

'Did ya see that soap go in?' said Chicken. 'Holy shit is right.'

'They really dirty?' I said, but Sue went on rubbing. 'Hey, Sue,' I said, 'they really dirty, or what? I'll do them.'

'Nay, nah,' she said, 'I was only kiddin ye. They're just old and ingrained, boy: country knickers. You sure could use some new things.'

'I suppose so,' I said. 'Hard thing to think of.'

'I had good clothes once,' said Chicken quietly.

He plonked his stone bottom on the grass, and trailed his toes to fish out the soap.

'Where was that?' said Sue, looking upstream at him. 'Here, you want me to get that soap for you?'

'Where was that? Good question,' said Chicken. 'Don't remember. I was in a band.'

'A singing band?' Sue said. 'A pop band? Or what?'

'No, ma'am,' he said. 'A gang of outlaws.'

'Shit, Chicken honey, they don't have any outlaws now.'

'That so? Yeh, I know. I was shittin ye. Got shit on the brain now with all this talk of it. No, it was a band all right, and I had this really neat suit I wore. I liked it, you know, I really did. It suited me at the time to have that suit. Yeh. But I don't know why.'

A clear fresh silence sat down among us for a moment. Not even an indifferent animal made a note or rustle. The river too was oddly soundless. We waited for Chicken to go on with it, but he just didn't. He scooped out the bright soap with his corned feet.

She danced for me with outrageous noncommittal. This time there was no doubt she had charted where I was leaning forward. She took all the little hooks out of her body and let it go. It went. She held out her skinny arms and tossed her breasts at a dangerous speed. She veed her steady legs, and dreamed her hands along her thighs, and for a moment fluttered them on her butterfly g-string. It was almost horrifying to feel the boulder of crashing lust that fell from the mountain top of my head into the splashed deep pool where my groin used to be. She stepped about to the clumsy music, like a horse that has been trained to make very unnatural horseless movements. The Americans have races with such breeds.

The Indian customers were vanished out of their stall, and only a broken neon of a smile, belonging to a strange little gentleman, broke the square of empty stools. Susan wasn't being very attentive to him, but he offered many dollar bills in succession, and she spun over to him as often as she noticed. He decorated her with them to such an extent that they started to twirl from her in singles, like the very last leaves on a tree in what she would have called the fall. I had watched this small man enter, and thought he would have done better at one of the gay bars, because his pants were yellow-grey and tight round his brief old bottom. He wore an exceptionally flowery Hawaiian shirt, whose buttons he had ignored until most of the way down his miniature but solid chest. On his breast-bone he showed a heavyish golden medallion that was obstinate in not catching the light, and which lay there secretively like a mushroom. His features looked pulled and taut – he might have been born looking naturally like the result of a score of facelift operations. The very substance of his eyes seemed to have been painted on his tanned face. The rims were black, painted so, and the china part a rich cadillac blue. They were perfect almonds, but drawn so levelly on him that you wished nature could have tilted them a bit, because they gave him the appearance of being ignorantly sketched by a young overambitious painter. On top of all this some invisible weight pressed on the crown of his sleeked-back balding hair, as if an axe had neatly and bloodlessly removed the uppermost shelf of his head, unless the grease was blood. But he observed Sue rather than watched her, so perhaps he wasn't so interested after all.

Ali was over keeping Mona company of a sort. Susan had been 'pissed', as she called it, before the small man had arrived, because she had had to dance for me and the Indians. The Indians had been a bit slow to work out the dollar method, since there was no one there to demonstrate besides me, and they feared to follow the example of one. Then when they were drunker they had gone too far, making everyone feel guilty about their money. It was an even slower night without them, and the girls emerged reluctantly from their dressing-room.

But now the medallion man had turned up, and he passed his dollars into their dance with the same attention that someone pays a bear when he feeds it with crisps to please his child. Perhaps the old fellow had a child inside him. He looked like he could afford the money anyhow.

Ali loomed at my elbow and tucked down to a stool.

'Got ta help 'em along,' he said, and he vied with the small man in attracting Susan over. She opened for Ali as crazily as for me, with the added spice of what passed for old acquaintance. Ali laughed with the sort of rumble that can be heard over bellowing music. It was daft to see this ordinary woman cavort and gesture, and hang off the pillars, for one topple-headed Irishman, a patriarchal rastafarian, and an ageing homosexual.

The last appeared to get tired of it after a while, and rubbed with a tight-bottomed confidence to the bar. Susan was finished anyway, and the girl with the bubbled breasts popped out. But when she saw only the two of us there, a bit exposed right enough in the big room, she strode over through the humming silence, and said:

'This is hell, boys, where is everyone?'

'Oh, maybe dey gone to da war, honey,' said Ali.

'They must have,' she said. 'You want me to dance, or what?'

'Ah naw,' said Ali. 'You just take a rest. I don't have any of dese dollars left, anyhow, an what I had were Mona's.'

'Mona's?' said the girl. 'Well she's a good old gal, for sure.'

'Should have kept a few for you,' said Ali. 'But Susan got dem all out of me, mon.'

'That's okay,' she said. 'He might let us go home then. What time have you got?'

'About two, mon,' said Ali.

'Yeh, that should do him. Where the motherfuckin perverts are tonight, I don't know.'

He was some unspecified character that owned the bar, or it might have been the doorman if he was also the manager. It wasn't worth it to ask. The girl was wearing a sort of swimsuit that came apart by some device. It was interesting to see this not happening, and the possibility of it happening bounced back in through the hatch of the dressing-room. She threw a glance at the Mohican as she moved to make sure it was allowed.

Susan had materialized beside the old fellow at the bar. It surprised me to find them talking in the closing lights, as if they knew each other. They clearly did.

'Hey, Ali,' she said. 'This is Stephen. He works in the house.'

'Right, mon,' said Ali.

'Well, I don't actually *work* there,' said the man, Stephen. He had an exaggerated English accent that possibly had never been in England. It could have been Boston or somewhere. Someone had told me they had peculiar ways in Boston.

'No,' he said, 'well, I do a bit of this and a bit of that, at any rate.'

He was eager and exact in his manner. If he was Boston and well-born or whatever, he certainly didn't baulk at us. The phrase 'rough trade' came to mind.

'Yeah,' said Susan. 'He just does a few things. A friend of the guy who owns it, really. Point is, he can help us.'

'Of course I can,' said Stephen. 'I am the soul of assistance. Let me see: I've been assisting those in need now for more than thirty wonderful years. Thirty wonderful years, my friends.'

He laughed to himself inside a pebbly and lightly polluted splutter. Ali towered up like a dolmen of black stone beside him. Ali turned off when people talked like that, I think. It hadn't the same pattern as his conversation. On the other hand, it was the same approach to the art, except it was a setter of tone like his was. And though someone like myself might slip into it for want of personal definition, this little creature wouldn't consider that, for the sake of his own performance. So Ali shut up and listened, and turned what was uttered over in his believing mind. Mona, as always, leaned on her elbows and listened without listening behind her agreeable worrying smile.

Moran cushioned his chin on his palms, where he sat knees-up on the rough boards. It was night, and the white-washed room had disappeared beyond the feeble gesturing of a factory-polished new oil-lamp. Captain Collins balanced back on his crude chair, and his cap was dropped thoughtlessly on his muddled papers. Even though there was breeze the lamp ticked minutely and remotely. It had been lit a full ten minutes ago by a struggling taper in Moran's fist. The taper still smoked pungently in his hand, because it was made of some tenacious waxy wood. The smell drifted full-strength into Moran's breathing nostrils. He had his mouth shut against it, but he admired the smell.

Captain Collins couldn't see Moran very well in the imprecise washings of the lamp, but he could hear the man's irregular breathing. At intervals he had been talking about his mother, and Moran felt sleepy with maternal notions. Mothers fascinated him, since he had had one himself. He thought to himself of Captain Collins lying on his back in some unknown room, and watching his mother, whom he kept calling *the nice old ma*, going about her business on some equally vague ceiling. What Captain Collins painted into the darkness didn't always tie in with this, but Moran made good attempts to ignore the tendency to talk about matters which began with: *When the nice old ma and myself used to go to Kenmare for our holidays*. Even so, some of the best elements of what the captain had to offer were contained within such narratives. So Moran listened to them, at the same time removing discrepancies that suggested something unique about his own childhood, and also, with a third hand, gathering such details as were awkward but valuable all the same for their own sake.

'Hmm,' said Captain Collins. 'I wasn't much more than twelve then, when we stayed in that extraordinary hotel. The nice old ma, you see, was a Quaker, and liked everything to be nice. She couldn't travel about with the old fellow because he always looked rough and useless in places like that. And anyway, her brother wouldn't pay for him to go with her. He called it her 'continuing education', whatever he meant by it. Idiomatic sort of character. Would have been a souper if he hadn't been one already, if you follow me. The woman was all of thirty-eight, I should have thought. Whatever year that was. Sometime or other, I suppose. Ever been to Kenmare, Moran?'

Not a squeak emerged from the shadows for a good half-minute.

'You're not asleep, are you, Moran?' said the captain, in a different, more real voice.

'No, sirr, I nivver bin,' came the monotone. 'Not thatte I

notissed.'

He referred both to Kenmare and sleep.

'You would have noticed, Moran my lad. You would have noticed Kenmare. The station at Killarney for instance is unforgettable. It has an enormous hotel built right beside it, where all the would-be quality stay. I seem to remember it is called The Great Southern, or some such boast. I would have thought the trains were a considerable nuisance, puffing in and out, and covering everything with soot, if the wind was available. But then would-be quality are the very devil for these places. Best hotel in Killarney anyway. But Killarney, you know, isn't all it's cracked up to be. Very seedy lot of trap-drivers to take you to the lakes. No, we just pushed on through the big dark trees – oh, very dark and big, Moran – and over the high pass in a bit of friendly moonlight, till we had Kenmare in our sights again. You needed two horses for the mountain, it was such a height. A bit like Switzerland, without the snow, and rain instead.'

The captain laughed nicely enough, and Moran nodded further down into that trough he always landed in when someone told him a story. It was like sitting in warm brackish water up to your neck. He liked it though.

'The hotel now in Kenmare was *really* grand, a wonderful affair. A big fire going under the splendid marble mantelpiece in the entrance-hall. Fires everywhere in the place, blazing away from dawn till midnight. Huge agreeable rooms, where the rustle of a newspaper in the far corner sounded like two valleys away. They wouldn't let you put your own napkin on your lap. A man to pour your wines, another man to bring the menu and discuss it with the nice old ma, another man to serve side-dishes, two men for the big things, and then another pukka-wallah to make sure everything was 'to your satisfaction'. I mean, it was like a bloody train-station after all, when things were in full swing.'

Captain Collins shot forward, either by choice or from being off-balanced by his energetic description of this hotel that Moran was having difficulty imagining. He saw a bewildering grey edifice without detail. And through the walls that were not very solid he could count the piled blazing fires occupying each room like guests. The sum of the size of the rooms was greater somehow in his head than the sum of the building imagined in

226

general. At the bottom of his image, and even a bit outside it, there was a confused group of girls and men attending to one severe quiet lady – who looked a little like his own mother, Sug – and a laughing boy. For some reason the boy in his skull was naked, although he tried to put clothes on him, for the boy's sake.

'Excoose me, siir,' said Moran, since the captain had stopped anyway. 'Bat wat arre ya werrin at dat teem, sire, if I maye enqueer?'

'And then there were the walks,' said Captain Collins, as if the question had not penetrated or were unacceptable, or uninteresting. 'Big walks through terribly green woods. Overgreen, really. That's a small joke, Moran. No dice, eh? And there was a salmon-leap there, that never had any salmon leaping, but if you stared at the water long enough, by god you saw them anyway.'

Moran was still struggling with the clotheless boy, and it was troublesome now to have these nonexistent salmon superimposed on the pageantry in the outside restaurant. The salmon leaped and tossed and twisted all over the flickering of the servers, but didn't seem to be noticed by them – politeness, probably. Then one landed with a soundless thump, like a dead hand hitting a white white coverlet, and the little boy gaped at it.

'Her brother, you see, never forgave her for marrying a Catholic. Actually, her brother as a rule never forgave anything, and wouldn't meet her again, nor would any of the rest of her family. But they seemed to relent in this matter of holidays. They couldn't bear to think of the poor creature without holidays, although it was evidently quite easy for them to think of her without family and old friends. You want to watch out for stuffy people in this wide world, Moran. Luckily I was prevented from encountering them by their complete despising of me, as the offspring of a Tague. Steer clear of them, Moran.'

The captain fiddled with a pill-box, and fingered out a couple of tiny pink tablets, by rolling them on the gathered cardboard rim. They were for what the captain dismissed as 'his unlooked-for condition'. In Moran's head, the captain, as he had been as a naked boy, leaned forward and stabbed the fat salmon with a silver fork.

Sixfoil Thirteen

As et wasse hes charg ta cercl, he didde, and lefte hes spiretted subjeckts fer hes fedde and freshent hors Jackk. It bloomt a simileer marnin as de wan befoor, an a gratlee simileer pooerfal drooseinesse botheret hem. An indade he wasse in a smal effecte afreed uf slepin, even tho he hadde manee roeds ta passe down, an Jacke didde kno dem welle. Bat it wase de men widdoot fealtee he fered, dat mite droppe on hem fram tal tres, or surgge uppe at hem fram de thickets an coover uf de riche grund. Stil hes facultees warre atackt mor by de softe girleishe fingeers uf tirednesse, dan anee fowel nastee robber-menne.

He hadde no jewls or monee anywaye, an al who knewe hes yerlee journee knew also his travelin povertee, an laft hem aloon.

An de silber feelin roosted in hes armes, an crept inta hes brest, an coovered hes shulders wid a blanket uf heat.

'Ah, sunne,' he sedde. 'Evven tho yer flames doo nat reche moi owel lant, stil yer heate will runne throo ta mee, yer seravanteman, an soothe mee trottin progresse.'

Bat he struggelt, and by hes stricte pooer wasse carfulle he did natte slepe. He sange a younge songe uf Owel his former tiem, a lital peece uf playfulle nouttin dat Owel hat stolen fram de tongue of de Frenche. He hatte made et tite an shorte, an it pleset Conn ta sprinkle et as he sat on hes sturdee Jacke:

> Aprille wull lappe ye roun
> moi swete Aprille Susie
> an ye wull playe an winke
> bat ye wil nat slumber
> manee brefe houers yel fil
> wid manee emptee hugges
> bat ye muste cum at end
> wher de sadde bitterne sendz

       atrocoos crees oot fram
          de weedee brokent rivver
       an lie dere in wrinklez
          fer wan poore crowe ta eet
       so doo nat wandere Su
          fram oot Aprilles booer

Et wasse anlee a tinee strem uf wordes fer childer, whan dey
wer slowe ta bette. Bat whan Conne trickelt et fer de somber
berds, an de greye depe shadez, he falt braverr an mar softe. He
remembert hes crazee muder sangin sech songes fer strang lul-
labee, an hes skinne titent wid happinesse. He smilt ta hes owen
hors in de moiste darkent wud, and no wan herd hes shorte
woodee lauf. He founde de tres veree thicke an joinet in dat
sectioon – de track wasse almoste closd, an covert wid leeves an
blak thik branschez. De leves lokt lik bats, dey werre soo darke
an rotten. Lang agoo dee tres hadde redde bigge flooers, becarse
he hadde ridden throo dem at dat fledde teem. Sum contagoon
livt nowe in dere herts an lunges, an dey wer halff ded in der
shooes, lik nobel beggers.

Whan dey beganne ta stande more distante frame ech odder,
he gessed he wasse neerbye to de nexte habitatoon. De singel
tres her warre mar blakent den de foreste. Der skyin trunkes
wer shrivelt an crampt. De leves war anlee memorees uf a brite
conditoon. His horse stepped again with contempt and horror.
He was almost sure now he was asleep and that he would see
the killed people of yesterday. He was certain when a body came
into his vision, up the mouldy muddy path.

And yet this corpse was not the same. It was as dark as the
wet dead leaves, and had sunk into the ground till its head and
feet were vanished. The turning collapsed chest and branchy
legs were spread like a cruel dance to his eyes.

'What has dis manne stumbelt upan?' he said to the rubbery
air. 'What badde deth wasse here, ta pluck hem inta ittes grimee
hugge?'

But Jack plodded on, and by accident his hind hoof crushed
through the ruined human chest. Conn heard the sound of wet
brittle carcase under him and groaned, as well he might. Further
on was another, and this one was not so badly mushed. Oliver's
path passed out of the drainy part and rose to a field of long

229

colourless grass. This stuff hung back and forward in the muscled talking of the wind. Here were ill things for his raw sight.
All ages of his people lay like dead animals in their patches of
rolled grass. And stuck, still, in the mouths of these unbreathing
villagers, was long pulls of the same grey grass, a small bit withered.

'Ar dese hoomans gon ta beest?' he said, as if they might answer him. 'Warr ye al on yer fore-legges, ta eet erbes lik cowes,
befar yer stomicks wud nat playe dis grazerz game? Warr ye nat
ashamt ta resembel sich sillee mater-uffe-facte creaturz as de
bulle an bullocke, an de milkincowe?'

The bellies under the stricken ribs ballooned out at him, as an
unuseful answer. They were such swellings that he wondered
that the bodies would not float up into the bleak sky. The child
in him wanted to prick these swollen bags with his small knife,
but the stench was too much a foe to his own sleek stomach. He
never saw such thin bad bones and skinny arms in his manly life
– and he had seen hungry dogs and sick cattle enough. He was
very afraid now. Here were his people turned into grazers and
such. And worse than this they were without life or speech. No
one could tell him what this troublesome sad happening had
been.

Further on however he nearly found his words. There was a
small group of one man and a young woman, and a clumsy
tottering child beside them. When they saw this whole man on
his horse, they stepped away to let him pass in his peace. The
shrunk man raised his arm in a silent greeting, and his eyes were
kept down. He was almost naked, but his rags and pieces served
to keep him from crotchy showings. The woman's belly seemed
to be with child, it was so bloomed. But also the child seemed
to be with child, which made the hairs on Conn's arms crawl
like insects. The man nodded his head three and four times. It
was not normal at all. It was a place of mad brains for certain.

The child with large eyes stooped to the ground and
wrenched with hardship a fist of grass.

'Wat isse et, moi childe?' oweled Oliever beggt. 'Whoi must
yoo, moi dere herte, ete dis seelee grasse?'

Bat he hadde slept widdout seein affter al, and sprange oot uf
hes dreme befar anyonne wud telle hem.

230

The railway tracks beat any threat from the stodgy sea by being a hundred yards high in the air on the cutting of the cliff. There had been undizzy men to build an inhuman wall where the natural slope of the cliff was missing, and the likelihood of a landslide good. Weather that forbid us to lie on the pastel sand, or to hurt our feet between cannonballs netted in slime, which we had to manoeuvre over to swim, allowed us walk under the solid clouds along the unparallel perspective of the tracks. Even out of sun, the scent of tar, cooked into the purply sleepers, hung about our noses. It climbed up from the ignored wood, made a twist in our nostrils, and insisted on being considered important and pleasant, and it was. When I smell tar on the boat-decks here, it always flings me back like a reversed person-age on a film-reel into the wallflower odour of the sleepers – the coloured signal of wallflowers, which in spite of themselves littered the soft banks, mixed itself in with the more assertive tar, and changed it from oil to water-colour in my eyes.

But are descriptions of this type defeating – do things become just patched up out of words, in a vocabulary of forgetting? Maybe such conscious seeing is wrong-headed and stupefying. I don't really know if I walked along there with my mother in any sort of weather, but as far as my memory is concerned I did, and if I didn't, *it* probably did. It acted and I forget. It's not funny – there are independent definers that also make use of my overbaked brain. It's a ramshackle central computer of which I am only a single questioner. Or I am so clumsy and ignorant in my methods that the data come back irritated and paradoxical. And when it seems most contradictory to me, when I know for a certainty that some item happened otherwise, then it's most true. I sometimes accept from another human that I have mis-remembered some common equation, but I never allow this small graciousness or pretended humility to my own elusive brain. I should make a start, and stop believing that memory gets things wrong, and accept that I, that is the controlling I, the I that for some bitter nervous reason believes it knows best, must often be in error. Hell, memory is the business itself as it unfolded, and happening with only changes of style or in non-style for ever. It is a darwin and I am those sensible ladies who

231

knew they weren't sprung from apes. So as always in my deistic afternoon of someone else's empire, it is more important to believe than to know, to believe in the hope of knowing later, when the unknowledgeable pinhead, who decides and goes on under the uncaring stare of memory, begins to get peeks through that stare, like a child suffered to peer for a moment through a seaside telescope, which whirrs by grace of the childish adult's sixpence. *Look, there is Howth town*, when to you it looked like a deserted cove. And you had Robinson Crusoe in there on some ancient burghers' plots.

Well then, memory is older and wiser than I am, and it has a supply of sixpences in its pocket for the metal finder. So better attend to what it has to say, and don't trot out dangerous guesses. Listen with the widest lugs I can grow.

These matters then come courtesy of the memory of Oliver Conn, and the poor juvenile man himself knows nothing except what memory had told him by way of story, and it carries much more than he does. It is a sort of familiar to his life, but neither avuncular or malign, neither supportive nor obstacle-minded. Neither honours nor disgraces, neither a familiar friend nor a familiar foe. It rides on my shoulders and I am just a vehicle among its fingers, a sort of stone that rain and weather can happen to. But it is neither lithographer nor paleographer. If something is covered over, this familiar is still the spirit of that something. It is in everything and everything, notices everything, retains everything, and remains everything. It grows with information, and I stay the few rags of a stock character, and the handful of notions a monkey needs to drink tea. Memory has no accent, like one of those people whose origins are vague and called neutral – but it also has all accents when it has been them all. A pervasive liquid traveller, who is as comfortable in third class as first, or uncomfortable. Neither tyrant nor guardian, something to fear and love – which reminds me of something, but of course I don't know what. A parent perhaps, at least in early years. Sun and years are fuddling my vision, but this bastard son of no one, or hermaphrodite of no origin, marches on without deterioration or confusion, an oracle of anything between blood and water. It doesn't seem to care, though it minutely distinguishes. And if it cared then it would perish too. So don't be bothered about anything, memory, or it'll bring such trouble on your head, if you have one, that who knows what would happen to me. Don't mind or celebrate what you see, my neutral familiar.

The railway track was a calm broad ledge on a Sunday. We stepped by means of the tightly-laid tart-smelling tracks. They smelled of mince pies. My mother sported her jeans which she had shrunk by wearing in the bath. The wet denim had turned her legs the same as a seal's skin when it flops out of its bound-aried pool in the zoo. They were dry and crisp now under the emphasizing clouds. The steel gleaming lines closed in the great distance before us, and the curling distance behind us. But as we reached the places where they closed, marked by a workman's hut or the roofs of the beach-shop and café, the journeying parallels remained miraculously open.

Where the tracks winced, or seemed to, at our backs, a figure followed, like a dog or a panther or a bear. My mother didn't look behind her at any point, but enthused about the many special features of the walk – the overgrown domestic grass and the danger of unscheduled trains. And the way the grey stony beach seemed solo and prehistoric from such an artificial height. Still the hairy creature stumbled along after us. It could neither catch us up nor lose us. Nor we him.

'You like?' she said. 'It is my palace for you.'

'Well, not for me,' I said. 'For both of us.'

'Yes,' she said. 'For you.'

A glowing old ship-deck of a place, under whose windows Lucerne or rather the old English Quarter roofed down to the wide metal-plate of the Vierwaldstatter See, and the sensible ridge of mountain, tree, and snow beyond the city. Here was the opposite of my Parisian bondage, from rot to royal flea: a broad easy apartment, whose rooms were at last near the size of the old Dublin half-tenement rooms of my childhood. And Xenia was delivering this clean shone ship to me with a clicking of her father's checkbook.

'It's bloody wonderful,' I said. 'No other word for it. Jesus Christ, Xenia, you found us a real paradise here.'

'Oh yes,' she said, and stuck her clacked palms together, so the girlish noise sprang out from her and went to live in the darkest corner. 'In the old quarter too. You say old quarter?'

'We certainly do, my dear, we certainly do.'

'Please do not call me dear,' she said.

'What?'

'Dear. That is like schätzeli, isn't? Yes it is I think.'

'Oh. Why not?'

My tone had descended to testiness in two grey seconds.

'It's not good,' she said. 'Okay?'

'Well, okay.'

But it wasn't really.

'What can I call you when I feel affectionate?'

'Call me Xenia,' she said, reasonably.

'Yes, but these words will just jump out of my mouth. I'm used to it.'

'I don't want you to call me names you had for the other girls.'

'Ah,' I said, 'come on. What about darling?'

'No,' she said, in the middle of the empty flat. The various angles of the sun came in the windows at precise Swiss intervals, and crossed each other a few feet from where she was braced. Her red skirt softened her long woolled legs. I was used now to how her breasts stopped lower on her stomach than most women's.

'It is all, how is the English? All little words, you know, Oliver, like eh, little dear or little darl.'

'No such thing as little darl.'

'Oh but then it is like human to animal, oh it is hard to explain. But I don't want.'

She was a mixture that moment of a soon-to-be-angry schoolgirl and a soon-to-be-angry schoolmistress, which just at that point seemed formidable, and I wasn't sure how to proceed. I felt quite differently about this, and didn't mind myself what she called me in affection. And anyway I didn't see that we were so big and wonderful to begin with. Perhaps it was measly and miserable to think that. But there was a presupposition that was bothering me, like a word on the tip of my lazy tongue. As often happened with Xenia, my notion wasn't presenting itself as a fully-fledged argument.

'I have to call you something sometimes. A shortening of

234

your name?'

'No,' she said, a little louder. 'No,' she said again, but leaning the word towards me with exaggerated quietness. 'It is what I don't want.'

'Look, I may have called other people darling and such, but I've never called you that, or yes, I have in letters, and you never said anything.'

The fine affectionate flat was beginning to lose its walls and definitions around us. We were floating above the city in an ill-defined cloud of yellow and cream paint. I saw the table which the unfaithful boy had picked for her, very exactly squared in the kitchen area.

'Let me use some other phrase then, something big.'

'What?' she said. 'Big what?'

'I don't know. Big animal? Or what do you want?'

'Big animal,' she said, laughing, 'yes, I like you call me big animal when you want. Okay.'

'Okay,' I said. 'Now what are we going to put in this huge great place?'

'I have the stuff from my room in Berne, and then there is things we can take from the apartment of my grandmother, and then we buy some more things.'

She pushed through her formula for an instant house, and I felt a slightly-winded suspicion of being a fairly useless ingredient in this arrangement.

'All right?' she said.

'Great,' I said. 'Perfect.'

Somewhere in the outer hall an urgent small bell came alive.

'They're here,' she said, and whirled out the door, and the glass door, and the second glass door, through the clean dust, and I listened to her clattering down the four flights of slippery stairs. I plodded more slowly in my unreliable shoes. She was used to polished surfaces from the country having snow much of the winter, and her shoes always had provision for that, quietly under her soles.

Her father and mother had driven up from their city in two laden volvos, which were parked outside our bushy blue gate like two sullen carapaces. One car had a tarpaulined trailer, with chairs and books and general ingredients for cooking and having a life. This was her life right enough in the cars and the trailer, and it would have been a vain search for my own among her possessions, unless you could count the old blue scratched suitcase that represented me as best it could. I thought of my own life in my own country with such things as parental cars at one's disposal, and bits of my mother's house transferring into flats of mine, in anticipation of settled times. Alas I had brought myself very far out into the sometimes warm but very real deep water of another person's life. Xenia was here in this town to attend her dance therapy school and I was here to be in love with her. Now that my life was saved, or so I irregularly and sweatingly believed, this prospect had a faint brush of the bizarre across it. Enter this picture, ye who dare, with strong heart and nothing to lose.

Her father again, with no effort on his part, and no obvious hostility, managed to tighten my shoulders as if mechanically, with an improvisation on the garotte, but I smiled with eventual horror, that hopefully looked like agreeable and urbane interest, and helped them haul Xenia's goods up into her, our, and my castle, sliding intimately on the soft waves of the wooden steps. At different times the castle would lose its second and more often its third pronoun – a fortification of definite solo tendencies, that could abide no unskirted king for long.

But when the cake-eating and coffee-sipping couple was talked to and dealt with in the whispers they desired, and cosied, and their little fleet of expensive upholstery was swept off the street below, we dragged in her big dark red carpet between the two of us, and spread it over the brilliant light-wooded boards of the bedroom. It fitted the room so snugly and beautifully, falling out of its roll with confidence, that we both cheered up in our separate gloomy doubts, and she hugged me like a daughter and pressed her unimpressionable mouth to touch my happiness. Who the daughter was beween us just then was hard to tell. I struggled not to call her darling or dear, and stared at the spread soft blood of the carpet, widening so opportunely before our feet. It was somehow a verifiably good omen.

It was a brief porchy town somewhere in southern Tennessee. We hadn't read off the name of it on the signboard as we motored in.

'Looks like a real bored little place,' Sue said, not bothering to lean more than an inch to view it.

'Can you get some cigarettes for us, Sue?' Chicken said. 'And some Bud maybe.'

'Sure,' she said.

He swished the car among a group of pick-ups and Fords, and let it lurch against the gear.

'I'll get out too,' I said. 'Breath of air.'

'Okay,' said Chicken. 'Right. See you in a minute, comrades.'

'Want anything else?' said Sue, sticking her head into the air-conditioned cave. It was hazy and different out on the pavement. The place claimed you as you fished into it.

'Nope, I don't. Don't like to leave the car in a town,' Chicken said, 'in case someone sniffs around it. They won't sniff around it if I'm sitting here to bite their noses off.'

'Oh sure,' said Sue. 'You just hang on there, Chicken. What cigarettes you want? Parliament or what?'

'Yeh, Parliament. Get me the soft pack if you can find it, okay?'

'Yeh, sure,' she mumbled, and we cut across the road in front of him. We had spotted a neoned store the other side.

The boy in there was rectangular-faced, and his adolescence had decorated his forehead with a galaxy of spots. He couldn't even grin properly, the sides of his mouth were so encaked. His lumpy white overcoat was streaked with some unidentifiable blue liquid. Perhaps he had had a spillage in the storeroom. He saw me looking at it and he looked at the stains, and he tried to grin again so I hunted up the beer instead.

'What beer you after, sir?' he said, stiffly.

'Budweiser.'

'Bud Light, sir, or the regular?'

'The regular,' I said. 'You got that?'

She rummaged about on the cigarette board, and cursed in a stifled way once or twice.

'Hey, fella,' she said. 'You got any Parliament in the soft pack?'

'Soft pack, ma'am? Well, maybe not. I don't know. You see any?'

237

He had swung like a puppy to serve her, and he raised his equally stained paw, and rubbed speedily at a group of spots on his chin. The finger he used fluttered on them, and then flew away, carrying the rest of the hand with it. The white arm was dunked against his side again.

'Well, you don't have any,' she said, more in anger than in sorrow.

'I'll fetch you some,' he said. 'Hold on there.'

He tumbled away into the storeroom, and left us with the whole shop to steal if we wanted to. We didn't though. Sue smiled cunningly at me and stared out the window, through the clutter of sun, and turned to the storeroom, amused, but then back to the window. A police-car had washed quietly in against the curb, and the driver was owling in the big shop-window at us.

'We're not doing anything wrong, are we, Owl? Just at this moment, I mean.'

'I don't think so,' I said.

'Well, just reassure me,' she said.

'No, we're all right, we're legal. Don't worry about it.'

'We could have been hauling something out of here, if we hadn't been lazy,' she said. She shook her moving hair and scratched an armpit briefly with a hitch of her shoulder. Two strands of hair got twisted roughly behind her ears.

'Fucker's making me nervous. Where's the bloody house-boy?'

The bloody houseboy, with his blue blood, re-emerged or reburst from the dark store-space.

'Got ya them,' he said, holding up a pack of two hundred. 'This is a rare cigarette, you realize. How many you want?' he said.

'We want twenty,' said Sue, 'and we want that sixpack, and that's it.'

'Right,' said the boy, understanding somehow that the tone of our adventure had changed. 'I'll wrap it.'

We left his garden of acne and pushed out into the street, with a small paperbag under my arm. The door was a little narrow and swung stiffly. When I turned with Sue we found the cop leaning against the backdoor of his extremely polished car. He raised an eyebrow at Sue and rocked up straight from the metal.

He had a funny touch of Chicken about him, in his hard burnt stance.

'Where are you two folks going?' he said. 'Where you headed, sir?'

I tried not to glance over to Chicken in the big wedged car. There was no sign of him in the front seat though, when my eyes inevitably dashed across that way.

'Out of town,' I said.

'How'd you come in?' he said.

'We hitched in, officer,' said Sue.

'How are you going to get out?'

'Same way we came in,' she said. 'If that's all right with you.'

'That's fine with me, ma'am. Out-of-staters don't do very well here, is all,' he said. 'I like to keep such as yourself movin.'

'Well see, we'll just wander down to the edge of town and thumb it,' said Sue.

'Better still,' said the policeman, 'I'll give you a ride myself. Then there'll be no possibility of confusion.'

He unstuck the backdoor for us and waved us in. His face was movie-starrish, but he had a fair mound of a beer belly to balance it.

'That's it, ma'am,' he said, as Sue bent in.

He slipped himself familiarly into his own seat. I looked over to Chicken again. The top of his head to his eyes rose in the shadowy front. The half of a head threw a vague nod at me.

We had an awkward feeling in the car, like a small stream of water that a horse's hoof has altered by printing into it. We sat stiffly in the bare cleaned vehicle. It represented for us an alien attention to what we thought of as ludicrous detail. Only the driver's seat was a bit worn-looking, and had a contraption of canvas stripes to keep the cop's body from sweating into his clothes.

'Conditioning's bust,' he said pleasantly. 'I keep meaning to get it fixed up. Weather's been coolish though,' he said.

'This is a nice little town,' I said.

'Not bad. Nothing ever happens. But then that's the way I like to have it.'

This seemed to put a slight caution on me, and I shut up.

'Neighbourly of you to give us the lift,' said Sue gently, robin-soft.

239

I could track his eyes observing her sharply in the rear-view mirror. But the gaze eased when it satisfied itself about something.

'You're welcome, ma'am,' he said. 'Glad to do you a favour. And it does me one at the same time.'

The clapboard and the signs dwindled away, as if some strange forester had chopped his way into the edges of the peculiar wood. He carried us right out to the entrance ramp of the highway.

'You can hitch on the ramp,' he said. 'That's legal. But don't go down on the road. Okay?'

'Sure,' said Sue. 'See you now.'

He left us with the bag of beer and tobacco, and Sue in her windy dress, and me in my polite smile. The blue car arced on the gravelly tar and crawled back into town.

'Well just friggin great,' said Sue. She backed into herself and opened her arms like a bloom, and said: 'Fuckin nowhere, fuckin nowhere, and he thinks it's Fort Apache or somewhere. Meddlin fuckin asshole.'

'I think Chicken saw us though,' I said, feeling suddenly crumpled and tired, as if I had done a day's work without pay. 'He'll be along in a while.'

'Still,' she said. 'I thought for a moment the bastard was going to arrest us.'

'For what?'

'I don't know,' she said.

After a division of an hour, Chicken's chariot hummed up and rescued us. The wide reassuring car seemed somehow much more stolen than it had in the morning. But it didn't matter.

It was a simple siesta-ing groggy Key West afternoon, and Ali and I had come down by the yellow-flowered road to sit on the planked pier that pointed a bit pointlessly towards Cuba, and to hang our legs from it. No boats, either pleasure- or fishing-, moored there, because it was open sea, and the reasonably happy blue water accepted the brighter thinner colour of a vanishing sky. The inks up there seeped away more and more, as the hour or two drifted, and the paper bleached in its own sunlight. The

240

sea transferred its flat bulk from right to left, so you thought the whole key was adrift and heading out into the Atlantic. Away to the right was a private shore of luxury houses, and to the left the public beach, where cheap fried sandwiches could be got – and an ageing gay sulked in the loo – and a big highwaylike pier that waded out into deep water, and rightangled there, and stopped.

Dope-pedlars liked to meet there, Ali said, because at night only the soft wool of the lamps was visible, and any car with or without headlamps could be prepared for if it set tyre onto the ramp. As we talked, a far-away stick of black strolled on motionless threadthin limbs into a corner of the marooned end. Like a piece of dirt in someone's eye, the figure seemed to float rather than propel itself, and it slipped into obscurity among the boulders of the pier's bulwarks. Ali followed this charcoal smudge with a superior professional concentration.

'He don't even have a car, mon. Look at him.'

'What's he waiting for, do you think?'

'He's waiting for no one. He thinks he's waiting for his customer, but it's too early.'

But along the wide palmed searoad, a large American-built car was trailing a closing tunnel of shimmer and exhaust. Ali was silent. Under my palms the grainy wood was warm and somehow soft – in the night it would be stone-hard. Two girls in parrot-bright bikinis treaded past us without heeding us. At the lip of our pier they stepped carefully down the seaweedy rungs, and flung themselves one after the other into the quiet stewing glitter. Their heads sleeked up from their dives, and they snaked in overarm straight out into nowhere. They turned about three hundred yards from shore and swam diagonally to the wriggling coast.

The big car meanwhile had got as far as the elbow in the large pier. It had paused there, and two men, or two straws we took to be men, detached themselves from the tiny blackness of the automobile. I supposed the first arrival had been luckier than Ali's doubting prophecy, because his figure reappeared clearly on the stricken whitened tar, and slid again in that odd legless way towards the similarly-floating newcomers. We heard the tiniest noise, like the top of an egg being tapped by the moon, but just once – and it sounded as unimportant as a seagull's bark.

'Shit mon,' said Ali.

The single man, who had not been let down, fell down instead, and his two customers flicked back to their car, and we imagined we could catch the swell of the engine as they reversed and calmly retraced their tracks.

'We didn't see that,' said Ali. 'You hear me?'

'What happened?' I said, very puzzled.

'It's useful for dat too,' said Ali. 'A little bit of business put straight again and no one the wiser.'

'But they just shot him. They just blew him away.'

'Mon, they have ten of these a month here. And it's not as bad as Fort Lauderdale. Forget you saw it. Forget it.'

'But they're crazy!'

'It's drugs, mon. The drugs people are really bad – really gone loose in the head. You can stay away from them and live a reasonably long life, but not in their company.'

Nothing happened on the searoad or the seapier. The black mark remained toppled over, and the car purposefully gained the further houses and gardens, and glimmered out of sight, the roof talking to the sun. No one came and no alarm appeared to be raised. We hung our legs and the sea moved from right to left, as if we were a great rocky raft, and the girls started to swim back towards us. Just nothing happened. There was no reaction on the part of the general scenery to this rapid smooth death, that had occurred as an item at the extreme range of our sleepy eyes. Its unimportance was bewildering. I felt nothing. It hadn't really taken place. The figure was there but if you let your gaze blur a little, the merest bit, it fuzzed and became part of the surface – it might have been a different-colour tar laid as a patch, or a trick of the light. Nowhere in my mind could I see it as a man of this or that height, with a well-placed bullet some-where vital in his corpse. There would be blood steaming from the wound, gathering in a widening invisible shape, and dyeing into his light summer clothes. He might be panting a final morsel of air. The sky might be unbearable, and exaggerated to a furnace in his shocked unable pupils. But more certainly none of these things could be unfolding, at such a distance – nothing could be real so far away and stagelike. It hadn't altered the progress of our inaction, nor impressed the seabirds, or been noticed by the only other moving intelligences in the vicinity,

242

who were even now pulling their varnished unattractive forms from the blind sea.

'What does he do now? Just lie there?' I said.

'What you want to do? Run over? And what? He's dead. Someone will find him who saw nothing, and they'll call for a cop, and the cop will haul him away, and won't find out who did it, or if they do it won't matter because the killers will be dead too, or I don't know. You can't do anything. These are mad people and dangerous and not important.'

I felt a short splatter of drops on the back of my shirt as the swimmers mutely passed. Their feet darkened the pale wood. Other bits of liquid pattered through into the sea. Maybe we didn't exist for them, like the dead man didn't for us. If someone crawled up now and blasted the two of us, we'd probably be left on these boards bleeding unimportantly into the water. It was a brand-new thought for me. It reminded me of what Captain Collins said once about Asian people – that at home in Thailand and so on they had no respect for human life at all, and killed each other freely and without bitterness. It was because there were so many of them, he said, fifty million in a small area. But in Africa, Asian colonists changed, because they were abruptly so few. But this didn't explain an unceremonious murder in an ordinary Florida afternoon. Cuba was the next piece of good land, and the whole shoaling deep of civilized America thundered up to the Great Lakes at our backs. There wasn't any way out of this. Ali understood it and I didn't. He knew there was nothing to understand. It had stopped long ago being humanly understandable.

When the war came to the south Batty Moran went to the war. The unfinished water-colour of Cobh had to be rolled attentively, and the rickety easel disassembled and its thin bits knotted with linen tape, and the few old bolts packed in a small safe thimble-box. All the captain's things vanished neatly into two handy leather portmanteaux, except for the books of Kipling and Conrad and Scott, which had to be left behind in a wooden satchel to wait for his return, or be shipped back to Ireland, whichever seemed more convenient. Captain Collins was very fussy about the cylinder that protected the painting, and the mess of the easel which was not much more valuable than firewood. He attached a talismanic importance to these, that was not extended to his trappings.

But Moran made sure his officer looked polished and shaved at the station. He spent a good half hour enduring the squeaks of the captain, while he tried to blade the hairs that were a little lost in the bumpy region of grog-blossom. Still now in the water-colour light, his charge's face shone red but bare, so it had been worth the steaming. Captain Collins stood stooped on the platform in his unexceptional height, and the apparent muddle of the troops eventually settled into the carriages, as impossibly as his things had into their bags.

Moran was happy to find that this train, though hard-seated and cramped, had ordinary windows and had been made, every bit of it, in Manchester. Beside him on his seat was an extremely small black-skinned man in an eccentric piecemeal uniform which Moran had trouble admiring. This man stared initially at the captain on the bench across from him, and then just as openly and severely at Moran. He didn't seem to think much of either of them. After seven or eight glances Moran realized that the man was a good deal older than his awake rather-critical energy indicated. He placed him, after a ninth longer glance, at about sixty. That was very old as far as Moran was concerned for anyone to be in an army, and he wanted to ask the trimmed man why he was on the train with them. But the man began to talk anyway before Moran could get going. There was the farth-est-off clicking noise now and again, among the man's precise and quite posh English. Posh was a word Moran had heard among the barrack men. It meant Port-Out-Starboard-Home, and that, it seemed, was the best way to travel on a cruise, if you had the money, and liked your belly as level as possible.

This chestnut face spoke almost as crisply and evenly as the captain. Moran was inclined to overadmire him for this trait, because it was something that Moran himself had ambitions towards. He was tired of people saying *What?* to him and laugh-ing, even when it was pleasantly, at his private way of speaking. The occasional click among the consonants and vowels only made the stranger more special. He talked to neither the captain nor Moran in particular – he appeared to be teasing some invisible personage that hovered against the window, which was covered in a gauzy powdering of yellow.

'You see,' said the man, 'you get on a train, and what's the first thing? Important people. You're sitting with important people. I'm just not used to it. Of course this isn't my country, and then again it isn't theirs. So maybe we have the same importance, except some of us don't realize it.'

He fumed on like that, good-naturedly, for some clanking minutes. The train nervously continued through the part of a great amber plain that it hadn't yet been nervous in. There was a pointless immensity to it, as if it was a usual insanity on its side not to have contented itself with a few miles of yellowness, and been done with it.

Moran noticed the captain absorbed in observing the speaking mouth, like a person, very still, watches a squirrel. He saw a shadow of annoyance in the brow, and then after a bit that cleared away, and the captain vaguely smiled. Moran was relieved the captain wasn't upset, and he was also relieved that he wasn't upset himself. He quite liked the old-young mocker.

'Can yoo egscews mee?' said Moran. 'Bat wat iss yer neem?'

The man stopped all his machinery. He shut it down. He spluttered forward in a lipped laugh.

'Oh you talk,' he said, 'you talk, my good friend. How are you, and how is your pretty uniform?'

'Ets foin,' said Moran. 'Ets veree gud, and tank yoo.'

Moran felt a small rough hand in his. The hand fumbled there for his wet fingers and gripped them.

'Henry Grant,' said the man. 'I am the Earl of Tanzania.'

Captain Collins turned his sunlit face from the glowering thumped plain, and fixed again on the bright man.

'There's no such thing, Mr Henry Grant,' said the captain.

'Oh captain, yes there is, and I am he. You are looking here at a proud member of the San race, or what you miserable people call Hottentot or Bushman. Which is why you think I am small, whereas in fact you fellows are ludicrously and wantonly enlarged. I know women in the bush who would choke and die laughing if they saw you!'

Moran was overcome by this vision of small women losing their very heart-beats in merriment. He saw them bodily and thinly and minutely standing on a piece of ground inside an

245

enormous bush, and their heads were banging backwards and forwards, and a horrible vicious laughter poured out of the berry mouths. He felt ashamed and horrified at his sudden size. He wanted to creep away into some littler body, like an ill-fitting crab. He knew in his centre that he was not truly the size he claimed ownership of, and was only the right shape for a smaller shell. He gazed astounded at Captain Collins, and the officer was swollen and miserably wrong. For the first time he realized it!

'Oh don't get so upset,' said Henry Grant, putting his shipshape hand on Moran's brushed sleeve. 'You'll never see those women. Don't you worry. They've probably died of hunger by now anyway, rather than laughter. Believe me.'

'Whoi hungerr?' said Moran, suddenly confused and hot that these powerful judges should be so carelessly lost. He needed them in his palm if necessary, to hear their scorn. He hoped he wouldn't stoop down and eat them with his teeth, if he had them at his mercy.

'There is a number of kinds of hunger, my odd young friend,' said the Earl of Tanzania. 'For instance, supposing you are a princess of the royal blood, and you are proceeding along your very own track, on which you have been thought special all your life, and you meet a young man much too tall for handsome, and he is all chalky and colourless in the face, and he doesn't bow or anything, or show the remotest respect, in fact he looks half-inclined to hit you with his stick – and in the upshot, ignores you. That gives a kind of hunger too.'

Sixfoil Fourteen

Moll, diss manne Micel datte de bishap hatte trapt an almoost torturt, cud nat be callt a badde fellaugh. He wasse nat a foole eeder, and did natte riez in hez wureld anly becorse his owen fadder hadd bene a thiefe of smalle tings, an soo hadd staint hes sonne. Bat Micell in hiselve wasse clere and ordinaire, and wud nat willinglee hurte anudder manne.

Dis daye he wasse huntin quietlee alonge de wied grene hille dat slopet at de backe of de tooer. He cud see som menne leanin an chattin on de walles, bat cud natt here dere mouthy speachez. He wasse aloon amang de rouff felds uf de hille.

Here he wisht ta cetch some animool fer hes ladee quene her supperr. He hopt datt perhapps de bishap mite forgivv hes burnt paw, and latte hem be. So dis present to de quene was bi politee as welle as al els.

He sette hes snarres, an putte hes own bodee in a gentel bushe, whar he cud reste and watche. De greye leves of de skirtee plante settelt ovvir hes worriet facc. Beforr him he hadde de barre hille, whar a softe clothey winde made litel cercles an tours throo de greye hete. He herede in hes eers de wordes an crees of de quene at eatin de nite paste.

She riz uppe amang de menne an al de serverrs an childer. And to gette der eyes, she stept apon de tabel, and stud streght, an wid herr legges sprad lik a soldeer. De bishapp satte in hes wizdim neer her, like a litul mouldet mounde of blak claye, al sileent an seeminglee widdot a carre. De quene heped in furs an cloth lookt as hotte as a cookt egge in a baskett uf woole. Her bodee livt unner de cloes, an de flocke uf menne sawe it der in de foully littel chamberrs of der heds. Sam wantted ta licke herr, and sum ta kille her − but moste turnt der eeres to her talke lik a grat beache uf shelles. Dese ears warr paintet bee wien an der owne mixtoors. An becors der larde wasse ganne, dey cud nat envisoon hem welle. He hatte becam a shadoo, unlik dis grat-

247

legged smal quaene dat wasse nat worthe de lov uf a worme. Dese menne ande folke war normalle and watery in der passoons, and wan Ollever wasse nat bafar der gaez, dey cud nat see hes diferoonce, norr kepe in der heds al he hadde completed and fashooned fer ther advantoog. And whan de quene she bellawed and screeched, lik a wicket owle uf de depest worste winterishe neet, ther bellees gript, and der faces loste the vigoroos blud of der drinking.

An Micel was wavt lik de reste, and he forgat.

'Dis lard uf yers,' she spatte, 'iss nat yer larde, becass he muste viset ech seesun de broken crued peple, dat live in filthinesse an oottside maners. He loves der goddes mare den yeers. Ower gott iss ta hem a litul pewlin forin god of odder peples. He wille cum bak an mebbee givv yoor yunger childer to de maws an de stomiks of dese sadde roarers. Hes greye cheks hav changt, and his midel an hert ar gon ovver to som unnatooral aspekt. He iss nat yer olde foin chappe, dat we al did love an fondel. Na, he isse a rogishe somtin-odder, an maebe ye lik dis, bat I do nat. It wulle kil mee, an it wull moider yoo. De bishap an mee hav no cravin fer demonns an changins. He hasse red hes bok in latinne calt Oved hes metymorfs, and ther it iss tru dat manne cann vert ta cretoor an clevir human godd. Bewar al dis, watchmenn, bewar, lisen to yer quene. Lisen to de honee an de songe uf yoor bishap. He isse no graspin manne. He wishoos ta serv hes lard. Bat hes larde is in dis waye ded. He hasse gon awae ta chang hes bodee an sole ta that uf a demonne. And ower god will nat havve demonnes ta rool. We muste shutte dis difrent manne awaye oot uf dis castel, and dreeve hem bak fram de arche. Lat hem den live wid de wud peple, iff so he wishes. Lat hem mudel in de dertee babee-crawlin mudd. Bat we muste nat havv hem on ower godlee castel an tooer. Wat saye yoor mouthes an braines ta dis?'

A glowerin sileence bitte inta de quene her fase. De bishap lat a peece of wint oot of hes arse an stud upp.

'Hoo does nat,' he sedd, very lowe, so dat som hadde ta lene ovver de tabels ta follow, 'who does nat shall go fram de hooly charch uf Room, an nat retern easilee. I wull excamunicat dese badde absentin kindes.'

De sileence becam a strange ponde uf thoght, and a dogge mite hev felte de slowe drift fram dislik to a deseer fer sens. Dey didd nat wishe fer der sonnes or gerls ta be et. An so de quene climbt downe an knewe dis seed wasse well planted, an mite gro gutt.

Micel dugge hes heels litely inta de erthe whar he nowe croucht. Everytin muste passe, he thoght, evven de gut manne Ollever. Perhapps, yess, dese olde gots hadd invadet hes cheste, lik a rivver of dangeroos hotte metall.

Won minet de hille wasse slopin wid emptiness, an denne twa greye hares ranne in across de anceent curve of a pathe. Wid som sorte of odde stupiditee, dey passt over de safe wied groun, an spunne an toppelt when de wiket snares pult tite on der leges. Micel burst oot wid hes bagge, an foght dese bigge crazee figoors inta de grainee fogge uf de darke clost linenn. He swept dem onta hes shulder, an sweted hoom wid dem. De creturs twistet an pummelt on hes back, bat he paid no heed.

In de stoen kitchen de pottes war redy an stemin fer dis gud hare soop. Micel wass happee in hes blut ta untee de bondes an grabb oot wan uf de animools. Fram de sacke he hault a yang greye dogge as spindlee an as dethly as a bowe. He dropt de howel tinge, an sprange up on anudder tabel. De too dogges lefte de bagge, and wagt der taels, an scoweret round de floor fer fallen food. De cookes laft ta finde Micel returnt wud dogges, an mockt his folly, de lik uf whach dey hat niver viowed.

'Wud ye haff de quene eat dogges fer her supper, Mic?' sed Jem Leery. 'Wat sorte uf feelty cuntee manne are yee?'

Micel made his mouthe nat telle, nat after de terrifeein storee of de quene laste nite. He did nat wishe ta bee murdered fer a magik-manne.

'Oh I amm a doltee calfe,' he sed, 'wat am I doin?'

'An whar do dese two fellas cum fram?' sed Leerye.

'Moi frend wasse drownin dese dogges at de rivver. An I hadde de sacke uf hares. We spoke an jokt a whiel an lefte doon de bagges. An nowe affter al dat, de hares ar at de botom of de rivver, and dese dogges liv. I wul drowen em in de welle.'

'Na, na,' sed Leery, 'dese are huntin houndes, an veree foin indede. Dese dogges cud kille a monster wid der tethe. Ye muste kepe dem an love dem.'

'An iss dat soo?' sed Micel. 'Den I wull.'

The wind was able to do something about the smoothness of the channel water, but it couldn't quite climb the hedges. We were over by the deepest corner of the garden, a bit squashed, and too close in some way to the caterpillared twigs and leaves. I could feel the extra intrusive nearness, that had come about by my mother placing our iron chairs without properly thinking first.

Through the leady interior of the hedge I could gauge the continuing action of the unfriendly wind. I was playing under a light covering of boredom, with a toy car painted red, and supposed to be an exact replica of a formula-one racing-car. I didn't know what such a car was, and anyway the seldom-mown lawn presented certain obstacles to smooth driving.

I steered the vehicle in around my mother's stockinged legs, and in the end irritated her. She spoke down to me mildly. She was reading from her favourite and often-read book, the ghost stories of M. R. James. She didn't understand the Latin tags at the end of some of the tales, and some day she meant to find out, and appreciate the plots even more thoroughly. As it was she appreciated them well enough. This man who had written the stories she considered a genius. She told me he was a genius. He was a schoolmaster at one time, and had read out the first goes at the stories to the boys under his care. I tried, but I couldn't imagine my present master doing anything of the sort. My mother also said she wasn't sure of Mr M. R. James' sexual nature. He was fascinating, but on the other hand had something of the closet queen about him. A closet was a cupboard and a queen was someone who kept England the way it was. This type of talk didn't help me to enjoy absolutely the journeys of the toy car across terrain it wasn't designed for. That ordered possessive tiredness, which had nothing to do with sleep, sat up in my head like a puppy and moved its crown. I could feel its hairy ears brush the insides of my skull. I sulked in a heap of grey school-clothes, that I hadn't bothered to take off. She didn't mind about such things. I thought briefly about the sausages and the fried tomatoes that were designated for tea, and then glanced out at the miserable exhausting corruption of the sea's surface.

'When is daddy coming back?' I murmured, like a choppy wave.

'Hmm?' she said. 'The end of the summer, I suppose.'

The end of the summer was a monstrously far-off border that had no windows, and couldn't ever mean anything because it was too inhuman and hopeless.

'And Dor?' I said. 'When's she coming?'

'With him, I suppose,' said the queen of toes. 'The same time as him. I don't know, Oliver, you know I don't.'

I looked up to follow the shadow of a seagull. My father and Dor, my sister, were standing in the archway that the hedges had for a door. I ducked my eyes down quickly to the car in my fist. The seagulls catapulted on up the sloped air in front of the fake castle, and skited in a blackened nervous flurry over the purple slates. I saw them in my hidden eyes, not in my real eyes. I judged their progress by their noise, like a radar did in a submarine. I hadn't liked to see my father and sister there, because she was growing out of his shoulder and they were both dark. Or else the archway was dark and they were just their normal colours – I didn't lift my eyes to check.

'They'll be back when the summer's over,' my mother said. She spread her finger over the green-covered book to stop the clever breeze from turning the pages too quickly, before she had read them. She knew them off by heart really, but only when she wasn't actually reading them. Then she appeared to have forgotten them after all.

I risked looking at her face under the loose waterfall of black hair. She was absorbed but not in reading.

'Couldn't they come for the summer, mummy?' I said, 'since the summer is the best time, and she won't have any school like me.'

'In England,' she said, 'the break is only six weeks. They don't have these huge holidays like you do. Don't you remember?'

'No,' I said, miserably. 'But it's no reason.'

'No, you're right,' she said. 'It isn't. Well, I don't know what to do,' she said. 'It's a pity the bloody landlord does, though.'

'Why?' I said. 'What does he say?'

'Nothing,' she said. 'Nothing at all.'

The gulls gave such a bawling pierced complaint, like a child having a knitting-needle stuck in its stomach, that I forgot myself, and raced my eyes up into the sky. I nearly cried myself: my father and Dor were hunched darkly in just the same way, but this time they were half-way across the lawn to us. While I hadn't been looking, they'd crept over like that dreadful game, where you close your eyes against the wall and count up to six, and then spin round, and if you see someone moving, you send them back to the starting-line, whether it's beside the tree, or wherever you decide to begin the game. But if you can't catch someone out, then they balance there at the point their run or leap has brought them. It's a game called statues, and it was the worst game to play in the world if you didn't like people stealing up on you. My father and Dor seemed to be intent on this game, except it was equally appalling either to watch them so they wouldn't budge, or hide down again in the circus of my hands, where lights and trapezes were. I stared as long as I could at the horrible way Dor's body slipped in and joined with my father's. There seemed absolutely no excuse for it. I couldn't tell if they were smiling or grinning, or what, because mostly they had a blank, rather dreary expression as far as I could make out, and it was the perfect match for this game.

I dug my stare into the grass in front of me, and swung it like a storm-lamp over the few green leaves with their snaily twigs, and up onto my mother's tennis-shoes, and climbed her silky legs.

'We can't really expect miracles,' she said. 'It isn't fair on your father really.'

I fixed my line of sight on her face, fumbling with that sextant as my boat began to sink – which meant that my father and sister were directly behind my head. My skull grew tight and crawly at the idea that he must have started to move again, and be even now approaching the last circle of my mother's influence. I felt my cheeks bursting into a plump redness as I goggled at my mother's dreaming mouth. Couldn't she see them at all? In a second his hand would reach out to tip me.

'I must ask what these tags mean sometime,' she said, for the hundredth time in my interested life.

In the afternoon of every day, after my walk up through the quiet houses, into the fringe of the forest, among the wide empty paths, under the marked pines, where the snows were

252

and I threw my head back up to the sky, for relief and in defiance – where the girl was, with her horse, heavy by the rough barn, and the ploughed field, and the dead football like a head in the stream, deeper in the forest, and walking-sticks to peel as I slipped, and over which the military jets scarred the chill sky – after this, in the afternoon, the housekeeper of the old man who mumbled below turned on his fading radio, for an exact hour after lunch. The machine, buried under the slippery boards and the intense rococo of his ceiling, hurtled up very slowly an always similar thumpy-thump bass music: only the grounding of the songs could penetrate the silent proper distances.

I imagined the details of the nonagenarian's flat, since I had to. I never saw him, or into his apartment, and only his housekeeper made herself known by the careful questions she asked Xenia about my legal status in the country. Seemingly it was a habit with such as she, to report in a natural concerned way any irregularity in the existences of fellow tenants in the house. All the other dwellers in the tall patrician building were rather crippled and ancient. The whole Englischviertel was an unlabyrinthine grid of doctors and the arks of autumnal rich Lucerners. There were specialists' plates screwed on every other gateway, and in my condition it was not a fact to please me.

Up through the Xenialess flat came the thick music, and I sprawled on the bed, and dreamed up repetitious scenarios for my demise. After some months of this, coupled with her return each evening to what I cooked for her – noodles and bacon and stripped cheese, apple-juice and soda water – and what I could think to say to her, and our at first communal baths, and eventually our single ones, and any of the other ceremonies that had had a speedy ritual thrust upon their surprised and unwilling shoulders, after a while of this reasonable life, the only perfectly reliable way for me to judge the passing of time was the mere tricks of the season outside the windows, through whose clothes and markets we walked at the week-ends, and the quickly-lengthening progress of my hair.

I wore it parted in the middle, as a new venture, so the curling blackness framed my face in a slightly girlish manner – it reminded me again of Degas' painting of the whore in her cups: alleys and pence on a marble table. I should have altered it to a more usual side-parting if it reminded me of that, but I didn't. It was gloomy in the bathroom with the big post-war water-heater – the war could only have beaten it by a year or two – and the disappointed scoured cream enamel bath. I fitted my face into the evening light of the mirror, and watched the hair grow through the afternoon. Or, under the light fixtures I had perched on chairs to place, in the first perfection of moving in, I lay out on the sky-blue couch, that we had carried through the amber streets from the amber ghosted flat of her deceased aunt.

Xenia told me her mother had opened a window after the death, to let the wrinkled soul of the widow escape out – to avoid the waiting shade of her oppressive husband at the front door. They had some belief or other in these matters.

At any rate the empty flat had not given up the couch easily, and we had filched also the three bits of mattress of the old woman's stately bed, which we passed our nights on, drifting without mayday on the shone floor. Xenia liked us to have little beanbags for pillows, and preferred to turn her tall brown back to me, and sleep undisturbed like a wombed creature. As I tended to panic stupidly in the hands of the dark, I oscillated between a gripped sort of isolation, which sometimes ended in my hands thumping the cold wall, and my odd cries waking her formidable self. This didn't go down very well: about as well as it would have gone down with me in other circumstances.

Sometimes we were more or less happy, or I was at least, counting the bushes by the tracked lake, or standing in the wet echoing blackness on a floating pier, and listening to the ducks complain about our human lateness. Incredibly old light was thrown out of the long shore-front windows, like rolls and roods of valuable carpet, onto the vanished shaved lawns. In Sunday daylight we leaned over the lake water – feathery and marbled – and watched black ducklike birds fishing blindly underwater for twisting escaping sprat. And we still haunted coffee-houses, established our favourites, the lame whore's one, and the one that sold an orange icecream beside the shallow part of the river. Sometimes we scouted for more stuff to grace the flat with, negotiated and grappled for a white hat-stand in an indifferent store.

Though these are not remote times, it is difficult all the same for me to remember her presence in these places. She doesn't survive much absence. But she is clearer in my documents when she is encouraging us to another severe spinning in each other's varied embraces. I grip still, in my careful dreams, her greyed panties in my fist till they tram into her cunt, and beat her up a blind bushy alley, like a mad child droving a calf. Her tossed head would turn and glare at me with dribbling rabid growling. Her lean danced buttocks bucked up at me so that my distant phallus, more faithful to her than to me, would delve her smell and her belching cunt – like a child's hand trying to scoop a sandy hole at the tide's overactive edge.

Is this what people do when one of them has lost himself, and the other hasn't noticed, and has gone on talking to him as if he were there. But he has drowned already in the bog's worst and deepest hole, and that shadow riding like a stone monster off a spitted rock of Notre Dame, riding on her back, is imaginary and obedient to the board of this imagination. She created me with her healthy unquestioning desire. A banana in her cunt and my inching phallus in her anus, clenched and spouting there, was as normal and good to her, as all unknown intimate but secret commerce was normal. Everything existed pure and clear, like banking, like weather in the wilderness, until the vicious weapon of question was applied to it, at which point I lost her shallowly, like a hand loses a handful of hair that belongs to a deeply sinking body. And when she stallioned up on top of me, with her stretched money-sacks for breasts, it was my palm crashing with a twisting energy on the bucking of her bottom that was obscene, not for her eyes. But then she claimed me and buried me into the dead leaves of the mattress. She pushed and pressed on my hips till the mattress let me drop further through the rotted bubbling mould. The flat hammer of her pelvis struck my phallus, and clamoured it through my stomach like a stake, and pegged it into the mushy floor, as if it were to steady a circus tent. And my head roared and responded, and my muscles sang and buckled in the heat, and all my body wanted to screw itself like a fleshy opener into the vulnerable wounding pickle-jar of her cunt. I gripped her grassy hair, and dragged down her lips, and ate them with steady enormous-tongued bites. I shouted out like a friend with one last instruction to a figure on the dock as the liner heads out into difference, and ruined her. And rose back against her like a murdered girl brought back to love her rapist. And she hoisted me up and up with her sensical love, and flew me happily over Lucerne, and greeted my risen face with a stretched vivid murderous resurrecting vowel.

But all today there's been a strange wind coming in off the fields, playing on Sue and me, upsetting the private mind. It has been impossible to think straight, with the wind, and in the end of the end I haven't wanted to think straight. And all of this day I've had cinemas, streets, the high walk from the circus square to the theatre, the big free school above it like a garrison, the helpful forest, anything to do with Lucerne, spinning and talking in my ears – her attitude sometimes in cafés, the real fall of her face, such a colour of forgetting around her pupils, that invisible thing that made her beautiful, how she got lost on her way home from school as a tiny girl, before breast and want, because she didn't recognize the bushes without the cars, how she stood on the crossroads, crying at the edge of her knowledge. It is all finished with, and over, never even happened in that sense, but the wind brought it back like faces, dead and buried, pressed against my window. I was again in those streets, not confused but painted, streets I have never been in like that, and the night tram hadn't arrived yet, and she would be on the tram. And I knew it for certain, that everything I remembered was wishful and wrong, the pattern and the man and woman it ought to have been. A little pillar at the end of the raised pavement held a light, like a smoker flaring a match in his cupped hands. And the broken-down drinkers were taking their beer in the frightened bar, and I could see their neat heads again through the curtainless windows, and catch their quarrellings and disappointments, catch them in my throat. The flower-shop was very dark, but still the blue flowers were bright in the blank dark window. The paper stand was locked so tight it was almost sighing with the constriction of its bands. Down the way the antique shop was evidently drowning, selling country furniture to citizens. The little park like a graveyard without any stones, just the huge deep yew tree stopping everything under it, like a forgotten disaster in the mind, and even the fag packet astonishingly dropped on the clay by a Swiss conscience, returned, and the knowledge that the slums for foreigners were never visited by me, though I was a foreigner, though not a stranger, and all the walking I did alone while she was at her school, and the hundreds of evenings we spent together in our mad way, flies in amber. And I just do not know why, and no one should have the impertinence to try and tell, why I was there, or why even I remembered it today in the lousy wind. I turned my head on it, but it was still ready when I turned, the far reach of the lake walk with its plaque telling you nothing in plain English, the whole fright that the Englischviertel was in because its name was a lie, an idea of Englishness, as remote as Ireland. Dank gardens and little sheds, where local sculptors hived, slippery walks again through the tall apartments, the grey mansions too, they came back, the snow by the brown stream, the outlandish notion of exercise among the pines, and the monument, a tiny one, to Aphrodite, which was just a horsetrough, and redundant at that, though not overflowing, despite the absence of cobs or shires. Ice on everything, even the lids of cankers on leaves, a sun for ice, stumbling among the trunks, the girls learning to skate to please their mamas, the pop music so stupid and beautiful in the distance, locals in their locality – her helping me once in my foreign shoes, between the blue trees and the rush of a field with a little ski-run, the slow descent on her arm, and her jokes, to the raw past of the city, where the tram and the fallen house were impatiently waiting. The woman who fell on the ice in middle age, just before the ski lift, just before safety, the mountain not wanting her. The rattle of German and French and Italian in the town at night, the glow always of the cinemas, friendly and like churches really, but never apart from her, someone I inhabited that planet with. How I got there, this was excluded from me today as a reason, and today I merely panicked, just a little, for fear I might not have escaped it after all. That I didn't want to escape it, that I had been there because I belonged except for the minor detail of not belonging in the least. The smartness of the people, their need for medicine, for everything that could be expensively bought, their banks, their restaurants in a drift of potatoes, the curtains over the doors in the bars to keep out the new nights. The great coloured church above the wide breathing river, the fall to the water. Xenia like an elaborate child pointing out the river of her childhood, the swimming they did there, she and her friends, in that enormous river, among the big boats, off the bridges at flood-time and

257

down to the lower bridges, like rats breasting its strength. Xenia saying *scheize* always, me not even able to spell it, or spell anything of her. The lunatics she taught to move, the old people on the edge of vanishing disturbing her so much she began secretly to smoke again, after she promised to stop if I would shave daily, to protect her chin from rashes. An aimless and talentless life, the slices of extraordinary cake, iced-over cake, the very look of the utensils in the kitchen, the cleanness of them, and the old engraved wineglasses she plundered out of her aunt's cupboards, and the bits and pieces of that home she winged to her own home and her own life, and how she left me in Paris and then collected me at the station in her own time. And those stations with the waterfall of panelling, the voices calling her intimately to trains, us to trains, to leave, to get there, to get home, losing you at last. That was a bravura wind today, and it lifted everything slightly, Sue's skirt among the rest, and spoke all day about Lucerne, and wouldn't let it go, and said I couldn't include what happened in the effort to include it. That everything like that was futile, nostalgia lying in its teeth, pretending I was only a spectator. The sitting in parks, watching the birds come down like euphoria to the clear earth, glanced at by so many eyes in private minutes, no pair ever considering another, the very key to their pain, that it might have worked if I had been intact, less poor, more steady, and then really have happened as I was remembering it, not nostalgia but forgotten happiness, watching the brown seep through the streets, touch the hats of the people, call to the windows, tell us at last what we were at, what we were doing out so late, waiting in the brown, the tram pulling in at last, with tears in its eyes, and Xenia so dreadfully calm and tall and good somehow against the secret flowers. And I didn't want her to be good, in anything, wanted to be steadfast in disapproval and exclusion, because in her goodness, if I had truly missed it, would be the impossibility of escape and survival.

Then at evening the wind stopped.

Chicken was black and moody, even broody. His sharecropper's features were dragged down, as if invisible weights had been tied to the stress points in his cheeks and chin. All he would say about it was, *I don't like Memphis.*

'What's on your mind?' Sue said.

'I don't like Memphis,' was the only available answer.

'We're not in Memphis,' she said.

'That don't stop me not liking it though,' he answered, 'and we're not far from it at that.'

Some miles down the road, the signs did begin to mention the closeness of the city. Chicken hung on to his large wheel with a grim fright, reflected for us to see in the rear mirror. He had a new denim shirt on, that he had bought mysteriously in the last little town. He had a swagger too in his head movements, despite his unknown trouble.

Sue rested quizzically deep into the back seat.

'Chicken, honey. You're making me pretty jumpy back here. What's the matter?'

'Woman there,' he said. 'Died.'

'Oh,' said Sue.

'But I didn't kill her,' said Chicken. 'I was even going to marry her.'

'Well, that's bad, Chicken baby. That's real bad. I'm sorry to hear it.'

I stared out at the lines of bowed electricity wire. They had set the tripod posts very wide apart, and clear black lines dipped over heavy black clay. We had driven through a surprising but brief pail-burst of rain, which Chicken claimed had blown up from the Gulf of Mexico. But how did he know?

'Hey,' said Chicken, suddenly getting all lively and friendly. 'Remember I said the other day I was in a band?'

'Yep,' said Sue.

'Well, Jesus Christ, but it was in Memphis I last played with those guys. I'm tellin ye.'

Sue crouched, warm and interested, and the cleaned fields and the scrubbed road flung rich touchable smells in through her lowered window.

'I wouldn't doubt you,' she said. 'Not for a minute.'

'Yeh,' he said, becoming momentarily sentimental, and his face dropping its weights for a difficult smile – Chicken's link to boyhood, I thought, 'good times,' he said, 'good times. The old days.'

'Why don't you like Memphis then?' she said, which was a fair question, except she seemed to have forgotten the woman.

'It's a mixture,' said Chicken. 'You can't get your hands on the okay without the bad. Ain't that right, Owl?'

'That's right, Chicken,' I said, but my heart wasn't in it. The land was so beautiful after the rain, and Chicken sounded mean and ordinary in his brightness, artificial somehow. The trees dripped with green water, and their whipped windy look was glossed by moisture, like a restored painting from a museum, set out to dry in some good simple daylight.

'You know,' said Chicken. 'I remember. Considering this rain we've just had.'

He stopped for a minute, and arranged what he wanted to say in little rows inside his head. I felt guilty for thinking him small, instructed myself that he wasn't.

'Well,' he said. 'I don't know. But I never did see such a flood as that year down here.'

'They get floods here? Really?' said Sue, and she looked out the window, as if there might be one passing at that moment, as if a flood were some sort of animal.

'Sure they do. They had a flood here, and we had money here. We had us a house up in the hills beyond the city. And our river there got up all swollen by the rain, and thickened in the rock sort of, and exploded itself, man, over the stone bridge between us and the highway. I couldn't say I've ever seen such water before. It was all muscles, you know, like a fighter in a big fight, shit, I'm tellin ye. We had a fair old flood that year, and I was singing well too.'

His last ten or so words had just started to gallop across the space between us, and his tongue made a yup-yup sound, it was spinning so quickly.

'Shit me, I'm dribbling,' he said. 'No. But my. I mean. You can't explain some things. You can't tell them to people. People last of all. It's just lies after a while. But maybe you two being friends of mine now. And all that. Well.'

Everything sparkled twice as vigorously as an innocent white sun spun from behind a flock of clouds, and dropped a mass of light on the country ahead. Still the green and white signs promised us Memphis in due course.

'You get drinking though, he said. 'You get drinking because it's nice to sing. And then it ain't so nice not to after a gig. And that was hard for me. But you still don't expect yourself to, how would you say, go completely out of gear. You eat your breakfast. And the woman's there to spruce you. And you're never a minute late for the stage. Until the day you are, and then, buddies, you're fucked, fucked all Bostonstyle, because they won't hire you unless you're a huge big man, saying nothing too much or too little, and I wasn't. I was just a happy little one, I suppose, and I knew it. But I drank all the same. Whisky in those days. Whisky for breakfast, whisky for love. Then the flood came up from the dry hills like that, so you thought you were looking at a big strong arm of a boxer, or whatever. I told you. And you had your day's bottle inside you, and you balanced on the bridge like that, like that, you know, waitin for someone to take you down to the city, remove you. Work. And then she comes out of the farmhouse with her bouncy little tail, boys. And what happens then? You can't remember! But they want to know. That's it, wanting to know.'

Chicken was quivering a bit, like an alcoholic in the early morning – any time of day, come to think of it.

'You know, Chicken,' said Sue, 'I don't give one shit in hell if we just go round Memphis here. And, you know, fuck it, who needs it?'

'Yeh, why not?' I said.

'I mean, who needs it, Chicken? Take this exit up there and leave it.'

'I will,' said Chicken, 'you're right. I'll leave it. And I was a good singer too but I don't sing now.'

'That doesn't surprise me, honey,' said Sue. 'I wouldn't either. Here, take this left here. Where's it head us?'

'Knoxville or somewhere,' he said. 'It's goin to take us backwards a piece.'

'That doesn't matter,' said Sue. 'Shit, it's all the same thing.'

We detoured then on a big circle of tar, with good ground the size of a small farm enclosed by it. But it was the highway, and the land was just scrubby and ignored.

'Hey,' said Chicken, 'now that I mention it, did you ever see someone go over a long slow waterfall on a big fucker of a flood? Did you ever?'

'No, I never,' said Sue. 'Thank God.'

'Well you don't see it,' he said. 'The body just disappears and rides that fucker all the way to the sea, or just as far as it can go without stopping, low fields, another state.'

Sue laughed like a toy fire-engine.

'And that's one ragdoll you've got for yourself then, I'm tellin ye. One hell of a pulped bag of bones. And no face or nothing. It was a hell of a thing to look at. Down that flood like a pill into your belly. Something ta see, I'm tellin ye, Owl. I'll never forget it, fuck me.'

He glanced back at me with a taximan's air, and speeded up, and inserted his car into a line of unexpected commuter traffic. It was late, and people were gong home somewhere to tea.

'Did a fair heck of years for that little party,' said Chicken, 'fuck me. Fuck me, fuck me.'

She laughed, like some nameless birds cry in odd parts of the world. It couldn't have been anything I had said to her, because I was still too nervous about being in her apartment to venture anything – let alone something that would work the miracle of making her laugh like that. So she must have been laughing of her own free will. Perhaps she let go every so often as a form of time-keeping.

Her house was a longish taxi-ride from the Bull Bar, and it was stuck up on a spare piece of land at the sea's edge. She had a crooked bushy view of an empty shallow bay. All along the road there were broken-down houseboats, either lopsided or propped on the dirty water. As a sort of joke, the other side of the road ran along a clean deep channel of water that was a road in itself for the expensive motor-boats of the people who owned the small estates there, with mooring at the ends of their gardens.

So Susan was neither slummer nor flaunter. The bottom damper part of her house was occupied by a battered woman, who watched you as you peered about for a bell and then banged on the swing-door.

I had no idea why Susan had asked me out there, but I had liked the long walk by the ragged neglected ocean. She didn't live that far from the palmed beach, where the burger seller got up so early, but it might have been another country. Just after her part of the key, the nondescript retirement homes began, and filled each side of the broad road, and could have been anywhere.

Susan showed me her three rooms and a toilet with pride. She paid heavily for her nowhere, but it still felt good to her. I had never seen her in daylight before: she was much younger than her workplace suggested she was. I felt my years like a crud of barnacles – as I was by the water – on my face. I let myself down into the canvas chair she put for me on her narrow balcony, and quickly knocked my fingers through my angled boiled-seeming hair. She surprised me again by making tea in two white big mugs. She propped hers on the wooden bar of the balcony, and then propped herself beside it. She wore a pair of paint-stained torn shorts, that were a few sizes too ample, and looked about twenty years old, and army issue: a bit like her. Her T-shirt wasn't much younger. Her feet were neat and bare, and on each foot her fifth toe was double at the nail, and joined at the root, so she had twelve toenails. But she didn't mind me counting them. She was still laughing and she was still proud of the house. I was proud of her house too, but I wasn't of my layers of age. I felt all the places I had been, and been wrong and right in, hanging from me in flags and mementoes and crutches, like the grotto of miracles in Lourdes, except I didn't think I was much of a miracle-maker myself.

On the other hand, Moll, it was a miracle of sorts to be on her balcony, and for there to be two or three hours of light left before she would even think of going into town to work. She had shorn her hair, I noticed, so it was short and boyish, and her legs were warm and comforting as they hung down from the old flaky wood. Someone had taken the trouble to groove four sides of the rail. The colour of the sky was a good cloth to frame her.

'You're going to have a bit of money when the stuff's got,' she said. 'What you think of doing with it?'

I raised my doubling chin, to look at her nervy face, with everything in its place. I wondered why I had ever thought to myself that she was plain. She wasn't. I knew the special journeys that her skin made all over the terrain around her eyes, and the strange scooped dip her cheeks took, just before her ears started. It was a hollow that shadow liked to butter in. She had a round wound like a halfpenny on the high fleshy part of her left arm, which she said was a bullet hole. She didn't bother to tell me where she got it. Perhaps it wasn't really one. It was the same as the mark of a clay mould, where the liquid was poured in, and which has to be filed when the piece is dried, if you want to cover over how the statue or whatever has been put together. It was her finishing point.

'I haven't been thinking about it,' I said. 'I didn't know there would be much money.'

'Oh there will, Bat,' she said. 'Yep. A couple of thousand each, I should say. Maybe you don't think that's very much.'

I considered what I had made in the army, Moll, and said yes, I thought it was a great deal at one go.

'I might slip up into Mexico. Or is Mexico down from here?' she said.

'I expect it depends on which part you head for. But Mexico is a bit rough for a lady.'

'But it's cheap, Bat, and I might get something going there if I plan it.'

I wondered if a few thousand would be any use at all for something businesslike, and thought probably not. But she was so young and awake she made me sleepy with her smoothness, and her teeth as hard as a turtle's back.

'What I wanted to ask you, Bat,' she said, picking a small cut sandwich out of a shell-blue plate, with a design of knives on it, 'do you think Ali would come with me, if I asked him?'

I hauled up my face to hers again. There was a shrunken elevator-boy on the bridge of my nose, and he pushed the buttons for me, and got my eyes on her. The jade water behind her still hot legs had nowhere to flow to.

'Ali?' I said, and would have liked to leave it at that. I felt his strength and his confidence like ulcers in my stomach. I felt like I had eaten Ali's confidence and it made me ill. I would have liked to groan and roll my head a little, but I held it, and the elevator-boy gripped my nose like a pair of wiry spectacles.

'He won't go,' I said abruptly. 'No, he won't.'

I didn't know why I let myself blurt it out. It was as true as anything I might have said, and as likely false as true. She set her soft feet on the floor, and made me raise my hand to protect my head by slamming her fist into the plate of sandwiches. In a moment I didn't know what was going on. I might as well have stabbed her, the way her body seemed to lose air and gain years. Maybe she was older after all. Or what had I done to her? I was claimed by silence. She glared into my silence, waiting for the life-belt. I fumbled it, and it fell out of my lips, and rolled without a sound over the end of the balcony into the dead sea.

'You bastard,' she said. 'You subtle little bastard. I've got your number,' she said. 'Take a walk.'

I gaped at her.

'Take a fucking *hike*.'

Her full-strength scream bulleted into my forehead.

At the station Moran stepped down stiffly with the captain's careless kit, and set it at a balance on the red dirt platform. Over to his vague left a file of men was leaving another train, on the opposite side. Moran sensed them even before he lifted his tired head, and he heard the words before the men got them out of their incredulous mouths:

'It's the Blessed Apostle, boys. Holy god.'

'Jesus, Mary and Joseph, so it is!'

Moran saw the fine small-treed country behind the rough carriages. The captain was still in their own train behind him. Only Henry Grant had heard the mocking astonishment. The grey-haired man paused on the sunny metal plate at the top of the steps, and regarded Moran bleached in the light beneath him. The muddled group of shoulders kept shouting Moran's Sligo name, which he had escaped from and abandoned, and beaten even, out of his own memory. Simple clear visions sliced in against him, and repeated, like a falling reaction of cards, between him and the soldiers. He saw Jane Smith burning like a dog in his hand. She spluttered brilliantly, like a whole table of candles.

Henry Grant thumped down to the platform beside him. He gripped Moran's sleeve again, as he had in the train, and pointed the taller man's clenched body in the direction of the plain of trees. Moran half stumbled where he was turned, and seemed suddenly catatonic, and the laughter and useless much-repeated jokes seemed only to hit against his uniform now, and fall as if he was armoured.

There was a town on the plain that he hadn't seen before. And instead of Jane Smith burning the town was burning. Out of the town, very clearly as in a painting, came a naked man, running with all speed towards the trains. Moran couldn't understand why he was able to see the floury skin of the runner in such detail. The whole thing was miles away, but also as deeply lined as an etching. He heard the beery macabre laugh of Henry Grant at his elbow, but the laugh was light all the same, and had true merriment in it.

The naked man was being pursued now by a figure with a lit torch in its hand, held up against the inquisitive sky. This second figure was burning like the town. His body was charred, like lamb done over an open fire, but his face was untouched, and black as Henry Grant's was black. But this man was taller than Henry Grant, and as the flames spread out behind him like a cloak, Moran could admire the gains the fast long legs were achieving on the runner in front. The white man had his red mouth open in a shout or a scream, but only the sky and the wide plain was the noise – Moran could hear nothing else. The legged and headed fire leaped all bumps and crevices in the ground, and the vivid chalked man pounded his limbs and o-ed the silent flower of his mouth. The black runner went at such a pace that he fanned the burning on his own body. A cross wind whipped now and then at him, and twisted and furled the lively tails of fire.

Moran heard the first man's scream, as if a radio playing the sound had just been turned on at full volume. Through this he still received the rhythmical knowing languaged chuckling of the earl. The scream started exactly as the runners reached the rusted first tracks of the sidings, and as they did the torch was lowered like a sword at the front man's hair, and Moran saw how small and out of scale the whiter figure was by comparison. The blue flames clenched the hair it was fed, and the runner's scream was framed by a dark explosion around his face. His hair might have been made of sulphur. The face screwed around on a soaked neck, and found the torch thrusting against its nose and eyes. They had stopped running now, and both the men were panting, and panicked, and half-weeping. They leaned on each other, as if it had been a sort of friendly race, and the fire caught on the fleshy fatty skin of the little white man, and fell around him like a dress. They blazed so viciously together that Moran could no longer make out who was who, and in a minute could distinguish nothing except an aureole and planet of windy flames.

When the fire faded and left nothing, even a few ashes, Henry Grant had not come down from the train yet after all, or had gone back up. When Moran swivelled he was not even on the metal plate, or rummaging, like he could see the captain doing, in the carriage. He set the kit he had in his hands down on the insect-crimson clay, and remembered the bunch of Sligomen, but they had gone. The train across the platform was an enormous line of goods wagons. He felt faint in the cooking heat, and swayed on his too-long-sitting legs. Out of his train soldiers were jumping and stepping, and handing down rifles and packs.

He wanted to ask Henry Grant about the runners, and hauled himself up into the dusty brown carriage. But the carriage had no one in it except the captain, and the captain was in a bit of a temper, because someone had crushed the rolled baton of his drawing. He was trying to smooth the page across his khaki-ed knees.

'Bloody hell, Moran. After all our trouble look what some idiot's gone and done?'

'Where's that black man gone,' said Moran. 'Did you see him, sir?'

Captain Collins nudged a glance up at Moran's reddened face.

'You look like you've been running about, Moran. You'd want to take it easy in this temperature. Do you know how hot it is? You're not in Ireland now.'

'Sligo, sir,' said Moran. 'Not in Sligo either, thank God.'

'Is that where you're from? Not much of a town, Moran. But it hasn't done you much harm. I wish I could say as much for someone's bottom on this thing.'

'Has he gone then?' said Moran. 'The man we were talking to, sir?'

'The little fellow? The earl of whatever? Didn't he go out your end?'

'I didn't see him, sir,' said Moran, 'maybe he slipped out past

267

me. I got a bit hot out there in the open. It's terribly warm in Africa, sir,' he said emptily.

'My very point, Moran. My very point. Oh bugger this stupid daub. I'll leave it.'

'No, take it with you, sir. We can straighten it out under your books when we're settled.'

'I'd rather not, Moran, if you don't mind. I'm fed up with it, and I can't be bothered to go on with it. For heaven's sake I can't remember what I'm supposed to be painting.'

'You'll remember, sir.'

'You think so?' said the captain. 'Well. I don't know.'

He lifted the creased damp page up to his face so it was hidden from Moran's sight. The head of the captain appeared against the magic lantern of the sun, as a silhouette.

'Maybe it isn't that bad.'

'It's very good, sir,' said Moran, 'and you'd miss it if you left it behind.'

Sixfoil Fifteen

The softe smoothe clover and smal white starree flouers spillet fram de buncht marked oakes onta de straet pathe dat wud bringe Conn hoom. He listent to de musik an de informatioon whach de dampe foreste likt ta throwe. He let de hooves of Jacke springe on de cutte soile. Behint themm, chunkes of clayey grasse flunge awaye fram his passag.

His domaine wasse clerly tite and tru, ande ass content as humanitee cud lette it. If they suffert, they suffert de saem as der fadders. It wasse enouff. His hert was grene and his bodee mostlee gud. He cud go hoom widdout regret: all laye faste behint hem. Ech godde restet lik a toade or a hare in ech place. They werr so muche fud in de earthenn jarrs. Hes springes an hes stremes an hes clovvered rodes, an hes wilde orcherdes, an hes vilooges, warre stil formed in de olde mathematuc. Der numbeers an shapes kept in der positioons. It was enouff.

The damme uf daylite was breched, tho it wasse middaye, an a feelthy darknesse bloomed lik de infectioon uf a wounde, an muche winde came gallopin uppe de pathe, an fram between de stiffe trees. Anly de thinne fishin-roddes at de endes of branches strucke across de aire.

Dis turnin breese stoppt, an denn, wid grater ambitoon, spunne in againe, lik de flailin ropes uf a great spiderr. Animools furred inta boles of oakes, an berds fluttered deepe inta holes an nestes. A thinne sparklin raine showered oot uf de clowds, an wove a lacey shawl againste de brittel ruinede lite. Olleeve leaned inta de strete droppes, dat mad a smal clatterin, lik madde fingers playin on an instrumente of stringes, manee manee stringes. Bat de stringes, wedder guttes uf cattes or what, wer icee an northerne. Theye cutte downe hes face, til he thoght he had a strange ironn webbe there. Hes horse thruste hes thick necke lower an forwarde. De winde foughte at hem, as if he mite bee a shippe. Deepe belleeish gruntes flew oot uf de cobbe.

269

Widdout firste gettinge less, de batterin stopt, an Jacke nerely fell on hes knes sans de force of de riveree winde ta butrez hem. Oliverr his eyes grewe wette an opent inta stretcht cercles. In fronte of hem on de roade a hors lik Jacke was steppin ta mete him, and on de clothy sadel lik his owen wasse a manne withe hes owen fetoors. De furz an al war de same. But moste odde of al wasse the coloors dat surroundet de rider. Al de foreste an skye an groun had receivet ther olde foin blues an redds an yellas. Conn shivert lik a childe or lovver ta se them. He cud havv callt oot to hes cheery godds, bat de figoor fritend hem an made hes mouthe hevy.

It alsoo lookt scaret an waree, an sed nuttin. He sawe howe derty an muddee de traveler wasse. Hes haire wasse lumpee and bearishe wid raine an rouff sleepin, bat Conn thoght de manne possest a happee aditoon to hes feer, becass de eyes hadde a pleasunt cavee colourin, dat a boye showes whan he iss plesed wid sum prospeckt, bat iss worriet to showe his plesoor, in case it mite be withhelde. Con liftet a wette arme, an twistet hes hand ta grete de silente manne, an de manne made the gestoor in mesurment wid hem, as iff he hadd knowne dat Conn wud doo it. Bothe horzes haltet wid one desicoon. A broken sudden horer loosenet in Conn his stomick, an he wisht ta shitte wher he percht.

'Wat ting maks yoo so pale, moi loif?' sed the riderr.

Conn cud nat answere. His bowells groweled insted, an chugged in hes gutt like a cowe trapt in a mud hoel.

'Yoo, moi lard,' sed Conne, becarse he sawe a princishe smatterin in de rainbowe uf de fello. 'Whar ar ye goin in moi naket tracke?'

'It iss moi tracke also,' sed the rider. 'Do yoo nat knowe mee at all?'

'I do nat,' sed Conn. 'I haff nevver sene you befor dis.'

'Whoi, moi prettee frend, I am unhappee dat yoo do nat finde mee in yer memoiree. Juste as de coloors nowe faed oot uf de leves an al supel grothes, so you seme to havv loste mee in yer labyrinth.'

'Wher ar ye goin?' sed Olleeve. 'Dis waye wulle anly bringe ye backe to moi castel in the ent.'

'It wull carree mee furder den dat, an no more. It wull carree mee inta yer firste tiem at bein a manne, and depe sporte wid

270

yooer quene, an codellin by yoor fader whan ye were veree breef, an inta de coeld winterr room whar yoo split yer mudder in torne skinnee sectoons at a cruell berth.'

'Wat iss dis nonsens?' sed Conn. 'Ar ye madde? It cannot be don ta slipp bak throo de loste an certaine rums an feelds uf what hass bene.'

'Nat bee yoo, in guet truthe,' sed de manne. 'Nat bee yoo, bat I cann do et.'

'Ande how?' sed Conn, bat in hes armes he did nat wante to knowe. Blak leches uf miseree hadde gott inta hes legges, an war drinken hes swete darke blud.

'Yoo can nat doo it,' sed the riderr, 'bat I can becass, moi dere, I am yoo. Dis hors iss Jacke, bat Jacke turnt rounde an walkin de udder waye. I haff bene yoo as oldt as crowes an parrotts an gredy turtles, an yoo after prinzship, an yoo in marchez an forestz, wid anlee yer hungerr an its hollo bellee fer companioon.'

'Don't, moi grete frende,' sed Conne. 'I do nat wishe ta here wat yoo halv don, or wat vicoos tings yoo haff endurt. Ried on an lat mee bee.'

'I can doo thate wid eese, moi loif, wid ees. Bat yoo cann goe gentlee an wid moi loff throo wat I knowe.'

'And whoi?' sed Conn, an in hes colde furr he wasse cryen.

'Becass it iss mine an yoors, and wat we meane an made fer owerselves, an tho it wull hurte yoo, it wull make yoo properlee mee.'

'Herte,' sed Conn, 'cud yoo nat turne aboot, an tak de saem chronicel fer seein twiss, an I wull turne olde Jacke on de roed an see moi dayes agin?'

'It wid nat wurk, sinc as yoo wud turne yoo wud vanishe, lik de coloors, an bee mee. Anly in de mirrer of what cums fer yoo alang dis tracke can you be sene by al. Wat iss nuttin fer yoo is vissoon an yers fer mee. Bat al dat is emptee an carried in moi hed behint mee iss solidd an a singel pathe fer yoo. Yoo jernee nowe intoo moi maggotee braine his lante, an I inta yoors. Butt, herte, dont crie lik thisse. I wante ta wrapp yoo to moi cheste, bat I can nat finde yoo lik dat, here at de midel line of ower lifes. Hushe lik a smoothe smal childe, an tak coorag in thatt yer yeers will be twic what nowe you haff eten, and de saem fer mee, or nuttin in de spinnin wurld can bee.'

'An wull I bee trapt an stampt bye murdroos hants, ande moi frame smasht boi fistes an kniffs? An wull I bee lonlee an smal?'

Bat de ryder wud nat, or wasse nat abel, ta saye. Hee proddet hes dubel Jacke, an Conn didd, an dey roed inta ech odder throo de mirrer uf raine.

Even though the sections of my life are no more than a handful in number, it's still astonishing that my mother rules only the first part. Here I am on another continent, as remote from her as a wild deer is from its keeper. If I am running from her I don't know it. I thought I had turned up in the world so she could be the world, and it's funny how long that notion stayed with me. I may have puzzled the vivid cloudy forever of the time behind me that had manufactured me, but it never entered my head to make any guess about the future. The future was only tomorrow and she was always there tomorrow, in fact she woke me into tomorrow, she called me. Like anyone else I realized I had been birthed and begun at some stage, but if I had been asked, and had to give a sincere reply, I would have had to admit I felt as if I had always been alive, and alive with her. I hadn't considered it, but I would probably have doubted anyone who suggested that everything had been there before me and without me. That just wouldn't have seemed true. The instinct of my empirical self did other more satisfactory prompting. I allowed that locations could be and were changed, and that the people I saw and half-knew and guessed at were for the most part temporary. But to have asked me to believe that they continued without me when we left them, would have been rather laughable and pointless. Why would they have wanted to? She wasn't there for them to respond to.

So she was the great definer and mapper, and because she led me with such confidence I followed her with equal confidence. If she thought a man passing had a face *like a mad man's arse,* then he had, forever. If someone disturbed her I loathed them, as if I had received the information of their stupidity by some simple electrical means. I have never lived with anyone so well since, and as an effort at peaceful communion it's only a pity that it came first, and couldn't have been worked up to gradually and sensibly – in consideration of the fact that most lovemaking and supposed love has been a bit of a mess, to say the least. It seems even now quite an attractive mode of life, if only she could always be fresh and sisterly in her twenties, and I scrubbed and laundered in my boyhood. Happiness needs decay to walk us out of it. But for people for whom sex is a brand of necessary suicide, being mother and son is suitable and bearable, especially for the small son, since he really has no need to hunt up disaster in the form of other people, and feels contained and even excellent inside the praise and one-time-only warmth of his mother. I'm grateful for that. But I have a hatred, or maybe a dread, of old sons still clinging to their even more ancient mothers. It gives me the creeps to think of it. Sometimes it's extended to a little corpse on a dusty mattress, and the quiet spooning son in his armchair, eating out of tins, tins being the affection of food. Well that wasn't ever for us. We were eminently sane and normal. Our sanity was a special prize. At any rate, I knew it would last forever, so there was no chance it could be in danger of change or decision.

I was that sure. And of course it did last forever, and has lasted and does last. She's still the captain and I'm still rowing our lost boat to safety under her brilliant guidance. You can love a really beautiful woman best as a man when you're not a man, but not a girl or a woman either. I've heard people talk to me about women being the best, and that they should stick together and to hell with men. Xenia used to reach that point in her least inspired and most dogmatic and probably miserable corners. It's almost true, I'd say. Sitting here at a lacquered desk among plants that almost stink they're so thinly perfumed, I'd almost agree. I don't think any woman I was with got much out of it. In later years they didn't give me much either – but then I've been thinning out in the small matters of hopefulness, and the spare generosity I started with. If I thought someone was a little cleverer than I, then maybe they got something out of it. But generally I haven't done any woman much good, except for her. And I can't explain it. I was better then, I feel it. It didn't matter about my father because she had me, and it didn't matter about my father because I had her. Maybe that was it. We both felt half-murdered by him, but we had a grand time together away from him. And we knew how to do it – or else she taught me.

She really knew how to have a good time. She could make an afternoon into a desirable accepted and undoubted history. We were like hunted deer all right, but as soon as we felt ourselves deep enough in the forest without the hunter, or he had stepped another way for the time being to hunt someone else, then we had the means to make the best of it. She had the knack of bringing a spinning moment right up beside a worst one. She could weave a disastrous morning right into the cloth of a fatherless afternoon. And then when we had to live without him, in the silly castle, by the seagull sea, with the oppressive landlord, all her years of solid practice just paid off. We were set for life, even if he did manage to be there, my father, now and then, or even most of the time for me. For her, it seemed he was as far away as the address she put on my letters indicated. This was power. Without him she had it, and could exclude even the shadows of him that penetrated to me. He couldn't haunt her because she knew his story, and she had translated the Latin tags to it long ago, and was expert in it, and able to ignore it, because it had always been straightforward and clumsily put together and the writer of it had had no true style. Compared to M. R. James my father had composed only one short narrative, which he had always repeated, and so he wasn't much of a threat to the old schoolmaster's supremacy. When she was given the bars of chocolate in the dim front room, in the melting shop, after our minted swim and our walk between the talkative swollen gardens, she paid no heed to the miserable black figure of my father trying to get between us, and say something that was urgent in his view, but useless and spoiling for us. The poor creature couldn't breathe and exist at that distance for her. I was sorry about him, because she was good at happiness and making such a thing for me, and that made him seem so inept and tiny. He could loom up as blackly as he liked. But her small size was bigger.

And then I think, maybe I am what she told me to be, in that, for instance, she warned me off marriages. Maybe she created me as the person who would always miss her – established her happiness as the only one, and pokered the eyes that would see anything else. Thankfully that is not true.

274

It took a great breath of courage to go in. The town was stone-raw and a little chilly: my ankles had ants of ice pouring over them, especially by the slow inch-deep sliding of the river. I had clutched my bones in a temporary suntrap for five minutes, in a hollow park with an asylum of gulls, and dreamed of going away to Greece or somewhere south, and anywhere alone. The two-bar sun and the squeezed first appearance of the débutante leaves, and the clattering cobbled square where I now was, with its cinema and its protesting daubs on the houses, seemed to be both in league and at loggerheads at the one time. The sun and the buds suggested I might stay and be overpowered by imminent spring, and the others the other. Get the hell out and don't look back. Whatever you do, don't look back. If you have the guts. I didn't have them.

The cinema was a discreet one, with small long posters on the columns of the doors. Only dowdy worked-out men, unsuitable for the country, seemed inclined to go in. Perhaps because it advertised a film with a former centre-fold of *Penthouse* as the star. I was so miserable it gave me an erection. Misery and boredom are oddly erotic, or at least unexpectedly arousing. I felt like I hadn't made love, or what I thought of as making love, for years, and in a strict sense I hadn't. I missed smallness and manageability and dishonest dreamy aggression. Maybe I wanted to fuck someone I didn't know. If fucking is being given the lead in the dance, then that's what I missed. But even so it made me twice as miserable to be glad now that I had worn my grey Donegal overcoat, that would hide my vagrant phallus, which was as bored as I was but had decided to do something about it.

I couldn't see the posters very well, but my eyesight was good – frustration makes you unblind – and I could discern a solid woman. And I might have asked her to marry me, if I could only have lobotomized myself and lived with her like that, in blunt excitement. I needed, on that bench, for my life to be a porn-movie, since it had stopped being any of the alternatives. That makes me grin when I think of Sue, but I didn't know anything about Sue. Then as now I knew nothing about anything, or nothing that wouldn't change, but I was sort of crafty

275

inside that ignorance. I had a matchsize light that I shone inside there.

The oldish coated men were drifting in, and paying their francs to a hand whose face, if it had a face – porn specializes in and even depends on disembodiment, butchery since metamorphosis is unavailable – was blocked by a sign taped on the booth window, so no one would actually have to look eye to eye. God forbid! There was something right about that sign.

No one came back out by that door, so the building seemed to eat the men. I was attracted by the idea. Building, eat me, I'm all yours, segment me as you please. Anyway I felt old and I had a similar coat on, and there wasn't anyone young about to define me better in the grey-blue streets. I was a private, a young recruit, in their little army. In that doldrum afternoon, the young were in university or school, or in coffee-houses, or at normal movies, or dead. Some of them took to the needle in a big way, that got them a small way – into the paid-for and godly incinerator.

This was the older men's drug I was staring at, though on the other hand, under the shockingly high sky, the woman on the posters was young enough, maybe younger than me. I thought of her trying to make some cash, to go to Greece maybe, escape her boyfriend, and having to do it with her ore, and the shafts that men liked to get down to it by. I was aware that sex films were shot in an exhausting pleasureless way by whores, and the cheaper brand of model, and I didn't suppose it could be much fun to be poked and repoked and licked by strangers. I supposed that might make a stranger of oneself, in that, unlike straight actors, you couldn't leave your character-part behind when you left the set – no world would let you.

I thought I had to go in and see this girl, or, as Xenia would insist, this woman. Of course this woman would be beyond the boundaries of Xenia, or require rescuing from the wicked desires of exploiting men. Well, that was true enough. It didn't matter a shit really. It was commerce. *Her* father ran a bank, probably serviced the accounts of killers and crooks, or at least some pretty shady types from outside the country. Just commerce! This girl with her colourful rounded picture, a trifle aided by an airbrush, in a half-winter square, was just a bit more obvious that his whispered politeness down a phone to someone who may have robbed people like himself, or even made a string of pornographic hits. I wondered.

Was this the only audience in the planet that never discussed what they had seen afterwards? Surely no one ever brought their girlfriend, or vice versa, there. And it was unlikely that these rainy men ever attended in twos. But you never knew. Maybe Xenia's father crept there, although she'd deny it for certain. And he wasn't the type. I was the type.

But I was inexperienced, and I knocked my money too loudly on the fingered counter – the swimming marks of the last hundred hands swished on the polish – and got a grunt and a ticket. When I swam my passage through the darkness of the seats, and eased down tenderly, the girl in the poster had her hand under the zip of a pair of shorts. She was wearing the shorts, and watching two other women commit a difficult act of sixty-nine together. They were exceptionally lovely in their bodies. The girl liked this and unbuttoned her blouse with her other hand, and made her breasts poke out. They were not real breasts. There were 'breasts', tits.

My mood changed, to put it mildly. It had been put to the test. I didn't want to marry her anymore. I wanted to lay her out on the floor, or failing that, watch someone else do it.

The fogs cleared in the cavernous auditorium, and my fellow admiring faces appeared around me, like a slope of large buttercups, or field mushrooms. The cinema was surprisingly smart and theatrical. As I peered at them, I marvelled how they managed to absorb themselves in the throbbing screen, and yet be very aware of not being alone, and erect sets of invisible blinkers on their ears, to block each other out, or to try. I imagined the blinkers as very worn and old and smelling of horses' cheeks.

This was strictly a matter between the glow and each man. They each were dreaming. They were old and they were dreaming. They were tired. When one of them woke up he got up, and sneaked with a hunched gait down the aisle, and in front of the hectic screen, and submerged himself in steps and a curtain, where there was a traffic-noisy door. As in most continental cinemas, no one smoked. Perhaps they only smoked after their star's coitus anyway. But that coitus never seemed to get post. I burst into blushing shame when an usherette carried the moon of her face to the wall under the screen, and stationed herself there a while, the most faraway look on her face that I have ever seen, with icecreams and lollipops and sweets. It was a great performance. No one budged. Over her torched black hair, the torched black hair of the performer's cunt squirmed and toiled. A manless phallus made a flaccid bendy noise in the greasy runnels of skin. It was a noise like a boot going into mud, a shoe kicking a rotten body, something so violent it was beyond violence. My heart was crashing about like a drunken sun. I had to get out or I would be murdered by anticipation.

Someone strolled down for an icecream. I skimmed from my seat like cream, and staggered, woollen with guilt, out into the unchanged moral square.

I wanted every girl I passed in the street, on my stiff progress home, to allow herself be edged into any alley, and be submissively but ruthlessly screwed. And I was the woman to do it.

A van came vomiting along the cobbles, passed me with its rear doors crashing, followed by a police-car, with an arm lolling out of it, firing off in the torn direction of the van, the bullets as disorientating as bombs. I was briefly back in Nassau Street in Dublin, looking at shoppers, bits of blackened shoppers, smoking on the tar between the green railings of the university and the hollowed shops. The van split its way through two cars at the crossroads, tried to recover, still at ludicrous courageous speed, struck a high stony slope, jumped back at the astonished home-going hats and umbrellas, and smoked a little.

'Hey, Chicken,' said Sue. 'See that paper there? Throw it over, will ya?'

It was very early morning. There were some men with caps that looked like they might be on their way to work but nothing fancy, and a grubbier young man, unshaven and morose. A chuckling little one, with a guilty confused expression, also hung on a stool at the counter, putting sugar into his mug — about eight spoons of it. He didn't drink it, but kept up the preliminaries.

The waitress moved back from the cooking-area, and planted her palms on the old clean counter, and gave him a look. He chuckled again, redly, and raised the sloping cup to his mouth, and the girl wiped her hands down her apron, and was wired back by a call from the cook.

Chicken yawned like an actor, and stretched his arms up into the warm room, and left his right arm up, and leaned a bit further to the counter, which was near enough to our table. He fumbled at the edge of the newspaper and couldn't get it – so he half-stood up and grabbed it, and plomped back into his hard pew and groaned.

He spread the local paper on the damp table and started to scan it.

'Hey, angelface,' said Sue, 'that's my paper first, honey.'

'Eh?' he said. 'Oh yeh. Sorry, Sue. Here you go.'

The waitress ducked out from behind the counter, that stuck like a rowing-boat into the middle of the café.

'What can I do you for this morning?' she said.

'Hey, I'll have a couple of eggs. Over easy, honey, an some toast.'

'You want some hash-browns?' said the girl. 'We do them good here.'

'Yeh,' said Chicken. 'Well, I will. Yeh. Gimme an order of them.'

The girl settled on Sue, and Sue raised her head at the silence.

'Me?' she said. 'You got some bacon?' she said. 'Yeh? Well give me a sandwich of that. And some coffee.'

'Oh yeh,' said Chicken. 'Coffee here too.'

'You want cream in your coffee, sir?' said the girl.

She was big-boned, but clear and handsome in her tanned face. Her hair was black and rich, and she had tied it up casually with an ordinary elastic band, so it flung out behind her in a stiff soft cone. It was thick sort of hair but shiny as chrome.

'Yep,' said Chicken.

She wrote on her pad in front of a comfortable strong breast.

'How about you, sir?' she said to me.

I risked a smile of an early-morning all-friends-together kind, and she gave the barest shell of a one in response.

'The same as Chicken,' I said.

'This Chicken here?' she said simply, nodding down at Sue.

'No, sir,' said Sue. 'That's Chicken.'

Chicken grinned up, twitching his brows like Groucho Marx, showing his teeth. They were as clean as the flesh of a fresh trout after baking.

'Okay,' she said, and turned away with a neat swing of her body. She baulked then, and swung, and her pony-tail swished, as if to get rid of flies, and she said:

'You want cream too?'

Sue glanced at me in brief confusion.

'Oh,' she said. 'No. He doesn't take it. Me neither. Thanks.'

'Right,' said the girl. 'Coming up.'

'She must be majoring in Poker-up-the-Ass,' said Sue, surprising me. I hadn't thought that at all.

'You finished with that, Sue girl?' said Chicken.

Sue hoarded the paper a little closer to her side.

'I've only just opened it,' she said. 'Hang your hat on it.'

The crazy man at the counter had a pyramid of sugar sticking out of his mug. He couldn't stop himself chuckling as the stuff spread down from the tip, and umbrellad thinly off the pile and on to his lap and the counter. The girl carried out someone's breakfast just then, and let the plate rattle in front of whoever it was meant for.

'Holy God, Jake,' she said. 'Will you leave the darn sugar alone?'

She pulled the bottle with its stainless steel pourer out of his mit, and plonked it emphatically down in front of someone else, making the stranger jump and slop a speck of coffee and laugh. Jake began to mumble like he had a speech impediment, and exploded with:

'S-s-s-some cawfee up here, miss, please!'

He almost screamed the *please,* but he did it slyly into his woodman's coat. He seemed to think she wouldn't know who had shouted. But as most people had thrown an eye or swivelled to look at him, he realised he was in trouble. But the girl just came down to him and took the full cup, and wiped the counter with a grubby rag.

'You got any of it on your trousers?' she said.

The man peered down as if his legs were a long way, and he was on top of the cliff of himself.

'Nope, I don't think so, Judy,' he admitted.

'Here then,' she said, and set another cup there, and streamed coffee into it from a glass bubble. 'Just drink it,' she said, 'and clam up for once.'

'Okay, Judy,' the man said, and he didn't chuckle but appeared suddenly very sleepy.

Our breakfasts were served up next and Chicken got the paper from Sue then, because she was hungry, and it took up too much room. Chicken went a few pages into it with his smoky stare, and then folded it back in a leisurely fashion, and folded it again and then again, and set the rectangle of newspaper beside his plate, creasing it down when it began to bloom, and started to eat with one elbow on the formica, and the other hand forking in hash-browns. I ate too. The cook had made our things very well. It wasn't greasy much and the eggs tasted new and the potatoes like potatoes. That was unusual, and we ate calmly and appreciatively. I was thinking how strange it was really that Chicken and I were shooting exactly the same items into our separate stomachs, when he said:

'What in fuck's this? You see this, Sue? You're going to be famous.'

'Me?' said Sue, with a laugh. 'What do you mean?'

She leaned over, and tried to turn her head upside down to see it. It was to encourage Chicken to spin the paper, but he didn't.

'Dublin, Virginia,' he read, in an old school-room sing-song. 'Yesterday morning the body of a well-known Dublin Virginia woman was found dead in her own residence. The body was badly decomposed. Mr Jesse Black, who found the body, said he had known Mrs Euphemia Jones for many years. She had not come into town for a good while, and he had been worried about her. The house was very dusty after the dry weather, he said, and there were a number of footprints that Mr Black could not explain. The police in Dublin are investigating. Police officer Pete Cruchback has said that fingerprints have been found on an old tobacco tin in which Mrs Jones, who was married to the late Judge Jones of the same township, kept small bills. The money however appeared to be untouched. A visit to the neighbouring farmer could shed no light on the matter. Holy shit.'

'They didn't write holy shit?' I said.

'No, I'm sayin it,' said Chicken, oddly.

'Where's Dublin, Virginia?' said Sue suspiciously.

'That's the damn woman we saw in the house the other week.'

281

We all stopped eating and stared forward like horses in the heat. Chicken spread his face, like he had a circle of muscle around his eyes and mouth. I had a lump of hash-browns in my mouth, and I let it sit there for a minute.

'What's this about finger prints?' said Sue.

'I seem to remember a little tin with ten bucks in it,' said Chicken rather sarcastically, 'and I seem to remember you pawin it.'

'Twenty,' I said.

'Oh fuck you, Chicken,' said Sue, 'so what?'

'So nothin,' said Chicken. 'But did you ever have your prints done for something?'

'I don't know,' said Sue. 'Well not in Virginia county anyways.'

'Oh fuck this,' said Chicken. 'I should have just left the both of you on the roadside.'

'Oh yeh?' said Sue. 'That's great.'

'Well now,' said Chicken, setting his fork on end, 'you can sound like an insulted sundaygirl if you want to. But if those redneck cops can get it together to find you, they'll find me.'

'Okay then,' said Sue. 'We'll split up if you're so chicken.'

'We're not splittin up,' he said. 'We ain't splittin, Owl,' he said. 'I'm not losing you two, I want to know what's happening to your mouths – like a vow of silence, friends.'

I started to chew slowly on the soggy potato. The mad man clucked and took a deep swallow on his already empty coffee cup.

'What sort of blammed name is Euphemia?' said Sue.

We finished our breakfast and didn't talk about it. The sun was beginning to boil up the air to cook sparrows in. We let it ride – on an owl-train that we hoped wouldn't be rattling back our way, beaming the convenient dark.

Well, Moll, you may never have seen such a place. But it had big dark marble for pillars inside, and there was a field of tables between the brassy bar and an empty stage. As well as our group, there was a varied crowd of younger customers. Not tourists though, but the children of anyone who owned a good home on the key, or had a boat. The girls wore the clothes that *Fast Buck Freddy's* showed in their windows, and usually the appearance of the dummies to match. They were glossy people with a serious bitterness in their froth. They were also some of the best interim clients to the drug trade, or so Ali maintained.

'Most of the stuff,' he said, 'will pass right through. A little of it, mon, goes up these people's noses.'

'Or worse,' said Johnnie, grinning.

Johnnie had changed his clothes to something approaching smart – but his hair was a salty ring under his shelly cap. Beside the circular darkness of his face, the puppyish dancer from the Topless leaned on his shoulder. It was her night off, and she had wanted to show herself off at the Copa. She said she was more tired of bare tits than she could say. Johnnie never came to her bar, so I hadn't realized she was the 'whore' he lived with, and she wasn't really a whore at all. He just called her that affectionately. Her name was Bub. She had a desperate line in cynical talk that she might have had from the age of seven. It sounded very tough, broken bottled, and she was.

'I *like* this place,' she said. 'It makes me feel like a girl.' She lifted her cheek briefly from Johnnie's seaweedy shoulder, and examined the nest of surfers and such behind us. 'But it's hard to find a good girl in this town.'

Johnnie sputtered loyally, and Ali deepened into the murk of the lighting. The waitresses here sported black outfits with every available part of their legs marketed in meshed stockings. Strangely enough they weren't as shapely as Bub or Susan or the others – they probably wouldn't have been given a gig at the Topless – so they seemed a bit over-reached and underachieved.

Bub called our waitress *brother* whenever she did some work for us. The other man at our table was a plain small man from Texas. He was the buddy of the Texan singer in the Bull Bar and he often drank there when he was off-duty. He was one of the policemen. As a policeman he surprised me. He was fond of Ali, or considered him in some way desirable or useful. Anyway he spoke to Ali always with respect and as an equal, which perhaps was a little insulting to Ali, come to think of it. It's true that Ali elicited this from most people but it still surprised me, from a policeman. He wore his grey shirt open to his stomach, and his chest had a few brambly hairs. He made you feel he had forgotten to button it up more than anything else. His head was square, a building brick, and his sheared hair sandy and pliable like grass – that is, not very pliable. He talked some sort of drawling brief language I hadn't heard before, but it was English really. He didn't use what crippled phrases he had unless it interested him. He was selective or else stupid.

Ali had his sunworn outfit on, but from the waist up he was fine, and anyway the young blond man who managed the joint had said hello to him with a slide of his expensive-looking lips, as we pushed in through the rivery willows at the bar. They were the well-dressed women with well-travelled-over faces like old roads. Stephen flowered out of the dark beside us in an extravagant Hawaian shirt. He looked like a photo of a lush rose blown up large.

'Hello, my dear people,' he said with his mouth tight. He silvered only as loud as he needed to to be heard by us. The policeman gave him a bleak nod and unexpectedly blushed. Stephen's medallion started forward like a comet on a string as he bent to greet the lady.

'My dear Miss Bub,' he said. 'How pleasant to see you resting.'

'That's it, daddy,' she said. 'Strain yourself.'

She offered a laugh like a boy's over the beer-bottled table. Johnnie reached for his stubby bottle and slugged at it and said:

'Hey, Steve, how's it goin? I don't see your boss much at the boats no more.'

'He's busy,' said Stephen. 'And what's more he's in New York.'

'That right?' said the policeman, and then shut up, as if for ever.

'By the way, Mr Hallberg,' whispered Stephen theatrically to the cop, 'what's the interesting gen on that killing on the pier?'

'Search me,' said Mr Hallberg. 'And the name's Ron.'

'I know it is, Ron. But your Swedish ancestry is so much more decorative.'

'It's still Ron,' said Ron, clicking his tongue.

'Yes – of course,' said Stephen. 'And where's our little star, Susan, tonight, Ali?'

Ali was rolling a thread of tobacco into a pencil-line of paper. He gave his locks the faintest flick. A kind of oil or sweat made his face gleam like pottery.

'Sit down, mon. There's a chair.'

Stephen sat as prettily as he could in his well–covered carcase and smiled at Ali.

'You're always so polite. That's what I like. A gentleman. All my best friends have been gentlemen, starting with my father. However, I don't work for a gentleman, and consequently New York is one of my favourite cities when I'm not in it and he is, and I'm here. So relaxing.'

He lifted his hands to examine the oceanic sapphire rings he favoured. He didn't allude to them, just admired or checked them.

'Hey, Steve,' said Johnnie. Stephen shuttled an eyebrow. His eyebrows seemed to have been applied with a stencil, to hammer them into place. 'What do you do for the boss man? You never told me.'

Bub stirred on the linened shoulder and said:

'Mainly Dick work, isn't that right, Stevo?'

Stephen chortled in his well-bred parody of a knowing chortle.

'I wish,' he said. 'Or you wish. One or the other. Or do I? And would you?'

Ali placed a rocky laugh on top of this, and it felt like a winning hand.

'There is no doubt about it, Stephen,' he said, 'you're a crude fellow.'

It sounded unnatural and largely inapplicable, but Ali treated himself to it all the same.

'Anyway,' said Ron into the noisy gap filled by the pouring difficult happiness of the younger drinkers. 'Who'd care one broken string why that guy was wasted?'

As this didn't absolutely follow, there was another gap while brains back-tracked to what it might be in response to.

'Dis man on the pier?' said Ali.

'Yeh,' said the policeman. 'Mean he was just another creep with another boatload of drugs, and we didn't need him in the first place. So fuck it. Who cares?'

'The law likes to find out that sort of thing, doesn't it, Ron?' said Stephen. How he meant it was anyone's guess. It sounded vulnerable and concerned, like a man in the street with a dog.

'Not a whole lot, buddy. Not a whole lot. What's the use in it? A dope-head gets himself screwed, bloodied up. Low-life. No point to him. He's just trouble to us. Someone jerks him away does us a favour. Low-life. And low-league. That's worse.'

'Pretty bad for him, right enough,' said Stephen. 'It's a business with a high body count, I've always noticed that. But also a high dollar count.'

'Anyways,' said Ron, 'that sort of corpse is a dead letter. Don't talk to me about it.'

'Cocksuckers' conversation, if you asked me,' Bub murmured.

The policeman bounced on his seat, and swung his beer between two fingers, and was quiet.

'What I've always liked about this town,' said Stephen to me, or me as an audience, he wasn't particular, 'is the democratic vulgarity of its insults. Do you find that, as a new arrival here, Oliver?'

I stared at him as if he was going to shoot me. I didn't dare risk a laugh or a word of agreement or denial. If I'd breathed I was sure in my slight drunkenness he would have bitten me with some polite fang. That he'd mistaken my name was no protection.

'Extremely unpleasant,' said Captain Collins. 'I mean, as far as the pit of the stomach's concerned. But if there isn't a crowd of our men up this way in a minute, I'll be very surprised.'

He dipped his combed red hair down from the grassy rim of the hollow. Moran said nothing and hoisted up his own stone head, like a flag or unlit lantern in the gentle bright afternoon. They were on a smoothly flowing hill among very tall trees, much taller than anything in Ireland but not so different either. All the time Moran was caught out by the similarity between that home and this home. He kept expecting it to be otherwise and confusing, but it wasn't as extreme as that.

The down-slope of their hill had more of the elegant thick-branched trees with a light covering of leaves. The leaves were shown up at the back by the dropping sun, and they looked like small fistfulls of pencil shavings out of a metal sharpener, or waste rags after dressmaking. They were green because all leaves were green, even when they were turquoise or amber, as men were always difficult. There was nothing and no one on the hill besides themselves. Moran slumped down again and stuck out his legs, and rested his palms on his horny knees. A mass of some sort of fly blew about in the windless air, making their own breeze perhaps, about two feet above the captain's head, but they never descended. They made a sound like a cyclist freewheeling downhill, so it belonged, that sound, to a hill. Moran felt this was satisfactory. He might have nodded into a green large sleep but he couldn't. He was frightened. The two dead men in the hollow with him made him glassy in his skin. He seemed in himself to be slidy and asleep, but dreaming in the sleep, and wide-awake there.

One of the dead men lay on its stomach and face, as if also sleeping. But the other was propped up and, except for the staring eyes and the tunic all shot up, he might have been on the point of speaking. They couldn't get his eyes shut. Captain Collins had tried but the man had been dead for hours, and the face wanted to stay like that. It wanted to be remembered, probably. There was a smell of shit that Moran suspected came from under the sitting man. He didn't wish to investigate.

He didn't mind the smell but he minded the stiff eyes. The flies came down onto them all right, and made a speciality of hurrying over the lack-lustre irises. The dead man was middle-aged, and had been a captain like the captain. Some of his fingers were missing at various joints, and Moran could only guess that they had been shot off as the man ran for the hollow. He hoped the man had run for the hollow, because that's what he and the captain had done, and Moran was a little uneasy about that. He didn't like running with guns behind him. He found it made him want to bite someone. It possibly looked funny too. The enemy had considered the other running captain so funny, that they had put bullets in his legs. Then after falling into the hollow, like a child playing in a sand-dune, the man must have plied his rifle for a bit, because it was still propped on the wavy rim. It had dry brown blood on its length, since the dead captain had received a fair number of bullets in the chest. All those bullets had made him sit up in that way, with an enormously odd look on his face. It was an angry look but also a miserable one. Moran wondered if the man had any mothers and fathers or even brothers and sisters. Maybe he was too old. Maybe he was one of the fathers.

Neither Captain Collins nor he had the slightest wound on them, because they had stumbled up the same hill at a different time. The flies were probably not waiting for them to die or anything, as in a story, but were the usual personal convoy of flies that always waited outside the door for you, whether in a town or the open veldt. Still the flies took the opportunity offered them and seemed to be eating the verymost outer surface of the dead captain's face. They might get down to the bone in time. How long would that take?

'Excuse me, sir?' said Moran. 'How long are we to stay here, may I ask, sir?'

'Well, I don't know, Moran, I don't know. We'd better wait till dark anyway. How long do you want to wait?'

'Sorry, sir?'

'I'm just joking. Not very funny maybe.'

The captain stuck two fingers in one of the tighter smaller pockets in his jacket.

'You got that pill-box with you, Moran?' he said.

'No, sir,' said Moran.

'Doesn't matter.'

Captain Collins leaned back against the grassy slope and for a moment appeared remarkably like the other captain. His eyes kind of glared for a brief space, and the skin on his face groaned without making a sound. Then the captain let himself sink completely, still master of his movements, into the curve of the hollow, and seemed to rest. He seemed to rest but his leather crossband heaved in an uncomfortable improbable way. Then Captain Collins died. Moran realized he had died because the crossband stopped trembling, and the lips fluttered once like the wings of a fat bird and the captain stopped. The captain remained dead for about ten minutes, and then he shuddered out of death, and reopened the shop of his eyes and stared sideways at Moran.

'What time is it?' he said, in a thin brown tone.

'Not any later, sir,' said Moran. 'A few minutes later.'

'Oh, come on,' said the captain, disappointed. 'Surely I must have slept for ages. I feel much better, and the sun has gone down completely.'

Moran stirred his boots on the firm grass – green grass, that might have been grey and brown too. The sun was precise and round, though a little dimmed, within both their views, over in the low sky, to the right of Moran. He thought about this for a while, and then said:

'Yes, sir.'

'Well, we can move off now if we're clever about it.'

Captain Collins stood up, but not very cleanly. He found himself abruptly on his hands and knees, with his face close to the warm odorous ground.

'God, I'm stiff,' he said. 'Get a move on, Moran. Come on.'

The captain didn't move. Moran thought.

'We could rest up for an hour more, sir,' he said. 'I'm very tired myself, sir.'

'Put me back then,' said the captain.

'What's that, sir?'

'Back, Moran. Lift me up and put me back.'

Moran scrambled forward and raised the captain under the armpits so that he embraced the bony chest. His burden was light as balsa wood. He propped it as close as possible to the captain's previous position.

'How do you feel now, Moran?' said the new voice.

'I'm fine, sir. I'll be all right in a minute.'

The sun was very near the tumble of the slow hill, and was having no trouble at all inching down through the great branches. Then the captain died properly.

Sixfoil Sixteen

Some monkishe manne in the stoney sky had dropped his inkpot alle ovvir de wureld of de waitin tooer. Thiss wasse de opinoon uf de hooley prayin bishopp. He satte like a fatt squerrell in hes smal chappel. Ther wasse noo glasse, Moll, nor nuttin in de longe arrowee windas. An so de thinne nite breze uf owels their breath, an de low signalle dey maed across de frozene cuntree, smatteret inn uponn hes eares an thinkins. He wasse taulkin too hes parfact godde in de greye peece uf hes sanctueree.

'Do ei doo wrange, moi got,' he sedde, 'in tryen ta stitche yer kingdome herr? Wat iss de fallin penaltee ef I ded nat? Oi amm a manne hoo es nat parfact, an dis I kno wal. I see in moi actoons a biter lacke uf hoolinesse an dignitee. Bat dis iss a cruell far cuntree whach ye havv givven mee fer a hoom, an I muste drawe inn moi breth amang difficultoos an barbaroos conflick. So her I aske, in moi poore humilitee an dread, whoi amm I soo widdout happinesse an gaine amang des peple? Whoi doo dey nat liuv der ordinaree bishap, an muste it alwayes be soo? Larde, I amm lonelye fer moi like, evven ef it iss in de dampe mistee localitee uf de ancent paganne Tiberr. Rame wasse colt bat nat emptee. Der wasse menn uf moi hert an minde:

> Lard, ef yee realized,
> ef ya cud fer moi loifteem fele
> howe oi misse oure stoopit raine,
> de forenesse uf de carters
> as dey haule ouwer empire inta our stretes!

Bat, larde, ef here I muste bee, ta change an tamper wid de wilde innocente doins uf thoghtlesse pagin menne, let it bee soo. I wull nat strugel or complaene. Bat al I begg is dis: lett no manne winne ovver me amang dese sadde people. Lat it nat bee, fer I amm no fleshe fer marterdum: I can nat be sante Larentio evvn fer yoo, fer moi bodee is badde, an will nat obeye moi smal beleef.'

De bishap stopt mumblin, an hes sounde, dat soundet lik de tellin of olde voises besoid a fier, felle fram his mout an laye lik a ded animool on de ruff rok floore. An in hes stilnesse he harde de dor shove ites gratin noiz acrass ta hem, an he spunne on de botom-polisht wud of hes sete. Anlee wan candel flutered on an iron spike, an it wawse lukin throo a mudde streme ta se hoo wass cum. Bat whan he cud spotte a lang berd an a talle manne, he falt it must be Owle, or els master luxifur. An he wawse serprized an worriet. Perhaps dis manne had crept in ta moirder hem.

'Iss dat Mazder Oool?' he whispert, as if he tawkt ta a finisht goste.

'Ay, bishap, it iss mee,' the gloomee celloing voiws sed, wid a holo eko.

Owel pacet silentlee too de bishap hes shulder, an ferder to de blak, bat briter, winda in fronte uf de puzzelt preest.

'Wat iss et, Owl, yoo wante ta saye ta mee? Or haff ye cum ta twiste moi oeld necke?'

De bishap herd a snakee werinesse enter hes blud. Owel wasse soo closlee tied in hes maner, lik a concentratioon uf a stoen, dat he mad de preest loos strengt.

Owel turnt, an hes lang chekes cawt de muddelt clowdee lite fram de slittet winda. How aged an thinne he isse, thoght de bishap.

'Holee Larentioo,' sed Owel, 'whoi muste ye plott an danc ta mak moi Olleeve oot uf kingdom? It iss nat wois an iss nat too yer honoor. I wud kill ye, bat yee ar anly an unpretee ratt, so I cann nat giv sich indignatee too moi handes. Doo yoo here me, moi blak mann?'

'Owel,' sed de bishap in de welle of darknesse. He paust fer a tickin peece uf tiem. De anger of Owele, dat came so quiett fram de poett his throte, chilld hem mar den de nite cud. He falt lik a smal child in hes bedd, an de whusperrs an de groanins uf tings arund hes rume. 'Owel, yoo must nat tink me soo wicket. I amm nat. Yer quene iss a grat womin, an wull nat be happee til she hass her planns compactet wid her faet. Trulee yoo muste see dis iss so. Yoo ar a godless mann an it iss hart fer yoo ta know dis.'

291

'Godless I amm nat,' sed Owel. 'I havv manee manee gots, batter an mur poerfal den yours. Bat I wil nat boste dem to yoo. Everee rivver an stoen iss a sete fer dem, an al berds flye an singe in der celebratoo. Dis is so an dis is tru. Wat I wull saye is diss: ye ar a softe uzerpin preest, an wul wante ruin fer wat is whole an wholenesse fer wat is ruine. Dis isse yer musik always an ever. An dis I here fram yoo even befar de menne an familee uf dis castel. Der iss noo forgivninz fer yoo amang moi gods, an yoo wull be a scremin rostet animool wan ye dee.'

De bishap gurgelt wid merriment ta listan to dis.

'Iss it mee wull roste?' he cride. 'Oh moi frent, no no. You havv it wrang an silee. Whoi, you wul be a marter to yer emptee caws, becorse whan de lard, yoor tru gott, findes ye in hes hante, he wul flinge ye lik a peble oot ovver hes clouwds an kingdome, til ye neste lik dat saem ston on a rivver-bottom, in hes river uf dradfal fier. Yer skinn, moi poete, wul pele in de endless hete, an yoo wil be one soree crien manne.'

'Hushe in yer bellee, bishap,' sed Owel, 'an lizzen. Perhaps too worleds lapp uzz rownd. I do nat kno. Perhaps ye are nat wat I kno yoo in moi hed ta bee. Yoo babel der lik a cesspit wid small bulbes uf dunge and shitt fer herte an braveree. Nivver minde wat I saye on dis, or yoo in aspeck uf mee. We wul forgit dis argooment ta saye dis: Larent, do nat mak moi Con ta fal, do nat engin hes defete. He iss a roundet lorde uf manee wuds an peple, an al hes fadders war too, an moi familee ded serv dem al wid pried an songes. It iss nat grat in de eyez uf enormoos kingdims an cuntres. I knaw dat gut an cler. Bat it iss parfacte an complet fer whoo persists here, in dis greye low lant widoot coloor an sunne. Jes go bak ta Roam, whar al is fer yoo, an leve us here whar al is fer uss. It iss nat much fer yer charch ta doo. It iss jes won smal acer ye wul nat havv.'

'Ah hert,' sed Larentius, 'yoo argoo wel bat bad. Al de wied wurled is fer moi savioor. Ower univerz wass sik of paganing, an we ar cum ta de roez uf Jesues, an evven dis tinee spot can nat be odderwise. De hott treless feelds uf de endes uf de ert, whar de boilin watter fals inta de bathe uf godd, in golde an silber shadoes, muste be hes too. Wat yoo saye iss wrang an hopeless. An eff yoo murderet mee, even den, or mor soo, wud dis plac became de provinz uf moi godd. Hes grate poer is ower mantel an ower coler.'

'Holee worme,' sed Owel, 'moi holee litul grubb, whoi muste moi foin Olivver be lambe ta dis sadd lionn, hes brite facc becam an onionn fer yoo ta beree an fede ta rootin piggs? Fer yoo ar flesh uf pigg, Larents, ass yoo wel kno.'

An Owel movt stifflee to de vage dor.

'Owel,' sed de bishap. 'I am soree fer yoo. Bat lat mee whusper dis. If Conn be lost fram hes lief an quene, it nede nat be soo wid yoo. Wee can be curful frends in ower nerbye age. Wat doo yoo saye?'

Owel gloweret in hes ponde uf blak.

'De frenshippe of a bogge es nat fer stoens,' he sed. 'I haff litent moi cargo by comin dowen ta halpe yoo. Nowe ye muste roe yer owen bote inta what wharlpoole an monsters yoo favoor.'

'Halpe mee, yoo saye, litel owel? Yoo mak moi belee chukel. Go out an sitt on claye. It wul soot ye wel.'

Owl noded hes berd, as ef he warr stirrin milke wid a fether ta skimm de duste, and den he walket awaye oot.

When my mother sang it was like being inside the machinery of a one-man band. The cymbals rose and clashed, and the bass drum flicked back and boomed in. The elbows of our rooms worked in and out, and lips sucked and wrenched on the kazoo. It gave our sitting-room a very occupied character.

I held on to the armchair while she fried up some spitting sausages, and cut clean cruel wounds in the unripe tomatoes she favoured, and a song sailed and trembled and anchored and sped up and tacked into smooth white waves from her launching mouth. The high seas were before it and it met them flamboyantly. Her top notes made the castle's roofs lift like my grandfather's hat greeting us on his vanished streets. Her low ones pistoned the cellars deeper into the rock and heathery roots. Middle registers blew out the windows like bubbles in a bubble-ring, and had the walls heaving with sighs and heartburn. So if I could have stood away from her and the house, on the hill of the park, and watched, it would have been the same as stopping with her in Grafton Street to examine the performance of a copper-hungry rained-on man. It was a melancholy procedure but a busy one.

She had written some famous songs in her early youth, and these were the most active of all. Some of those verses would have permanently dislodged the slates, if they hadn't been eager to settle back in their places to hear more.

I was a fool about this. Her songs were done sadly, but I foolishly cheered up to them. She especially liked to sing very high and wanderingly: she made journeys on summits of music that made me dizzy and open-mouthed. It was like having someone sing right into your ear so softly, but thinly and exactly, that they are changing the construction of your body with these nervous messages.

Sometimes I worried the police would come and take her away, because her songs were dangerous. They had things about lonely Sundays in them, and much of the most seditious ones was in Irish, and could have meant anything. They were love songs, she told me, and I feared that these were the sort the police would object to most. I saw their country feet standing on the gravel outside, locating our windows, and greatly troubled that my mother was going to bring down the landlord's walls.

Then when the real feet did come it was twice as real as reality, because I had imagined them to the point where they had been already real enough for anyone's taste. He was a polar scrubbed person, with a remote resemblance to the cabbage I had objected to eating the night before. I preferred the cabbage now.

My mother was still singing as he knocked on the purple door, and she didn't pause in her verse to open it, but opened it on such a lofty note that I would have laid a bet the chimney had uprooted, and gone cometting over Dublin Bay.

'Hello,' she sang, 'Hello, hello, hello!'

She reminded me of Harry Bellafonte singing his best piece, which was, as far as I knew, called *Daylight Come and I Want to Go Home*. Day-o, day-o, day-o, he sang, Calypso-style, and my mother echoed him shamelessly to greet the policeman. He obviously didn't have any voice to speak of, so he spoke instead:

'Got ta bring ya in, missie, or else blow you away.'

This was idle as he had no gun.

'I wish I was in Artai Chuain!' lowed my mother.

294

'Missie, even ef ye war in Tombstone, I'd still hev ta haul ya in.'

The policeman had a difficult-to-understand Wicklow accent. I recognized it from my exile there with my Great Aunt in some very old weeks.

'Veni, veni, veni,' sang my butterfly mother. 'I wish I had me a handsome boatman,' she added, with her hand fixed white on the panelled door, 'to ferry me over, my love and I.'

I decided to learn to row at the earliest opportunity.

'That's me,' I piped from the armchair. 'Don't forget me, mister.'

'Who are you, son?' said the policeman, gravely or gravidly. 'The love or the boatman?'

'I had a little pony,' shrilled my mother happily, her knuckles bloodless, 'his name was Dapple Grey.'

'Dapple Grey,' wrote the policeman in his notebook, while my mother hummed continuously, like an organ or a bagpipe, just so there wouldn't be an unpeaceful silence.

'Does that have an *e* on the end, ma'am, or can I take it as it comes?'

'I am young and easy,' replied my mother.

'This is how it is, ma'am: you have one hell of a bad kidney of a landlord underneath you. Now *I* ain't sayin you're treatin him unkind, but he is. Ma'am, I'm only a cun'ry boy, but that sure is a sweet little ole singin voice you got there.'

'I have a bonnet,' my mother emphasized, by way of proof, 'trimmed with blue.'

'Yep, I cin well believe that, ma'am. You ever hear tell of an outlaw called Jemmy Conn?'

My mother shut up. She didn't want to seem suspicious.

'Ring a bell?' said the policeman. 'Or not?'

'Well,' said my mother calmly, but with a sunny red face, like a soapsudded palm. She got so bright I expected to see bits of molten rock and segments of rock take off from the burning surface of her cheeks. The moon, that was her other half, cooled her. 'Well that depends of what sort of bell you mean,' she said. 'It doesn't ring a steeple bell. It doesn't ring a front-door bell, no. And it doesn't ring the little bell that is inside any normal telephone. It doesn't ring a fire-engine's bell, as Oliver will be the first to tell you.' I could see the policeman wondering who

Oliver was. 'And it doesn't ring the bell on the alarm-clock or the cooker. It doesn't ring.'

'How many bells do you have here?' said the man.

'Thousands,' said my mother. 'One thing always reminds me of another thing. Yes,' she said, 'I've always heard, man and boy, a lot of bells.'

'So, which bell does Jemmy Conn ring?' he said reasonably, not really expecting a useful answer, and thinking more of the stroll back to the station up past the hotel with its crinkled bushes, and the big black gates, and the bottled walls, and the smooth tar they lay for the better districts, and the.

'It rings the drowned sea-bell of my husband's love,' she said, into what he was thinking.

'Not the sort of bell that would interest the authorities. Often as a child I ate sandy sandwiches not far from here,' he said. 'So I'll say goodbye and be down the road.'

His head and brimmed hat sank.

'A typical landlord's lackey,' said my good mother when he was gone and wouldn't be offended. 'A face like a mad man's arse. That fellow needs a good boot up the earhole. It takes one to know one, but one what? He didn't have bumfluff on his chin, but he looked like he wanted to have it. Remind me to repeat that joke for the next twenty years. Unfortunately, lackey derives from the Arabic for judge.'

It was the best morning of all my life. I lay under the gentle blankets in my habitual pool of piss. I had warmed it with my bottom and back: just as the narrow nailfree plank of sun floored my chest and warmed that.

The river allowed itself little by way of movement. It was passionate though, in its hesitant minimal gestures, like a very shy very young and beautiful child trying to be easy and acceptable in his father's arms. The bridge might have been fifty years old, but by comparison with the river, in the matter of age, it looked like it had been built a thousand years from now. It carried its existence and the existence of its trams and figures, briefcased and hatted, with a deal of fictionality. It didn't lack presence because it was green and metal and quietly ornate but it lacked the present. Who passed over it passed through the future. So its trams and travellers and motorcars inched and inched and flowed and inched with traces of reality, but not the full shilling of things happening.

The river however knew what was what and illustrated it with its small dances. The ducks up here were in wired enclosures, because they were exotic ones and foreign ones, and crossbreeds, that the more regular birds might have eaten on the lake. Xenia and I had seen swans murdering the strayed chicks of the wild ducks. If a chick was adventurous enough to strike out for ill-defined wastes, the mothers chased but they had to cross the distance first – and a swan could drown a baby duck in no time. Small lungs maybe helped. But up here the ducks were protected and lonely and meshed.

Across the passing water there was a restaurant on a piece of jutting water-walled land, with green railings to stop customers dropping in with the brown stones. There were white paper lanterns in the wood of trees, among which the green tables were set to grow. I had been over there with Xenia, and one of the tablelegs had rooted and leaves had fanged the table. It was just an accident. Aside from the lights in the trees there were pale full moons also. These were the one or two lamps on old iron poles that they kept alight even in the moony afternoon. The waiters served the distant diners smoothly and probably expensively – we had only risked a hot chocolate each, just in case.

The laundered waiters served the rubbed men and women, and the steps going down to the river on this side served the late afternoons of the young people who gathered there, pinchbeck coins in a spilling bag. They liked leather jackets with big sizes, and well-worn before they bought them in crammed old-clothes shops. They liked scarves wrapped many times around their necks, and narrow and tight trousers, and short eccentric haircuts. Their faces were fresh and a bit Germanic and northern to the last dropping ear-ring. They used to assemble in their now bulldozed clubhouse, and had been washed up on the river-bank – the only section of the city that they were tolerated to possess. Sooner or later the police would arrive, and harass them daily till they tested out new ground. They could only find their allocated place by standing and sitting. And if their fathers mysteriously and quietly made a decision that they had been free somewhere long enough, then like cloths of disturbed birds they lifted and changed. It reminded me of walking down the West Pier in Monkstown and forcing the peewits to flash their bodies white and flash them black, all the way down in front of you, with them never daring to cross your path, or fly around you and go back. The young of Lucerne shifted at the paternal tread of the town's decrees in their regard, and I wondered what would happen when they were finally in the last possible corner of Lucerne. They would give up, I supposed, and grow their hair a little, and knot the good ties, and enter the simple danger-ous drug of banking.

Their drugs for the moment were in needle-shape and pill-shape. Whatever couldn't be got into a syringe or compounded, they smoked, not on the river steps, but the sales went on there. I warmed myself a few feet from their edge. And wanted to be among them and couldn't naturally be. I didn't have their splashes of words, much less their secret idiom, and less than that their confidence. So I sat in Xenia's briefest panties under my black corduroy jeans and watched the intelligent river. I was tired out and very happy or euphoric. I felt lazy and relaxed and very old. I was as old as her dead grandmother, very feminine but strong. I was soft and breasted like the female ducks, slightly and feathery. I was so well-disposed to everything I might have devoured a passing fish, raw and with relish. I could feel the tight strings of her panties holding me together. Best friend I ever had, I thought. A sort of black rocker of your balls and the river so low it was the opposite of flood. I was easy with that feeling of low water crossing the brown stones, and myself a sort of girlfriend to it. I shouldn't have been talking to the water, but I was anyway. Fuck it.

When I balanced up to walk away slowly, the strings pulled into the gully between my arse-cheeks like a finger-nailed caress. Caress be damned, I thought. I strolled away from the unseeing young, and across the square where the small circus had arrived to entertain the children of the town, who were not yet aware of the larger circus they already belonged to, and were beloved animals in. Sweet-apple children in their humane and best cages. If you let them run wild they might eat things, things like other children for a start. I moved gently, not swinging my hips, but with the loose falling gait of a girl. Xenia's blue Chinese jacket waved a little on my breast. The sticky Turks were making bratwurst under the stripy tent, fingers of meat in deep bread to carry into the cinemas. I felt spongelike, up the swung hill and past the grey mansion, and the barren acre of the first supermarket. On up the road with the railinged bare gardens, and the antique shop with country furniture for city houses.

I drifted into our supermarket and lifted a basket with a tearing of wires from its neat stack. Chocolate and pork steaks and noodles for my love and me. That makes three of us. A hot blast of air struck the side of my face like a huge light tongue. I toppled briefly but didn't fall. I couldn't see the tongue anywhere when I glanced for it. I couldn't see. I stood in the middle of the low aisles with the empty basket in my loose hand, and the arcane panties held me but not together. My hair streamed like absinthe each side of my face, and my head was on one side as if I was listening for something. If I could have screamed without notice I would have. Chocolate and pork steaks and noodles. Personal stockings or tights, racks of them. Murderous cabbages. The girl to pay at the cash-desk. Words to offer. I stiffened under the water of the emporium, its colours choppy. Perfect hurrying housewives outdid me with their choices. Plastic river. *Is your hate then of such measure*. I fled out into the masculine town.

You look for permanence and they give you a fire, a fire in your paw. Watch out it doesn't burn right through. These were imperfect thoughts, but they were the ones I had just the same. I remember them now because at the time on the bright grass I thought they meant something. Maybe they do, but not to me. At least I hope not. I don't like things I don't understand meaning something, it's a type of slyness. I was down among the boats today, and the harbour seemed deserted, but as if it had been deserted for a long time. All the boats looked decrepit. The merest wind would have swamped their timbers. That wasn't so true. It was just my mood, I suppose. The boats are kept well enough, and today all sections of the world had wind in them so the boatmen just stayed in the bars. My trousers flapped like narrow sails as I put my face into the buffeting, on the scraped dust at the water's edge. The sea heaved up against the harbour bulwark like the breaths of a breasty woman. I thought about home because of the wind, but not necessarily the sea at home. It was the high bogs in the mountains that came back to me, where I must have walked some time or other in a similar blow. Up there the water in the pools was very black, like a trout's eyes when they dry. The eyes used to gawk up at the speedy sky. The harbour at Key West was very otherwise to the mountains around Mayo or Sligo, but they were equal as diagrams. For instance, the men who drove the cattle into those shelfy secret pastures were sailors too, except their boats were cows. It was the same bitter friendship they had with the beasts as the boatmen had with their launches, and the harbour might have been a stormy small plateau of bad ground, with the herd scattered and nosing at the tough grass like those nosedown boats. I didn't know though. I just felt that. It was a private picture between me and the empty character of it.

Then I walked up through the bars, without going in, and got myself a triangle of middling pizza, which I tried to improve with a paper cup of coke. I didn't see anyone I knew, even in the slight way I know people here. I wandered back through the tossed eucalyptus trees, beside the peeling white Baptist church. The bells were sounding faintly because of the wind washing into the tower, like a buoy signals its bell in the indelible swell of the ocean. Of course the sun is in the streets also, and would be too jealous of the storm to let clouds come between it and Key West. The animal plants are shrugging in windy sunlight outside the stiff porch, like blasé men stuck in their gesture. The bushes are very off-hand today.

And then I was thinking about thinking about permanence, and about a fire. All the pleasantly-designed hydrants here are painted green, which is a sort of contradiction of growth against rust. But it suits the key somehow. The most surprising thing I ever heard was someone saying once that rust was really a very slow kind of burning. An idea that Chicken would have considered unnecessary and unhelpful – his car's principal disease was rust.

Sue and I stretched ourselves on the bright grass, and he got out his sack of tools, and went to work on our chariot. We were marooned in some everywhere place with a dense defensive forest divided by a neatly-laid shallow of tar. It was one of those precise neurotically-measured American roads. The forest only wanted truck with Indians still, and it didn't know the Indians were gone, so it stood off from the clean raised road by about twenty feet each side. The shiny smooth grass had been sown on this. It must have been a special breed that didn't inch very high, or else some machine had been sent out from the nearest town to trim it. The car leaned slightly against the slight slope, and the huge blackbird's wing of the bonnet was propped up into the noisy air. All the noises were small ones. They didn't intrude on Sue's sunning herself. She lifted her bottom and gathered up her dress to let that yellow cat lie on her thighs. A little nose of pubic hair peered out. She groaned like a man and placed her head on her layered palms, and stared at the sun with her eyes closed. She raised her chin to it. The light seemed to wash her with some brand of flow, because her spar of hair trickled back from her face, and twisted on the grass like lost gold, the fool's gold of my best Sue.

Chicken chose a long screwdriver with a yellow handle from his kit. The handle gripped the sunlight too. Chicken put the screwdriver in his mouth and made a silent gesture with his face at me, as if to say, this is some fucking job in this heat. He stripped off his newer shirt, and dived his glistening combed head into the shadowy bonnet. His jeans moved and ticked to his torso's shiftings, like they were phantom trousers with a life of their own. I laughed to myself, and heaved myself up, and tried to part a path through the cottony temperature, and made some headway as far as a turn in the yard-brushed road. Here I was made run by the dipping bank to the first muddle of the blocked trees.

I stepped over brambles, and was embraced by a few more, but got to a tiny clearing just appropriate enough to squat down in and relieve myself. That position of having your belly on your thighs more or less, and your colon pointing in the right direction, is a better one than plonking your arse on a bowl. It is more friendly to your poor channelled body with all its agonized and untalked-about functions. There is a pleasure in shitting in the woods, and a simple sad pleasure in the cloudy smell that visits your nostrils for a moment, as it passes up to join more unmentionable substances in the upper atmosphere. So odd that a mere hole in your corpse, and an item of smell, should be so ostracized and hidden under wraps. This thought pleased me under the many directions of the branches. It completed me temporarily. I had read it somewhere, and now it formed a brief entry in the always altering catalogue of my triteness. Unlike many of my opinions however, it was sufficient unto the act. I stood up contentedly and gazed up the road idly. I clenched – I saw that I would be visible to Chicken and Sue beside the car if they looked carefully. But Chicken wasn't looking at me. He was paused by the extravagant roll of the front mudguard, with his coconut head directed at Sue on the grass. He did throw a spannered glance down my way, but mustn't have spotted me in the brown and green, because he knelt very softly at Sue's side, and his mouth said something. He landed his hand like a fastidious bird on her thigh. Sue's head bloomed like a gold rock, and she chucked her legs away from him. He said something more that was only a sort of coloured morse from that distance. He walked on his knees to get close to her again, and she spoke up into his face with a spring-trap force. I caught Chicken's laugh as he jacked to his feet, and threw the screwdriver in the bag, and the bag in the trunk, and banged the bonnet home. We were obviously ready to go.

We were playing against a man with seven fingers, and a well-turned-out blackhaired man who looked Indian. He had rounded delved features, like a rough carving on the prow of an old European sailing-boat. That's how he seemed in my eyes anyway.

Ali had no Romantic notions about American Indians, and was playing severely and even, I suspected, to win. He wanted to win that night, because he knew he had the special feeling that no amount of beer can diminish. He could be as pissed as he pleased, but he had the humming unsmiling sensation, and no stroke could really miss. If it missed the pocket he aimed for it would go in somewhere else, or snooker the opposition. One of the sugared laws in his day-to-day history.

The two other men being on the platform with us made it complicated for me to speak with Ali in the slow useful way I could and liked to when we played pool alone. The fingerless man and the possible Indian had very amiably suggested a doubles game, and we had leaned through four such already. Our bottles bathed in their shallow discs of spillings on the awkward stained-wood counter. We were lifted as usual above the rest of the drinkers, whether bored or drunk or calling to the singer, by the small elevation of the greenly-lit platform.

The country singer had just finished his break at the bar, where he had seemed a little lost and untalked to. Only the most desperately pally of the customers ever talked to the singer. He had some songs about that, or about other things that were really about that. The policeman Ron was away over by the cool entrance. He was preoccupied with a pair of plain terrified-looking tourist women. He was treating them like royalty or at least his idea of that. It may have been working, but mostly it meant the singer had to sink his few whiskeys alone.

But the singer kept smiling with his country-star expression, set for the night, for life, towards all probable offers of better places to sing. If they didn't come tonight, he wouldn't mind. He'd go back through the fresh fished dawn to his morning sleep, surfacing, and last another round at least. He wasn't tough but he could bounce, and though all scars and disappointments showed in his voice and beerbelly, still the face was prepared, and wouldn't disgrace his first album when the call came. He was still in there – and the Bull Bar was an important spot to play, in the meantime, in the mean time. Hank Someone-or-Other had started there. He had a song about that too. Maybe it was someone else's song, but he gave it as his own or better. He gave it as the anthem for all his tribe. He made you admire Texas, which wasn't always an easy thing to do, after you had met a few of the punchier ones. An ambassador for his country and his music, dust and dust-notes, in a pair of loose boxer's shorts and a filled ballooning T-shirt.

His voice reminded me of what a fish suggests when a fisherman drags a barbed hook out of it. Everything good and operable gets torn, and half the belly arrives out through the gullet. The worm may yet be moving, but even it is unsavable after the hook, and anyway has been drenched in the fish's stomach acids. It didn't mean the singer was hard to listen to – it just made you admire Texas a little more.

Almost the first person I had met in Key West was the bar-maid, and here she was as alien or more alien than that travel-drunk first night. You think someone is going to be a great friend or a lover or a wife or an enemy, and they're still standing there strangely and unapproachably and in the end you wouldn't want to get near them anyway.

Susan had rented me now, whether she liked it or knew it, and at that moment the most immediate effect was an improve-ment in my pool game. Like Ali I would have found it onerous and dangerous to bet on a miss. I gripped the notched wood and clumsily lined the shot, and felt the shrugging tightness of the cloth, and realized my sureness, and searched softly for the next ball after to be tracked with the white and equally disposed of, and my arm moved for me gratefully, and nuzzled the white, and one of our colours knocked from the cushion it had taken a fancy to, and spun correctly and confidently two-thirds the length of the table into its predestined pocket, a planet among planets. I found I had forgotten to track the next one even though I had glanced and thought about it, but the ball scooped anyway, and angled round a few stationary ones, and appeared back for the spot-ball of its choice, like a collie rounding sheep.

Ali imitated a statue just inside the boundary of the light and held his cue loosely, in the way he did when the end of the game was acceptably in sight. He threw a lighthouse beam of his own over at the Indian, not for any clever purpose other than to exer-cise his neck. He just may have been seeing how the opposition was taking it, but they were very well-mannered city people down for a short holiday, and pool to them was recreational. To Ali it was slightly religious, prophetic, and he had known a lot of trouble from disappointed fanatics at pool tables. So he glanced over just in case, and I removed the last two spots with a grace I did not possess, and had the sullen black ball search after them into the labyrinth of the machinery.

'That's all we can take from you guys,' said the seven-fingered tourist, but with unaffected good humour. I felt as if I had been in Key West for ever, and Ali looked like he predated it by some thousands of years. The pool-playing statue. They let their dollar bills float onto the table, and palmed us goodbye, and Ali leaned over the cloth with a careful carelessness, and just for his own satisfaction and the rightful punishment of a ball, sent one cricketing into a corner pocket.

'Ali,' I said, the clean shot nodding in my head. He had laid an egg there with his energetic stroke.

'What, man?' he said without straightening. He left himself on the table as if he had forgotten such a distant possession.

'Do you think Susan would care for me at all?'

I had meant to go round this question, and trim it a bit with some camouflage, but it issued itself, and was stamped and bonded before I could call it back.

'One more game, mon, all right?' he said. He was fond of one-more-games. He troubled the machine, and picked the balls like apples, and triangled them, and stopped for an oddly long time at the end of the table while the country singer told us about San Bernadino. I remembered Susan's Mexican ambitions.

'You like this woman,' said Ali. 'That's good man.'

'I'm a bit too – you know. I think about her a good deal. I was wondering what you might have noticed. Or whatever.'

'I don't notice anythin,' he said. 'I said before she liked you.'

'But I don't want to buy her,' I said.

'Hey, she could buy the two of us and not notice.'

'Yes, I mean pay for her.'

'Pay for her?'

'For a night.'

'No, of couse not, mon, no. No, let me break these.'

He brought himself and what he knew around the border of rain-green baize, letting his hand slide along the bank of the cushion. My head drooped unattractively. The policeman had gone and so had the tourists, but maybe not together, and maybe yes. I was far gone to a reasonable extent myself. I didn't mind. At least she was in the same town for the moment.

'Woman,' said Ali, 'woman, sweet woman,' and smashed the tight formation.

If Moran had ever found his way back to the war, he would have been informed by a bullet or a noose that he had lost it.

Like most of his previous supposed enemies, the other side won a technical victory. As his own army had then no opportunity to go out and look for him, and the victors didn't know he was there in the first place, he discovered himself a free if unknown man between these two states of friend and foe.

He lost his uniformed self in an ample trackless land, and had to pick up another clothy character from the fresh snakey ground for purposes of survival. Survival in that mysterious climate entailed mostly the satisfaction of his hunger – to have sheltered from the elements would have meant dying of sweaty suffocation. He became a creature part of whose personality was made of simple heat. He enjoyed the company of grass fleas and smudging grey lice, that seemed to proliferate magically as he crushed them, like the defeating segmentation of worms. He knew if he paused in his daily lice-hunting he might turn into an animal clothed clumsily in a material of soft writhing wool.

He distrusted the water in the rivers and the lakes, and got only the fruit of the afternoon rains into his throat. There was a variety of accommodating plants that gathered this for him. To try and coddle his soles he had to tear up more and more of his beloved uniform day by day. He was bad at knots with his naturally muddling fingers, and so left a fading trail of khaki scraps. A diagram of his progress would have been an ambling peeling kite pulling an enormous impromptu ribbony tail, without colour or join. He wasn't going anywhere that he knew of but didn't get afraid. Any notion of fear had been left to dry on the ground with Captain Collins.

After a week he no longer sported his shirt, and after another he was strolling along in his underclothes. This was a set of combinations that he had already cut the arms and most of the legs from soon after arriving in the country. His lice seemed to resent this increasing nakedness, because the pleasant sun was too much for their untanning skins. They massed under his sweaty linen, and in his bewilderingly itchy hair on both his head and crotch. He stopped every hour or so and sat in under a firm imperial rock, where shade hid too like a bear, and raked with healthy fingernails into his lower belly and scalp. His skin had turned so dry it didn't bleed under these attacks. It grouped in soapflakes and capped the heads of his fingers.

He ate blindly whatever trees had growing on them, sometimes leaves and sometimes fruit. None of these made him ill but one of the blue fruits had him laughing emptily the rest of the afternoon of his eating it. The same afternoon he found a giant lizard that he could hold in the palm of his hand – so he kept away from the blue-skinned pearlike lunches, and settled for what satisfied him and didn't interfere with his normal discomfort.

He had the idea of crunching the blue fruit and rubbing it all over his half-reddened and half-browned skin, but it didn't deal with the lice as he hoped, but only gave him a greater population to cull behind the rocks.

As he didn't fear anything he methodically circled the obvious glittering snakes with his eyes fitfully on them, and when he saw lions in the difficult distance he climbed trees till they were long gone. If someone had told him that lions could manage trees as straightforwardly as a domestic cat, he wouldn't have tolerated it. It couldn't have been true because he wasn't afraid.

He considered himself very small in the layered richly-curtained nights, and very big in the small exact daylight. He didn't go in big wandering circles but in a reasonably accurate line. He suspected fear was a circle of some kind, and supposed he was lucky so not to be bringing it with him. He saw his fear lying on the dry grass beside the captain's death, like an offering at a grave . It was the biggest thing he had had to give him. His fear had been considerably bigger than any one thing in the new landscape, larger than any of the muscled trees, or the boulders or the snakes, or even the far-off lions which might have been any size up close. It hadn't been bigger than the captain though, and so had been able to lie neatly on the ground at his side.

After three weeks his Sligo skin was heavily deepened, especially when he puckered it between his thumb and fingers. It felt a bit leprous and raw on the top of his shoulders, but each night soothed that, though each day full of distance tended to stoke it again. Soon a crust formed on this wound, compounded with sweat and dirt and blown clay, and he carried a kidney-shaped plaque of thin armour on his back like a species of two-legged armadillo. His hair was bleached to light brown at the ends and he wore a wetted leaf across his fried-up nose. He devised a manner of tying two large leaves together so they joined hands around his neck and flapped coolly on his angry scab. He had no more cloth for his feet, but they had considerably hardened on the only occasionally gritty surface. Most of the days he had a helpful cloak of supple grass to tread across. Sometimes the cloak must have lain in shallow puddles because his soles slapped on it, and ooze tubed between his toes. For this sort of terrain he cut himself a long leanable-on pole, which he debarked with his left thumb and nail as he wandered over dryer places. Then it was friendly to use it to totter along with generally.

Although the berries and the fruits were tasteless and filling they were not good for replacing the given-up strength at the night-time of every day's walk. Morning was troublesome to wake up into, and his legs grew more mindless and disinclined to carry him smoothly — it was like depending on two snakes for support, who were always trying to escape into the grass and abandon him.

When he came to the town his eyes felt lidless and jumped in their sockets moodily every few seconds. The town was a great plantation of corrugated iron which the sun banged off so possessively that the heat far exceeded the temperature of the plain. The angry rolls would have buffeted him over if he hadn't had his staff. All the small dwellings were silent and eyeless, as he was himself almost. He plodded deeper into the grassless cauldron and found himself noticing a blossoming echoing clamour. It didn't echo among the houses but against the thin cupped hollow of his skull. It was sucked in behind his worn eyes, and was bounced there as if by an idle child.

Sixfoil Seventeen

The quene prest herselff hevilee on herr hazilwud stoole. She cud fele her leggs as weytee as boughes. She wass halv astonisht dat shee did nat crak throo de flagges. A curten uff swet waterfallt doon her forhed an chekes. Her hare splitt in de midel, an stuk oot fercelyee lik a hedg. Al her brest an stomik tremblet as iff softe hott stone mite flowe upp, an burst at her mouthe. Her tweestin eg-shapt eyez satt on her fas lik stoens. She tonged her fatt dree lipps, an heldt on unner her shakkes to da rimme uf herr stule. Her nipels warr flyin lik arros, an wanted ta pulle de reste uf herr oot de darke winda, and inta de hevy nite. Softlee in her bellee her lief stirrd. Her musels leened on itt an gave a sorte of nastee plesur.

Der wasse a seegul on de mossee ledg sudenlee, whach started ta screche inta her roome, bat shee wasse too fritenet ta bullee it awaye. She stard wid her longe fulle eyez lik oweled jewels. De gulle wass veree bigge an clumsee. It cud hardlee perche on de ledg widdoot slippin off, an dat gav mor merderoos bawlin to ittes beke. She wiped her shulder quiklee wid one hant, becorse it wasse itchin herr. She lokt at her wineskinn brests, whach jumpt fram her wid a grate cargoe uf juicey milke. Stil she felt de hevinesse of al de wureld chooz her hed for a restin plac. She wobbelt on de cushin of her bottim, an shivert lik a yong hors. She semt ta herself ta hav juste been boorn oot of her ded mudder. De swet wass de saem in de darke as blut, an she wass fatted an reddent lik a babee jest cum oot.

'Mudder of mercee,' she whimpert, 'wat havv I don ta yoo?'
De wetnesse burnt oot uf her haire, an washt her bak.
'Pitee mee,' she groant ta de berde, 'pitee mee.'
Bat de berde onlee roared wid strengthe.
De cretur wass quiete nowe, an stud wid his pebblet eyez open on her.
'Havv I dun wrong?' she askt dis gul. 'Hav I putt somtin ta

309

finishe mee amang moi storees?'

She tore awaye her cloes, so dey spred on de floor aroun herr, like a strangge feld of furree flowres, and strecht oot her armes to da berd and sed:

'Iff yoo want ta devoor mee, here iss moi milkee bagges. Stabbe yer beke inta dem iff ye deseer.'

She groped fer a knief on de tabel at her sied, an ranne de blaed agenst her lefte brest. Bludeed milke shotte fram de cutte skinne, an swampt wid a noisee voloom on her lappe. She hackt de reste of de brest, til her cheste wasse burnin wid rawnesse, an flatte – bat de nexte momint dis had nat happent, becorse whan she opent her gaze in mumblin horrer, she wasse hoel, an der wasse no wicket knief in her grippin hante. Bat de berd watcht stil.

'Yoo see wat I wud doo too mysel,' she sed. 'Yoo see wat madnesse an uselessnesse I owne insied moi hert.'

She rockt on her botim, forward and bak, til de gulle lookt dizzy and crosse. It mewed lik a kittin.

'Ahh, yoo ar rely a catt – is dat itt, moi graye animool? Yoo ar a veree funee ting.'

She lafft wit a sesonin off biternes, an shook ouwt her wett hed. De tinee planitz uf water fledd ovir de rume, an evin arrivt on de seegul his winges in a hailin patter. De berd shook too, an a smaler ringe an cercle uf droppes sprad aboot hem, bat cud nat go bak to de quene. Shhe rored uppe at de ceelin:

'Mudder, mudder, yoo haff putte som ferce smiel insied mee. Lat mee givv it berthe or I wull di!'

As shee clamoored, shhe raized herr bodee upp, and staggert bak agenst de colde blak wall. Der she stud wid her legges parted, an a serpriezed pattern on her scratcht face. She plact her pamms on de dampe wal, an watter broke fram her cunte, an trulee painted de ruff flor. She dipt, an her vois dipped, an she callt oot ta nowan. Her bellee squirmt an billowed on itts hott whit surfis. She lookt at dis movmint, an did nat knowe it. She felt somtin turnin an thrashin in dere, an den it began ta eese inta her legges. Bat it cud nat go dere, so it pusht for clere aire. Shhe called an made a stormee clatter in her throte, like a brethe suckt bak throu irron. She clutcht her hed bothe sieds, an heavt on her bellee.

'Get oot, get oot, get oot,' she sange wid a hideoos mizeribel

310

cello. De seegulle fluttert hes bodee. A widenin splatter uf stuff an water an yella splurgt fram de quene her cunte. She thrust her hande in her mouthe, an bit it soo vicooslee dat her tethe founde her secrete boenes. De bowens scremt merder an soo did shee. She wasse thenn so legless an weke she slithert to de floor, an met it wid a slapp.

In fronte of her wasse a blak rooty ting, twistin and retoornin on itselff quiclee. De quene pantet an rubbt her bellee, an strokt her pamm on it wid newe affectoon. She gigelt lik a tinee boye. Stil her strange childe travelt in on itselff widdoot stoppe. It smelt lik a rottin fishe, bat hadde no eyes or mouthe or rele hed. It wasse darke blak an wette, an veree faste, bat onlee in ittes owen hepe. She thoght perhapps it wasse a litel lik a grasssnak. She lafft at it, and wantet ta touche et. She lent off her thighes an pettet de tumblin masse. It stoppt movin an bete in one place lik a dogge affter runnin, or a childe affter lonelinesse. De gulle sprad itself an hopped down inta de rume. It stalkt on itts thinne yello legges, an approacht de quene an her bab.

'Go awaye, stiff sadde berd,' she sed. 'Dis ting iss mien, an yoo wil nat dine off moi progenee.'

She swiped her hant at de berd his necke, bat she wasse too distante. She smackt her hanse on de flagges ta friten et, bat it onlee swept a few fete away an den hurriet bak.

'Pur litel babee,' sed de quene, 'wat wil I doo wid yoo? You haff no fete or handes or anythin. Ar yoo boye or womin? Wher is yoor smal face an gentil eyes? An whar is yoor fadder his bellee? Ye haff no noes evven ta smell mee. Wat wil I doo wid yoo, moi badde fellaugh?'

She duckt her hed an peerd in carfulee at de coills. She murmured wid lovin rymes, an restet her lippes agenst de broodee coils.

'Oh moi dere,' she sed, an spatt oot agen. 'Yoo taste lik ded mete.'

As shee pult awaye in her desguste, de berde lurcht inn an grabt parte uf de ting in his grippe. He yankt at et and et thrasht wid grat energee agen.

'No, no, moi berde,' showted de quene, 'leve it doon! Do nat ete moi babee.'

Bat de berde half-flewe and halv-fell to hes ledg, an carriet de hevy thik beste wid himm.

'Oh master gull, yoo hurtte mee nowe,' she cryed. 'Hee iss nat pretee, but he iss de chiel uf moi bishap, an Oi wud luv hem wel.'

De gul loste hes clutche on de blak snake, becorse a peece of it cam awaye, an de gul gobbelt et wid apetiet, an mad annudder lunge fer de twistin bodee. Dis tiem hes beke wass gentil, an hault de hoel cretur onta de legg, an off inta de blanke nite.

'Moi childe, moi childe,' de quene whispert, an lafft greedilee inta her biten handes.

As I banged down the stairs I found the room without my mother. The cotton back of the couch billowed quietly, and the door pointed at me instead of being pleasantly closed. The sea and the island hung in the windows, like pictures on the cream and blue walls. The table was all ready for breakfast, with the rough red–and–black tablemats, and the battered aluminium cof-fee-pot. The sideplates with the lost fishes on them had been set like little lakes to the left of each place. There were two places. Worst of all there was an egg frying in the pan, but no one to look after it. It was spitting with annoyance and had formed a lacy brown rust to lie on. I scooped it with the scooper, whose fingers were burned and shortened from being always left in contact with the cooling pan. There was a series of deft ridges up near the handle for the same reason where it rested on the hot rim. It was a well-known object in that kitchen, even a bit famous.

I made the blue tongue of gas swallow itself, and examined for a while the Highgate scar on my knee which was now darker than the rest of me and moonshaped. The steps I had run down to get it, and the leaves I had slipped on, ran harshly up the back of my head, so I didn't think about that, and travelled the enormous roses of the carpet to the exact door. The stairs there were narrow and panelled, and there was either brown air or brown paint on the grubby walls. My mother stood in the fussed light from the cramped window on the lower landing, in a small noise of seagulls. She was just finishing talking to a dim figure there, a man in courteous black. It might have been my grandfather except he didn't have a trilby, and it might have been the schoolmaster except he didn't have a seedy bare head. He had a cap like a policeman's cap. I set my fingers on my arm like my sister Dor used to do, and squeezed the skin. It didn't hurt enough to wake me so I twisted it. My mother was wearing her pair of black tight trousers and a cashmere sweater. Her black hair seemed to exist about three feet to the right of her inside the wall, possibly because there was no panelling there, only gloomy white gloss. The man submerged into his own affairs again, and my mother came at her normal tomboy pace up to recover the room and me. I had an inspiration.

'Am I going to school?' I said.

'Not today,' she said. 'Go in and I'll get your breakfast.'

I trailed over to the table. It used to be waxed by the previous tenant, but the window weather had scummed the fingernail-thin shell. The table-top was therefore not slippy, and anchored your elbows well.

My mother exploded the gas, and dropped the leathery egg on the pan without remembering she had left it cooking. How far would she ever get without me, I thought. A long long way, I knew. She got some life into the egg again, and crusted some old potatoes from the night before with a light brown armour, summer armour.

'Do you want fried tomato?' she said, with her woolly back to me, something from the zoo in the park.

'Ah ha,' I said, a bit surprised. Only my father ate fried tomato, apart from herself, that was. It was making me dizzy and heavy-lidded to think of this complete school-less day in front of me. There was everything to do. The caterpillars to check and the bloodsuckers on the rocks to be horrified by – endless.

'Ol,' she said, with my plate in her steady hand. She stopped and slitted her eyes at the window, with her other hand balancing her already-balanced body on the dusty sill. She'd have a black hand after that, as I had experience of it.

'Well, eat this,' she said slowly. 'Don't gobble it,'

She brought a blue-and-white striped mug with a thick character for her coffee. I didn't care for it, except for the grainy smell. It reminded me of logs rotting in a rainy wood, the same grassy ironed-clothes mixture. She sipped at it, using the point of her top lip as a cooling instrument. She dipped the sluglike part into the milky brown, and the smooth folding point gathered the cooler air vigorously and prevented her burning herself. Her elbows settled on the sticky wood, and she settled a stare on the island outside, that was really a stare which ended a few feet in front of her clear brown eyes. A tiny liveable-in Martello tower framed itself carefully in each retina. If I could have switched and gone there to either of them, I would have, instanter.

'Em,' she said, and sat the barely-drunk coffee down, and glanced a little guiltily into my chewing face. I hilled my cheeks at her, to help her. 'Your father's em, finished with coming back – I mean he won't be back.'

I chewed on. I doubted this. I was certain she was wrong.

'And Dor,' I said, 'where's Dor?' My voice was indignant, but less than it might have been because of the tough egg. The sea below whipped itself in its own bowl, and passed the island, and ignored it.

'She'll stay in England. She's got a hamster.'

'What?' I said.

'A hamster,' she said.

'What's that?'

'I don't know,' said my mother.

'Where is Dor?' I said. 'Tell her to come back.'

'No,' said my mother. 'She'll have to stay with her great aunt and uncle. I can't manage her here.'

I couldn't really remember Dor so I stopped talking about her. I knew I had liked her very much and she had been an expert at a number of things. I could read her spiral-bound notebook now, but a spiral-bound notebook wasn't everything. I knew she was very big and clever and perfect but she wasn't inside me anymore. But still I missed her, I wanted her back. But I stopped because I couldn't remember her. It seemed rude and cruel to ask for someone back that you couldn't imagine. I cried instead. I didn't cry very often, so these tears were sound-less and came flowing generously out of reservoirs that had brimmed a good length of time, tailored time. They queued on the end of my nose, and then cast themselves off to drop brightly, and break on my empty plate. There they lay in broken circles on the standoffish grease.

'It's funny,' she said, 'very funny'.

'What is?' I said.

'The way policemen talk to you. As if you were ninety, or nine perhaps.'

I felt a bit hunched over in my chair and recalled this was a wrong position, and tried to straighten up my back but the sight of my mother's voice wouldn't let me.

'You'd think they wouldn't dare come up the stairs and say what they say.'

She was talking in her low mirrory tone that she kept for bedtime stories. This pleased me suddenly, and I smiled and placed my arms on the sludgy wax, and then smiled again. I feathered there happily and let myself hunch as much as was necessary. I felt quite ninety or nine myself, if I was to tell the truth.

'Funny,' she said, 'and then it comes like this, and it doesn't surprise me, because he always had it in him.'

Some theatricality prompted me to drop from the chair, and circle what I could reach of her with my arms, and mechanically pat her back. She didn't even cry then, which disappointed me. I was a bad patter maybe.

'Even so,' she said, 'never to see someone again is.'

She didn't say what it was. Anyway I felt confident she was wrong, and proud of my knowledge, but suspected it would be crowing to mention it. There was little point telling me he wouldn't be back. He had been hanging from a rope all morning in my bedroom.

Xenia's magazine lips spoke more to the lightly-whipped lake than to me on the rusty rail beside her:

'She was with my mother for holiday in the lake house, and then one night when everyone was gone and sleep, my mother heard a big noise in the top part where the bedrooms are, my grandmother who is you see my father's mother and not hers, and so not completely in her affection.'

Xenia let this part of her sentence snake out over the water like a cast line. I didn't see the splash. A wooden passenger-boat with yellow lines on its sides and a sleeked look, like a rock-and-roller, was steaming up from some unpronounceable port of

315

call on the lake. We could see it pull from the faraway pier and start to straddle the crossing waves, and champagne its road.

'The grandmother was found by my mother so, in the toilet, with only a nightdress on, and a few short feet from the bowl, but there on the floor and walls was a big bomb of shit like water. My grandmother had exploded before reaching the bowl, and my mother looked at her, and my grandmother weeped, isn't it, and my mother cleaned it all up, and scolded her, isn't it, like she was a child of my mother.'

Xenia had some meaning for this story and some meaning in the act of telling it to me now. As an introduction to her grandmother, whom we were just about to meet, it didn't have much to recommend it. This frail childlike shitting creature would be on this night-club of a boat. I stared down at the rusted water and the rusted rocks under it. I looked at Xenia's face then, trying to remember it, and shook my own face at it without her seeing me. Trim dark bushes walked off politely around the lake. Little broken-down dogs followed them as if the shrubs were masters, carrying their fleas and Brazils of fur, fardels of neurosis. I sighed but the greedy breeze got at it, and happily nudged the sigh another way.

I was nervous of her grandmother, and Xenia was nervous of me being nervous, and somehow ruining the day for them both. It was a burden but I restricted the sketching of it with these blown-sideways sighs. They were theatrical but probably genuine.

The boat when it arrived had all the character of a paper hat. It looked frivolous and sinkable. We handed over our square green tickets, and left the exercising dogs, and drummed about on the metal stairways looking for a grandmother. The second-class restaurant was full of one child and a uniformed nurse – admirably brushed out of existence by her navy-blue breast. Some other grey-suited passengers polished the chilly rails with their elbows above on deck. Then we discovered a large white low-ceilinged room, with one small neat woman at the far end pretending to be enjoying the sun at two long windows. There was no sun. She had her right cheek turned to the lack of it. Still it looked graceful somehow and antidotal to cloacal anecdotes. Dylan Thomas has a poem about something bringing him somewhere by the shadow of his hand. I felt a complete cloaked shadow from tip to toe and would not have liked to face a mirror to check. But the grandmother faced us with brightness and eagerness. Her head was a good substitute for the sun, being round and yellow. She called Xenia by some other name but seemed to recognize me perfectly. Though I had never met her I took her plump hand in my own shaded one, and let her speak to me in German for a while.

'You must give him English, Omi,' said Xenia. 'He is not Swiss.'

'Ah,' she said. 'You know, I do have English but I forget a lot. Many things. You do look Swiss. But so handsome,' she said to me, being an interpreter of shadows. She was agreeably coy and her lightly-dressed body spun stiffly in her hard plywood seat. Her lashes were very long, like birds' tails, and twisted up like the bed of an egg-slicer. She was wearing flaggy black trousers, and her legs were seemingly the same thin old woman's legs that Xenia had. I couldn't know that for certain without causing some clamour in the restaurant, empty as it was.

All the square tables were cleared and shone viciously. The disturbed lake was moving now under the throbbing keel. I saw her standing in the surprised bathroom, but I also saw her sitting like this talking quickly and apparently instructively to Xenia, so one image calmed the other like a hopeful second opinion. Xenia gathered opposite her and leaned her muscled smile into the old woman's information. Xenia's babyish voice had reasserted itself for the moment – it was the instrument she had used for me when she still approved of me, and so I supposed she must approve of her grandmother. Strange music, first-class.

The boat brought our tiny trinity to a number of thrust docks, and in the very heel of the lake Xenia and her grandmother prepared to get me off.

On shore the grandmother peered at my black shape against a dull restaurant and said, like a lamp:

'I learned my English first among the skiers in Biarritz. That was some time ago.'

She said 'my English' as if she spoke a language peculiar to her or to a vanished sect.

'Now,' she said, 'we will walk up and view my old house.'

On the dock behind us the stranded restaurant leaned, with wind-torn umbrellas outside it, never taken in from the summer season. The town was white-washed hotels and medieval shops. The hotels were made of glassed-in balconies where orders for chocolate and beer were given, with tight lips clear behind the frostless panes, and children threatening to become chaotic, unSwiss. We drank in one such for a while, and I admired the ability of Xenia and the old woman to speak the language of the country. After even one winter in Lucerne, I was losing a clear feeling about anywhere that I might have once called home. I feared my English was deteriorating or perhaps improving in the dialect of pidgin that Xenia had mistressed – instead of her syntax straightening, mine was beginning to meander, and feel uncertain and unlikely in my mouth and ears.

A thin paved path struggled up to a vague castle at the cone of the town, leaving the neat long streets behind to ribbon the flanks. We headed for the smudge of battlements. Halfway up, the grandmother plucked Xenia's arm, and Xenia said:

'Hold on to Oliver too, Omi.'

And Omi giggled and said:

'But he might not want that, and I do not wish to seem forward.'

Xenia gave me an orange-quarter of a smile, mixed with half a worried scowl, and I said:

'Please. Take my arm.'

I angled it for her and she swept briefly from Xenia and settled there, and walked on up with me serenely and silently, a strip of feathered flotsam. She opened her other hand to the misty view of a distant unrecognizable Lucerne. She turned her eyes up at my face, distantly and unrecognizably. She had the air and story of an old station waiting-room. On the summit she said simply:

'This is what I miss, you don't mind, do you, Oliver?'

Her voice had become watery and clean, and she was light and slim beside me, trailing two world wars. I was troubled by how happy being valued again made me. Here was the material of my crudest and most constructive notion of romance.

'This, my dear, is my old castle,' she said gently, as if we were about to claim it, and live there, like Lear and Cordelia, reversed or not reversed, perverted.

318

The big cricket under the stopped bonnet ticked confidently. We were pulled in under drifted streetlamps, that ringed some sort of depot in the town. A mauve light washed up the street in front of us like a slow tide. The yellow-grey of the lamps pierced columns into it. The light so built a huge palace, and the unspecial town looked embarrassed to surround it.

Sue was petalled in the far corner of the back-seat, a night flower. The pinky yellow air was extremely heated, and a sweat pool was gradually staining her back. She was dipped in a shallow half-sleep, a lily in grubby water.

Chicken shifted from foot to foot in a glass phone-booth, like a mummy in a showcase. He was having to grapple a little with the apparatus to make it co-operate. I saw his palm thump on the coinbox, and a foot strike at the see-through coffin, but I couldn't hear him. It was so late the owls thought they were in the country, and skimmed stony sounds into the deep glossy sky. The world of the owl seemed upside down. They might have been some other birds – I wasn't an expert.

'Who's he ringing, do you think?' I said.

I had to repeat it to make Sue's otter head rise with a small shock.

'Oh, what?' she said.

'Chicken's calling someone. Who do you think it might be?'

'Don't you have any sense, Oliver?' she said, pleasantly.

'How do you mean?'

'Honey, nothing that Chicken does has a great deal of whatever attached to it.'

'How's that?'

'Don't be such a cow-bell, Oliver honey.'

She placed her cheek on the warm leather again, and was still for a bit. Then she swung her legs down and levered up and boarded back on the seat.

'I can't fuckin sleep,' she said. 'Who's that bastard calling up at this hour of night?'

I laughed.

'That's what I asked you.'

'Yeh, well, who is he? I want a motel and I want a bed and I

319

want a shower. And in the bright morning I'll want you, honey, so hold on to your hat.'

I laughed among the leather and the cold smell of leaked petrol.

'It's a fuckin hard job, this,' she said. 'And it's not improving my language.'

'You always curse when you're tired,' I said.

'Oh so, you're the expert of when I fuck, are you?' she said.

I couldn't work it out and the tone upset me.

'Hey, I was joking,' she said. 'Big old weed. Do you hear me?'

'I hear you,' I said.

Instant coffee, instant milk, instant happiness.

'You know, Owl,' she said, and slid her way over, so she rested beside me but didn't touch, 'if you're thinking of, you know, heading off again on our own, well I don't mind, not me.'

The tick of the engine got into the lamps outside and they ticked too. Then the flood of mauve ticked. And my heart ticked.

'Whatever you wanted, Owl,' she said.

'Are you fed up with Chicken?'

'Ah shit,' she said, 'excusing my language, but maybe I am. Dancing there like a bird on a lectric plate. Maybe I'm fed up with being cooped like an eating-hen in the back of this bus. You know? I wouldn't mind walking about fifty-two miles. You know what I mean? I mean I could walk from here to the coast or wherever we're headed.'

She had made her face up with a small cache of lipstick, powdered cherry, and face-powder and eyeshadow and such, that we had bought back up the road. The seat had put a hand to her cheek and struck some red on to her smile. Her eyes rested like minnows dropped back into a trout river. They were deep blue in a running brown light. I suddenly looked attentively at her nose, and realized to myself how much I preferred it. I couldn't remember ever liking it or even not liking it before. It was straight but slightly swollen, and the nostrils were tiny inverted teacups made of best china. Everything about it was carved and curved, and it twitched very slightly like an animal when she spoke. The nose was beginning to take her over, so I

320

said:

'He mightn't understand that. He thinks we're staying together. I mean, if you want to tell him, go ahead, and I'll be quite happy to do it.'

'You couldn't tell him, Owl,' she said, 'could you not, baby?' She was pleading.

'When would I tell him? When would you like to go?'

'Whenever,' she said, and leaned away again, and set herself straight in the heat. 'I don't know,' she said, 'I just want to get out on our own. Don't you?'

'I don't mind,' I said. 'I'll come with you if you want.'

'I'll come with *you*,' she said. 'You're the boss. For fuck's sake, Owl, you just do what you like, and when that's done I'll still be with you. Okay?'

She said it cleanly and without malice like a farm woman twisting a chicken's neck — but she didn't intend it that way. The words she said had crossed on top of someone else's in what seemed the long-ago. So I swilled out the long-ago as best I could, and she said:

'He's been talking there a mighty long time, and we've been steaming here a mighty long time, and sooner or later it's going to be too long. You see, Owl, if we were on the tarmacadam now we'd just sneak into a little field, with a bunch of barns, and sleep with the owls.'

She was plucking the chicken now, but she still didn't mean it. The trouble was, I didn't know how to broach the thing with Chicken. He was too silent and too presupposing. The trouble of it lit up on a board in my head, and flashed at the back of my eyes.

'It's getting like me sitting in my mother's old house in Virginia, and the whole world of traffic going by, and me sitting and the stupid clock booming, and me getting pissed at everything, and fuming there.'

'I know,' I said, 'you're right. We've got to make a move and go. Maybe he won't mind, Sue. I'll tell him. I'll tell him tomorrow.'

'Whenever,' said Sue. 'Don't worry about it. Come over here, honey, and hold your girl.'

Corny as it was, it was the correct thing to say to me. I suppose I just liked corny commands, or liked any affection that

321

came from her. I moved over towards her, like an iceberg setting off on a big thaw. She put her very hot palm against my right cheek, and drew my face down to hers, and kissed me like an actress – she just touched her smudged lips against my mouth, and left everything there, and then took it away. It was delicious though, a sort of lovely underkiss.

'You're my old man,' she said, with a drowning dog in the well of her throat. Her cooler arms hydraulicked up my shoulders, and she pressed her breast on me, and made a silver mine out of my eyes and dug there with hers.

'You ever think of leaving your wife and really getting married?' she whispered.

I chuckled again. I knew this time she was playing since I wasn't married, but sometimes I got so stupid I needed such knowledge, or I reacted oddly.

'Yes,' I said, 'now that you mention it, I have.'

'You have, old bear?' she said, with stagy surprise.

'Sue,' I said.

'Yep?'

'I'm not joking.'

'Look,' said Stephen, flicking at his loose left ear – they were both a bit loose, 'you'd want to get a move on with this, Ali. My good boss man won't be away for ever, and we'll have the season going in a little bit, and then friends of his may be rocketed down, even without him.'

'We'll do it, mon, take it easy,' said Ali gravely, like a reproving grandfather.

'Of course you will, my dear friend,' said Stephen. 'Yes of course you will, that's not in doubt.'

He sucked without much finesse at a thin brown cigarette. The bar was well customered that night, and the music was up too loud, to encourage the girls, and encourage the wallets, so we had to hunch a little at the counter to misunderstand each other. Ali was not a pal to hunching, and he hunched without much effect or enthusiasm, which made him hardest to decipher. Stephen's smoke forced out of his lips, and jagged and fattened up towards the dark roof. He stuck the filter against the ashtray, and sort of spat the last marble of smoke, and licked his upper lip where a shred of tobacco had rested. Immediately, he said:

'Then we have this nice buyer friend of mine running up a hotel bill in Miami. Now I haven't asked him, but I don't suppose he's putting his feet up in a dosshouse. The wretched Hilton would be nearer his mark. I'm not a rich man, Ali, and if you can't manage this little task I'll be stuck even for the hotel. I mean, my dear boy, I worry about these things. I'm lying in my little bed in that big empty place, and I think first of all of the swimming-pool. Supposing, I think, I fall asleep and in my foolish dreams walk out on to the lawn and fall in the pool. Then I think of the wall, and how low it is, and how Ali and Bat here and even Susan, if she's going in with you –.'

'No,' said Ali, his word muddled by a heavy bass, a piece of wet charcoal.

'Well, as you wish. I haven't asked you and I don't want to know really. My god, do you think the police might torture me if they find out?' he said to me, in seemingly unfeigned fright. 'I was reading about a fiendish torture the other day that the Chinese went in for, a box of paste over the head that stripped the flesh off your.'

Ali foiled the thumped bass with a thick laugh.

'No, no,' said Stephen, 'well, let me think, what was I saying to you, Ali? Well, when is the basic question. When. If you're trying to interfere with the smooth working of my blood system you're doing a fine job. Did I ever tell you, Bat, about my blood pressure? It is a simple story but a depressing one. No? Well, never mind.'

Mona danced blankly and restrictedly behind the bar. She looked much older than a few weeks ago. She looked a hundred and two. Maybe she was. She stuck her chin out at me as part of her seductive dance.

'Aren't they great tonight?' she said.

'You mean the girls?' I said.

'Oh yeh,' said Mona and danced on.

'Where's the Mohican tonight?' I said.

She twisted over and leaned on the counter and just let her rump dance.

'You know,' she said, 'he had ta go home and see his mother.'

323

'Really?' I said. 'So who's on the door?'

'Ali,' she said.

'Ali,' I said, 'our Ali?'

'Yeh, yeh,' she said, and squeezed her eyes in a silent laugh. 'Just for tonight. Which is why maybe we have so many customers.'

'How so?'

'Well, he ain't stoppin anyone pushin in. But it's up to him, and we're gettin away with it.'

I pulled back from her and tucked myself on to my stool again. I had been forming a sweating barrier between Ali and Stephen. As soon as I shifted Stephen's sleeked head dived into the space again.

'So when can you do it, Ali?' his very red lips said.

'Tomorrow,' said Ali, 'when the Mohican's back. I got to work tonight.'

'I didn't mean do it tonight,' said Stephen with a tulipish pout. 'Tomorrow will be the right time. I'm just glad to have it settled. Well, I'm going to my bed. Take care of all your selves. And give my affectionate regards to Susan. I didn't get a chance to speak to her.'

'Take it easy,' said Ali again, but as a goodbye.

'Night-night, Mona love,' said Stephen, and Mona flagged him a minute wave.

'So, mon,' said Ali to me gently. 'We can do all that tomorrow.'

'If you have it worked out, we might as well,' I said, glumly.

'Yeh,' he said. 'Then we'll go to Miami with Stephen. And then – do what we want.'

'I just might go to Mexico.' I said, as a gesture against the odds.

'You could go to Jamaica,' he said, like he was giving me a gift.

'I could,' I said. 'Maybe after.'

'My father has a good house there, and always a room for me. Go to Kingstown and live in my room. Tell my father I said you to, and he'll put you in there. Do it.'

'Thanks, Ali,' I said, bewildered.

'No,' he said, 'you do that, mon. He'll look after you. Jamaica is a great place, and if you want to stay in my room, it's there for you.'

'That's good of you, Ali.'

'Right,' he said, as if it were all settled, and going to be done.

'You won't go yourself though maybe,' I said.

'I don't think so. I might, mon, in a while. I might go down to Rio. I might go to Canada. I don't know it, and it's there.'

'It's a pity we couldn't just come back here and go on as before.'

'You like this town, mon?' he said.

'I like these people. I feel easy here, It's not easy to feel easy. It's a bit of a novelty for me, and I've got used to it already.'

'That's a pity, mon,' he said, 'but you can't come back here for a long time.'

He said it with simple finality. He made it sound like a banging door. Can't come back, and so no more easiness. He made me desperate in three seconds, but I sat on it. The whole thing was nothing to him. It wasn't even enough. It was just a little troubled place which he was going to get himself out of. He knew he'd meet me again somewhere. I wouldn't have the same name or the same appearance, but for him it would be me, or as much of me as he paid any heed to. He looked like a hangman and stared at his beercan, and tossed the small beer around inside it.

'Susan won't come into the house then?' I said, in the bruised cocoon of music. In the corner of my eye a man fell over woodenly as he moved towards an empty space at the cockpit. Someone picked him up and thumped his back, and cast his own head to the winds, and roared into the smoke. It was the seven-fingered tourist and his Indian friend, on holiday, strangers again to us now, as is the way.

'She never was,' said Ali. 'No, she just set this up, and she'll come to Miami with us, but not on the same plane. Just as you and me won't be on the same flight. Those planes are only little cigars.'

The sandy sea-ridden airport rushed back at me. Key West, I supposed, was closing for me, like a complete life. I was on my death-bed here, and would have to bear myself unwillingly into the next life, some unknown shadowy life on the mainland. I wouldn't go to the unclear cell Ali had offered me in Jamaica, I knew that. But where would I go? With Susan to Mexico? That was the best thing. It had better be that.

Since Moran had walked so far, there was no reason in his boiled head not to walk on further. He was stopped by the rim of a thickly-gathered carpetpile of people. The noise was the booming of a loudspeaker, or rather a number of them in delayed competition. Moran clambered on to a handy tree-stump, and balanced himself there by placing his stick on the clay, and a hand on the reduced height of the top of it. He expected to be spoken to, but people only glanced back at him and then forward again. He didn't seem remarkable to them. Many of the figures in the crowd were flagged with coloured cloth, and plain grassy khaki, but many others were mostly naked like Moran, and held sticks as he did.

A far-off finger was raised on a highish small platform – the finger was a man, and this man was producing the bullish sounds. Without being precisely aware why, Moran understood immediately it was Henry Grant. No creature on earth could also have that smiling acceptable arrogance that survived even the mish-mash of the speakers. Anyway Henry Grant's odd music had been constantly in Moran's ears, and the real sound was only a jazzing of the imaginary. Also it had to be Henry Grant, because Moran didn't know any other Blacks, and yet he was sure he knew this distant man, so that proved it to himself. He found himself extremely at his ease on the stump. He had no desire to move or eat or drink or talk. He could conveniently have become the replacement to the vanished tree. He stuck his stick more firmly into the dust as if to encourage it to root, and gripped it to encourage himself to graft on to it. In the meantime Henry Grant was making the loudspeakers whisper and thunder, wasp and weather. It was some sort of chant or speech, and it reached Moran a little chopped and prepared for the cooking-pot:

'My yee-ers in prison will not be-be a story for my grand-children-ren but-ut a gun-un for you my broth-others. They have-av pinion-ioned these claws but now the-now the eag-le flies-ies free-ee and flies in sorrow-sorrow for you my-my brothers.'

Everyone in front of Moran gave a surge that didn't contain much movement, and a song was delivered back to Henry Grant. There were no words in it from Moran's box of language, but the held crying note excited him in such a way that he almost let the stick fall forward and punish someone's skull. He steadied himself, and the water-coloured crowd cut its note with a huge ceremonial scissors, and stared at Henry Grant again, and took the whitened light on their crowns.

'I will–ill have my country for my coun–country. We will rule as free–ee men brother with–ith brother sister with ster.'

The crowd called out to Henry Grant and Moran tried to become the tree. They wanted to tell the small fleshed post against the platform something that Moran didn't know about. Still he felt he ought to be there, and did his best to cheer the stump under him to some kind of vigour. Henry waved his small arms above his small grey head, and rocked himself. The arms of the crowd flew up like a sudden thorny wilderness, that Moran was glad he didn't have to trek over. It was the worst terrain he had ever seen. All those boulders, with rough and mobile plants tearing their way out of them. He felt he was better where he was – not that he had any idea where that was. A treestump in Africa, somewhere. Then he wondered if it was appropriate or not for all his life so far to have led to this, or whether perhaps it hadn't led to this, but this was leading to something else. Well he didn't really need something else. He had never seemed to himself very clearly defined, or drawn against the ground, but now, and blissfully, he was nothing. He was an animal that couldn't even resuscitate a dead tree. He was certain he couldn't do it. He had killed the staff, and the townspeople had killed the tree, or it had died from lack of tilled clay at its base, the burnt air had embraced its girth too toughly. Feet had trampled its lungs to death. The tree had been dependent on isolation in the bush for reasonable survival. Well, there was nothing he could do. His body was fountaining with sweat. He could do nothing. He was finished. He had never begun. Nothing was the best thing yet he had ever been. He wanted now to remain like that. But the tree was very very dead, and some time or other he'd have to get down off it, since he couldn't help it, cozen it, or join himself to it. It was over and now he was expected to continue. The people sang and sang to Henry, and Henry over the crippled microphone, blackly, sang and sang to the people. They might have done that all afternoon, and still Moran would not have existed. As proof of his nonexistence, he started to cry, but very copiously and generously. No one else was crying, he was the only one. The trickles of moisture bought tickets for his burned cheeks, and his narrowed neck, and his hardened chest, and one full drop treated him like glass which he was not, and tobogganed down his leg, and dripped from his left ankle, and put a soft halfpenny on the hacked bole. After a minute there was in all twopence there. Moran lifted a grimed hand and held it over his eyes. The crowd kept singing. It wasn't untrue singing though – it was a sort of talking. Henry Grant and the audience had left all odious fragmentary language behind, and their new notes were whole and destructive. Moran didn't know where he was crying from, but wherever it was, the huge song was inside there, turning the handles and taking off stops. It climbed down into his engine of happiness, and worked it till its valves were threatening an explosion. It accelerated Moran on and on past all guarantees of the manufacturer. He might have died a number of times, except only that he didn't. The machine held good. Now there was a machine inside the machine to reach, which would be hard to reach, and which if ever entered would be able to explain the bigger one. The song let Moran be more than he was, like a fair master lets a dog be human in his own house.

'I am human in your own house,' whispered Moran, because he couldn't become the tree. Now he was something better. He was less than the tree. But he was changed into a man.

Sixfoil Eighteen

'Yoo wante yer mousee oates,' sed Olliver, as Jacke kepte attemptin ta trott. De blak wall uf hes castell roz lik a parcell uf ded fier oot uf de scufft footet grasse. Conn restet stoenilee on hes hors his woern bak. Jacke needet ta be fre uf hes weit, an he needet ta be fre of anudder unsene weit dat boldered hes shulders. De wied darke gaet wasse prest agenst stoen, an shutt agenst travilerz, so Conn scremt uppe de walz fer sumwan ta lat hem passe inn. Highe heds stard doon at hem an he sed:

'Yoo lazee boyez, leve off yer playe an unblok dis arch!'

Bat wan manne calt doon:

'We can nat, lard Conn, we muste kepe ower loord oot.'

'Openn moi gaet, ye nastee cattes, or Oi wille brek boens dis daye!'

'Noe, noe,' dey sed, 'we ar soree, bat it iss pert of vanisht lawes dat saye yoo arr lard here. Yoo arr nuttin here nowe, an wee morne dis, butt can doo nuttin ferr nuttin.'

'Hoo is dat? Iss dat, iss et moi grey cooke an fiter Jem Leery?'

'Yas, it es mee, grat Conn, bat nat yer cooke or yoor fiter noo. I amm bat cookk an sworderr ta yer simpel quene.'

'Diss iss no gaem fer a weery manne,' sed Conne. 'Wud yoo nat shutt dis gabb uf quenes, an lett me att sum morsell uf moi fudd?'

'Derr iss no fude or no drinke eeder fer yoo nowe, lard Con. Yoo muste pasther an sucke somwhar els.'

Bat denn de gaet didd shudderr, an handes pult et openn, an handes at de ende of carful armes, tyed on ta bigge bodees, crept oot lik stronge ratts ta mete Olivverr.

'Gat doon fram de quen her hors,' sed der capten, hoo wasse a cusin ta Conne bee hes gratmudder.

'Go an putte a dunkee hes shitt in yer mout, Cavnagh. Wat is dis stoopit storee uf clost wud an newe orderrs? Iss dis nat de castel an tooer uf Conne, whach iss yoor famlee as welle as mien? An amme I nat de litul parfact hed of al ower blut?'

'Yee ar nat,' sed Cavnaghe, whoo hadd no hare on hes hed at all, bat hoos arms whar blown upp lik pigges ther bladderz. He helt a smoothe ironn sord, whach indade whass wan uf de oweld weponz uf Olliver hisself.

'Doo I nede ta remoov yer cloody hed, ta chang ittes wether?' sed Conn. 'Or wul ye hied behint dat fowlishe grup uf moi tribesmenne?'

'Dey ar nat yern at al,' sed Cavnagh, wid a badde sneere. 'Yoo ar nat here. Yoo ar gon inta sum ded storee.'

Olivver slidd off Jacke an de hors bumbelt on throo de menne ta gaen hez stabel. Olivv helt uppe hes owen greye sord.

'Poore Cavnagh,' he sed, 'poor Cavnagh, dat I muste remoov fram de jois an pesters uf hes claye. Cum, steppe agenst mee, Cavnagh, an I wul chang yoo fram pott ta pickt–over bittes.'

Cavnagh an hess blak–letheret menne walk doon de sloep an struk at Olivver. A flatt slap uf Cavnagh hes sorde founde de dulle belle of Conne hes eare, an he fal dowen, thumpinge. Oliverr his face staret uppe at de lower skye, an hes eyez warr veree coyned an rounde. Wan sadde–lukin manne pickt de sord fram hes nested fingerz.

'Yoo ar a breef hero,' sed Cavnagh. 'Wat wul yer poete doo wid so smal a conqueste on moi parte? Hee wil saye yoo foght fram noone to neet an al de nexte daye.'

Cavnagh lafft ovver Conne, ande smal ironne berds tosst aboot in de winde uf trobelt Olivve hes vizoon. Metil hants tuk hem uppe. Jem Learie, lik a wurm in hes simpil trechrie, let lowerr a pare uf roeps fram de tooer, an de lowlee menn notted ech ta ech riste uf Conn. Dene Lerry an hes helpres drew softlee on de rop, an whiel sum pult an udders beloe lifted, dey war abel to hoiste Oleev a fewe fete fram de grount.

He racoveret fram de sord ittes cracke to de newe pane uf hes draggt armes. His shoulders an toppe armz stuk oot fram de rouff walle, an he wept fram ets strangnesse. Cavnagh gave hes potatoe laff agen, as a small stele musik.

'I hoep ya wul nat be too unhappee der, moi lonlee Olivver, becarse yoo wil staye der fer al dis nite an daye, til de quene says "lat hem doon".'

Deye passt inn throo de breethin doore. Idel menne watcht hem fram de caztelatunz fer a whiel, bat denn dey loste interezt

330

an der hedz dismooned. He herd hes castel humm lik a hieve, wid al de normall coursins uf a daye.

'Dey haff forgottin mee alredee,' he sed to hes torment. 'Oi haff onlee yoo nowe ta companioon mee. How quiklee I havv passt fram lorde ta theef.'

He whispert in hes windoed eyez fer sum sart uf madd slepe.

'Whoi, helo, moi hert,' sed a womane her voiz unnernethe hem. He hault uppe hes sighte itz hoodz, an dropt a stare on herr browen hed.

'What doo yoo doo, daft gerl?' he sed. 'Wat doo yoo doo to wan mann, hoo gaef yoo a towerr to haff in equall?'

'Ha, noe, moi prettee guerrier, yoo did nat giff me anytin, an lik yer oeld fadderz I haff taken diss plaez fer moi selff. Yeer rool wass veree lange, bat wat will I saye to yoo nowe? Only dat it iss ovir, an yoo ar too.'

Conne tryed ta reche inta her pooled eyez wid hiz.

'Whoi, moi Olivver,' she sed, 'yoo look lik a sicke dogg wid a belee ful uf ded pupees. Wull yoo misse yoor gentil woif, yer wolff, moi dustee luv, or natt?'

De bishap roolet oot fram de sprad gaets an sed:

'Ah, hee iss hoom at laste, iss hee, moi quene an masterr?'

'Yas,' sed de quene, 'hoom an hunge.'

'An hunge on hes hoom at dat,' sed de bishap happilee. 'Poor chicken he iss noew, dat muste wait fer hes blut ta drippe fram al hes chanels befor de pott.'

'Dat iss a gut idea, lard bishap,' sed de quene. 'We kan roste dis poore manne whan it iss daye tomorro. We wull haff a smal celebratioon uf yer hoom–cumin, Conn – an yoo can bee mete fer us al.'

Evven in hes rencht herte positioon, dis thoght wasse veree nastee, an agen, agenst hes beter effertz, yonge water stremt fram de dertee cornez us hes lashez.

'O Con, moi dere babee,' sed de quene in a tinee childishe lovlee murmurr, 'moi dere wan, moi gentil hunterr, doo nat crye. I wul mak de fier soo smal yoo wil nat burne quicklee, an soo it wul nat hurte yoo muche, and whan yer hert iss cookt, I wil toothe et myselv.'

De quene cud nat stoppe herselfe makin a noiz lik an ovvere-xited hors, which wass her laff uf desir. She cud nat stoppe et jist ass Conn cud nat stop hes ters. So Conne criede badlee an

331

she chortelt badlee, an it wass a sorte uf mokeree of bravnesse an unioon. No, Moll, he wasse nat braev wid hes armes so hardlee strunge, nat in hes chekes or hes mout anywaye. He foght fer breth, an dis made hes armes dragg mor, an soo he cried onn, an den he fadet. No sound frooted from hem at al.

'Hee iss gon inta a slepe of a kinde,' sed de bishap mousilee. 'Do nat wake hem.'

'I wul wake hem if I pleese,' sed de quene, an flunge a greye rocke at her lorde. It struck hes cheste an bounct awaye, an nerlee knockt de bishap his forhed.

'Oh watche yer style,' he sed.

'Donat spek lik dis ta mee,' de quene spat, a magot in an apell, an echoed on hes fac wid her smal fiste.

'Here,' said the master's check suit, 'hold the tongue of this and ring it when I tell you.'

It was the early morning of school, rather than the very different early morning of a free day. All the foreigners had turned up for the repetition of this dreary slow-motion show. The inside of the master's pinked mouth was flaking and damp like a chalky cliff. He probably swallowed a deal of chalk dust among his squeaking gestures at the board. He was certainly from Cork, as he claimed, and he loved an extraordinarily unusual language called Theirish. All the books were in English, as in normal and previous places on both sides of the taxi-ridden sea, except for one monstrously tedious and frightening one about Daithi and Maire. Daithi and Maire were obsessed with the objects in their house, and kept on and on pointing them out to each other. It was a language for little soldiers. You take the house apart like this, and then, oops, dear me, how do you put it together again. But the words had letters pretending to be other letters, so that when you went to open your gob to read from the book, it magically was supposed to be something quite other than what you hoped it was. English was hard enough without this mean game the master played with the letters. There were fullstops lost on top of b's that were not b's, and many of the words had to be given a footless tick over one or other of the letters, to denote god-knew-what – but it was a curious caned crime to unpluck one of these darts, the last spears of the grime-ridden tribes.

The master could prove he was lord of Theirish because he had a little silver washer on his lapel. His cheeks were a little green and mouldy which also was connected. The check of his jacket was stroked by the green of card tables, which made him look like a frondy riverside plant.

Even the foreigners at the other desks around me had a hard time with this language, and there was a silent noise like insects dying all during Theirish class. The other great tract of ruinous landmines was the Catkism, which, like the master's jacket and the unrusted washer, was linked with Theirish in some way, even though it was all about god and delivered thankfully in English. These gods had apparently made the whole world whereas before my mother had had this distinction. Therefore it was a pack of lies. The book reeked of the most spoilsport information, and cast a metal gloom over everyone as we learned to sing it. The words didn't sing very well, so the master left out all notes except one quite high up, and made us render the shebang on that alone. We were embarrassingly below Alfred Deller's offest day, but luckily the master was easily the worst, and keened out the book of mumbo-jumbo like he had sat on a spike, or broken his neck by slipping in the bath, which was easy to do.

I had never tackled such subjects before. There might have been some justification in my mind for Theirish, since at least it demonstrated the comparative simplicity of learning to read English. Against it was the fact that no one in the wide world spoke it, or knew it, or learned it besides us. I hated and distrusted Daithi and Maire but their threat was turned inward against themselves, and they were only frightening because they were frightening to have anything to do with, in the way of contemplating them. But the god and gods generally in the Catkism were at open war with me, and told me without a please or thank-you what I had to do or not do, and what would happen to me if I didn't or did. The book smelled of spilled old jamwater, and the paper was unpleasant, and the words clubbed together like weapons. They had one bang of a nerve, those badly-printed gods. The other boys knew a lot more about them than I did, and had always known it. Every Sunday, instead of going for a walk, they muttered into a building, against their own better wishes, and the master's brother sang endlessly in yet another murderous local language, and they shouted up at the blackened man from time to time, probably to relieve the strange white gloomy boredom that afflicted them, after the first five minutes. Absolutely nothing happened except up behind an iron fence, until the whole town blocked the passages, like so much mucous membrane in a noseful of sinuses, and inched up towards the master's brother, and ate the thinnest most tasteless biscuit, called Marietta. It was explained to me that this biscuit was part of the dead body of a man from Jerusalem, which was somewhere in the mediterranean sea, which was so far away it was nowhere at all. It was astonishing. I had had my doubts about it, but to know that I had swallowed a large-size tiddlywink of a piece of someone's corpse, a desert traveller, was very troublesome to accept, especially since my mother never went near the place, and for very sound reasons, I thought. Everyone was mad, with their rotted bodies and their unplayful languages.

The exception to all their dangerous customs was the drawing class. This was conducted in much the same way as the one in England, though here they sketched mostly cows and fields, and in England cars and houses. It was a point of reference, something shared, an evolutionary link between the kind of insect I was and the kind they were. So I drew as much outside the drawing-class as in it. This inexplicably was punished – you could be punished also for what you drew in the class itself. Cows and fields and faces were all right, as long as they were done with no particular cow or field or face in mind, especially face. The master detested being portrayed himself, and threw an unknown child from the room for trying it, when detected darkly. So I never drew the master, even though he was very easy to draw because of his jumbled teeth, and was standing availably at the top of the rows anyway.

I tried to remember my mother on paper for some classes in a row, till my drawings were examined, and my head was clipped for including 'boozams'.

'What are they?' I said, though I had a fairly accurate notion of them – you can't draw what you don't at least recognize the name of, the soft of good-nights.

'This part,' he said, placing his inked finger on my mother's chest.

'But she has those,' I said, pleasantly.

'Who has?' the master asked, equally agreeably.

'She has,' I said, 'my mother has.'

The foreigners began to hoot and cackle artificially.

'What sort of monstrous brat are you,' said the master, 'that you draw these on your mother?'

Like Daithi and Maire, I didn't understand him, but he terrified me. He was like a hedge infested with rats. You couldn't walk past him without a danger of some characteristic of his going for your throat.

'She has them,' I said, 'she has them,' as if repetition and a raised voice might get it through to him. The thought of her without them, deprived of them somehow by the master perhaps, was vile. Then he showed me how his stick worked – there wasn't much to it.

Then, after the policeman called on my mother, I tried to remember what my father looked like. I made a big black beard and a big long nose and his round mirroring spectacles, that had not made the world. The master named me the filthiest little boy he had ever come across, the ruins of a good Irish lad after my English education, and expelled me for a week. He had done something wonderful for me at last. Agus amen.

I had a simple trick of a whistle that Xenia called 'our bird'. The bird lived mostly in the big wicker-basket under a window. It was the window I could see the postman from, if I angled out over the perfect street. Somehow I thought of the postman as the same nationality as myself.

I was stretched beside her, looking at the basket in the early-morning greyness. Out of a stubborn wish to be held by her, I had kept myself awake through a small night of my life. I didn't have the least reason to offer why I was in this particular bed in this room in this city with this woman. I had arrived in her colours on an unimportant pretext of imminent death, and since I hadn't quite risen or descended to it, the suspicion that this type of existence might go on without end, or even for another week, was wormwood and woodworm.

There had been an expensive argument in a bar the night before. We were drinking among gays of uncommon unattractiveness – one especially kept posturing to himself in the big wall-mirror. He was not beautiful, and he did it without loss of interest or change of attitude hour on top of hour. His acne was as baroque as the mirror frames.

Xenia and I were both stealing into an uneasy drunken garden of our own, and the only thing that was holding good was the late daylight strolling through the town. The narcissistic gay with his dead scallop of fawn hair couldn't enter our gates exactly, but he seemed to leer at us through them. A much older man, for whom the performance was infinitely repeated, was watching us, instead of the shaper who would have preferred it. The gentleman was got up in a very English suit, of a foreign European kind. His cravat was golden rather than gold, and his square face could look at you with a cinematic sexual composure. I felt ill-temperedly attracted to him, which made me miserable and exultant – to be admired, to be admired. Xenia elbowed the counter as if she wanted to shove it out of her way, or shove herself out of her way. The cigarette-case eyes observed her through invisible but sharply-focused opera-glasses. When he swung away to drink his coffee, I realized through the motes and insect noises of drunkenness that he was a constricted bunched man. Only his full face existed, the rest of him was vague and narrow and badly drawn. I would have to trim the face from the surround, and hang it in our apartment as a friendly moon. What service would the moon want in return?

Xenia swallowed a sentence she meant to bring out. She gobbled on it emptily. She had a special owlish stupidity to drape on her extraordinary features when she had put too much beer into her unlikely frame.

'Will you ask a beer?' she said.

'Let's get out,' I said. 'Let's take the tram and go home.'

She signalled a barman over, with a loose insignificant tap that he responded to at once.

'Yes, madam?' he said in English. He had just bottomed on to his shift, and thought we were tourists, because we were drinking like tourists.

'No,' I said, quietly. I had fifty deer running across my field of vision when I said it.

'One beer,' she said, also in English. Perhaps she was a tourist.

'No,' I said to the barman. 'We're going. We've had it.'

She twisted herself neatly amid the storm of conversation. She was much more sober that I had thought, because she said:

'Don't. Don't tell me.'

I knew what she meant to say. The broken mirrors that her eyes had suddenly become said it anyway. The elegant gay laughed at us. The barman fetched her her beer – he guessed instinctively who was paying. I sprang away, circumlocutively, as a kind of banal reply, into the full neon-marked night. It was simple and fresh, and the city had raised itself up in its own hands. I plundered my paths home, and she was there before me, silent and innocent, having more straightforwardly sat for a franc on a tram. There was no conversation. She put herself naked into bed, pulled out again and shoved on a T-shirt and some dancing tights, and removed herself from me into sleep.

So now I was awake among the debris of my own thoughtlessness, and the possible coal-beds of tomorrow. I didn't mind about my stupidity. I knew I was stupid and wrong, and only a cautionary footnote in any textbook of marriage or union, even a common law marriage like ours, but I no longer knew why I was being stupid and wrong with her. Certainly she didn't desire my limited company any more. So why didn't she say it, and toss me out into the train-times of Europe? If she didn't give me any money, I'd hitch. Yes, I'd hitch, when the sun returned from wherever it had briefly been visiting.

I slipped out of our strange rectangle of padded floor, and tried to curl boyishly on the wicker-basket. It couldn't be done, so I hunched there, and watched her Javanese dolls get their day-time colours back. She surfaced at seven to get herself break-fasted and scrubbed for her school. I wasn't in the flat, to judge by her manner. It didn't surprise me. I wasn't certain of it myself. I saw the broad tarred autoroute flowing up to Basel and the border and on to Paris, and back to places where I might feel I was there.

'Xenia,' I said, as if I had never mentioned that name in my

337

life, and as if I might be summoning a mythical tall-story monster from the remote island of the next room. She didn't come the first time, but the second summmons decided her to thump barefoot across our boards, and wedge herself on the blue couch, unsittable-on at the best of times.

'What?' she said.

'I want to go away for – three months or so, I don't know,' I said, 'and then I'll come back.'

She looked at me and all trace of idiocy was gone. It had never been there. She flung out a brown one-time-only painterly gorgeousness. She was bright and subdued like our old rooms in a former candlelight. She inspired cliché. She seemed vulnerable and good. I was stricken, like a pigeon whose wings have just been torn off by children, and who prints a few trefoils and looks ridiculous, and starts to scream quietly.

'Get out,' she said.

'Only three months,' I said. 'I have to.'

'This is your idea about caring for people, is it?' she said, in almost perfect syntax. She shook her head. So I told the beautiful face I had forgotten by living with what I was thinking.

'I don't love you,' I said. How simple it was to say the opposite, and how unthought-of her reaction. For the first and last moment in our time together, her face dropped. It fell away into the floor and probably landed on the old man's dreams below. I laughed with embarrassment. I could have murdered her father in front of her with the same effect. I had just never seen her ordinary like that, or with any quietness, even the quietness of hurt, before, and it embarrassed me. So I offered the room a laugh that must have sounded like vicious crowing. It was done and everything was done, and I didn't have the ninety-nine years it would have taken to rectify it. Why had she shown herself now, why not ever and always?

'You are not very much, are you, Oliver?' she said. 'I am leaving my apartment now, and when I come again you can not be here.'

She strode away, the oddest dancer. I packed in disquiet, euphorically, on automatic.

We could smell it now in the treacled air that washed into the pot of the car – the drowned smell of near-tropical real estate and the seal's estate beyond.

'Oh jiminy,' said Sue, pushing her hair back from her forehead, as if she was already cooking on a littered beach.

'Yea-hey!' hooted Chicken, and drummed his palms on the ebony wheel. 'Would ya look at this fuckin ocean!' he said, as we scorched smoothly round a corner, and a hot-plate of liquid beamed at us from its broad owned miles.

'Whey-hay,' said Sue, 'what in holy fuck!'

She bounced herself on the seat and embraced me remotely, and then made the seat dip and shake me again. Chicken darted glances at this unknown ocean, and Sue examined it and catalogued its simple sameness.

'Big mighty fuckin job,' said Chicken.

'We got a big mighty fuckin job with us now, man,' said Sue, 'you said it, Chicken!'

'I said it,' said Chicken, 'hot shit in hell.'

'Can't we stay here a while, Chicken honey?' said Sue. 'Stop the blazes car.'

'Hell, Sue,' said Chicken, 'let me get into town. Not sure I want this big black wagon ass-up on the side of the highway. This is an eye-open state down here, and I aim to let it sleep on my account.'

'You tellin me that, you fucker?' said Sue. 'I want to swim!'

'You'll swim,' said Chicken excitedly, 'you'll swim, baby. Let's establish our little selves in town, and we'll come back out.'

'Oh jesus, man,' said Sue, and quietened again. But I could see now her blood had woken up, and she couldn't hardly keep her mind still. She burst at me with:

'Hey, Owl, you like swimmin too?'

'I do,' I said, 'I love it. I love the beach.'

'Oh I love it, Owl,' she said. 'I've been missing the sea for ever.'

'Ain't you never seen it before?' said Chicken.

'Oh hey, I seen it on the movies. I mean, I have seen it before, boys, but I was never here beside it before.'

'Holy shit,' said Chicken. 'You mean this is the very first and only time you've hit the coast?'

'Well, that isn't so strange, Chicken sweetie,' she said. 'I was miles from the coast where I was. There's a whole world of people that've never seen it.'

'Oh god, Owl,' said Chicken, 'I don't believe it. Can you believe that? Sixty years old and she's never seen the sea.'

Sue leaned over and thumped his left shoulder and made him swerve and laugh.

'I ain't sixty, you asshole. What you take me for?'

Chicken laughed up high in his timbre. It was real laughter though.

'Hey, Owl,' she said, 'you ever been happy before?'

'No,' I said, 'not like this.'

'Yeh,' she said, 'happy. Happy is a good word. You ever heard of happy, Chicken?'

Chicken shoved his head out his window and yelled nothing and everything at the sea:

'You old fuckin big sea ocean, we're comin ta get ya. Watch out, you old sleepin whore, because we're going to put our dollars down!'

'It isn't any whore,' said Sue, very seriously. 'What you callin it names for?'

Then she released her brand of laughter too, and they shouted and bounced, and the car S-ed and danced on the empty highway.

'Make the car swim, Chicken!' said Sue. 'Make it swim! Stick it over the cliff, Chicken!'

Chicken clutched the engine, and pestled down a gear, and flowed into the slow lane. He kissed the chambers with gas, and the old machine responded, and roared for us. He eased off the clutch, and the black car vomited itself across the fast lane, and ski-ed over the burned-grass island, and thunked its back-axle briefly and jarringly as it descended on to the northbound laneways.

'You crazy fuckin aceman!' screamed Sue. 'There's cars comin this way!'

The astonished wheels reached the dead shoulder that bordered an unseen cliff, and Chicken hauled the steering round before the front wheel could get a taste of the last feet of grass, and skewered his extended self at an angle back across the two lanes. Even in the rear seat I saw the breaking shock on the faces of two oncoming drivers. Chicken had thumbed a switch of some sort, and the approaching faces glowed like reading-lamps. Out of the sharp shadow of the hill they rushed, and into the rich changes of the sun going for a deep swim away over to our right, and into the unreal exploit of Chicken. He gained the neutral island, with a dab of time to prevent a meeting of the imaginary and the real, and belly-flopped on to our own tarmac. The car's frame seemed to bend freely at the back, and Chicken wrestled his spinning front, and set us straight again. We sat behind him in utter schoolroom silence. We didn't move the least muscle except the punchbags of our hearts. There might have been a terrible snake in the car that we had to be careful not to disturb. There might have been an absorbing deadly film showing on the windscreen in front of us. I noticed that I had my fingers clamped on Sue's arm, like I wanted to insert them finally into her flesh. I let these relax but she didn't notice. She started to sing:

'Well I've done all I can do, and I can't git along with you, gonna take you to your mamma, pay day.' She let the smoky sun provide a chorus for this.

'Mississippi John Hurt,' she said then. 'Great fella for songs.'

'Didn't frighten anyone back there?' said Chicken, now his coast seemed clear.

'Nah,' said Sue, 'He didn't frighten us, did he, Owl?'

'He didn't frighten us,' I said.

'I terrified you, right?' said Chicken, and laughed with difficulty. He sounded mysteriously guilty and unsure of himself.

'Hey, Chicken?' said Sue.

He said nothing as he fed the gas regularly, with a calm level foot on the accelerator. 'What?'

'Chicken,' she said.

'What?' he said, with an edge of annoyance.

'Chicken, you're one hell of a fuckin pilot,' she said.

'Yeh,' he said, with enthusiasm and relief. 'Yeh, I'm okay, right?'

'There's only one trouble,' she said.

'What's that?' he said, like a straightman on a poor television show. She let him have it. She yelled it with her mouth flowered up to the still roof:

'This ain't a fuckin airplane.'

341

'Oh, I don't know,' he said, completely recovered, and not minding. 'Shit, I should say this here bus is a bit of a crossbreed, wouldn't you say, Owl?'

'I don't know about the car,' I said.

'Hey, hey,' said Chicken, 'the sunny man, the funny man. I know what I am, buddy. I'm a mongrel, but my pa worked and my ma cooked, so eat your heart out, buster.'

'I haven't got one any more,' I said, weakly.

'Damn right, you haven't,' he said. 'Damn right there, brother.'

The city started to begin. It kept on starting to begin for a good few miles. Then it began for a while and then it was all around us. It was new and dusty, but every few houses an older building was rooted, a real tooth among artificial sets. They hadn't been painted that recently, but they were handsome, and we scouted for one that might be masquerading as a cheap hotel.

The Copa, as we walked by it, shone out onto the pavement like a cinema sunk under neon.

'She'll meet us there later, mon,' said Ali.

'Susan will?' I said.

'When we have the stuff in your room, we'll glide in there normal as cowboys. Right?'

My room. I supposed it didn't matter.

We stepped from the cleaned-up shop façades and fountains and pavements into the place that its sign described as *Jamaica Village*. The street and houses reversed twenty years in the space of a football.

'Hi there, blood,' said Ali, and offered his arm in greeting. He got an irritated glance from the passing black man, black and intent, he had tried to sell it to. Ali let him go, and probably forgot about it. I puzzled it only for a moment. It was unexpected that he seemed less accepted in this part of the town.

The white paint on the irregular long street was not so proud as to cover any one area in entirety. It leafed and a blackened wood showed through, grained like banana skin when the top smooth layer has been stripped off – there was that same rainy juicy smell of green rotting into brown.

The second man we saw wore an old grey suit, without any shirt or shoes. He was a large man and still the suit sailed about him. He was extraordinarily drunk, his body pitched against a wall like a paperclip. But his face was calm and aware of us, too aware, and he called out like a popsinger:

'You lookin for weed, man, lookin for weed?'

Ali flicked his hand up at him and the man flicked one of his down in return.

There was a lot of damp black dirt under the fingernails of the street. One small shop was cowled in blackness. The forms of the tight room were only vaguely outlined by the wood it was made of. There were three middle-aged men propped on three bentwood chairs. Two had walking-sticks, whose knobs perched like lightbulbs in the clothy interior. It was a bar, but nowhere I'd be allowed to drink. They didn't look at us, but talked on carefully under their vanishing straw hats. They would have been in serious danger of looking like a piece of a film set, except that the crew was gone off years ago, and the dust had gathered, and the hats had lost essential bits, and the faces were a bit swollen. Those people were a long way from home and they were sitting right in it. I feared them, as my own past. I feared them like a child fears the magician who can make the cards disappear, because he might be next. Better not to catch the magician's eye. I kept close to Ali and my shirt rubbed his clothless skinny arm. His big rubber sandals made his feet look like tennis-rackets in their stretchers.

Under a broken-hearted tree, younger men were laughing and idling over a game of dominoes. They had a square card-table without its baize covering. One had his chair turned backwards, and his endless muscled arms stretched down from where his underarms rested on the chair-back. His face showed three crushed folds when he blanked up at our passing. The chin curved affectionately to meet the forehead, and yet it was a nor-mal handsome face. It gave my own the feeling of a bare dry bog. I rubbed my hands down my cheeks quickly.

'It's a funny place down here,' I said.

'Why, mon?'

'I don't think they appreciate me.'

'No,' he said, 'why should they? You're painted all the wrong colours, mon.'

'Should I be down here?'

'Well,' he said, 'this brings us out to a side street of the house, that's number one. Number two, there's whites comin down here all the time, for the girls and the dope and whatever.'

'Black girls?'

'Sure, black girls. You want me ta fix you up after?' he said.

'Ah, no, no,' I said. 'Never mind. I don't feel like it.'

'Sure,' he said, 'whenever.'

It was an uncluttered easy night, but all the slim blue of the sky was leaned on somehow by an unexpected weight, in an upper section of it. The palm trees strained under this, and heaved without moving to keep the blue from falling and compressing their trunks. The dipping leaf-blades, and withered fruit-feathers at the stems, wouldn't even dare let the tree's breathing stir them. They reminded me of propeller planes in an airforce base, a film. And then, by accident, I made out at the end of the street a plane parked in someone's garden, as if I had madly forced it to appear. Up nearer, other elderly craft revealed themselves, and raised up on wooden blocks were heavy surly-looking torpedoes. Behind them a lighthouse, designed like a giant beehive, swelled, and threatened to puff cigarsmoke from its tower.

'What are those things?' I said.

'That's the navy owns them,' he said. 'There's a base in there behind all that. You didn't know that?'

'I didn't know it,' I said.

'This is the side-wall of our good house here,' he said. 'You want to be real careful from now on, real careful.'

'Are you sure it's late enough?' I said.

'Sure,' he said, 'any time after dark's fine for this work.'

'Are we to meet Stephen?'

'You jokin' mon? He don't want anything to do with us from now on. Far as he's concerned, he knew us a little and we robbed him. He don't want to lose his job, mon. He likes that job and I don't say he shouldn't.'

'Isn't he even in the house?' I said, as we paused on the still-warm pavement by an old yellow-brick wall.

'He's there. Don't worry, mon. He'll sleep through it.'

'Sleep?' I said.

'Yeh, mon, with his eyes open, you know. He lives over here

344

in this extra part. None of the house has anyone. All we have is fifty cats in the grounds and that's it.'

'Fifty?'

'Fifty, and cats don't bite, you ready now, mon?'

'Whose house is it?' I said, disliking myself for being suddenly too full of questions, peering up at the exotic trees, and then even more worriedly at the small panes of the lighthouse's observation room. The sea was a good two hundred yards or more down the street, where I heard it washing clothes fretfully against either concrete or a rocky breakwater. So they must have reclaimed all that land for the base, and once this house may have had a gentle view out onto the Bay of Mexico, and a terrifying view during a tornado storm. The torpedoes slept gloomily and frustratedly on their wooden hammocks.

'You're askin me?' he said. 'All this time and you never asked me and you were right those times. What you want to know this for, mon? It won't help you, and it won't help me, and it won't help the guy we're stealing from.'

'Okay, okay,' I said, 'never mind that. Listen, Ali, don't mind me. I know we'll be all right and all that. Just fire ahead. Go on.'

'Sure, mon, sure,' he said.

He stuck the rim of a sandal in between a line of bricks, and bellied himself over the parapet. I was left alone, with the blackened faces lost in the night behind me, and the relics of a dead war in front of me, local and global at the same time. So I followed quickly, the smooth top scraping me under my shirt. I was bound to Ali now, and would be till we finished up in Miami and got our money. What I needed money for I didn't know. I felt as if someone had planted a needle into my backside, and fed some agitating drug into my everyday peacefulness. My heart was completely out of control, and veering and tottering up the stony path to my mouth. It would be looking to climb out in a minute, but I crept after Ali's bowed-over spine, and his careful carved elbows slightly spread in the cat-filled hush. The shrubbery and wild border of the garden were easily parted, and had no thorns. If only, Moll, I could have said the same about me and my stupidity.

Something was happening over in a sea-distant worn edge of the crowd. It was only an unmomentous shifting in Moran's eye, but he turned this unsubtle instrument on the cloudy and as yet soundless fluctuation. Henry Grant, in his tininess, flickered too, but only to go out and disappear like a black light. Much of the crowd gave small jumps to see over other peering heads, and the collective singing note they had been able to construct fell away into a more usual smashed litter of voices. The voices ran like a shallow river over shuffling pebbles. Then someone started to fire what sounded like little hot bullets into the stream. The great stretch of water boiled up and stormed about, squalling. A legged flood of black hurried past Moran's stump, and was parted by the solid wood, but all these figures had to return the few feet they had gained, because their enemy had stolen up the path that Moran had come by. Moran presumed it was their enemy, because now he saw a small woman fall on her back – a policeman had skited a piece of melting lead into her astonished brain with his pistol. Everyone stopped and everyone moved and then stopped. Moran counted calmly the capped heads of twenty or thirty policemen where he stood, and all about in a barrelled circle a crown of enemies bristled.

In the faces of the crowd Moran made out people he had known. It was because he was tired and wanted to sleep now, and the policemen upset him. They upset him but they paid him no heed. A man with colours on his breast, and a better brighter hat, arrived at a clumping run. He also stopped and waited while the people waited.

Moran noticed the corked features of an almost-forgotten Jane Smith. He could barely remember her because he had never seen her so young. Her body was still firm, and though it was a bit ridiculous like his, it was pleasant. He liked her again. Then he remembered her beating him and had to pause in his liking. She was frightened and her belly was sweating to show it. A policeman aimed at her and exploded his gun just under Moran's elbows. The bullet seemed to punch Jane Smith, because she was knocked back three feet, and was put sitting on the dirt holding her wound, in the heat. She took her palms off it, and leaned to see over her breasts at it, and it was a tiny bottle-top of red tinsel. The crowd had shuddered like a huge cow when the bullet was loosed.

346

'Are they only cattle?' thought Moran. 'Are they only stupid cattle? They must be.'

Then he recalled what he liked in Jane Smith, and he forgot she had flailed him. He couldn't look now at her surprise and suffering without receiving it himself.

'Shoot,' said the officer, and the raw cordon of men shot at the full circle of men. The men shot the men.

'The men are shooting the men,' said Moran to himself, like a line from a schoolbook, but he had never been to school properly, he knew, only the muddle the army had given him. He wondered what it was in other languages. Perhaps it was the men shoot the men.

It was inaccurate because the men were also shooting the children and the women, so it would have to be, for the sake of accuracy, the men shoot humanity, or samples of humanity. He didn't know how to put it. He was dry all over like a rock. He was burning. His feet were happy. People died. Everyone had been dipped in ink, red ink, like sheep cleansed of body-lice, and the policemen were not satisfied that they were clean so they killed them. But didn't they know what corpses did after a bit, thought Moran? Corpses are one of the dirtiest things under the sun, and especially under a factoried sun like this, he thought. He thought of course it was the same sun wherever you were, or so people said. Not these people maybe. These people were eating bullets with little new mouths all over their bodies. But they didn't try to run away.

'They are like cattle,' said Moran. 'My friends and my companions are cattle. Look at them all. I can't even remember their names. I wish the policemen wouldn't shoot them though,' he said.

The remaining cattle in the crowd were finding it onerous to stand now, because the dirt had mixed with blood and become red mud. There was a cowlike groaning going on over the clearing.

'My beautiful cows,' said Moran. 'Please don't shoot my beautiful cows.'

But the policemen had started and now they had to go through with it. The wounded would be bothersome in the heat, and the whole would be bothersome in their talk. It had to happen so thoroughly that it would be as if it had never happened. It had to be an absolute, so that other similar people would be so horrified they wouldn't believe it if they heard of it.

'But there is no such thing as an absolute,' said Moran, in the afternoon. 'For instance, I am here, and they don't shoot me. They are letting me watch this. I wish they wouldn't. I wish they would shoot me too.'

He even felt this when they shot the Sligo bishop, who was the last man at the centre of the soggy mess. Every one of the policemen bulleted the bishop, or so it seemed, and his body was grimly and greyly there one moment, and a sort of gurgling mince the next. The bishop left the spot he had understandably taken refuge on, and scattered in handkerchiefs among his fellow cattle.

'They are just cattle,' said Moran. 'I wanted them to be humans. I was almost human myself, just being near them.'

The police fired round after round into the soft ruined arms and faces, and then the bulldozers grinded up in their puffed cloaks of dust. For many afternoon hours they worked on their trench, and when the shocked sun had almost decided to turn away and go, the digging was finished. The shining scooped blades, like trailing wings, worked on the drying bodies, like gardeners expertly trimming grass in decisive true lines, with their mowers. They bulldozed the corpses into the long silent pit. The chatting policemen smoked in groups, family men, house-holders, and brushed off the friendly flies, and section by section they climbed up into trucks and jeeps and went away. They went away idly and thoughtfully, like cattle.

'They are like cattle in those trucks,' said Moran. 'What is the point going away to their wives, when their wives are being covered over in the ditch? They are like cattle,' he said.

The bulldozers, with ceremony, switching back and forth, and putting strange gridded marks on the sandy earth, smoothed over the slightly bulging ground that had been the pit.

'They are burying their wives and children, and themselves. What cattle,' said Moran.

His stomach boiled inside him. He started to choke, like a stupid cow that has swallowed barbed wire.

Sixfoil Nineteen

Sum berd hoos lunges war fillt wid water, an hoo horned to Conn throo dese colorles deepes, endet hes songe dat hadd bene a geometrie of Conn hes paine. Somtin newe or veree olde laye on de drye dirte belo hem. It sat in de tres an evin cud flye acras de hoel skye. It fallowt de thousante jurnees of leves, an sanke in de stoen of hes loste wals. It wasse de sunne, an al her colers.

'Yoo ar late,' he whispert, wid his throte al dustee, 'an yer merinesse moks moi estate.'

Bat stil de sunn had manee hants, an she heldt hes face and moddert et, an smootht hes armes. He sercht in de wal for a redee ledg, an found sudnelee he coud balanz on a peece of olde werk der.

'Yoo ar sech a silee mann, Oleever,' he sed. 'Sech a ruinin mudeld ting. Yoo havv almoost lat yer armes bee rippt fram yer brethin sholders, an nowe yoo finde a footholt dat wass alwaes der.'

Hes formerr oakes shrugged der bodees in an intricet breze. It wass so erlee dat anlee two hobbelt gotes rummiget aboot fer wedes an uder fuud. Bat a cokk let loos hes broken promisez fer cries, an evertin stracht an movt. De tres roes fram slepe an dried der dewet limbes wid carfal danzes. De gotes ignorad al dat, an grubbed awae. Smal speckelt fliyes cam lik inseficiant cloods, an botheret hes skinn, bat did nat biet. Anlee hes quene cud trulee bite hem nowe.

He falt lik a yang boye wakin upp ta et hes porridg. He wantet ta rushe doon lik a dogg to da rivver an thumpe hes bodee in. Ah, dat coolnes an madnes wad soot hem welle dis marning. Insted, he wass de silee objecte uf hes owen quene, a weree dekeratioon fer her spoort. Whar war hes goodes an dayes, dat dey did nat scratche her wid insecs an destroye her filty slepe? Bat hes woreld itsel wass dremy an silente, an evin in hes hardshippe he lovet hes plac an centir. He lovet itts bittes uf memoire, an al hes fader hes pathes dat it mapped, an al dese wilde contemptuoos sparras an sparrahoks an blakberds dat made breef marks on al de grounde, he lovt dem alsoo. An hes henz an gese dat grumbelt oot fram hes gaets, after de handes uf hes uzeles menne hadd unpenned dem, dese he had luv fer too – he cud nat unluff dem becarse he was tormentet. It wass nat tings he cud ete thate wantet hes ruoin, bat tings dat cud ete himm, humins so daintee wid der mouts an practisses, hoo wud berne hem nowe, an flinge hem in ashez awayye. Wat badd cookes dey were, hes somtiem fellaughs. An al hes dayes an lange frettet neets hadd been madde a lange argumente ta dis consequenze. Fer certenlee he hadd pickt hes woif oddlee an wrang, an hes bishap too, an yas, yas, Olivver, al hes whiet menne as wel. Hes inosent sordez-menne an farmirs and buuter-makerz and smithez war evertin ta hem, bat he waz litul to dem, he wasse a strawemanne ta scare de crowes from a endroite dat hadd no croppes, a buncht bundil uf boens to marke an enemee dat wass wance der cheef.

Den, widdoot greetin, a horer shooke hes corp. He witheret in hes knockt an pecefal streng, an wantet ta cree oot fer aide an sum smal luff. Befar dis oorge cud livv in hes mouthe, de quene an fatt bishap, an manee menne sich ass Jem Lery an Cavnagh, poored oot fram de smal doore withinn de coortyarde, an Micel struggelt inta sunlite wid dem, tryen ta holde hes dogges. Jem Lerree an an udder manne carriet a veree bigge bagg, dat squiermt an madd darke shoots fram withinn. Dis sacke dey laft ta rolle an murmur undder de shadoee arche.

'Wat arr dey doin?' Con sed, ta nowan bat himselfe. 'An whoi doo dey nat remarkk on dis hominge sunne?'

De bishap stud bye de movin sacke, an sed in hes frogged fed vois:

'Boi graez uf hes lordshippe, moi exclent godde, in hes spar-kin hevin, an hes dominoon ovvir manne an beeste, bothe nowe an for evvir.'

He haltet an pullt fer brethe. De quene in Conn hes eyez semt dejectet an sickk. Her hed sunke lik a melon on her looz shoul-derz. Her ownn gaez wass de gaze uff a manne fer hangin. Dis wass funee to Oleever whar he percht.

'Moi por litul quene is sadde,' he sed to de ropes dat squeeset hem, 'shee iss sadd becarse she iss nat upp here wid mee. She

350

wantes ta be here an happee.'

'It iss a good marnin,' sed de bishap, 'fer al uf creatoon an al god hes werks. Here we haff sunn becaurse de rool uf Oliever, whach wass nat goddlik an troo, iss finisht. Dis sunne iss a fysik an happineese to yoo an moiself. Here in dis bagg is a greevin manne, hoo wud nat luv hes quene, a manne hoo wud nat luv godd hes goldnes and wud nat lov hes bishap his silbernes, a manne dat spatt at Roome an her ancent mitynesse, har newe hoolines, a manne mor fitt fer de companee uf pagann Tulleey an hes wordee crewe, den poepes an mityee holee folkes, a manne nat wrange in himsel bat wrang whar he dweltt, a mann too ful uf wat iss ovvir to be generess to wat has juste cum, a manne hoo prefert de greye particuleer ovir de colored everydaye. I praye here fer dis manne hes soule an saye, manne is butt grass sinz he etes de munchin cowe, an I amm a poore an badd mann hoo wil studee to be udder – bat here iss a manne whoo wud nat cree oot befar gott, bat wente skemin an diggin in de graevez an boltholtz uf hes ded demonz. Nat a badde manne, I saye, butt an oeld wan, whoo cann nat bee becass he iss nat, who we muste nowe retarn ta erthee conditoon, bye meenz uf deese two dogges dat ower gud servante, Micel, strainez ta hold. Fer dese doggs ar miracels by hes owen admissoon ta mee, an anlee a mirakel can cuur diss seelee poete.'

Olivver, wid hes armes sprad lik an nighte berd, sed den:

'Hoe, bigg bishapp, wat doo yoo doo wid moi poet manne der? Iss he in dat sacke?'

'Dis iss a holee ceremonee,' sed de bishap, 'yoo muste nat speke.'

'Mudd an gutts on yer diner, bishap, what iss in yer cruel sacke?'

'It iss yer dangeroos Owle,' sed de bishap, 'a manne hoo –.'

'I haff herd enoug uf yer mann hoo dis, an mann hoo dat. Leve yer strang bawlin aloon, an lat hem oot dis momint, or I wille hawnt yoo wid dremes uf wormez an deth. Owle is a olde stif manne, hoo can nat be in sackes widdoot hardshipp.'

'Ah, smal Conn, yoo can doo no sich ting whiel god livvs, an alwayes he livvs. I haff no hatrid of yoo or anee manne, bat yer sool, an de sowl uf dis unreppentint berd widin a chepe bagg, deye ar tings fer burnin an etin bee animools – an den we wull ete perhapz in absent tiem ta cum yer absentt soels, an mak yee

351

trulee menne.'

'I amm manne enoug, moi badd crazee heepocrit,' sed Oliver, 'bat doo nat tuch hes tanglet holee hairz.'

'Holee, iss hee?' sed de bishap. 'Micel, good sonn, lat goo yer hownds.'

Owle in de bagg roret lik a berr, an de bishap ranne bak to de quene an al de menne kept agenst de wal. De doggs swisht der tales, an snifft at de belloin sak. Wan gafe a growle and an angri barke. Dey bitt at de thrashin mateerial an ript bitz fram et. Der muzzels mined inta de brethy insiedez, an sanke tethe in pertz uf Owel. He wass al tied an wilde. Conn sawe de redde showtin fase, an shoutet too:

'Moi Owle, moi Owle!' he scremt. 'Don't lat moi Owle bee hert!'

His voiz whass as hie as a boyz.

'Larent,' he sed, 'saef moi poete befar hes blut iss in yoor purss.'

Bat de thinne jawz of de huntin howns founde oot Owl hes face, and ate de owld chekes in thre bietz.

'Yoo feelthee houndes, shoo awaye for yoor graez,' wepte Con. Den Owle stumbelt uppe widdout hes faez, an hes harde nose wass sharpe, ande hes eyes widdout lashes an liddes war rounde. Der war no clevir cordes on hes legges, an he kickt at de snappin bludee dogs, and spedde off lik a spancelt berd inta de trubeld wud, rooined bat stil ootraged.

And my mother is to be so, and this is to be my mother, a solid absolute, because it is not precise. Nothing is wrong in that boy's view because his gaze is absolute. Sleeping was a little life, and waking was a little life. That dangerous hooded adjective of being small. And I had no ambition towards anything and by common consent that's considered little. Better to be a murderer than a child, though the child is the absolute murderer and the absolute victim.

I murdered myself and became someone who could sit alone in a room, with a wooden life, and a fridge holding on tight to my cans of coke. It purrs unaffectionately and thumps tinily, and puts a small saucer of ice, like a spread possessive palm, under each can. So be it, and the bicycles parting the clay on the road, and the dresses just past the smell of being clean. And the black cheeks turn at me where I crouch like a cat among the big leaves, and the small athletic girl washes herself now under the outside shower. She makes a sound like hands sprinkling coins, the coins of the world, and to say I spent these days watching for myself among the lost and little other days, that held other matters and other purposes, is to admit that I am divorced from them. And they were little, they were no doubt little, they were little. Absolutely so, dust after planets not before. Mother, my mother, my cotton mother, pray for me under the clever harbour lights of M. R. James and his safety. Pray for me in the power of your cashmere and your jeans. Have your child return from the cold corner and the warm corner, collect him from the difficult school gate, where he makes his effort to wait. Mother, my mother, it is warm here in Key West, and my falling body is warm from the fall, and I haven't forgotten that you made it for me. I'm still pushing it around the world, my mother. It goes like a clock, never misses a tick. You made a good body here, my cotton mother.

My head nods and the room is asleep behind me, where the big bed idles and dreams, and the long chair waits for a long woman who will never come. Mother I have tried among all people, among everything, lampstandards and canals, even among your appointments, to sing against the fathers of all places, as you were able and worked hard to teach me. Mother, the fathers bow down to me and I cut off their little heads. It is hard, it is hard, it is hard, but your knife works cleanly. Mother, to have stopped my own years might have held yours, and I didn't. Look at me, mother, through this glass, look at me in this floating room, which I have gained with dollars, and will lose easily, and thankfully, by loss of time, not in my life, mother, but in my morning. Let it be that all our walking, and our admiring talk in dreams was the best part of something lengthy and disturbing and rotten at the ends. Let us remember the unripe tomatoes and the bananas too green for good taste, let us remember that we ate as we wished to, and paid no attention to advice and fashion. My mother, let us put 'Oh' in front of our names when we think of each other, let us commit all the indiscretions of affection from passionate to maudlin, let us

353

reserve parts of long days for the gamut of stupidity and humanity. Mother, not to hurt, yes, it is a simple notion, and I've seen you make toffee with it. Mother, mother, I am not calling you, I am not hurt. The weather is indescribable, like a phrase on a collector's postcard. Mother, there is no instrument that I can use to talk to you, there is no pitch telephone or government service, no diplomat can be sent now from this small country that defines my boundaries, as ambassador. The water from the tap is fresh and expected, and it hits the blackcurrant juice with an expected vigour. Look, mother, the hard juice rocks like a tide at the base of the speckled glass, and the sea moves against it. Look at my hands, here on this table, look, you formed these too. Look, I spread them and watch these fingers, that have dug and dialled and thumbed and eaten. Into this right hand you placed apples and hard pears, hard pears and apples with hard green skins. Why did we never eat apples with red cheeks? Or those soft sweet pears that everyone covets? We wanted unripeness, and we wanted the sea to be lost like that, in its own deep water, and we wanted that trouble and the safe house against it. Mother, this is simple, and muscle is grass, and all the things there in the rooms, the painted plates and the blind couch and the sunk chest of clothes, were once hung in symbol from a full ring, and any one of them opened any door to any other. You see my carelessness? In that I've dropped all those keys? And where the hell are they? I should look for them, shouldn't I? Where could they be? I've been careless with our keys, my safest mother – to be lost from you, not to be burdensome to you, not to be abnormal or unusual, not to be illogical, and to sever the tie when the ceremony told me to, it was these considerations that had those strange keys dropping into mud, and rusting like chameleons, for other people to pluck up from the small suck of the ground, even children, and wonder what doors, and where, those shaped sea-weights fitted. Mother, cotton child, it's a long walk from you, in that it doesn't curve back like walks used to, and had to, or they were not walks.

Why set out from home on straight roads, like important railway-tracks, when these are ruinous and all the destitute are travelling on them? Look at that enormous ignored night up there, mother, over these board houses, and every house. And this is the owl-train stilled by the yeared distance it has to travel.

Ten million miles of track make the train seem stopped when you look at it, but really it rushes as efficiently as it can. Many remains are piled in there, you can feel the red heart of possessions in the furnace, from any point on the flying carriages. Mother, look at this distance. I'm so terribly sorry, but here I am, and the tracks don't ever turn back or circle. I can say to myself, jump off, Mr Moran, but it's going like the devil, with the devil's eyes and horns up front, through a featureless landscape, or one so blurred by speed that I can't catalogue it. And I promise myself a curve soon, hunched in my allotted seat, and I promise myself a confident jaunty stride when our pretend castle is approached again. That's me on the gravel between the extravagant rhododendrons, and that's me with my face briefly on the glass door. Never mind! Good god, it was a long walk after all. I just made it, mother, look at the silver air cutting into the silver water. This is owl-light, mother. The owls made this.

With how sad steps, O moon, thou climbst the skies, with how sad steps, O foolish-either-way Oliver, thou abandonest thy bag in Lucerne station and climbst her hill, how silently, and with how wan a face, even though the platforms rattled with a discovery that at first had made my slack feathers preen – there were easy-moving people in the world. I had forgotten them. But while I recognized them now, I couldn't become leagued with them so smoothly. There were hours to wait for a train, and each beat of those hours registered a slightly different or an enormously different opinion in me. I counted such fine reasons for catching any train going anywhere. She had left, mysteriously, money in the hall, and that seemed a showing, first-class, of how she felt – get rid of him at any cost. But I could also think that, since she had gone to the trouble of leaving money, it might have been prompted by a desire that I would not suffer on the journey. In some manner it was a form of care. On the other hand – well, the real trouble was, those hours had too many hands, an Indian goddess among the skiers and the porters.

I had platform thirteen all to myself, and then I had a curious feeling all to myself. I identified it as a liquid of panic, some little-tapped category. It froze me and heated me by turn, and then it passed into my head, and my head multiplied it by signals to all corners of its empire. I gripped on the ordinary wooden station-seat like that for another hour. The possible train berthed and sighed windily, and like a man in distress for a toilet, I jerked up, and hurried out under the high glass and metal domes, and into the placid home-moving crowds. As always when I was in a rush I didn't take a tram. A tram never hastened, it just sat you down, and though it would actually arrive somewhere faster, it took longer in terms of personal energy to get you there. Walking was a sort of rowing, and the brain was hindered by it.

I was fearful that Xenia might have rushed off some place, and done something imaginably vicious to herself. I saw her seducing three strangers in a row, and getting terribly drunk, and murdering them all, and then. I dreaded that what I had done to her was irretrievably damaging. Then the idea of her sitting quietly alone somewhere, suffering the maps of the abandoned, occupied me like shovels of coal, and powered me up the hill. In other words, I was suddenly horrified by the threat of guilt. I suspected I had carried out an action of a post-sleepless night with all the finesse of a violent thief. God in his remote heaven, it was a long hill for such notions. Now it was as if someone else had left her, and I was trotting to her aid. If only she would forgive the other man, I might fetch her wine, and cosset her, and heal everything over in a night. The great idea was to do it quickly, have it as if it had never been scripted and filmed, reverse the reel and reinstate that impossible present that I had barbarously made past in three minutes. What would we be doing if I hadn't acted? I had thrown away the bathwater with the baby. I inconveniently valued that grubby water, of stealing about the lake on Sundays, and buying bratwurst from the immigrant Turks, and munching it, with their rough warm bread, in a cinema queue. But I hadn't realized I valued it till the basin was upside down, and the water lapping onto the flagstones. The thing was to pick up the howling baby and wipe it off, and fill up that basin again smartish. It might never notice. The howls might stop.

The main field of terror was the hill. As long as I was speeding up the sluggish hill, I would feel all this, and Xenia might already have returned and be just sweeping out her door. I assumed she would hurry right back after work – in the hope I wouldn't have gone, even? Oliver, Oliver, you are thinking like a valued man. Unfortunately you don't know any better and the house is reached, the bell is gained. The bright disc is being thumped hard and continuously. Show enthusiasm. Show contrition. Show business-like acumen – show bankerliness. Why are you so upset, Oliver? Why are you sweating and pained and so uselessly miserable? Why is your face so floury and your skin so moonish? Come out of your great ship, O Stranger, and get me back into our fortunate doldrums and we'll rattle our charts.

It was soon too lonely to ring the bell. I stepped back on to the flowerbed, injuring nothing, and stared up at one of her end windows. It was ridiculous that that morning I had keys to this place, that it was home among the small hours, and home before a run of frightened words. That the same keys were either snug on the kitchen-table, or possibly knocked to the floor by Xenia. My thumb melted on to the button, as I urged the bell again, and at last the big brown door opened.

'Xenia,' I said, 'Xenia!'

Her face had aged thirty years – it was the old man's housekeeper, in a life. She looked very tired-out in that life, and with a reflex animal reaction on her lips:

'What do you want?' she said, not malevolently, but like a shadowy silent movie given sound, a spookiness illustrated convincingly. She was such a contrast to Xenia in appearance, and so close in that second in her manner, that I was confounded for that second – as if I had been gone after all for thirty years – and waved my arms restrictedly at her, but really at her words.

'Just lost my keys,' I said, with the confidence of an escapee.

'No, you didn't,' she said. 'No, no.'

'Let me in,' I said. 'I lost my keys.'

'No,' she said. 'Go away. I don't want you coming in. I don't like it.'

She made me lost. I wandered about in what she had said, and made some burnt effort to stamp through it.

'Look, I'm going up to my apartment, so please take the chain off the door.'

'It is not your apartment,' she said.

She sounded like she was on a cliff, and I was a very foreign seal on a rock far below. She did not want me coming up, ever. She would never need to climb down.

'What do you mean?' I whined.

'Ah,' she said, 'I know about you. You have no money. Isn't that so? And you have been here for four months, and it is not the law here for that.'

'Is Xenia up there?' I said. 'Would you mind letting me in to see?'

'I would,' she said, 'very much. I am going now to phone for our police.'

There was a great relief in her attitude, but I knew the one couldn't last without her presenting the other, so I banged on the door-panels after she shut them. The door seemed to bang much harder on my hand than I could on it.

'Merciful hour,' I said, to the brown paint, and backed down onto the lower level of the road, and tried to see up into the great deck of our apartment. Then I noticed the volvo at the curb, and felt as if the stone sets in the roadway had punched me, rapidly. I stared at our window – our, our, our. Give me my life here back, give it!

At our bedroom window, where the bird lived, singly, in his basket, her mother was iconed, like a ghost of herself. There were other figures up there, a trinity of resistance. Xenia, what is this murder? Surely murder for murder is a bit lacking in love? Xenia, down here, among the low! I am standing here as patiently as a village fool. Put everything back in their places. Turn on our lights. The city is deepening and our rooms will be getting dark. Call me up to flick the switches! Let's boil water for the noodles!

And then I ran. There were wheels being pressured on the nearby corner. A siren was politely screaming, discretely, Swissly.

Chicken inserted his sunned face into our very white hotel room. Actually the big ell-shaped room was painted cream, but the four o'clock sun refused the colour. Sue hopped about quietly in a darker corner away from the door, where a tall mirror was awake – she was putting on clean white socks after establishing a new swim-suit under her dress. It would make her very smooth and strange to touch, I thought. She stood lightly in her socked feet on the glowing wood boards, and turned her hidden face when Chicken spoke to me:

'Ol,' he said, and then he noticed the room, 'hell, shit,' he said, 'what they given you here, some sort of presidential job?'

'Same price as you,' I said.

'Yeh,' he said, 'weird town. Always was. Damn sea below there, and I'm looking at a glass tower.'

'I'm going down to swim,' said Sue, like a bee.

'All back out there where we were?' said Chicken, with some resistance.

'Nah,' said Sue. 'They got a pool near the city beach which's part of the hotel.'

'Oh right, because that's a million miles back, the other place.'

'Anything in the paper?' I said, since he was gripping one under his shortsleeved arm.

'Hey? No, nothin,' he said.

'Comin down, Owl?' said Sue.

'I'm going to sleep a little bit. That bed looks very comfortable. And I haven't been getting much rest in the car.'

'Okay, boys. See you now, sweetie,' she said, and took her showered body out past Chicken, and walked silently, in sailor's slippers, down the stairway.

'Okay, shit,' said Chicken to me. 'Catch up on the latest story. Very nicely written. Good stuff for the punters.'

He ruffled the folded paper at me, and tapped on a little item with a thumb.

'That's who?' he said. 'Who's that gettin nasty about?'

'Susan Bateman,' I said. 'They're talking about Susan Bateman.'

'That's the follow-up on the Virginia story. Now just you tell me what Sue's second name might be.'

'Never asked her. Or I forget maybe. You think this is her?'

'Do I think? Missing person, fingerprints, dead old dame, police search. Jesus, Owl, they could be in the city now. They might even have a photograph.'

'They didn't publish it, if they do,' I said, gripping the neat paper as if I were checking the racing results.

'Maybe they were too busy sending them out to every station in the country, man. I don't know.' He dropped his lack of knowledge on a low-legged blue couch, an awkward thing. 'Somethin got to be done about this, and I don't know what.'

'Well, Chicken,' I said, 'Sue and me were already thinking of going our own way, so that might be the best thing.'

He gawked at me. His hands stalled on the odd reliefed material of the couch, and the angle of his back became even more strained and uncomfortable.

'What you sayin, brother? What's all these plans I-haven't heard of?'

'Don't get upset about it, Chicken. We've had our ride and it's been great, but we don't need to be going around for ever. Stop staring at me.'

His face cleared like a piece of troubled sky at the top of an air-vent.

'Yeh,' he said, 'yeh. Maybe you're right. Anyway, I'm leavin the old car. It's givin me the creeps every time I start her up.'

'That's a good old car,' I said.

'Sure it is, she's the best. But you know, like I said, she ain't just as legal as they like.'

'No one's stopped you yet.'

'Fuck, Owl, if you can't agree about it just shut your mouth. Just shut the fuck up. If I want to ditch the car I'll ditch it. Keep your shit out of it.'

His anger knocked about the room. It came back and curled at his feet. I stood there, over by a square pleasant window.

'Ah hell,' he said, 'I'll miss you both. I'm just lettin off steam here. Don't mind it.'

'No, it's all right,' I said.

'Yeh, thanks,' he said. 'Go on. You sleep.' He clattered his boots. 'I'll do likewise. You won't want to be splittin for a day or two, I hope?'

'No, Chicken. A day or two isn't going to.'

'Yeh,' he said, at the cool door. 'Bateman,' he said. 'You remember it now?'

'I don't think she ever told me. It really worries you?'

'Not the old lady,' he said. 'We didn't do nothin to her, and they can't prove we did. I don't want no talk with a cop though. I don't want anything to do with such a conversation.'

'Well. Maybe you won't.'

'Ah-ah,' he said. 'No maybe about it. I won't and I won't. That's it. Sleep well, buddy.'

I had a dream, on the wide fathomed bed, of Sue in a wide fathomed pool. It was a simple meaningless dream, as most dreams are. She dived in and swam through it, with her precise and unsplashing strokes. If the dream meant anything at all it meant I probably loved her, or I didn't want to be away from her, if that's something different to love. And when I came to think about it, I wasn't much concerned about the police or the articles in the papers. They were small-time small-town small-people articles, and in my small drowsiness when I woke, I only wanted to see Sue, and to hell with the rest.

It was near to a green richly-smelling night, and I dressed alone in the generous empty room, and pushed down the old black stairs, and out past the snoozing deskclerk into the almost liquid air. I felt like a calm rowing-boat being footed from the shore.

There was a sun-warm diving street that slid all the way down to the ocean, and I knew the pool was there somewhere. In every doorway were selections from a hundred idle families, laughing and yapping and sunning themselves in the cheap last beams. They drugged me with a drug of ease.

By the slapping lightly-oiled water, a boardwalk edged the town, and a rise of four or five rough wooden steps was arched by a sign that was daubed with the name of our hotel. Though the slatted surround of the pool was still a surprising fish-slab of bathers, I saw Sue immediately, where she stretched virginly by herself, in her plain black suit, on the bare slats. I dropped a cloth over her eyes, and she elbowed up.

'Hiya handsome,' she said, inaccurately.

'Handsome yourself,' I said.

She rose, and tried to reach up and punch the first bare stars with a yawn. There was a muddled smell of pool-water and lotion and wet cloth, and the frosted salt smell of her warm skin. She put her dampness around me, and her hair was stringy and strange, and I felt on her thin back the impression of the fortunate wood she had lain on. She set a dewed kiss on my shoulder, and rubbed her cheek minimally against the vague blot of the kiss.

'Baby,' she said, 'baby,' and lifted the sunned country of her face, and made it a moon to mine. 'I do love you, little animal.'

She was brief and hushed under the worn palm-trees, and faraway somehow from the mess of lingered bodies. I brushed her shoulder like a servant cleaning his master's coat, but in slow-motion, and without a necessary word in my head. She didn't want a word. Like me she wanted the accidental fortune of what can be called love, but is more likely mere fortune, and to be counted in minutes. But when you have the minutes, well, you have them a little emptily. But they hold you. They celebrate you, despite what you have done to disqualify yourself – as if this love was a faithful mother, with killers as her progeny to console.

If Ali had popped out a bomb, and detonated it on the humid cropped lawn, it couldn't have sounded louder in my ears than the great rip of wood he executed with his screwdriver. The screwdriver was too big to be dainty, and its plastic handle looked horribly yellow and dead in his big dark hand, as if he was working on the window with a long-legged crushed canary. His own caved eyes were another instrument picking invisibly at the stubborn pretty door.

'You'll wake Stephen,' I said thoughtlessly, and got no answer from his concentrated torched face. The house rose up in deep ruby brick, and where there was no grass there were black meshing branches. On the lawn, as promised, a troupe of cats had separated from each other, as if after an argument of prima donnas. The place was impressive and battered and rich, and within its brick walls it insisted on being considered as a world apart. It didn't need the sea or the town or the land-sailing bars. We had passed the hollow lights of a considerable blue-rimmed pool, which had an odd pillared annex to the energetic house at one end of it. A catwalk crossed from the annex to the first floor of the house, where a shaded balcony lived ghostily, behind ornamental iron and under hanging plants, and among what looked like simple iron furniture. The whole house was closed in again after the closing-in of the garden, a Chinese ivory ball inside another. To think we had to enter this sealed confidence was bad for my heart.

Ali appeared distressed at his blunt hacking job. Perhaps the carpenter in him disliked to disfigure the panelling. Then he pointed the screwdriver into his old belt, at his fleshless side, and took my hand lightly, and led me in like father and son. He let go my hand, and left the door a little agape, like a lazy mouth through which, in ages to come, we might be able to escape. Everything in the hall ticked with silence. There was a patient table of white hats and yellow hats, which all floated on the chamoised rosewood surface. Ali's low gritty voice unwisely flew out into this perfectly sober space, and crashed disrespectfully against mirrors and personal resentful objects.

'I'm goin by a little map the man gave me,' he rattled. 'Up the stair, mon, through the big bedroom, and along the balcony, and into the study.'

Every word wrecked a few more hostile feet of quiet. Only remote, possibly spidered, corners slumbered on, too important and too nicely stuccoed to raise eyelids to us.

'There will be two boxes to bring out, and that's the whole thing. Do not worry, mon.'

'No,' I whispered.

His eloquent feet dragged tincans of footfalls after them, and we made it to the bridgehead of the stairs. Neat wooden halls wandered off in three directions. Ali panthered on through the only open door, and beckoned me through a bedroom that screamed with privacy and an angered peace. The bed sank ornately and woodenly under its mound of woven rugs. It looked like an engine that would kill you with heat. There was a peculiar little chair made out of barely-shaped wood like thick vine, or olive.

The balcony seemed enormous only because it was out in the air. The things I had seen on it from the lawn were mostly tubs and boxes of flowers. Thin armlike pillars withheld the ceiling from the blue floor, and the warm worm of old daily life at the centre of this green apple. Ali padded, thunderously in my ears, though his steps were mouselike and expert. The pool swam below me, and I was shocked to see a towel abandoned on a little bush beside it. I saw in my head some swimmer drying himself off with it, maybe weeks ago, and flinging the vague towel there to dry. I was moved by it. There was a life lived

363

here very different to the gaps I leaped day after day. People came out of comfortable sleeps and stirred up mornings with a noisy swim. I imagined those people with my hands viced on the rail, till the sun nearly glowed out and the strokes were nearly real. The old wooden table, by the little gate to the cat-walk, spindled and black, might have been where these unknown beings ate breakfast, perhaps early in the day, up with the wet light, like young children.

I snuck after Ali, and paused in a door. The small room was lined with glass cases, some like tables on the floor, and some flat and screwed against the walls. The heavy light from the balcony edged a few feet in and gave way to darkness, but the trench of poor brightness that the door constructed was col-lected dimly in the glass of a case facing me. Ali for his own reasons was taking books and ribboned manuscripts off a large plain table, and thrusting them all-anyway into two cardboard boxes that Stephen must have provided. They would be quite convenient between the two of us. When Ali bent over he grunted. Again, for a moment, I wondered what age he might be. One of the manuscripts had painted on the top page, in large clumsy silver letters, *The Engine of Owl-Light* – as if a child had printed it – glinting, a message without any meaning.

The facing case was full of photographs, and because I couldn't see them properly, and because there was an aspect all the same to the figures in them, that brought something back to me, I approached it like a nervous dog looking for a pat from a stranger. At first glance I was sure one brownish posed portrait was of Captain Collins. Some feeling chose me with its hard hand, and chopped me. But then I noticed that the uniform was different, and I was equally sure it couldn't be. But still the long hatted face was terribly like him, and I stared frustratedly at the other cases. The damp murk was defeating.

'Come and help, mon,' said Ali, leaning over, and with his face lamped on me. He sounded peaceful and content. I flicked through every image of the captain that I still had in my brain, and matched them against the silent half-lit case.

'Turn on the light,' I said.

'We can't do that, mon.'

He straightened now and watched me.

'Whose house is this?' I said, but as I said it, I knew the picture wasn't Collins. It was just an ordinary face like his, and what it had in common was its being framed by a uniform, and its being thirtyish, and simply young. But I couldn't steal from any room that had such a photograph. My courage didn't go that far.

'We can't do this,' I said, and was troubled to find him still assessing me.

'What can't we do? Why?'

'I don't know why, Ali.'

'What you talkin about? What you gapin at that cabinet for?'

'Who is this person?' I said. 'Who is he?'

'It's the man who lives in this house, mon.'

'But it's forty years old at least.'

'Yeh, mon, he's old. He's an old difficult man, like you.'

I looked hard at this long-ago. I got lost in it for a second, then I flapped away from it.

'What's this?' said Ali, aggrieved, and justly, and a trifle vicious. He didn't have a notion what was wrong with me, and nor did I. It was like being slapped by the past, and the past saying bluntly, *I'm more important*. I knew it wasn't, necessarily, but it spun my head. Ali had lost me. I couldn't carry anything away from there, let alone fly it to Miami. I would never be able to carry it back. And I would want to.

'That's a nigger, sir,' said the soldier.

The nigger was asleep across the road, so the lieutenant told the driver not to run over it.

'I can't get round him, sir,' said the soldier. 'He's right bang in the middle, and look at all that sand, sir, on both sides.'

'Well pull him out of the way, for Christ's sake,' said the officer. He was a clerk at home, and he liked the army for its blotting-paper qualities. On normal paper he was a dot, but out here he could fairly say he had been spread a little. It was dusky on the road, and he wasn't surprised to find a nigger cluttering it up. Niggers did that sort of thing quite well. They stunk to heaven too, and he was glad the driver was there to heave him away.

'I think he must be dead, sir,' said the driver across the bonnet, without much enthusiasm. The driver lifted Moran's wrist and paused. 'How do you do this, sir?'

'Do what, man?'

'Feel a pulse, sir.'

The lieutenant despised the driver because he had no university degree and he had no chin. It was a cliché in respect of aristocrats that they had no chins, but this time round the lieutenant had one and the driver didn't. The driver barely had a face at all – probably had to make do with whores for his needs, the lieutenant idly thought. Poor whores.

'Is he breathing, driver, is he breathing?'

'How would I tell, sir?'

'Kick him.'

'Kick him, sir? I can't just kick him.'

'Kick him gently, driver, like you would your mother.'

'I'd never kick my mother, sir, in any manner.'

The lieutenant sat back in his seat and crossed his hands on his knees. He felt the lip of his trouser-crease under his warm palm. He also felt the great dam of sweat under his arms that only the sodden khaki of his shirt was containing. The least bit of exertion now and his whole tunic would be awash.

'Anyway, sir,' said the driver, 'there's nowhere to kick him. He's all burnt.'

'What do you mean, burned, man? Do you mean by fire or something?'

'No, sir. Sunburn, sir.'

'They don't get sunburn, you idiot.'

'This one did, sir. He's all peeling. And his hair's straight, sir. It's very dirty but it's straight.'

'Christ Almighty.'

The lieutenant gave the door a shove and it screeched but decided to open for him. He stuck his bright boot on the deep red dust, and stamped down to the driver, who was feeling the nigger's hair.

'Don't do that, you clot. He's probably running with vermin.'

'Well, sir,' said the driver, under a drive of honesty, 'I'm not as clean as I was when I set out, myself, sir.'

'You've got lice?'

'Yes, sir.'

'In your hair?'

'Body lice, sir.'

'Oh God, well see you wash in that whatsit stuff when we get back. Look, just toss this fella into the ditch. It can't do him any harm and he won't do anyone much good using the road as a bed.'

'I don't think he's asleep, sir.'

The lieutenant gazed down at the length of flesh. They were such odd beasts, these wild men, and not a stitch of clothing on him.

'Where's his other arm, driver? Or has he just got the one?'

'It's underneath him, sir.'

'Bloody hell. Right, let's give him a yank.'

But just as the driver and the lieutenant had an arm raised each, and Moran's face was hanging gently from his body, the nigger spoke:

'Is that you, sir?' he said.

They dropped the arms and stood back a bit from him.

'No,' said the driver. 'This is a casualty, this is, sir. This isn't any nigger.'

'Christ, you're right,' said the lieutenant, normally, 'get my rug from the boot, will you? And I'll try to give the poor fellow some water.'

He unslung his bottle and twisted off the stiff cap, and took a short slug himself, and then knelt fastidiously at Moran's baked head, and let a splash of tepid liquid strike the peaceful dustiness of the scummy mouth.

'You are in a mess, my lad,' the man said. He and the driver rolled Moran in the plaid knee-rug, and found the weight very little trouble to carry to the backseat of the big car.

'I think we'll have the hood over, if you don't mind,' said the lieutenant.

'Yes, sir', said the driver, pleasantly. 'Do you think he's one of ours, sir?'

'I should say so,' said the lieutenant. 'Most definitely one of ours. I think one could tell by the English, don't you?'

'Sounded a bit foreign to me, sir,' said the driver, who was from a suburb of London himself.

'He's exhausted,' said the lieutenant sharply. 'How would you expect him to speak distinctly in this condition?'

'Yes, sir,' said the driver, and since he had shot his bolt, he

367

tumbled into the worn bucket of his seat, and surged them away.

Moran lifted his lids under the leafy half-light. He remembered the captain.

'What time is it?' he said sadly.

'Em, nearly eleven o'clock,' said the lieutenant, graciously. In four words he had recognized not that the poor exposed creature was foreign, but that he was lower-class. 'Thank God for that,' said the lieutenant out loud.

'Has he come round, sir?' the driver shouted, pluming the track behind him. The noise of the engine seemed much worse now the hood was up.

'Yes, yes. Not to worry,' said the officer. 'He'll be all right now. I'm giving him some water. Here you are, my lad, get this down you.'

But Moran just stared out at the straight grateful road.

'What time is it?' he said again.

'Well,' said the lieutenant, 'never mind that.'

He gave a quick smooth to his forehead with a hand, smudging himself.

'What's your name, son?'

Moran didn't say what his name was.

'Just carry on there,' said the lieutenant. 'Rest yourself. We'll have you into camp now in twenty minutes.'

But after a minute of these twenty, the lieutenant's curiosity got the better of his kindness.

'Do you know how long you've been.' He waved a hand at the unknown and uncatalogued greenery on the right side of the road. Various items of deer, unknown also to him by their exact names, moved off as quickly as extraordinary bounds would allow them. A great bounding country, Africa, really. 'Wandering about there?'

Moran turned his peeling solid face to the lieutenant.

'Nasty,' said the lieutenant.

Moran smiled at him. The lieutenant laughed unhappily. But his disgruntled good spirits returned to him, as if by telegram, and he said cheerily:

'And your regiment? Do you remember? No. Well never mind. My God, you look like you've been through the wars. But then, there is a war, isn't there? Or was. I didn't see any of it, except for you. I'm transport, you understand. Sanitation.'

There was nothing in the world that Moran could do now except watch the flies explode against the windscreen.

'Are you not thirsty?' said his companion.

The driver craned his neck back jerkily, and Moran met his eyes, and the driver stretched his mouth and said:

'Cheers, chum. All right then?'

'I'm all right,' said Moran.

'Great, man, great,' said the driver, triumphantly.

Moran took the water-bottle delicately from the lieutenant's bird-white hand, and drank from it very softly. The lieutenant was amused, and he laughed, but this time he wasn't unhappy.

'Is it really that late?' Moran said to him.

Sixfoil Twenty

I didn't even know there was a phone in our room till it bleated, and there it was, obvious, white, and flat on the side-table. Sue woke in my arms and craned round to the noise in surprise.

'Will I unplug that?' she said clumsily.

I laughed in the clear dark room.

'Let's see who's ringing us,' I said, and leaned over her and lifted the whole apparatus, and balanced it on my chest, and got the receiver to my head.

'Owl,' said the receiver, 'hi. Chicken here.'

'Chicken,' I said, and laughed again. 'What're you ringing this hour for?'

'It ain't this hour,' said Chicken's canned voice. 'It's around three, and if you two weren't screwing each other, you'd be down here too.'

'Where?' I said, glad that Sue had downed her head again, and shut her eyes. She wasn't interested any more in what Chicken had to say.

'Listen, Owl, get over here, will ya? It's a place on Ely Street. Get a cab. Number 3001.'

'You're joking, Chicken. What the hell for?'

'I'm in trouble here, Owl. Don't bring Sue with ya. She'll only get her head beaten in. She's too much of a fighter.'

'You're really in trouble, Chicken?' I said, and was afraid suddenly.

'Yep, and I can't wait all night for you, either. Because what trouble I have is going to be on my dear back in about three minutes.'

I noticed Chicken pronounced his g's over the phone.

'Okay, Chicken. I'm on my way. Hold on there.'

'Listen, listen, Owl.'

'What, Chicken?'

'You or Sue got a gun or anything? I mean, it'd come in useful

370

just now.'

'Jesus, no, we haven't, Chicken. Are you insane? Wait there.'

'Got ya,' said Chicken, and the line toned out.

'I've got to go, darling,' I said, and pulled away from her. She woke again.

'You goin to the bathroom, honey?'

I dragged my trousers on, and wrapped my shirt quickly around me. For some reason I had to get all the buttons closed before I'd let myself leave.

'Chicken's in a fight or something, down-town. I'm just going to jump in a taxi-cab and bring him back here. There's no chance I'll be doing any fighting for him unless someone insists.'

'What do you mean, Owl? I don't get it.'

'It's all right, baby,' I said. 'Just you sleep. I'll be back in a little bit. I won't be longer than an hour. I've got to hurry.'

'Okay, honey,' she said. 'Hey, honey,' she said, as I unlocked the door.

'Yeh?'

'Don't get yourself killed out there.'

'See you in a little,' I said, smiling at her joke.

When I was out in the corridor and the door was closed, I heard her call:

'Hey, you want I come?'

But I didn't have time to answer, and I thought of her staying up on her elbows for a few moments, and settling back down then on our nicest bed. I didn't think Chicken was in very bad trouble because it hadn't been in his voice, but since I was on my way, I might as well make sure.

The streets were well-served by big rounded grey taxis, and I ducked into the cavernous bare back of one, and gave the number in Ely Street.

'That the singles' joint?' the man said. He was youngish but his toupee was as offbeam as his radio. It was playing some anonymous jazz music, and he was trying to eat a burger and drive me to Ely Street with the same hand. The other hand was attached provisionally to his other elbow, which was getting the air on the open window.

'I don't know,' I said. 'Probably.'

The man angled his toupee and took a look at me in his rear mirror. His denim shirt had dandruff on it as big as mica, his shoulders as irregular as a boulder under the blue. I didn't know wigs could have dandruff.

'Yeh. It is,' he said.

He drove with due consideration for his engine, and was in no hurry to take off from traffic-lights.

'Nice night enough,' he said. 'Where you from?'

'New York,' I said.

'Nah, nah,' said the man delightedly and nastily. 'Nah, you ain't from there. I'd know if you were. Nah. Where you from? You from Canada or someplace?'

'England,' I said, 'I'm from England.' I didn't want to risk Ireland, in case it encouraged him.

'No shit?' said the man. 'Do people still live there? Ya see, I knew you weren't a New Yorker. Shit, I know my places. Now, my grandfather was Irish. You ever been there?'

'No, never.'

I felt as if I were denying my religion to Cromwell.

'Yeh, he came over on one of them coffin ships. I bet he was pretty shook up when he got off. I mean to say.'

'I bet,' I said.

'Yeh,' said the man. 'Here's the joint. See? It's called the One Night Café. You'll like it.'

I thrust his dollars at him and crossed through a noisy herd of people on the street, into the bar.

There was a throng of bodies in there too, and a blues singer, drunkenly saying something, with a smile, into a mike that leaned down to him from his piano lid. Everyone appeared very happy, ended-up. The women were curiously alike, and were dressed like country-singers, and had their hair so tended it looked like wigs. Then I realized the blues singer was not black at all, but flushed in his face, and he was mouthing a maudlin country tune. The men were booted and trim, and even when they were short it didn't prevent them leaning confidently at the bar.

Chicken wasn't visible straight off. I searched for the phone, and found it towards the rear of the room, where there was a fire-door leading into an alley. The door was open to let air in and people out.

About fifteen couples were on the ground out there, between the big square trash-cans and the bright street. They were short for space, so they had to writhe not only against their partners, but also, in a neighbourly way, against other couples. Zips were down and skirts were dragged up, and they were sluggishly fucking each other on the concrete dusty seaside ground. Occasionally abrupt throat-noises squeezed from them, but for the most part it was surprisingly quiet, snakelike. There was some other sound out there, because the alley borrowed the endless horning and shouting from the full street, like the business of a tide. I watched them, and hoped Chicken wasn't among them somewhere, turned into anyone, because it would be a hideous task to sort through the tangles. Their clothes were so new, and the faces so shaved and made-up, and brightened, like plastic. They seemed impersonal, and patently didn't know each other from Adam or from Eve. The didn't want anything less makeshift than the alley for their searching, because it was the simple logic of the singles' bar brought as quickly as possible to its fruition. I cursed Chicken, and then started to my self-disgust to have an erection. So I pushed through the drinkers and chatters, and beckoned the bar-man. He pressed his voice through his nose, and his head through the noise, and said:

'What's yours?'

'Did a guy called Chicken leave a message here?'

'What?' he said. 'A guy what?'

'Never mind,' I said, 'never mind.'

A guy called Chicken. It sounded like nonsense. I made a last glance around the terrified polite bar, and stepped out into the lurching slack street. A patrol car inched smoothly along the white concrete. As far as they were concerned, everything was in order. Perhaps it was.

I got a taxi and was carried in silence back to the hotel. I was angry with Chicken, but worried about him too, and hoped he had rung up again to say he was safe, or had battered his way home, by whatever means.

'Did he ring?' I said, as I pushed through the door, forgetting she might be sleeping, hushing the last word. I was a bit upset after my journey.

Sue was resting, with her thighs on the floor, and her arms and head on the end of the bed. She was looking directly at me, with her mouth a tiny bit open, the lips trembling. Her last noiseless remark was earthed by the screwdriver nailed into the back of her soft head. Her hands were white and open, poised to run, like young rabbits.

'Moran,' he said. 'Where are you goin?' I had stepped for the humming doorway. The cicadas were suddenly loud and important out on the great lawn. For the first time since I'd known him, he moved to block my path, and now that he thought he had to, he did it thoroughly, stonily.

'What's all dis craziness, mon?' he said, as evenly as a crater. I put my hands up against his chest, like a girl.

'It's too,' I said.

'What you say? I can't bring all dem books out wid me.'

'Jesus, Ali, take half of them.'

'What half, mon? How would I take half? We have a deal for dem all.'

'Choose the best of them, Ali.'

'Choose them, mon? I know nottin about dem. I can't even hardly read dis English.'

I pushed his chest considerably out of the way, but the body came swaying back like a branch, saying urgently:

'We need your room, mon, we need your room.'

'Don't bring those things near my room. Don't. I won't have them there.'

'You won't?' he said.

He shifted a yard sideways against the big table.

'Then it's over,' he murmured. 'A pity, mon. So where are you runnin now, mon?'

'I'm going down to the Copa,' I said. My teeth felt much larger somehow. They were like palisades against Indian wars, Irish wars, African.

'What for, the Copa?' he said. 'What's for you der?'

'I'm asking Susan to come with me, out of here. Get us both to someplace.'

'No, mon,' he said. He slipped a book along the table and held it out to me. 'Mon, just like I can't read this book, you can't have dat girl. You don't know where someplace is.'

I was ashamed by two melted moons that crept out of my eyes.

'You can never have her,' he repeated, and nodded his dreadlocks, so they knocked about like silent chimes in a breeze.

'I'll ask her,' I said. 'Take care, Ali.'

'Hey, Mon,' he said, as I engined out on to the balcony, low on fuel, lowly. His words were avalanching at me. 'Hey, mon, don't give your friendship to anyone,' he said. 'A good man can live without dat.'

'You're right,' I said.

I unlatched the light gate and crossed carefully over the catwalk, and reached a steep narrow fall of steps down the arm of the little annex. They were the same as the stairs on a ship. I thumped across the catted lawn, and rolled over the lowest part of the wall, trying not to look back at the balcony in its curtains of blue dark. I ran slowly with my best lope towards the sea, passing the exact widened gates of the airforce base. I didn't know why I was heading towards the water, but had an idea that I could circle the houses and gardens, and go along the edge of the Jamaican Village. I didn't fancy the centre part on my own.

The mooned sea moved without moving to a lip of old concrete, plastered onto a rocky beach. The houses diminished as I went, in the height of their roofs, and the well-kept wood deteriorated a little more with each gate, as if the skins of the inhabitants darkened with each household. Soon I was walking and panting between the Jamaican Village and the broad drum of the ocean, the chocolate foreign ocean. I glanced behind me, and at the windows mostly lost behind flowering bushes and small palms. A little grey boat tapped its feet against the pole it was moored to, about ten yards out in the water. For a moment I considered it as a refuge, and then I wondered why I was seeking for one. My instinct was to crouch and cower and cover myself, and wait for the world as I knew it to get old, and go by.

'I've let him down,' I said, to the heavily-cracked pavement.

The road itself was a swathe of dirt. My head had a clamour of information, but all in languages I didn't understand. The night was so empty it was emptying me. Distantly a man was singing inside the dry wood-fire of a radio, an old radio with a youngish man singing, *Everytin's goin ta be alright,* over and over to a falling and rising melody, that travelled past my bewildered head, and went on over the flat sea as passionate as a single wave, to Cuba.

The further I walked the more the distance in front of me was increased. My progress was antlike and minute, but still the held houses rumbled by me like rolling-stock. After much too much time, I found myself, or lost myself, out of that quarter, and away at the sea-bed of the street that became the main street further up.

There was a plaster and painted object lost too on the pavement. It stood about seven feet high, and was armless and sad-looking, like a big smoked cigar. It gave the latitude and longitude of where I stood, and told me either proudly or plainly that America ended here. I could believe it. The kidney-shaped beach behind it had been concreted over, and a small jetty guarded the cove against the Old World, and other obscurer worlds. There were no boats. The sea was the colour and texture of whaleskin, and the low fish of Cuba was out there somewhere, below the soft brushstroke of the horizon, its casinos unplugged, falling off the end of America.

So I turned back into America, and at each streetlamp the air acquired a little more glare, because more and more houses added to the light by being restaurants and motels. The Southernmost Motel In The USA gave way to the Southernmost Bar, their neoned names the first words of this world. I brought the southernmost silence of my life into the first singles and clutches of people. The damp warm silence of where people lived and slept changed to the dryer hotter mutter and calling of a long night winding-up. Stories had been shared and boredom had been endured, loneliness had lasted another night-time, and some had found a temporary break from it, that would serve as an emphasis to it later – I was beginning to think like the Texan singer sang.

A trio of men was still playing pool, on a pool of green under a bamboo shelter in an open-air bar. A lit woman was leaning on her black counter, with her bottles behind her sparking and signalling like a ship in the bay. She wanted them to pack it in and go home. There was nothing to be done that hadn't been done before, and nowhere to reach that hadn't been reached. The end of America was just down the street, lost in the reflecting darkness, but the end of a pool game had more importance. The lights of the cinema ahead cleared and focused, and gained their letters. No doubt it was the southernmost picture-house, but it had the grace not to say it, being the source-house of all America anyway, an image-flickerer almost holy in its potency, without which no moment or dream of the inhabitants had any quality.

The sky was so separate when I happened to stare up at it, that it made the street seem a film-reel badly imposed on another. The washed blue was going one way against its moon, and the street flowing in another. But the actors were idle and had probably forgotten their lines, the director was dead from importance, and they were insisting by their jumbled actions that there was no story to anything, and no sentence was worth completing to its full-stop – they frustrated their storylines and axed their own dialogue, and the cut words were left on the pavement like litter, hamburger wrappings made of silver paper, and leaflets to save you, and Marlboro packets, and the little robbed woodpiles of matchbooks. Here was this tossed eloquence on the street, or hitched up as neon, and here in front of the disappointed crowd was a young woman, lying on her breast on the inlaid pavement, in front of the Copa. She was dancing still, with a small chaste jerking of her limbs, a clockwork animal fallen over, left. The funny position, and the screwdriver searching in the back of her head, stopped the dance being beautiful.

The litter of words that the breeze blew against her said that no one had seen anyone do anything, that she had tumbled over just as she left the bulbed door of the Copa, that the screwdriver had appeared 'by magic' in her head. No doubt they were pro-tecting Ali – everyone liked Ali, and anyway, who really cared that much about safety and order? And wasn't it just another drug killing? On the other hand, if the screwdriver really had just probed suddenly into her, of its own apparent accord, nothing could have been more suitable for the southernmost murder in the new world. But I, in my love, doubted such per-fection. Someone had done this, whether he had been there or not, some hand, somewhere, a wing and a prayer – Ali's, Chicken's, anyone's.

The pavement made a young noise under my hard brown shoes. It reminded me how long it had been since I had run for any distance. Whatever I passed seemed to be erased by the sweep of my body. All the times I had tracked both ways along this route were being stamped out by my loud feet.

The police-car wasn't following me, so I slowed and clumped along. I had already reached the kunstmuseum, so that meant the brown shoemaker's and the xenophobic café were gone for ever. The civilized flower-shop had had it too, and so had the exhausted balconies of the once broad and desirable street. I was heaving for breath and I was drunk from oxygen. A neat wood-pecker of a pulse was beaking away at my temples. I walked down between the picture-galleries, and tried not to stare at the valuable sunny canvases in the windows, the productions of happy artists. I crossed the new river by the stone bridge, where we had argued once about Virginia Woolf, and then drunk the sweet orange concoction at the second-favourite café, which had made us both orangely sick. She had shown me some special windows in a church not far from here, and I couldn't remem-ber the name of the very famous artist who had taken the trou-ble and the money to make them. I had disliked them, dully.

I looked accusingly into a shop-window where I had bought her silver earrings, as silver was the only metal that could com-pete with her colouring. She had liked them. She would wear them again without thinking who had given them to her, I was sure.

There were few cafés I passed that had not at one time or other served her black jacket, and her powerful smile, but I saw these things as if I had never known them before, as if this mem-ory of them was inaccurate and hallucinatory. There was some-thing false about them, as if I had more or less made them up, like I made up my father and sister not being there as a child, when they all too really were there all the time. I had never given her earrings at all, and we had never ordered chocolate in the hundred cafés. We had never patronized this string of cinemas, even though I remembered walking back with her from *Death in Venice,* and not talking, tranquillized, and going to bed cloudily, and sleeping better than I had for months. I knew it had not happened, it was only a memory, entire and original unto itself. It hadn't happened but I hadn't been there.

Fear had shut me off, and I was meeting myself again for the first time after a long time. I couldn't greet myself with much enthusiasm, but it was simpler to have myself back. I began to walk quite differently, with a kind of containment, a box in a box. The inside box was empty but it was not unprotected.

It is the continuation of that feeling that lets me be with Sue now – Sue couldn't have gone off with someone whose self was temporarily or permanently away. I couldn't manage this road without my bare but almost sufficient self, and Sue can't do anything in the world except keep this scrap-wood together.

I stopped among the most expensive shops in the city centre. No one lived here, and the long shopfronts were lit for nobody but myself. Everything was closed, and I had no idea what day of the week it was, or what time it might be, and again I could only vaguely recall what I had been doing here in this city, and felt foolish and freed. I had either just arrived, or had just woken in a place that a dream had described in shifting detail, and which had to be faced now as it really was.

There were mannequins waiting alertly and smartly in the streaming windows. They were poised and rich and would never have to be sorry about anything. They were so fortunate they weren't even smiling. They had no philosophy and no poetry, they didn't need to say that being alive was not meant to be easy and they didn't need to court any gods. They were suave and safe and perfect and wordless, like the moments in people's lives stilled in the photographs of some celebration. I stood in the middle of the road, between the tram-tracks to carry people north and the tracks to bring them back south. Xenia was perfect like the mannequins, and I knew she was flawlessly human like them – and what a changeling she had located and taken for herself in Paris, what an animal she had kennelled in her flat! And she was fine and I never needed to see her again.

The moon poured down a theatrical light on my head, and made a brief clear shadow on the sets of the road. The culled trees that lined the avenue were clutched and vigorous, and exhaled a storm of green, all the way to the empiric station. The station's brave roof was tiny and confident in the distance. Perspective made it easier and smaller. I thought of the snow still up in the mountains, and the paths up there unlit but bright

379

under this same moon, illuming the sensible coffee-stations. The moon was very eloquent, and apologized for being so beautiful, but I let it be. People had made the lot of it, even the meaning of the moon, and snobby tempers may have dressed the mannequins and angry architects been disappointed in the builders, but all in all the world had conspired to show something excellent, and succeeded well enough. The street was all the hands that had made it, and the effort of it and the success of it were extraordinary. To see how good it was, was so joyful I felt guilty about it. I felt ashamed to notice it, while its owners and begetters were sunk in the sleeping-quarters of the town. It was too valuable and I started to laugh at myself, but it was a very stupid laugh, and I put my hand stupidly to my mouth to shut it up – but the laugh was bent on stupidity, so I let it loose rather than kill it.

There was something black and white at the shadowed foot of a shop-entrance, and I trod over to it. The light sailed me over helpfully. The black and white thing, colourless, like an animal from an old film, was a magpie. Its few long tail feathers were bent up along its back, as was its neck and head and black beak, as if entering this coloured world had been too puzzling for it – everything changed except itself! Its beak was closed and there was a white scum over its round hidden eye. Its claws loosened gently and then twitched shut again, like a baby's hands against the air. Its stomach jumped tinily too, but without disturbing its general position on the dark green slab of the pavement. I thought I should stamp on its head to kill it, and stop it suffering, but wasn't sure that was right. I remembered how chickens could canter round after their heads were removed, and decided the magpie was dead. These were just a few last movements it was making, independent of its brain, as its body cooled off. Indeed, a red bead of blood sparkled on its nostril.

While it flew, it would have been a bird of ill omen for me, without a mate. I would have whispered, *magpie, show me your mate,* as my mother had taught me. I didn't wish it to show me its mate now. It looked complete against the absolute steps. It was not alone. It looked mated to itself and exultant and lucky.

He couldn't be found anywhere. Even when I closed my eyes he wasn't there. He had carried Dor away with him too.

As an outside chance, I settled myself for an hour in the hedged garden, and stared at the arched opening. It remained a cramped vista for the weedy bank, climbing to the castle on the far boundary of the clear lawn. There were daisies and buttercups, as an army against the grass.

I missed seeing my father and sister and I missed the fear they had brought with them, or rather I missed that part of family life, such as it was. It was better to have them and be frightened of them, than to have many empty places which they had so faithfully inhabited. It seemed they had been hanging about for ever, and it was getting harder for me to remember any time when they had truly been there. I could recall them doing things and talking, but I couldn't recall myself being there with them. All that was a kind of story-book, and it didn't seem to prove anything, whereas more recently he had so shocked me that these events were detailed and applicable-to, a feeling of things going on could be got from them, that was now suspended.

When my mother and I went somewhere we were not in danger. I could no longer see more than she could, and there was nothing to protect her from, if the worst ever arrived at the worst. I was reduced in status and made young again, and I felt the limitation of being young without secret knowledge.

I would have given much for my father to be lurking or looming in the landlord's tiny tool-shed. I chanted mad words, made-up words, for him to appear inside as I danced across the lawn to it. I doubled back three times to the granite steps, and tapped the broken stone pillar at its foot three times three – a solid ritual that would work for most things. It could keep spiders from being in the bath when I crept to use the toilet, and prevent me being thrown around in the playground, if the taps were very carefully counted and attended to. It could make my mother agree to cook toffee, or agree to have cocktail sausages for dinner. Since it could do all that, it wasn't much to expect it to make one mere father materialize in a small tool-shed. It was no use whatsoever though – the mower's blades were thickened with once-wet grass, and the grimy can of oil sat up on a crossboard. A pair of brown-bladed shears was hung on a yel ow string, and an old pile of *Life* magazines clotted in a trussed bundle on the strange ground. There might have been any number of serious spiders in there but no sign of a father. I sighed a bit obviously, and sat down against the dry tarry door. The grass was able to grow as high as it liked against the shed, because the mower-blades couldn't attack it, and the shears were blunt.

I tugged at a dried stem and slipped it into my mouth. It tickled my lips when I pulled on it, because the stem was furred with tiny stiff hairs growing the other way, silverly. I was angered, and would have snapped at my mother if she had been near. I wished she were near so I could. I rested my thin arms on my green knees and my chin on top of that. I must have looked diminutive and daydreamy against that unknown shed, but I was bigger than the world and plotting viciously. I tried to remember what I didn't like about my mother, and how I could make her angry too. I realized it was difficult to make her angry, but I felt like having a good try.

Then the sun got the better of me, and I forgot about how I might be successfully nasty, and creaked the iron gate, and let the granite steps bring me to the rocks. The last two steps were slimy. They needed care when the tide was just gone out. But the water was low, the stone undressed, and the sun had crusted the weed. When the sea covered the knees of everything again the green hair would shift healthily, but for the moment it was a cross between cardboard and eggshell. My feet left burst prints in it.

The best pool was a deep cone of colourless water, with only a bare saucer-sized bed of pebbles at the bottom of its steep rough cliffs. What the tide abandoned there had only one skin-brown weed to use for shade. Its roots sucked on the rock like a seagull's foot deformed. Its stem was polished, and if it was like the weeds that had to dry above pool-level, sticky too. The plant was like a full false beard, and in the beard were transparent and articulated characters, who were shy and stagy and courageous at the same time. They were elusive to chase, and the height of the water was a little more than my rolled-up sleeve could avoid, as they knew well, but once gripped they made a wonderful soft squirming in my palm. They thrashed and stilled and pouted, and their eyes were like the smallest

382

inkblots in the world, the sort that dried out to leave a hard raised mark on my copybooks. They didn't die when I took off my shoes and grey socks, and stuffed my feet right down to the bed of grey pebbles. The blond small hairs on my legs softened in the water like the sea-weed. The angle of the submerged part altered itself to the rest of me, so my legs suddenly wooded away oddly.

Down on the rocks I was almost as low as the channel water, and it looked much more powerful and personal from there. It pretended to be blue, but really it was a ruined colour, though like blue, with thousands and thousands of round lighter discs chained mathematically but changeably on top. It was the type of construction that would have made an excellent eiderdown or coverlet.

Then my mother's voice inserted itself into the glitter. I glanced back over the higher more-boulderlike rocks, and up the neat military-looking wall, and over the round journey of the hedges, and found her face and arms leaning on the hot sill of the kitchen window, high up on the house's flaking façade. I could imagine her hands pressing on the grainy stone.

'Oliver!' she said. Her voice hit a few obstacles, and dropped on them like scraps of metal, but it came on none the less to where I was playing.

'Coming!' I said, and one of the see-through fish seemed to nibble at my foot, so I hauled them both up.

'Oliver!' she called again, so the three syllables were cut up by the heat. The gaps widened, and reached me half-broken but still mine. I shouted back louder and better than before, and then more quietly but still effectively, she said:

'Oh, there you are.'

I stayed sitting on the sunny rock and waited for what she might want.

'I think I'll come down,' she said. 'Is it still warm in the garden?'

'Yes,' I said.

She withdrew from the blue gap and left the window pulled up. It was strange that the room inside could stay so blue and the sun so white. I thought of her bringing down her chair and a book, through the private half-life of the stairwell, the wood of the house hugging into the swelled walls.

Below me the ingredients of a world cooked in their pool. One day I would get a boat and row myself over to the island. It might be a nice place to live and, after all, it had once been my father.

'Do you want to come up here?' my mother said, arriving at the wall. Dor sprinkled herself down the steps to me, laughing when she noticed my foot-prints in the weed.

'What are you doing?' she said.

'Your father will be home soon,' said my mother, idly. 'Now what shall I make for dinner, in this heat? Cold meat?'

'Yes!' we said.

De quene wass changt.

'Resst in yer chare,' sed de bishap. 'Yoo ar a smal pece tyred.'

'No,' she sedd, 'I amm sickk.'

'Ah, it iss theze wayted dayes,' he sedd, an smooht hes belee gentlee.

'Wat arr we dooin, rippin dese poetts and kinges?'

De bishap sercht in hesself fer de reesonz.

'Wal,' he sed, 'it iss nat dat wee doo nat luv ower Ollever. Bat he iss an herronn to ower crowes, an we muste bee natur driev hem awaye fram ower territoree.'

'Wee shud lat hem goe nowe inta de wuds. It wul nat doo uz harme.'

'No, no, dere quene, he wil bee a rebell an a monsterr to uz der. Lat uzz jest lite de gud hepe uf wud yoo havv stackt unner hem, and put thiss daye ta reste.'

Otseed de door, Micel wass treein ta gett ther wordes. Owl his bloode was stil on hes leggs, whar de dogges hadd smered et. He semt lik a wilde dogg ta hemsel, as mich ass dey, and wass tryen ta makk hes pantin les in de echoin pasag.

He rann ferst ta de stares goin bak doon to de coortyarde, an den changt hes ideea, an ract wid a scutter to de twistin stone stepps to de ramperts. He pult hemsel upp dese, an stuk hes eyes oot at de menne watchin der. He sawe de two nottet ropes lact on an iran ringe, whach wass holdin Ollever bello. He thoght uf hes lief an hes meanz ta ete an drinke an slepe, bat stil he hadd to rooin hesself. He walkt oot veree slawlee, an broeke

384

inta smal songe as ef too hes owen pleasur. He wass nat frends to dese towermenne, so he did nat saye anytin. Whan he wass beseed de ropz, he fingert hes smal kneef whar it wass silente in hes clothes, then he stoopt an slict at de too cabelz, til wan pluuckt off, an Olleever, somwhar at de ende, lat oot a yelle of hurte. De secund clutche uf strandes frilled an unwounde, an snappt agenst hes blade.

An ax madd two halv appels of hes skulle, and far unner hem Olleve landet on de highe piel uf stickks an logges dat wasse ta roste hem. De manne hoo had cloven Micel hes hed, leant ovvir de perypit an callt doon ta Coon:

'Staye, mastir!' he roret. 'Doo nat runn fram uss!'

He wud haff killt Olivveer, sinz he wass a pal uf demonz, bat he nedet, an al de menne der needet, at leest hes bodee at de towerr to make dem alieve. Bat Olivver, tho hes armes war like flamin branchez, canterrd awaye on hes astonisht fete.

De menne on de toor did nat movv agen, sich wass der maners. Bat soon somwan had to telle de quene, an shee scremt in hes faec ta heer itt. Her talke uf bein gentil ta Olivver her manne smokt uppe ta joine odder passin vapers. De bishap felte lik a foolishe pigg. Shee rann oot de lowe dor, an doon inta de fronte uf de castel, an he palmmed hes hed. He wass always strokkin sum pert uf hes corp.

'Iss et badd?' he sed to de rume. 'Oi tinke nat. He wass jest alowe anceent sorte uf fellaugh, an hes pooer wass nat so magniffisent. Beseed a smal prinx uf Rome he wass a mous. Evven a poore cityzan uf dat damlee citee, iss uf grater skolarshipp den Conne. Nowe lat hem sinke inta sum smal historee widdout wordes, whach noe tendere-mindet scribe wud wante to giv. Wat breef nede der wud bee fer sich a privat tale, concernin a saveg lorde an hes wors witt. Dis wul bee a clene gudd plac widdoot dem. An nowe menne cann giff demselfs ta praier an juztic.'

Oot in de yarde, de quene circlet aboot, an hisst upp to de tooer hoo hadd losst her captif.

'Micel, moi leddy,' sed de axmann.

'Pulle hes throte fram hes necke!' she scremt. 'Noe,' she sed, 'keepe hem faste, an Oi wul haff moi triks wid hem.'

'Oh, moi ledee, he iss ded nowe.'

'Oh Kristes hes blut,' she spatt. 'Iss der no rode fer moi angr?'

Den she wass dissy, an leent agenst de castel, dat wass nowe herz, an al herr grate gaem wass fer litel, Moll, becarse she hadd no childes fram anee mann. She livt in beter helthe an saentlines wid her bubel uff a bishap, an wud nat sufer hes smal fingerz to soothe herr. Yass, Moll, a grat saent she wass in de yers dat foloed, an shee wass almoste worshippt bee de peple as barbarooslee as anee of de brokken gotts.

Wid de godz wente Olleeve, as you kno. Amonn wass hes ferst helpir, an affter hes frende. De trieb uff Amon tretet hem as a prinz, an did nat suffir anee harmz ta curss hem. Conn hes pried wass heelt boi dese feelthy folke. He hadd a rocke he ust ta sitt on, in memoree uff al rockee places, an ass a sorte uf fortunate chaire. Heere he watcht de spidderz refoos de harde saef shell uf de laedeeberdz, and wisht he had sich a winged shelle hemself. Wan daye he sawe a squirrell fal fram a longe waye doon a tree inta de rivver. He studd upp and hurriet doon ta helpe dis dafte cretur. Bat itt wass swimin boi natur in de watter, an recht de odder banke, an slipt up anudder tre.

'Dat wul be mee, lorde squerel,' he lafft. 'Dat wil bee mee.'

Bat it iss tru, Mol, dat al hes affterchilder waz lowlee menne an gerlls. He hadd hes passed–ovvir triboot-gerl fer hes woif, an daye bredd sevenn sonz an wan doghter. Dat loif wass dificelt an colde, an ther woreld wass a musik uf deseez an owels.

Whan Conn wass olde, he wass a litel madd alsoo, an ovvten tolde storees dat hadd nat been soo, ande he sed too hes childrenn dat deye war cheftenz an uf beste blut, bat it wass nuttin to dem. Dey hadd to kill de beestes, an shivver, an argoo wid de reste. An soo, Moll, diss lineage sanke, as deye saye, inta de mudd. Deye war lik ootlawes an eegiptianz in der wayes. Certanlee, tho he wass madd, he wasse lovt. Yas, thiss iss tru. An hes storrees war askt forr, as bein de beste iff nat de wizest. Hes armes in olde yers whar veree crippelt, becarse de dampe gott in de wrenches of hes laste conditoon in hes castel.

Soo hes armes hookt bak lik fetherles winges, an hee lafft ta see hemsel in siche a staet. Becorse den he was de saem as hes lovlee poete, masiter Owle. Always he sed he herd magister Owl hooin an tellin a kinde uf tiem amang de darke tres. Bat dis wass anlee hes madness.

Stil, Moll, no wan sawe Owle agen, an probablee sum silee animool had hem fer supper, an de grounde hadd de restt fer puddin. He cud nat haff livvt wid hes fac torne off. Bat it iss plesent, Moll, issent et, ta tinke he mite haff gon ferther, as madde no dowt as Conne ande as rooind, in tiem? Watevver wass de caes, he wud haff died at de ent, and trulee, Moll, dese two creturz onlee livv in mee, as yoo doo too. Ande soo I haff toldt-moi childishe storee ta a womin dat hass nivver bene, an yatt Oi lovt herr.

Having been a largely extra citizen of Ireland, Africa, Europe and America, Moran went back to Sligo with fifty pounds and an unshakeable wish to be left alone. He didn't have to work too hard to achieve this.

He was sixty when he walked into the town he had hated most in the world, and he was a curiosity that the townspeople had to relearn. The bishop was long dead, and no one seemed to recognize him. Certainly anyone who had known him as the Blessed Apostle was either perished or gone away.

He took possession of a disused bridge carrying a grassed-over road that had been superseded by a larger one on another route. The bridge had only spanned a dry gully, and he made a house out of one side of that, under the arch. A policeman came out to talk to him once or twice, but Moran was so silent and simple that he was, as he desired, left to himself.

He was obviously not an idiot because he could do his shopping as well as the next man, and the countryside was well-stocked with bachelors who cycled into town on a Wednesday, without uttering more than ten words to the shopkeepers. Moran had only his legs, but he carried a linoleum bag like the rest of them. Here he put cabbages and potatoes and bacon and dripping, as it was handed over the scrubbed counters to him.

The children of his dead tormentors treated him as was his due, a poor single man living on his army pension in the best habitation he could muster. He suspected the town had changed, and it was as good as if he had never been there before. It was possibly the one place on the globe he could be truly unknown – he believed in the principle that lightning never strikes twice on the one tree.

He had nothing to look forward to, so he made a virtue of

each day, or did his best at it. Often, though he was old, he was not lonely, and as he expected the summers were the easiest season. He had always had a taste for a bit of sun and wild animals and grass, and he enjoyed these things like books. Every week that he got through with a measure of peace made him stronger for the next. He was completely without virtue perhaps, but on the other hand he lacked significant vices. Perhaps Moran had no true ability to love other people, but he didn't love himself either. Apart from a longing for women, which he didn't feel anymore, he had never aspired much to the companionship of other travellers, or if he had, he had met with such little success that he began to think a thing like that was impossible. Most men were more powerful than he was, and there didn't seem to be any area in the departments of life in which he excelled or even glimmered, so the neatest thing for him to do was retreat, and retreat he did.

In winter he felt like winter, and he always expected to be dead before the end of it. To be dead was a sort of solid respectable phrase which he never bothered to entertain himself with. Since he had nothing to give up and no one to leave, he couldn't really imagine it, so he left it alone. This was a bit irritating for me, but I endured it for his sake.

He spent a great deal of his mornings talking to a woman he called Moll, and I often used to pretend that I was she. This shouldn't be seen as a sign of weakness on my part, but actually a type of generosity. I found it light enough to assume the character of a patient interested woman, and as he never knew anything about it, it hurt no one.

I have always taken a superior attitude to Moran since this was appropriate, and it would have been ridiculous to pretend ever that he had much to recommend him, besides his affectionate ignorance. But still I know I was well fond of him, and he was harmless enough in himself for me to be a bit agitated when the weather was very bad, or he seemed unhappy. He had a way of being unhappy without being foolish that was perhaps quite rare. Of course he was foolish in everything else, and he wasn't often unhappy as I say. Still, he had a few good qualities.

I feel apologetic for him – or rather for myself, in that I was so long with him – because he appeared so trampish and was so unsought-after by other people. Of course I had to stay with him, but that was a grotesque combination at best. It's not very encouraging to like someone whom no one else even takes the trouble to dislike. This wasn't so in his youth and middle years, and in those rather arbitrary years it might have been possible for him to rise above his abysmal stature or perhaps be elevated by some pleasant accident. But he was a bit of a Jonah in his own boat, and I minded that from time to time. He didn't seem to care at all. And now that he was over sixty and beyond meddling with, there was really no one but myself to notice it.

The catalogue of his pleasures was childish – tall grass, shades of grass, good level-headed sunshine, a clean river, shades of water of this, river birds, grass birds, night birds, especially the owl. He had a preference for owls that he never lost, even into his last day. He liked them because no one ever saw them, or rarely, and only when the owls chose it. He liked them because the owl had a steady informative call. It was so regular he sometimes wondered as he listened to it whether it was real at all, or just some important part of the general soil, a natural clock for the likes of himself. He thought of owls in the plural sometimes although he only ever heard one, but he heard it for so many years, in so many places, that he could calculate there would have to be more than one such engine. Unless owls were similar to the moon, in that the moon was singular but lived everywhere. He supposed there had to be more than the one – all the same he hoped the owl was like the moon, and called over the world, but was still alone. He would believe it if anyone ever told him about some plurality of owls, but until he was told he preferred to think of just the one, when he could.

The best nights indeed were the ones when the sky was open, and the moon got in, and filled everywhere with its light, and the owl thrummed in its machinery. That simple note plumbed Moran, and represented far more comprehensively than a book all the oddments and jumps of his life. It was comprehensive, but at the same time trimmed and compact, and he could almost think of his life, as he listened to the owl, as something that he could hold in his own hand. He could lie back, under the bridge, behind the lengths of wood, and the moon could come in there, and he could hold everything like a toy.

That's what made me fond of him really. But he got away from me, he slipped away, in some way free of everything, in a better way free of me. And he heard in his heart the mysterious perfect heart of the owl.

Fiction in Paladin

The Businessman: A Tale of Terror   £2.95 ☐
Thomas M. Disch
'Each of the sixty short chapters of THE BUSINESSMAN is a *tour de force* of polished, distanced, sly narrative art . . . always the vision of America stays with us: melancholic, subversive and perfectly put . . . In this vision lies the terror of THE BUSINESSMAN'
Times Literary Supplement

'An entertaining nightmare out of Thomas Berger and Stephen King'
Time

Filthy English   £2.95 ☐
Jonathan Meades
'Incest and lily-boys, loose livers and ruched red anal compulsives, rape, murder and literary looting . . . Meades tosses off quips, cracks and crossword clues, stirs up the smut and stuffs in the erudition, pokes you in the ribs and prods you in the kidneys (as in Renal, home of Irene and Albert) . . . a delicious treat (full of fruit and nuts) for the vile and filthy mind to savour'
Time Out

Dancing with Mermaids   £2.95 ☐
Miles Gibson
'An excellent, imaginative comic tale . . . an original and wholly entertaining fiction . . . extremely funny and curiously touching'
Cosmopolitan

'The impact of the early Ian McEwan or Martin Amis, electrifying, a dazzler'
Financial Times

'It is as if Milk Wood had burst forth with those obscene-looking blossoms one finds in sweaty tropical palm houses . . . murder and mayhem decked out in fantastic and erotic prose'
The Times

To order direct from the publisher just tick the titles you want and fill in the order form.   **PF1**